STACY M. JONES

Missing Time Murders

First edition

ISBN: 978-0-578-66182-7

This book was professionally typeset on Reedsy.
Find out more at reedsy.com

For B.W. - for the stories that inspired this one

Acknowledgement

Special thanks to my family and friends who are always a source of support and encouragement. Thank you to my early readers whose feedback was invaluable. Sharon Aponte, a wonderfully-skilled graphic designer, thank you for bringing my stories to life with amazing covers. Thank you to Dj Hendrickson for your insightful editing. I am always grateful for the city of Little Rock for allowing me to borrow your landscapes, businesses, and city streets and adding my own twist – sometimes moving streets and locations to fit my scene but always still reflective of the area. To the detectives and medical examiner that I call for fact-checking - thank you always for answering my countless questions so patiently with your expert knowledge.

Thanks to my readers who have been with me since the first in the series and new readers just finding my books – I hope you enjoy reading these stories as much as I enjoy writing them.

CHAPTER 1

"**G**ood morning, sunshine." I leaned over my boyfriend, Det. Luke Morgan, in the bed we shared in our house on N. Tyler Street in the Heights neighborhood of Little Rock, Arkansas and kissed his cheek.

Luke stirred in his sleep, reaching an arm around my back and pulling me down on top of him. I rested my head on his chest and breathed him in, the woodsy scent of his soap still on his skin from the shower he had taken the night before. I snuggled into him, allowing ourselves a few more minutes before I'd absolutely have to rouse Luke from his slumber.

We had brunch plans with Luke's parents and my mother and her boyfriend, Jack Malone, a detective from New York. My mother and Jack were in town for a few days to join Luke's celebration. He finally brought his sister Lily's killer to justice. It had been a challenging case for Luke, starting with Lily's disappearance in college seventeen years prior and ending nearly six months ago with twenty-four total victims uncovered, and thankfully, justice for all of them.

Jack and I had worked a cold case in my hometown in upstate New York while Cooper, Luke's best friend and my investigative partner, had tackled one in Atlanta. It took all of us putting the pieces of the puzzle together to bring the killer down. It had been Luke's relentless pursuit of justice that had driven the entire investigation.

All of the families of the victims had come together last night to honor their loved ones while also celebrating Luke who had led the multi-state investigation. The close of the case also garnered Cooper and me a special consultant status with the Little Rock Police Department, which made Luke's life easier all around. It meant I could butt my nose into Luke's cases if there wasn't a conflict of interest for us. As a private investigator, I had wormed my way into previous cases so it might as well be legit.

After the celebratory event, Luke slept beside me soundly for probably the first time in the history of our relationship. His sister's death and his earlier attempts to solve the case had always weighed heavily on him. It was what drove him to become a detective in the first place.

Luke snaked his hand into my long, thick auburn tresses and massaged my scalp with his fingertips, something he knew drove me crazy. I planted a sweet kiss on his chest.

He sighed sleepily. "How long have you been awake?"

"About an hour. I texted my mother and gave her directions to the restaurant. I told her we'd meet there at ten. You have about an hour before we need to leave."

"An hour is longer than I need." Luke laughed and rolled to his side, draping an arm over my hip and planting a smacking kiss on my forehead. Within moments though, his eyes were closed and breath even again.

It was good the Little Rock Police Department had given him some time off to regroup after the case. Luke earned it. After the killer was arrested, Luke had worked night and day over the last few months to help the federal task force that had been set up to match victims' remains and notify families. It was a long and arduous process.

Luke playfully pinched my side. "Can we skip brunch and stay in bed all day? I can just snack on you." Luke planted a round of kisses on my face and then closed his eyes again. There seemed to be no rousing him from his sleepiness this morning.

I nudged his arm, but he didn't look at me. "We promised we'd meet them. My mother and Jack are going back to New York this afternoon. You can nap when we get back."

I pulled out of Luke's grasp and planted my feet on the floor. I shrugged off my tee-shirt and pushed down my sleeping shorts, standing there naked in front of him. I cleared my throat once and then twice until he opened his eyes.

"You're teasing me. You should be in bed next to me instead of standing there." Luke pulled the covers back in an invitation.

"Not happening. If you want all this, you're going to have to get your lazy bones out of bed and come shower with me." I turned on my heels and gave my backside a shake before I walked to the bathroom. Luke groaned loudly. I didn't turn back to look but heard the rustling of sheets and his bare feet slap on the hardwood floor.

An hour later, we stood on the sidewalk in front of the restaurant in the Riverdale neighborhood, waiting for my mother, Karen, and Jack. Luke's parents, Spencer and Lucia, had already arrived and went inside to grab us a table for six.

Several people nodded hello as they walked into the restaurant. A few shook Luke's hand and congratulated him on his recent success. A local news station had covered the event last night, and Luke had even given a rare willing statement to the media. It seemed more than a few people had already watched it.

"You're famous," I teased.

"Not hardly," Luke said absently while reaching for his phone. He read a message and looked down the street toward the river.

"What's up?" I asked, following his gaze.

"That was the station. We've got a young woman dead inside one of those apartments down on Riverfront Drive."

"Homicide?" I asked. A few years ago, Luke had worked himself up to the lead detective in the homicide division. There weren't many detectives, even across multiple states, who matched his closure and conviction rate.

Luke squinted and read the text message again. "I don't know. It's just a suspicious unattended death. They are treating it like it could be a homicide. The text doesn't say much. The body was found in Riverstone. That's one of the newer expensive apartment communities though, so odd to say the least."

"Do you want to go?" I hoped he didn't. I wanted Luke to have a break.

"No, but maybe I'll stop down after brunch just to check-in." Luke reached for me and pulled me in for a kiss. "I can tell by how you asked that you'd be disappointed if I went."

I rose to tiptoes and kissed his full lips. "It's not that. I want you to have a break. You're going to burn yourself out."

"Do you have to make out in public?" my mother scolded as she and Jack walked towards us.

I laughed. "Yes, always." If the red hue that showed up on my skin had been apparent on Luke's dark complexion, my mother would have seen how embarrassed he was being caught like that. Instead, Luke let me go and smiled at her like he hadn't been doing anything wrong, which he hadn't.

My mother reached her hand out and squeezed Luke's arm. "I'm just teasing you."

The four of us made our way into the restaurant, navigating around tightly packed tables until we found Luke's parents patiently waiting for us near the window. After taking a seat, we ordered quickly and enjoyed our brunch, chatting happily. I was pleased that my mother and Luke's parents were getting along so well. It was like we were all family already. Jack was a good addition to the group and for my mother, who hadn't dated in more than thirty years.

During our meal, Luke checked his phone for updates. His mother scolded him twice for having the phone at the table. He apologized and put it away, only to be unable to resist when another message came through.

As brunch wore on, Luke's face became more and more constrained. I figured the suspicious death was proving to be more, and the break I thought he'd have would have to be put on hold.

CHAPTER 2

Private investigator Cooper Deagnan slowly opened his eyes and focused on the ceiling in his bedroom. He closed them again, the morning light too much. His brain thudded against his skull causing such pain he rubbed his forehead gently with his fingers. The pain grew more intense the longer he remained awake. It was at least a nine on a scale of ten if a doctor were asking.

Cooper stretched his long limbs under the covers, first his legs and then his arms. He debated getting up to grab some medicine and a glass of water for the headache, but only for a second. He had no desire to move so he closed his eyes and tried unsuccessfully to fall back to sleep.

The previous evening's celebration with Luke and Riley had been one of the highlights of his life, but strangely now, he couldn't recall all of the evening. Cooper didn't think he'd had that much to drink, but he was hard-pressed to remember how he had made it back to his condo. It had only been a few blocks walk from where they had been, but still, he didn't recall a thing. Cooper brushed if off. Maybe he drank more than he thought. Cooper yawned and turned to his side.

Every synapse of his body snapped awake at the same time. Cooper came face to face with a woman. Her eyes bulged and her mouth grotesquely gaped open. Dried blood caked the woman's face from the bullet wound in her forehead. He didn't need to check for a pulse. Cooper froze in place, both confusion and terror filled him. The butt of a gun pressed against his middle. It pointed right at her.

Blood splatter and brain matter marked the wall behind his bed. Cooper dry heaved. He thrust himself back and landed with a thud on the floor. He stayed there like that on his hands and knees, waiting for the contents of his stomach to rise out of him.

Cooper tried to catch his breath, breathing slowly in through his nose and out through his mouth the way they had taught him in the police academy. It was a technique he had used frequently back when he had been a detective and he'd have to go to a particularly bloody crime scene. He didn't have the strongest stomach for it.

Cooper breathed in a steady rhythm over and over again until his stomach settled. His eyes watered and wetness streamed down his face. He wiped his eyes with the backs of his hands. He slowly looked back up at his bed and dry heaved once more. He repeated the breathing again until his stomach settled. Just as quickly though, terror replaced nausea. Could someone still be in his place? He listened for sound but heard nothing, just the stillness of the morning.

Cooper pushed himself off the floor into a standing position. It was then he noticed he was still dressed as he had been the night before. He forced himself to look at the bed. She was naked from the waist up. Cooper couldn't see more. The covers had been pulled up to her middle.

The terror returned. He couldn't understand the scene in front of him. Cooper raced out of his bedroom into the wide-open living space but found no one and nothing disturbed. From where Cooper stood, he could see every angle of his kitchen and living room. He scanned the rooms until his eyes settled on the front door. The bolt lock lay horizontal. Cooper had never even locked the door last night.

Cooper froze in place, trying desperately to recall anything from the night before. The dead woman in his bed wasn't a stranger. She was someone Cooper knew – intimately. Her name was Holly Reed. Cooper had had sex with her several months back right before he had left for Atlanta to help Luke on the case. It had been a one-night stand that had lingered. She had texted and called and showed up at his place when he was gone. She had sent him threatening texts that he'd pay for not going out with her again. She had made a real nuisance of herself. Cooper hadn't led her on. It was what it was, but she had become clingy, obsessive even. Now she was dead in his bed, and he had absolutely no memory of any of it.

Cooper raced back to the bedroom, steadied his stomach, and yanked the covers back. The gun. He reached his hand to pick it up and then stopped himself. He didn't want to have his prints on it if he hadn't been the one to fire it. He noticed then that Holly was completely naked.

Cooper left the gun on the bed and walked to his closet. Pulling open the door, Cooper stepped inside and moved to the back to the wall safe hidden behind a row of pressed shirts. He punched in the code and pulled open the door. His gun and other contents of the safe sat in place. Cooper slammed the safe door shut and raked a hand through his hair.

Cooper slowly brought his hands, palms up, to his front and peered down. They were free of blood, but if he had fired that weapon there might be traces of gunpowder residue. Cooper debated only for a second. He had no idea what was happening to him, but he didn't kill that woman. At least, he couldn't remember killing her.

Cooper jetted out of his bedroom and beelined for his bathroom. He didn't even flip on the light. He turned the handles to the sink, pumped out three shots of hand soap and scrubbed. He promised himself he'd touch nothing else, but he wanted any gunpowder off his hands. He scrubbed until his hands were raw and wiped them on the towel behind the door.

As Cooper made his way out of the bathroom, he locked eyes with his reflection in the mirror. It stopped him cold. He was acting like a guilty man. He'd just washed off evidence if, in fact, he had fired the gun. Now he'd never know for sure, but neither would the cops. It was right then he thought of Luke. Cooper winced. It was his best friend who'd investigate or maybe they'd assign one of the other detectives, but either way, Luke could be involved.

Cooper stepped back and leaned against the wall, taking in his reflection. Why couldn't he remember? He recalled being at the party, but it was fuzzy after that. Adele, the woman he had met in Atlanta whose sister had been murdered and he had been involved with for the last six months, had texted him to ask how the party was going. She had a criminal defense case wrapping up in court so she couldn't be there for the celebration. She was supposed to arrive tomorrow – Monday night. What would he tell her? Cooper shoved that thought aside. He'd deal with it later. It was the here and now that pressed him.

After getting Adele's text the night before, Cooper remembered he had stepped outside of the event venue into the spring night air to text Adele back. He had walked down the street, not even a block, farther into the River Market district and stepped into Kepler's – one of his favorite bars. He recalled ordering a beer and grabbing a table in a corner near the front window. The place hadn't been crowded. It had still been early in the evening.

Cooper stretched his memory, feeling some things start to gel. He had sat there texting Adele and drinking his beer. He couldn't recall the conversation though or even when he left. It was like walking up to an edge and then nothing. Sitting at that table was the last memory he had from the night before. Cooper shoved himself off the bathroom wall and went in search of his phone.

Cooper checked all his usual spots and then found it on the counter in his small galley kitchen. He picked it up and scanned the text messages. He had talked to Adele. The texts back and forth were right there, but his texts had become erratic. They made no sense and ended all together near ten-thirty. In her last messages, Adele had expressed concern for him. Cooper scrolled back up to where the text chain started and scanned through them quickly. His stomach dropped. Anger, even rage, had filled the lines of later texts. He complained about Holly. He railed against her.

He checked his call log. He had four missed calls from Adele from later after they had stopped texting. But he had talked to her earlier that night. There was one call that lasted for nearly half an hour. Adele had left him several messages, too. He'd have to listen to the messages later. He'd stalled for long enough.

Cooper took a deep breath and placed the call.

"911. What is your emergency?"

Cooper's voice caught in his throat. "There's been a murder. A woman is dead in my condo. In my bed. I woke up and found her there. I have no idea what happened." It sounded like a lie even to himself.

CHAPTER 3

As the six of them stood in front of the restaurant after brunch, Luke hugged his parents goodbye. Collectively, they had made the decision that Riley would spend a few more hours with Karen and Jack before their flight while Luke checked out the crime scene. Det. Bill Tyler had texted him several times with updates, and it quickly became apparent they were dealing with a homicide. Luke was itching to get to the scene.

Before they parted, Luke asked Riley, "Did you text Cooper this morning?"

"No, he seemed pretty tired last night. He had received a text from Adele about her upcoming visit and then he left. I hadn't had the chance to tell him about brunch. Did you?"

Luke shook his head. "He was gone last night before I could ask him."

"Do you want me to reach out to him?" Riley asked.

"I'll catch him later. He just took off so quickly last night, I didn't get a chance to catch up with him."

Riley reached up and gave Luke a kiss. "I'm sure he'll text you later. He's probably just sleeping in. Don't work too hard today. Remember you're supposed to be taking some time off."

As they parted and Riley went with her mother, Luke grabbed his car from the parking lot across from the restaurant and drove less than a mile down the road. The resort-style community, which had only been built two years earlier, had seven floors of apartments in a huge building shaped like a rectangle. The center offered an open courtyard with a pool and cabanas. Luke had never been inside but had seen photos in the newspaper around the time the place opened.

The uniformed officer stationed at the entrance to the parking garage recognized Luke and opened the gate for him. Luke pulled his car through and navigated his way into the parking structure. Det. Tyler had told him they were all parked on the sixth floor so Luke looped around the parking deck roadway until he reached that level. He pulled his car into an open spot, gathered his things, and moved with efficiency toward the entrance of the building.

Luke found Det. Tyler standing at the elevator talking to a crime scene tech. His brow furrowed as he pointed to a sheet of paper in front of him. As Luke approached, he realized Det. Tyler held a rendering of an apartment. It sketched out each room with dimensions and square footage.

"What do we have?" Luke asked, nodding hello to the crime tech whose name he couldn't quite remember. The guy took the rendering from Det. Tyler and went back into the building through the door next to the elevator.

"You really didn't need to come out for this, but glad you're here." Det. Tyler reached out and gave Luke a slap on the back. "We received a call early this morning about a strange smell coming from the sixth-floor hallway. The first call came in around five and then several more calls followed. Since it's Sunday, the office isn't open and no one could reach the staff who works here. Officers came out and started searching. Given the structure of the place, it was hard to pinpoint where the smell originated. The first call came in from the floor above and then another from below. There were a handful of calls from this floor. Finally, they zeroed in on an area. After checking with other residents, they pinpointed the apartment. The first officers on the scene found the door unlocked."

"Were you onsite for that or just the officer who took the call?"

"Just the officers here," Det. Tyler explained, "but after they went in and found the woman, they stepped back out and called us immediately. She's been dead for a few days. The body is bloated and discolored. Looks to me like she's been shot."

Luke scoped out the garage until he spotted the familiar Pulaski County Medical Examiner's Office van. "Ed Purvis inside?"

Det. Tyler followed Luke's gaze. "Yeah, he got here about thirty minutes ago with his team."

"Let's go in and check it out."

Det. Tyler pulled gloves out of his pocket and handed them to Luke. Luke snapped them on as Tyler opened the door for him. The smell of decay and death hit Luke in the face like a brick wall as soon as he stepped inside. He choked back a gag.

Det. Tyler shook his head. "I don't know how anyone is still in their apartments right now."

Luke coughed. "You have any idea of the age of the victim? You said she'd been shot. Any idea if that was self-inflicted?"

Det. Tyler walked down the hall first, showing Luke the way. "She didn't do it to herself. There's no weapon at the scene. I couldn't tell her age for sure, but by the look of her, probably thirties. I still haven't found a wallet or identification. The rent here goes for well over fifteen hundred a month so unless she had someone paying her bills, she has a decent job to afford it all."

The hallway turned off to the left and right. Det. Tyler turned left and Luke followed. Halfway down the hall, Luke caught sight of the crime scene tape. He was glad Det. Tyler had been outside to greet him and show him the way. One door was no different than the next. The industrial beige walls and overhead lighting created a maze-like effect.

Det. Tyler and Luke made their way past the throngs of officers milling around and stepped into the apartment. Luke scanned his eyes around the living room. It wasn't a large space, but the victim had it well-furnished. Nothing seemed out of place. Photos of cityscapes in black and white hung on the walls. The turquoise and black checkered pillows were arranged on the couch and chair. Nothing had, at least from what Luke saw, been disturbed. They made their way down the hall, past a small kitchen on the left and bathroom on the right and entered into the bedroom in the back of the apartment.

A queen-size bed sat against the back wall and a row of windows took up space on the right. A dresser with a mirror and chest of drawers were positioned directly across from the bed on the wall that had the door. The victim had been tidy. Even in her bedroom nothing seemed out of place. No piles of clothes or shoes. Barely anything, except a jewelry box and photo, on top of the dresser.

Ed Purvis, Pulaski County's Medical Examiner, stood over the victim's body. She was naked from the waist up with a blanket thrown over her lower torso. Her head was turned to face the windows. Blood had seeped from her nose and mouth. Although decomp had started, the round dark wound in the middle of her forehead was apparent. Dark bloodstains marked the floor next to the bed and the purple sheets beneath the victim.

"What do you think?" Luke asked Purvis, walking up behind the medical examiner and peering down at the victim.

Purvis turned and gave Luke a nod. "Good to see you. You've been a busy man. Glad to have you back."

"I'm not back officially. I'm supposed to take a couple of weeks off, but I was right around the corner with Riley. I thought I'd stop in since I was here. How long has she been dead?"

"I won't know officially until I'm back in my office and do the autopsy, but probably four or five days. I don't see any signs that it's a suicide. That's what it was first called in as because nothing in the apartment had been disturbed, but your guys have since done a thorough search, and there's no gun."

Purvis pointed to the back of the bed and then down at the sheets. "From the angle of the blood splatter and her position, she was shot right here on her back. She might have been asleep. I'm not seeing any struggle at all."

Luke took in the scene, moving around the victim's body, and noted some of the evidence Purvis pointed out.

"I don't know what this city is coming to," Purvis said, disgusted. "This is the third shooting like this we've had in a few weeks."

Luke raised his eyebrows. "I've been so busy that I hadn't heard about the others."

"There was a homicide last weekend in one of the downtown lofts. Det. Tyler arrested a guy who was with the female victim at the time of her death.

He claimed he didn't remember anything from the night before and woke up with the deceased. He did call 911 though. Then a couple of weeks back there was another shooting right down the road from here. They think it was a robbery or someone who knew the victim. Not much was disturbed much like this scene here. The door was unlocked so they figured someone got in."

As Purvis talked more, something caught Luke's eye. He moved around to the other side of the bed and reached down a gloved hand to pick up what at first looked like a large silver button. Only it wasn't a button. When Luke flipped it over, he looked closer. It was a round watch face without the wrist strap attached.

Purvis hitched his jaw in Luke's direction. "What did you find?"

Luke held it up. "Could be nothing, but it's a watch face. Let's make sure it's bagged."

Det. Tyler cleared his throat from the doorway. He held up a cellphone. "Luke, you're going to want to take this call. Units have responded to a 911 call from Cooper. He woke up to find a dead woman in the bed next to him."

CHAPTER 4

"Repeat what you just said." Luke wasn't sure he had heard his partner correctly.

Det. Tyler held the phone out to him. He insisted, "Just take the call. It's Captain Meadows."

Luke locked eyes with Purvis and compelled his feet to move. He grabbed the phone from Det. Tyler and briskly walked through the apartment, stepping out into the hall. He held the phone at his side until he was a safe distance away from all the other law enforcement personnel that remained at the scene.

"What's going on, Captain?" Luke asked in a rushed breath.

"I'm not sure exactly, but Cooper called 911 to report that he woke up this morning in bed with a dead woman next to him. He called to report it but gave few details. He was clear that he did not kill her, but he said he has no idea what happened."

"How did she die?" Luke ran a hand down his face.

"Gunshot wound."

Confused, Luke asked, "How can he not know what happened? He didn't hear the shot?"

Captain Meadows breathed out loudly. "Listen, I don't know the details. You just need to get over there. Purvis there with you?"

Luke looked back at the victim's apartment. "Yeah, he's here."

"Bring him with you. I'm requesting that he handles this one specifically. His team can take the case you're at now."

"What about the conflict of interest for me?"

"I thought of that, but Luke, we are swamped. There have been three gang homicides on the southside of the city in the last week. Det. Tyler is working the case you're at and two others from the past few weeks. I figured even if I told you to stay out of this with Cooper, you wouldn't listen. Take it for now, and we'll worry about the rest later. Cooper might talk to you and tell you what he wouldn't tell someone else. Just make sure to follow procedure. We'll have extra scrutiny on this case so we don't need any mistakes."

Luke stood frozen, unsure of what to do first. It didn't feel real. Luke scrambled through memories of the night before and his last moments with Cooper. Nothing of significance stood out. Luke walked back to the apartment and made his way to the bedroom. He handed the phone to Det. Tyler.

"Purvis, any chance your team can wrap this up here? There's a deceased woman at Cooper's condo. Captain Meadows is requesting you."

Purvis craned his neck to look back at Luke. "I'll be right behind you. I've already called in more staff. I'll meet you over there."

Luke headed back out stopping only briefly to update Det. Tyler what Captain Meadows had told him.

Det. Tyler shook his head. "This sudden convenient memory loss seems to be common. I had a case like that last weekend. The guy I arrested on the scene claimed the same thing."

"Did he do it?" Luke pressed.

"If he didn't, he sure looks guilty. No other possible explanation."

Luke made his way out of the apartments, pulled off his gloves, and headed towards Cooper's condo, which was in downtown Little Rock, a short drive from the Riverdale neighborhood.

Once there, Luke found a spot to park on the road and walked the block to Cooper's building. He took the elevator up to Cooper's floor. Once the elevator doors opened, Luke stepped into a circus of uniformed officers and crime scene techs and navigated down the hallway to Cooper's unit. Through the throngs of people, Luke spotted Cooper sitting on the couch with an officer by his side.

Luke pushed his way past and entered Cooper's residence. Cooper stood as soon as he saw him. "What happened?" Luke asked, his voice not sounding like his own.

Cooper didn't even hesitate. "I don't know. I woke up this morning feeling completely hungover. I rolled over to my side and there she was."

"What do you mean by 'there she was'? You just woke up and there's a dead woman? Do you know her?"

Cooper looked down at the floor, not making eye contact with anyone. "Yeah, she's someone I spent the night with once a few months back before I left for Atlanta." He brought his gaze back to Luke. "Riley met her. Actually, Riley met her the morning you got the letter from your sister's killer."

"What's been your interaction with her to date?"

Cooper looked around the room. "Do you really want to do this here? We can go down to the station and talk."

"Wait here." Luke headed into Cooper's bedroom. He stepped around an officer standing in the doorway and was immediately struck by an eerily similar scene. The woman's body was positioned similarly and the gunshot wound nearly identical to the victim he had just left. The only difference was this victim looked to have been in a sitting position when she was killed. Again, the scene offered no sign of a struggle.

Luke snapped a few photos with his phone around the room, taking in the rumpled bedsheets, discarded clothing on the floor, and the victim's blood and brain matter on the wall. Luke bent down to more closely examine the gun on the bed. It was a Sig Sauer P229 Legion Compact, not too unlike his own service weapon. Luke knew Cooper had a Glock, and to his knowledge, Cooper only had the one handgun and no others.

"Make sure you are careful bagging that," Luke instructed the crime scene tech more out of habit than need. The crime scene techs in Little Rock were the best in the state.

Luke started to make his way out of the bedroom but only made it halfway up the hall when Purvis entered the residence. Luke waved him back. Stepping back into the bedroom, Luke asked for the room to be cleared. He promised the crime techs they could get back to work as soon as the medical examiner had taken a cursory look.

Luke gave Purvis a moment to look around the scene before asking, "See any similarities to the scene we just left?"

Purvis nodded slowly. "It's nearly identical. Does Cooper know about the other?"

"Not that I'm aware of. I'm taking him down to the station to talk. If you find anything of interest, send me a text."

Luke left Purvis and walked back into the living room. He caught the tail end of Cooper's conversation with the officer. Luke interrupted, "Did you say there are cameras in the hallway?"

Cooper stepped back so Luke could join the conversation. "I did. The recordings are only stored for a short period of time though so you need to get ahold of them immediately. Someone else had to be here. When I woke up, I found my front door unlocked. I swear to you, I didn't kill her."

Luke scanned the rest of Cooper's place. He didn't see anything out of place. "Where's your gun? The one on the bed is different from the one that's registered to you."

"I don't know where that came from. Mine is in the safe in my bedroom. It was one of the first things I checked this morning. What you asked me to hold is still there, too. I haven't been robbed."

Before Luke could respond, a voice behind him asked, "Did you do all that before or after you called 911?"

A man with short dark hair wearing a tailored suit leaned against the doorframe. He stepped forward with his hand out to Luke. "I'm Don Jennings. I'm the new assistant prosecutor with Pulaski County."

Luke eyed him suspiciously but shook the man's hand. At six foot, Luke and the man stood eye to eye. He was a slight man though. Luke guessed he had probably forty pounds on the guy. Both of the man's hands could have fit in his own. "Det. Lucas Morgan," was all Luke said.

Jennings stepped back appraising them both. The disdain evident on his face. "I know who you are. I'm surprised you'd be assigned to this case given your close friendship with the suspect."

Luke ignored the insinuation. "We don't normally have anyone from the prosecutor's office involved until we are further into a case. Can I help you with something?"

The man folded his arms across his chest. "No, nothing now, but I'll be watching this case carefully to ensure the Little Rock Police Department doesn't protect one of their own. Just because Cooper was once a detective with the police force, doesn't mean he's immune from a murder conviction."

Cooper started to protest. Luke could see the red rising from his neck to his face. Luke reached a hand out to stop him. "We show no favoritism to anyone." Luke escorted Cooper past Jennings, brushing against him as he passed.

CHAPTER 5

Cooper sat in the small interrogation room at the police station. He'd never been on this side of the table before. The room, with its beige walls and overhead lighting, seemed distinctly more cramped and confining than it did when he was a detective. Maybe it was now, unlike every other time he'd been in the space, because Cooper wasn't sure he'd be free to leave.

Luke and Cooper had gone to college and joined the police force together. They rose in the ranks and became detectives months apart. Cooper found over time that the confines of police work didn't work for him. While Cooper loved the investigative challenge, he hated the bureaucracy of it all. He preferred working on his own. That's why he quit the force a few years ago and opened his own private investigation firm. Riley had joined him last year after she moved from New York. He liked having her as a partner.

Since starting his business, Cooper had been taking private cases and absolutely loving it. The cases ranged from cheating spouses and child custody to tougher missing persons, cold case homicides and the occasional criminal defense. Sure, he had to testify in court once in a while, but he had no boss to answer to. He could hunt for the truth without the pressure of case closure rates and the media breathing down his neck.

Now though, Cooper knew it was Luke's job to rule him in or out as a killer. If he were standing in Luke's shoes, he'd suspect himself, too. All Cooper wanted to do at that moment, other than take a long, hot shower and put on fresh clothes, which he hadn't had the chance to do that morning, was get out of this confining space and put all of his skills to work finding the person who had killed Holly and set him up.

Cooper knew as he sat there that he might be watched. The interrogation room had a camera in the ceiling, and the whole room was wired for audio. Luke hadn't taken his cellphone away, which was good because Cooper needed an ally.

He pulled his phone from his pocket and punched in a text to Riley. *I'm in serious trouble and need your help.*

Cooper set the phone down and waited. Riley wasn't emotional. She nearly always remained levelheaded. She was probably the most logical woman he knew. Some might say even logical to a fault. That's why she made such a good investigator and even better friend. Riley never became unhinged. She stayed calm and rational at all times. Cooper needed that right now. As much as he tried to remain calm on the outside and keep his words and responses measured, sweat pooled at his back and his hands shook as he typed.

Riley responded faster than Cooper thought she would. *What's going on? Girl trouble? lol*

Cooper typed knowing that one day this conversation could become evidence. *Something like that. I woke up to find Holly dead in my bed this morning. She was shot. At the police station now. Luke is about to question me. You know I didn't do this so we need to find out who is framing me.*

Riley sent several texts in response: *Are you serious? What happened? Are you okay?*

I don't know. I have no memory of last night after a certain point. I went to Kepler's after the event but can't remember anything about last night after that point. I just can't remember.

Riley wrote just three words, but the text carried a powerful message, something that hadn't even occurred to Cooper. *Were you drugged?*

Cooper recalled his last memory sitting at a table, drinking his beer laughing while he texted Adele. He still couldn't remember anything after that. But if he were drugged, it couldn't have been from that beer. He chatted with the bartender as he poured it. It never left his sight. If he were drugged, it had to have been later in the night.

Cooper asked: *I don't know. Can they test for that now or is it too late?*

Riley responded: *A urine analysis should show GHB up to twelve hours and Rohypnol up to twenty-four. Request the test immediately.*

I'll go and ask Luke. Will you help me find Holly's killer? It wasn't me, Riley. I swear to you I didn't do this.

Of course, you didn't. I'll help however I can. But I don't understand something. Luke and I were at brunch with our parents. Det. Tyler was at a scene right near there in Riverdale with the suspicious death of a woman. You said the woman was dead at your place?

Cooper hadn't thought to question where Luke had been prior or why the medical examiner looked so frazzled. He hadn't heard anything about another case.

Cooper typed back: *They must have come from that scene to mine. Any idea what happened there?*

I really don't know. I haven't heard from Luke. Cooper, should you really talk to Luke without a lawyer? I know he's your friend, but this is serious. You know Luke. He's going to be harder on you than most suspects.

Suspect. There was that word again. Cooper had been avoiding even thinking about it. He was a suspect in a murder investigation. A murder that occurred in his apartment and in his bed, no less. Even if he didn't go to jail tonight, could he really go home? Could he ever go back again? Cooper may have lacked family, but his residence was his safety net, or at least it was before last night.

Cooper typed just a few last words to Riley. *I want to talk to Luke without a lawyer for now at least. I haven't done anything wrong. He knows I haven't. I know you've never spoken to Adele, but she knows all about you and Luke. Please call her for me and tell her what's happening. I'm going to talk to Luke now.*

Cooper sent one more text with Adele's phone number and then stood. He carried the phone with him as he opened the door and stepped out into the hallway. There was no one in sight, which was good. He slowly moved down the hall toward the detective's bullpen where he assumed Luke would be at his desk. His phone chimed again. Cooper stopped mid-hallway and put the phone on silent before reading Riley's text.

Cooper, I hope you know how sorry I am this is happening. Anything you need, you know I'm here. I'll call Adele.

Cooper thanked her and put his phone back in his pocket. Riley didn't need to say what she said. Cooper knew that. He didn't have much family. His father, now deceased, had been married several times and there had been a horde of stepsiblings in and out of his life, but no one he ever attached to. His mother had passed when Cooper was just a baby. There were no aunts or uncles or even cousins. Luke and Riley were the closest family he had.

Now it was Luke's job to figure out if he was a killer. It put them on opposite sides of the table for the first time in the history of their friendship.

Luke sat at his desk with his head down focused on a file in front of him. Cooper cleared his throat. "Luke, I just talked to Riley. She told me I should get tested immediately for GHB or Rohypnol. She said it could be why I have memory loss."

Luke stood; annoyance was written all over his face. "I wish you hadn't involved Riley."

Cooper sighed loudly and moved closer to Luke. "Come on, man, she'd find out later today anyway."

"I'm in a complicated situation here, Cooper. You woke up this morning to find a woman you have a history with dead in your bed. Anyone else would probably be arrested right now."

Cooper held his arms open wide. "You know me better than anyone. Come interrogate me. Give it your best shot. You're searching my place right now. I came down here willingly. It was my idea. I'll tell you anything you want to know, but I'm telling you I don't remember a thing about last night. At least test me before it's out of my system. I need to know why I can't remember. What Riley said is the first thing that's made sense since I opened my eyes this morning."

Luke didn't say anything. He stood with his hands on his hips, mouth set in a straight line.

Cooper pulled his phone out and offered it to Luke. "Take it. Read my messages to Adele last night. I'm coherent and then I'm not. I talked to her on the phone, too. Call her and see what she tells you. I haven't even told her any of this is happening. She'll tell you but look right in the text messages. She wrote it. I stopped making any sense at all. Something happened to me last night long before Holly was murdered."

Luke hesitated only for a second. He didn't take Cooper's cellphone but instead turned back to his desk, picked up the phone and placed a call.

Turning back to Cooper when he was done, Luke explained, "Someone will be up soon to take your blood and do a urine test. Let's go talk while we wait."

CHAPTER 6

I sat in my car in the airport's short-term parking lot staring at my cellphone on my lap. I just dropped my mother and Jack off for their flight. I walked them in as far as I could go before the security checkpoint and hugged my mother goodbye. I only made a few feet away from her when I got the text from Cooper.

His message caught me off guard in such a way that I had to sit down on a bench in the airport to process what he had told me. I couldn't wrap my mind around the words Cooper had written. I read the text at least fifty times, desperately trying to make sense of it.

I knew Holly, well of her, anyway. I had met her briefly at Cooper's apartment the morning I went to tell him about the letter Luke had received from his sister's killer. She had been possessive of Cooper even then. Later, Cooper had confided how much she had harassed him after he turned her down.

I couldn't believe that Cooper had killed her, but it also stretched my imagination to understand how someone had drugged him so easily. While Cooper did engage in the occasional one-night stand, I'd never considered him to be reckless. In fact, Cooper was far more of a rule follower when it came to our investigations than he'd probably like to admit. I was the one who was sometimes willing to break the rules, much to the chagrin of Luke and Cooper. Sometimes things had to be done for the sake of justice. Sometimes you had to get creative.

It was his rule-following personality that had me convinced that Cooper hadn't killed Holly. Not only did I think Cooper wouldn't hurt a woman, but

I knew he wouldn't have ever gone home with her. Cooper had fallen head over heels for another woman. I knew beyond any shadow of a doubt that Cooper would never do anything to jeopardize his relationship with Adele. He'd never let Holly back in his apartment let alone in his bed. Through and through Cooper was a gentleman. He'd never cheat. I knew that much about him if I knew anything.

At that moment though, I didn't know what I could do to help. Cooper was being questioned. His condo would be swarming with cops. I was hamstrung to do anything at the moment.

Cooper had asked me to call Adele and that's what I would do as soon as I got home. I drove the route back home in a fog. I traversed over familiar streets without even so much as a passing thought as to where I headed. It was rote memory for me at this point, and my mind was pinned on how the situation the night before could have unfolded and what exactly I'd tell Adele.

I pulled into my driveway and slipped my car into park. Coming home held such a different feeling than the promise of a great spring day that I had felt when I had left that morning. I unlocked the front door, dropped my purse on the couch and went to the kitchen to pour myself something to drink. Once I settled at the kitchen table, I looked at my phone, dreading the call I was about to make. Adele needed to be told though. I punched in her number and it barely rang. Adele answered immediately.

"Adele, it's Riley, Cooper's friend—"

She interrupted. "Is Cooper okay? I've been worried about him since last night, but I didn't know who to call. He's not answering."

"He's not in any physical danger, but Cooper is in trouble." I tried to make my voice even. I didn't want her to panic, although she probably should.

Adele groaned. "I knew it. I knew something was wrong last night when I was texting him. I called him and then he called me back. When we were talking, I thought he might be really drunk, but he said he hadn't had much to drink. He was yelling at some guy. It sounded like total chaos and then he hung up. I couldn't reach him after that. I sent a few texts and called. I hoped he went home and slept it off. I've been sitting here worried."

I hesitated, trying to find the right words. "Adele, Cooper's at the police station right now being questioned. When he woke up this morning there was a dead woman beside him in bed."

Adele gasped. "Was her name Holly?"

I was taken aback. I had no idea Cooper had shared his history with Adele. "It was. What do you know about her?"

"Nothing until last night. Cooper complained that she was in the bar. He thought about leaving. He admitted that right before we met, he had a fling with her. One night, he said, nothing serious, but that she had been harassing him since. Cooper said he had decided to stay in the bar last night and finish his beer because he was tired of the whole situation. Cooper insisted he wouldn't give up his favorite spot for anyone. But then things took a turn."

I had no idea that Adele would be such an asset piecing together the events of the previous night. Cooper had given me no indication. "What do you mean took a turn?"

"Cooper was different," Adele started, frustration apparent in her voice. "His texting became erratic. I thought maybe he had downplayed what he had to drink earlier in the evening. He started spelling things incorrectly. But more than that, Cooper stopped making sense. He was rambling and incoherent. I can't explain it better than that. You'd have to see the text messages. I called him then. Cooper didn't answer, but he called me back."

I got up from the kitchen table and dashed up to my home office. I needed pen and paper. I wanted to take notes. I asked Adele to hold on until I got caught up. I asked her a few more clarifying questions that filled in some blanks for me up to that point, and then I asked her to tell me about the call.

Adele breathed out slowly. "Cooper slurred his words. In fact, it was hard to understand him at all. There was a man, too. I don't know his name, but Cooper was talking to him while I was on the phone. He asked Cooper a few times why he didn't like Holly. He pressed Cooper about how he could have a one-night stand like that but then drop her so casually. Cooper thought it might be a friend of hers, but the guy also told Cooper that he gave guys a bad name. That he made it harder for everyone. Cooper just kept saying he was sorry, that he didn't mean to hurt anyone."

"Could you hear anyone else?"

"It was getting loud in the place at that point. I couldn't really hear Cooper at all. I heard a woman, too, but no idea who she was. I couldn't understand what she was saying. It sounded like a couple of people were ganging up on Cooper. He was so out of it at that point he was barely making sense."

Delicately, I asked, "Didn't it bother you to listen to people talk about Cooper with another woman, especially since Holly was right there in the bar?"

"Riley, I don't know what Cooper has told you, but he and I are very much in love. Actually, he asked me to move in with him. I know it's really fast, but we live so far apart. When you know you know, and I know without question how committed Cooper is to me. So no, it didn't bother me. What bothered me was how out of character Cooper seemed last night. I was worried about him."

I was shocked to hear Cooper had asked Adele to move in. Not that it was any of our business, but Cooper had never told us. "I think it's really important for you to speak to Luke. He's going to want to know everything you just told me."

"Riley, does Cooper have an attorney with him?"

"No, I told him he should get one, but I think because he and Luke have been friends for so long Cooper didn't want one."

There was some movement on the other end. A book being slapped down on a desk, pages being flipped. Adele's voice was strong and insistent. "If you can reach Cooper, tell him not to say anything. I'm licensed to practice law in Arkansas. I was planning to arrive tomorrow night, but I'm going to see if I can catch an earlier flight out in the morning."

I didn't know what to say. I really had no idea Cooper had become this serious with her. "I…" I started and stammered, trying to get my mouth to catch up with my thoughts. "I'll tell him. I can pick you up from the airport if you'd like."

Adele told me she'd text me when she arranged her flight. I had no idea if what just transpired would make Cooper happy or not. I certainly hoped it didn't add complication to his life.

CHAPTER 7

Cooper followed Luke back to the interrogation room and sat at the far side of the table away from the door where suspects sat. It was an odd, disorienting feeling for Cooper knowing he was quite literally on the wrong side of the table.

Luke dropped a file down and pulled in his chair. He locked eyes with Cooper. "Help me to understand what happened."

Cooper stared at Luke blankly. He was overcome with emotion and blinked back tears.

Luke said, "If you want to speak to a lawyer, please do. I'll understand. You have a right to one. But you and I both know I have to ask you some tough questions. Start with meeting Holly initially and bring me right up to last night."

Cooper quickly wiped the tears out of his eyes. He let out a breath and told Luke the story. "I met Holly at Kepler's in the River Market one night. I was having dinner there, and she was with friends. It was a weekday night. I had just come back from a child custody case and wanted to wind down. I don't remember all the little details of our meeting because it was fairly unremarkable. She noticed me first and came over to my table. That much I do remember because she was quite forward, more so than women usually are with me."

Luke pressed, "What do you mean? What did she do exactly?"

Cooper shrugged. "Holly brought me a beer. She sat down at the table without asking if I wanted company. She told me she thought I was hot. She was forceful about it. Holly wasn't shy. That probably should have been a red flag for me. I found her attractive, and I don't know, maybe I was lonely. Maybe I hadn't had any in a while, but I flirted back. She kissed me right in the bar, and when she suggested we go back to my place, I went willingly. We hadn't even known each other for two hours. It was an incredibly stupid thing to do."

Cooper looked across the table at Luke and knew he was being judged. Luke had never been cavalier like that about his personal life. Cooper wasn't usually that easy either. Yes, he'd had some one-night stands, but not like that. Yes, he had a time or two met a woman in a bar and taken her back to his place, but not like that.

Cooper met women, they talked and flirted and enjoyed each other's company. He never went into something with the intention that it was one night. Sometimes he found they weren't compatible in bed. Sometimes they never called him back. More times than not, women simply didn't understand the erratic hours he worked and wanted more consistency in life than a private investigator could afford. Making plans wasn't always in the cards.

Holly was different, but she didn't deserve to die. She had her own reasons for doing what she did. Cooper certainly wasn't one to judge her for her choices. And he, in turn, didn't want to be judged for his. Luke's look of disdain for him said it all.

"What happened after you went back to your place?"

Cooper raised his eyebrows. "I'm not going to detail the sex."

"That isn't what I meant. Did you talk or was it just sex? What happened the next morning?"

Cooper measured his words carefully. "Holly was all over me as soon as I closed and locked the door to my place. She didn't seem interested in conversation. The sex happened nearly immediately, and again an hour later. In the morning, she was different. Softer. She wanted to go to breakfast. If I recall correctly, Riley was on her way over, and I was rushing to get her out of my place. The first time I had any hint that maybe things were a mistake was when Holly got out of the shower and she left. She gave Riley a dirty look and kissed me like she had the night before. It was a possessive move that would be a precursor of other things to come."

Luke reached down to the folder that he had brought in with him and grabbed a pen and a small spiral notebook. "Tell me more about that. What interaction did you have with her after that night?"

Cooper thought back, wanting to remember correctly, knowing how imperative it was. He raked a hand through his hair. "I only saw her twice more in person. Once was actually when I had lunch with Captain Meadows. When we were leaving Doe's Eat Place, Holly walked in. She grabbed me and kissed me right there in front of everyone."

"Captain Meadows see that?"

"Yes, it was actually embarrassing the way she just grabbed me. It completely threw me off guard."

Luke jotted down a note. "When was the second time you saw her?"

"One night I stopped into the Flying Saucer. She came up to me, and we interacted. We had a tentative date planned for the following Friday. It was something I had said when she left my place that morning, that maybe we could see each other the following Friday. I had to cancel because I was headed to Atlanta. She wanted me to cancel my trip and was really insistent about it. I told her that it wasn't possible and that maybe we weren't a good fit if she couldn't understand my work. She told me I'd pay for how I had treated her, and she walked away."

Remembering the time at the bar jogged a memory for Cooper. He leaned forward. "Actually, there's a bartender there who told me to be careful with Holly. He said a friend of his had gone out with her, and she had keyed that guy's car."

"Got a name?"

"I think it's Drew."

Luke jotted a few notes down. He looked back up at Cooper. "Was that the last time you saw Holly before last night?"

"The time at the Flying Saucer, when she told me I'd pay. I have a vague memory of Holly being in Kepler's last night, but I don't recall speaking to her. I don't even understand why this all started back up again. I slept with her months ago before I left for Atlanta. While I was gone, Holly texted me a lot, and I blocked her. When I got back, she texted me a few times from a different number, and I blocked that, too. Honestly, I thought it had stopped for good. There's been no sign of her over the last two months."

Before Luke said anything further, there was a knock at the door. One of the crime techs waved Cooper out, ready to take Cooper's blood and do the urine test. He left Luke sitting at the table. When the door closed behind him, Cooper breathed a sigh of relief that maybe this test would give him some answers.

Cooper returned nearly thirty minutes later with a small Band-Aid in the crook of his arm. Sitting back down at the table, he explained, "They said we should know the results within forty-eight hours at the latest. They took a strand of my hair, too. They said that roofies can be detected for up to thirty days. I had no idea they could do that."

Luke just nodded. "I just messaged Captain Meadows, and he confirmed what you said about Holly kissing you at Doe's. You don't recall talking to Holly last night so we'll get to that, but tell me the last time you recall having direct contact with her in person or via text."

Cooper searched his memories until he landed on the last conversation. "Holly texted me a photo of herself sitting outside of my condo when I was in Atlanta. I told her right then and there that I didn't want to see her anymore. I apologized and said we'd just be better off going our separate ways. After that, she sent a series of angry texts over the next month or so from her phone and then another that I ignored. I eventually blocked both numbers."

Luke squinted at him. "What do you mean outside of your condo, like your building?"

"No, she was in my building leaning up against my door."

"How did she get in? The outside doors to your place are always locked. You need a key or passcode."

"I never really gave that any thought," Cooper admitted. "Maybe she saw me type in the passcode the night we went back to my place."

Luke tapped his pen against the paper. "If Holly got into your building once on her own, it means she could have done it again last night."

"I didn't even think of that."

Luke breathed out a quick breath. "That's not surprising. It doesn't sound like you were thinking at all when it came to this woman."

Cooper's head snapped back like he'd been slapped.

CHAPTER 8

"You can cut the sanctimonious crap, Luke. We went to college together. Don't sit there and tell me you've never had a one-night stand because I know you have." Cooper glared at his friend.

Luke didn't say anything for several more moments. "Of course, I have, but you seem to make a real habit of it. Didn't you ever think that your lifestyle might lead to danger or could set you up for something you weren't expecting?"

Cooper let out an incredulous laugh. "Yeah, like an unwanted pregnancy or sexually transmitted disease. I don't think it goes through any guy's head that he shouldn't have sex with a woman because she might turn psycho or end up dead in his bed. I can tell you with certainty that never crossed my mind."

"That isn't what I meant." Luke softened his tone, but the damage was done.

Cooper felt the heat rise up his neck and face. He was ready for a fight and pounded his fist on the table. "Then say what you mean."

Luke dropped his head and looked at his notes. "What time did you leave the party last night, and where did you go?"

Not that Cooper was expecting Luke to apologize, but it would have felt better if he had. "I left around nine. Adele had texted me, and I wanted to sit and chat with her. I went down to Kepler's and grabbed a beer. I sat at the table I like near the window."

"What time did you return home?"

"I don't know." Cooper wasn't sure if Luke didn't believe him about his memory loss or if he was testing him.

Luke held Cooper's gaze. "What is the last thing you do remember?"

"Having a good time texting Adele. I kind of recall drinking another beer, but I don't remember ordering it." Cooper reached in his pocket and slid his phone across the table to Luke. "Read my text messages. You'll see a little after ten, I started sounding strange. Some of the words are misspelled and sentences don't make any sense."

Luke reached out and took Cooper's phone. He read through the section of the text messages. Cooper watched as Luke's eyes got wider, confusion blanketed his face. Luke popped his head up to look at Cooper. "You really do seem incoherent at times. I see that Adele called you and then you called her back right around ten-thirty. I'm going to need to speak to her about that call. What do you remember about it?"

"Nothing. If my phone didn't show that I spoke to her for nearly thirty minutes I wouldn't have even known we talked."

Luke slid the phone back to Cooper. "We are going to need to get your phone records. Are you okay with that?"

"I'll call my phone company right now and hand them over to you myself. I'm not trying to hide anything here, Luke. I really want to know who killed Holly as much as you do."

Luke leaned back in his seat. He looked to the ceiling and exhaled slowly. Making eye contact with Cooper again, he asked, "What do you remember about last night after that?"

"Nothing. I have no memory. It's wiped clean. I don't know when I left the bar. I don't know when I came home. I don't remember what happened when I came home. Luke, I swear to you, I don't remember anything. I've tried to recall. There's nothing. Trust me, I wish I knew. I don't even know if I had sex with Holly last night. I couldn't even tell you if I cheated on my girlfriend, but I woke up fully dressed in the same clothes as last night so I don't think that happened."

Cooper leaned forward and stared directly at Luke. He pointed his finger. "But I do know I didn't kill her. I'd feel it. I'd know that much." Cooper started to tear up again. He swallowed fast and blinked back tears. "I couldn't kill her, Luke. I've only taken a life once and that was to save Riley. I still think about that every single day."

"That was justified, Cooper. You know that."

"I know, but it doesn't mean that it doesn't stay with me. I could never take an innocent life. Think what you want about me and my careless personal life. Yeah, maybe I enjoyed being a bachelor too much, but I could never kill someone – let alone an innocent woman."

They were interrupted by another knock on the door. Det. Tyler stuck his head inside, gave Cooper a nod, and said, "Luke, can I talk to you for a second?" Luke got up and left the conference room closing the door behind him.

Cooper sat back, wiped the wetness from his eyes and closed them shut. He took a few deep breaths, trying to push the image of the crime scene in his bedroom out of his mind. He couldn't help but wonder if he missed anything when he went through his apartment before he called 911. He did his best not to disturb the body so he didn't touch Holly at all. Cooper knew he had nothing to hide but he hated that cops, many of whom he once worked with, were going through the intimate details of his residence.

Cooper's phone vibrated in his pocket. He looked toward the door and then pulled out his phone. There was a text from Riley and from Adele from earlier. Both texts said pretty much the same thing. Don't talk to the cops and that Adele was on her way. Riley had indicated that Adele told her she was licensed to practice law in Arkansas. Did Riley and Adele really think he needed a criminal defense lawyer? He texted Adele back first, apologizing and telling her he couldn't wait to see her. He thanked Riley for her help. Cooper didn't disclose to either that he was sitting talking to Luke at that very moment.

Cooper slid his phone back in his pocket just as Luke turned the handle on the door and pushed it open. He had a glossy photo in his hand. Normally, Cooper would have asked Luke what Det. Tyler wanted, but he knew sitting where he sat it wouldn't be appropriate. Instead, he waited for Luke to speak first.

Luke put the photo down on the table facing Cooper and slid it in his direction. "Do you know this woman?"

Cooper glanced down at the photo of the dark-haired woman smiling back at him. He didn't recognize her, but he picked up the photo to have a closer look. The photo looked like it was taken at a Christmas party. There were people in the background standing in front of a lit Christmas tree. The woman wore a red dress and was smiling happily for the camera. Cooper was sure he didn't know her. He set the photo back down and nudged it toward Luke. "No idea who she is. Should I know her?"

"Before I came to your place, we got a call to go to Riverstone apartments for a suspicious death. Cops found this woman in her bed with a bullet wound through her forehead much in the way you found Holly this morning. The victim's name is Casey Perry. The medical examiner believes she's been dead for a few days. We won't know the exact time of death until Purvis has time to complete his assessment. Where were you Tuesday and Wednesday night of last week?"

Cooper sat back and crossed his arms defiantly. He scowled at Luke. "What do you think I'm running around Little Rock killing women now? I saved Riley, put my entire life on hold to help you catch your sister's killer, but now suddenly I'm a serial killer?"

"You know that's not what I mean. I'm just establishing your alibi. Please stop taking everything I say the wrong way. Cooper, I want you to go home tonight as much as you want to, but I have to ask these questions. It's going to be my job to inform everyone why I'm not arresting you. Make that job easy for me."

Cooper didn't relax his posture. "If you recall I was with Riley nearly all of Tuesday afternoon and the both of you Tuesday night. Wednesday, after ten in the morning and well into the night I worked a case. I have a video with time and date stamp to prove that."

CHAPTER 9

I paced the floor much of the afternoon. I hadn't been able to sit still. It took everything I had to force myself to my desk long enough to type up a report that needed to be on the desk of a family law attorney in the morning from a recent child custody case I had worked. I had hoped typing the report would have taken my mind off Cooper, but it hadn't. The report seemed like an annoyance I couldn't wait to complete. It took up mental space that I should have been using figuring out who set up Cooper.

I hadn't heard from Luke all day even though I had texted him at least ten times. I was pretty sure he was ignoring me, not sure how to address his feelings over the entire situation. Maybe he was just busy, but even so, he normally would at least say hello and tell me he'd call me later. There was no response from him at all.

The afternoon had turned into evening. I wasn't even sure when, or if, Luke was coming home. I decided to start some dinner just in case. I dug through the cabinets and pulled together some pasta and store-bought sauce. I added some hot Italian sausages to the sauce and added a few spices. It wasn't a fancy meal by any stretch, but it served its purpose and would be easy enough for Luke to reheat.

I had just sat down at the kitchen table and was twirling spaghetti on my fork when Luke unlocked the front door. I resisted the urge to rush him with a million questions. He yelled to me that he was going to take a shower and would be back down in a minute. I put my fork with half-twirled spaghetti back on my plate and got up to grab a plate and silverware for Luke.

I fixed him a plate when I heard the water shut off. By the time he threw on shorts and a tee-shirt, his dinner was waiting on the table.

Luke entered the kitchen, smiled down at his food when he saw it and came around the table to give me a kiss. "I'm sorry I didn't get back to you today. Nothing seemed like the right thing to say." Luke sat down and took a sip of his drink.

Not that I wanted to start right in on him, but I wanted to know. "Where's Cooper?"

Luke took a bite of his food and chewed slowly. I wasn't sure if he was meaning to keep me in suspense or not, but it had that effect. I picked up my own fork and started to eat.

When Luke was done, he locked eyes with me. "He's at the Marriott tonight. He couldn't go back to his place. After talking to Captain Meadows and running it by Det. Tyler, we determined that we don't have enough right now to arrest him. We took the clothes he was wearing as evidence, gave him some of my extra clothes I keep at the station, and I escorted him myself to the hotel."

I dropped my fork, clanging it against my plate. "You don't have enough to arrest right now as in you're looking for more evidence to arrest Cooper or you're looking for the actual killer? The two aren't the same."

Luke put his fork down on his plate calmly and sighed loudly. "Riley, I can't get into this with you. I'm letting the evidence guide me. I still have a job to do. Do I think Cooper is a killer? No, but I have to go where the evidence leads me, and right now, there's a lot of evidence against Cooper."

I stood up, pushing my chair back forcefully. I couldn't believe what I was hearing. "You're letting the evidence guide you? This is your best friend you're talking about, not just some random guy you golf with occasionally. Cooper is family. You know he didn't kill that horrible woman."

Luke looked at me with pleading eyes. He reached for me, but I stepped back out of his grasp. He withdrew his hand and explained, "I don't think Cooper intentionally killed her, but I think it's been firmly established that he wasn't in his right mind. Now, whether he killed her in a fit of rage or even by accident, I don't know. The point is nothing has been ruled out or in right now. None of the evidence is back."

"I don't understand how you could suspect Cooper at all." I knew that I was being unreasonable as soon as it was out of my mouth.

Luke stood, knocking his chair back and tipping it over, sending it crashing to the floor. He raised his voice at me for the first time in our relationship. "You don't understand how I can even suspect him? Are you kidding me? Cooper woke up in bed with a dead woman who had been shot in the head, Riley! The gun that was used to kill her was between them. If all that wasn't bad enough, Cooper claims he has absolutely no memory of how he got back to his place or how the woman ended up dead in his bed or even what the heck he was doing during the time the murder was committed. I'd be out of my mind and completely incompetent at my job if I didn't at least consider his actions suspicious."

I knew Luke was right. I wanted to reach for him and apologize, but I didn't. It all just felt out of my control. No matter the circumstances, Cooper wasn't a killer. That's the only truth I knew for sure. I didn't do any of the loving things I should have done at the moment to reassure Luke I understood. Instead, stupidly, I dug in deeper. "That's why you should be out there finding whoever killed her so you can answer all those questions."

"You're impossible sometimes, you know that," Luke growled. He looked down at his plate of half-eaten food and back up at me. He huffed a few more times but eventually calmed himself down. "Riley, the last thing I want to do is fight with you. All I can tell you is that this is killing me, but I have a job to do. I've been on such a high these last few months, and this morning, it all just came crashing down. No one, not Captain Meadows, not Det. Tyler, not anyone at the station believes Cooper intentionally murdered this woman, but we have a job to do."

I resisted the urge to throw my arms around Luke and tell him that it was all going to be okay. I couldn't switch emotions like that and quickly calm down like Luke. I was angry and didn't know where else to direct it. I folded my arms across my chest. "How is Captain Meadows even allowing you to be on the case?"

Luke shook his head. "I'm not sure how long I will be. We are understaffed and have had a few murder cases recently so the detectives are spread thin. I think he knew I wouldn't want Cooper's fate in anyone else's hands, and I don't, Riley. You have to believe me when I say I'm going to follow the evidence, but I'm going to do my best to protect my best friend. He's like a brother to me."

Luke bent over and picked up his chair and sat back down. As he pulled himself to the table, he met my look. "Are you going to calm down and finish eating? It's good. I'm grateful you cooked."

I didn't budge though. I wasn't even sure why I was being so stubborn.

"Come on, sit," Luke urged. "I'll tell you about the case I went to right after brunch if you can keep it between us."

He was bribing me with information. I sat down begrudgingly and picked up my fork from my plate. At least the spaghetti was still warm.

Luke took a quick sip of his drink and wiped his mouth with his napkin. "The case this morning was eerily similar to what we found in Cooper's apartment, but that victim had been dead for a few days."

"Do you mean you think they are connected?" Even if Luke believed Cooper had killed Holly accidentally, I knew Luke would never think Cooper had killed multiple women.

"I don't know if they are connected or not. I won't know until we get the ballistics back on each case, test the gun for prints and so forth. It was striking to me that neither scene looked like there was a struggle. Also, Cooper said that when he got up this morning, he found his door unlocked. The officers first on the scene at the other said that the victim's door was unlocked as well. Seems to me, someone is letting the killer in willingly, but he doesn't have the key to lock the doors on exit."

CHAPTER 10

Luke hadn't slept well. He tossed and turned and couldn't find a comfortable position all night long. Riley hadn't slept well either. In fact, Riley had gotten up around three in the morning and went to sleep in the spare room. She assured Luke on her way out of the bedroom that she wasn't still angry with him, but he had his doubts. The last thing he needed was a battle at home, especially when he and Riley really seemed to be in a good place in their relationship.

Luke had skipped his morning run, grabbed some coffee, and left for work. He leaned over and kissed Riley on the cheek while she sat at the kitchen table before he left. She barely said two words to him all morning.

Luke canceled his two weeks of vacation, again, and had asked for a morning meeting with everyone to go over the cases as a team. Luke hoped Purvis or the crime scene techs had something for them to run with today.

A couple of uniformed cops had canvassed Cooper's neighbors while still on the scene to see if anyone had heard a shot or saw anything suspicious. Luke expected those statements to be on his desk, and he planned to follow up on any leads. He also had a call out to Cooper's building security for any security video recordings. As he drove to the station, Luke made a mental to-do list as he carefully went back over each crime scene in his mind.

Luke pulled into the station parking lot, gathered his things, and moved quickly into the building and up to his desk. Although Cooper had said the drug test results should come back in forty-eight hours, sometimes it came sooner, which is what Luke was hoping.

He was disappointed to find that nothing was on his desk but a file of neighbors' statements. Luke flipped through them quickly and was surprised that no one had seen or heard anything – not even the gunshot. In that close quarters, it would be nearly impossible to not hear a gunshot unless the killer used a suppressor, or silencer, as they were more commonly known. He'd have to check with the crime scene techs to see what evidence had been collected at the scene.

Luke did a thorough sweep of his desk in case a crime scene file or Cooper's lab reports had been put under something else, but there was nothing. Luke glanced at the clock. It was nearing seven-thirty and probably too early for anyone to be there yet, but Luke placed a quick call to the crime scene unit and left a message.

When he was done, Luke grabbed a few pertinent files and his coffee and made his way into the conference room. He pulled the dry erase board from against the wall and positioned it at the head of the table. He wanted to write information about each case side by side and compare. He didn't know if they could be considered connected or not, but homicides like the ones they had yesterday weren't the norm for Little Rock.

Sure, the city had its share of violent crime and homicides. It didn't fall on the top ten of the country's most dangerous mid-sized cities for no reason. But homicides of white women in upscale condo and apartment communities were not the norm by any stretch. Little Rock had a gang violence problem, and as such, a good deal of the crime was concentrated in the southeast parts of the city. It was why the cops were stretched so thin lately. The police department wasn't getting accolades from residents. There was always something more to be done. Luke understood. It wasn't a complaint so much as more added to the stress of the job.

Luke flipped through his files, going over questions he had and notes he had taken until Det. Tyler and Captain Meadows arrived at eight. They joined him in the conference room.

"How's Cooper holding up?" Captain Meadows asked as he sat.

"I think about as well as can be expected," Luke replied evenly.

"Did you record his interview yesterday? I'd like to see it if you did."

"I did," Luke said. He was embarrassed to admit how harshly he had judged Cooper, but it was recorded for all to see.

"Let's get down to business then." Captain Meadows tapped his finger against the table. "Det. Tyler, why don't you start."

Det. Tyler flipped open the file in front of him. He looked it over as he spoke. "I don't have anything back from the medical examiner yet, but the first victim yesterday is thirty-five-year-old Casey Perry. She's lived at Riverstone since its opening two years ago. She was among the first tenants. I was able to reach her parents. Her father and sister came to the morgue last night to identify her. They had been concerned because no one could reach her for a few days, but it hadn't set off any alarm bells because Casey had a hectic life and would often take a few days to call her parents back. Her sister was more concerned because she said Casey would at least text, and she hadn't connected in a few days. She didn't go to Casey's place because they generally gave each other privacy and space. Casey also travels a lot for work. Her sister felt guilty for not checking on her sooner."

Det. Tyler flipped a couple of pages. "Casey works as an insurance agent at a large firm right on Riverfront Drive. She could walk to work from her apartment at Riverstone. I reached her boss last night at home. He said Casey had last been to work on Tuesday. She had planned to meet up with some friends for dinner, but he wasn't sure where. He said that Casey had been discussing restaurants at the office that afternoon, which is the only reason he knew of her plans for that evening."

Captain Meadows interrupted, "Wasn't her boss concerned that she hadn't been to work the rest of the week?"

Det. Tyler closed the file. "As luck would have it, Casey was supposed to be on an afternoon flight to Portland, Oregon. She was headed to a work conference. No one had any idea that she didn't leave. Everyone assumed she was there and would be back on Monday. My call came as quite a shock. Her boss said whatever we need, they'd provide it."

"Did Casey have a boyfriend?" Luke asked.

"Not that I'm aware of. Her sister said that Casey had been married in her early twenties, but the divorce had been more than ten years ago. Her ex lives in St. Louis, and they were on okay terms. Nothing to suspect that he'd have anything to do with it."

"What else do you have?" Captain Meadows asked, his face drawn and pensive.

"Not much else right now. I'm still waiting on the official time of death. Once I have that, I'll start retracing her steps. We've canvassed the neighbors, and no one saw or heard anything unusual. I assume a silencer was used since no one reported a gunshot. I have calls out to her friends. Her sister and her boss provided some names of people to talk to. Other than that, I'm just waiting to see what the crime scene analysis shows me. I should know more this afternoon."

Captain Meadows hitched his chin to Luke. "Do we have any reason to suspect Cooper on that one?"

Luke shook his head. "Not at all. I showed him the victim's photo. He doesn't know her. Looks like by what her boss said, and the fact she missed her flight on Wednesday, that she was killed Tuesday night. Cooper was with Riley and me most of the night."

Captain Meadow raised his eyebrows. "All night?"

"No, Cooper went home probably a little after eleven. He told me yesterday he had a surveillance case at ten Wednesday morning. He said he has surveillance photos and video with time and date stamp."

Captain Meadows laid his hands on the table palm down. "That would mean there are eleven hours where Cooper is unaccounted for during the most likely night in question."

"In all fairness," Det. Tyler started. "There's no reason to suspect that Cooper had anything to do with this one. He doesn't even know the victim. Did he give any reaction to her photo, Luke?"

"None," Luke said definitely. Turning to Captain Meadows, he asked, "Do you think the cases are connected? Is that what you're driving at?"

Captain Meadows expelled a breath. "I'm not driving at anything. I'm just trying to rule Cooper out. There's a new prosecutor, Don Jennings, who thinks Cooper should be our number one suspect. Actually, I got a call from him this morning, wondering why Cooper wasn't arrested yesterday. I'm just trying to rule Cooper out completely. But yes, the cases could be connected. If we rule Cooper out of one, we can more easily rule him out of both."

CHAPTER 11

Luke couldn't disagree with Captain Meadows' reasoning, but he also knew that his boss wasn't looking at anything other than victim type and some minor similarities to indicate that the cases could be connected. That didn't tell them much of anything. Luke spent the next hour going over the details of Holly Reed's case for Det. Tyler and Captain Meadows. But like Tyler's case, without ballistics, crime scene evidence, or tracing the women's lives further, Luke didn't have much to go on. He certainly couldn't say with any degree of certainty if the two murders were connected.

Luke had something else to focus on, too. "I understand why Cooper is the number one suspect, given where Holly was murdered and who had access. Plus, Cooper's history with the victim didn't help his cause, but I don't understand why Don Jennings is pushing so hard on this case. I understand he's new and probably wants to make a name for himself, but this isn't normally how we work with the prosecutor's office."

Det. Tyler spoke up. "Any chance Cooper has some history with him? Jennings was a criminal defense attorney before going to the prosecutor's office, which isn't the way most lawyers track in their careers. Usually, it's the other way around."

Luke shrugged. "I really don't know, but Jennings did say he knew Cooper. Cooper has never shared much with me about his cases. I know he and Riley work with a few criminal defense attorneys though. Neither Jennings nor Cooper offered up an explanation of how they knew each other, but it certainly wasn't my focus at the crime scene. I was frankly taken a little by surprise that Jennings showed up there at all. Who even notified him about the case? It had literally just happened."

Captain Meadows bit at the inside of his cheek, making a popping sound with his mouth when he let go. "That's a fair point, Luke, and I don't know the answer. I'm going to dig a little into that. I don't appreciate him digging around in our cases right now. We've never had that kind of intrusion from the prosecutor's office before. We've got enough on our plate. I don't even know if Jennings has been assigned either of the cases should anything end up with a prosecution."

Pinning his eyes on Luke, he asked, "What do you think? Do you really think Cooper could have killed her? Having no memory of it certainly isn't a good defense, but Cooper has never struck me as stupid."

Luke broke eye contact with Captain Meadows, hesitant to say what he really felt. His job was to remain objective and not make conclusions before all the evidence was in, but he definitely already had an opinion. Luke just wasn't sure he should voice it.

Captain Meadows waved his hand at Luke and read his mind. "It's just around this table, Luke. I know exactly what you're thinking. Just say what you have to say."

"No, I don't think Cooper could have voluntarily committed this murder," Luke explained. "First off, Cooper would never intentionally harm anyone. In self-defense, sure, but to just kill someone even in rage, no. Secondly, you're right, Cooper isn't stupid. Even if I could believe that Cooper could kill a woman, and I can't, he certainly knows how to get away with murder if he wanted to. He's not going to do something so obvious as killing a woman in his own bed."

Luke stood for his last point. "Lastly, it just feels like a set-up, especially if Cooper was drugged. But that's what's tripping me up. Could Cooper have killed her drugged and completely not in his right mind? Could it have been an accident? Did someone push him into doing it? There are just too many unknowns for me right now."

"You really think Cooper could have killed her by accident? Doesn't the fact that a silencer was probably used negate that?" Det. Tyler looked up at

Luke skeptically.

Luke paced back and forth in front of the dry erase board, something he did when he ran through a case step by step in his mind. "I can't account for that. We don't even know right now for sure that a silencer was used. But let's just say someone drugged Cooper with GHB or Rohypnol. Why? Did Holly do it to sexually assault him? If this were a woman given the drug, that's exactly what we'd be considering so we have to consider it. Did she drug him and get him back to his place and he acted in self-defense?"

"I'm following," Captain Meadows started, "but where did the gun come from then? You said Cooper's was still in his safe."

"Yeah, that's tripping me up," Luke admitted.

Captain Meadows offered up some questions of his own. "Could Holly have brought the gun with her? Maybe Cooper grabbed it in a struggle. You said Purvis said it looked like she was sitting up when she was shot so could they have had a struggle in his bed, Cooper rolled over on top of her, grabbed the gun and shot her?"

"I guess that's one scenario, but if a silencer was used, that negates that as well. A silencer gives way to premeditation."

Captain Meadows agreed. "Do you really think Cooper shot her, dropped the gun on the bed and went to sleep?"

Det. Tyler answered before Luke could. "Women have been sexually assaulted and then gone back to sleep in the same bed as the offender, got up the next morning and not even realized an assault occurred until they were back home. So, yeah, these drugs are that powerful so that is possible."

Luke knew that Det. Tyler had worked in the special victim's unit before they had become partners a few years back. He had far more knowledge about sexual assault cases then Luke did. He looked down at the detective. "Have you had cases like that before – where a man was given a date-rape drug and sexually assaulted?"

Det. Tyler shook his head. "I can only think of one in my entire career, but research in the field and anonymous surveys and such show that it's more prevalent than thought. It's hard enough for a man to come forward and admit rape, but many times they just think they had a hard night of drinking and don't even consider that they might have been a victim. Sometimes later, they get flashes of memory or once they start piecing the night together, it might occur to them, but most never consider reporting something like that."

"We don't even know for sure right now if Cooper was drugged though, correct?" Captain Meadows asked. He grabbed Holly's file and flipped through it, scanning different sections.

"No, I haven't received the report back yet. I'm basing it off his memory loss and erratic behavior. I wouldn't have even thought of having him tested, but Cooper had texted Riley. She's the one who suggested if he really had missing time that might be the answer. We have her to thank for that. Honestly, it didn't even occur to me."

"I wouldn't have thought of it either," Captain Meadows admitted. "Tyler, didn't you have a similar case last week where the perp claimed memory loss?"

"I did and was going to bring that up. Scott Davis has been arraigned for the murder and pled not guilty. He has fully cooperated and sworn over and over again to anyone who will listen that he didn't kill her. Similar to Cooper, it was a woman that Scott had seen casually a few times. They left a bar in the River Market Friday night and went back to her place. She was shot, and he claimed memory loss. It seemed like a real open and shut case, although we never did find the murder weapon."

"Did you have him tested for drugs?" Luke asked.

"Didn't occur to me. You know these perps say anything," Det. Tyler explained.

"Cooper said something about a hair sample might show these kinds of drugs longer than the other tests. It might be worth it to double-check."

"I'll call Scott's attorney," Det. Tyler said.

Luke asked, "Purvis said there was another case where a woman was shot in her bed and the apartment door left open. There were no suspects in that one."

"That's my case, too," Det. Tyler responded. "It's exactly what Purvis said."

"Is it possible we have men skipping out in the morning worried they will be charged, especially if they can't remember anything from the night before?" Captain Meadows proposed.

"It's certainly possible."

Luke looked around the room. "We have four similar cases in three weeks' time?"

"Looks that way," Captain Meadows said with an edge in his voice.

"What's the plan at this point, Cap?" Luke asked. "Am I running down leads on Holly's case and Tyler taking Casey's?"

Captain Meadows closed Holly's case file. "That works for me, but I want you to work together on this. I want you both to go back over the evidence of the two past cases. I'd rather us work together and give consideration right up front that the cases could be connected and rule it out instead of the other way around. I think we will be on the lookout for more cross-evidence that way. I don't want anything to slip through. I also don't want to force a theory. If it's not connected, we run it that way. Got it?"

Det. Tyler and Luke both nodded in agreement, grabbed their respective case files and headed back to their desks to start running down leads. Luke hoped the forensics were back soon. Everything hinged on that.

CHAPTER 12

At two in the afternoon, I was back at the airport to pick up Adele. I parked in short-term parking and made my way into the main entrance. I checked the board to make sure her flight was on time and then headed to the baggage area and planted myself on a bench across from the baggage conveyor belt.

I had wanted to see Cooper earlier in the day, but he was holed up at the Marriott and didn't want company. He said he was working through his plan on how to catch Holly's killer. I reminded him that he'd be getting in the way of the Little Rock Police Department and essentially stepping on Luke's toes. I wasn't sure that given Cooper's current predicament as the primary suspect, angering the police would be the best idea. Cooper reminded me that because he was the prime suspect, he had no choice.

Not that I didn't want him to investigate. My argument was that I would do it for him, hopefully under the radar. I just didn't think there was any reason for Cooper to stick his neck out. I hoped that once Adele talked some sense into him, Cooper might reconsider.

I didn't know Adele well enough, or hardly at all, so I wasn't sure what her thinking would be on the whole situation. I was still in a bit of shock that she and Cooper had already talked about moving in together. Cooper told me he had kept it to himself because he hadn't wanted to jinx it. He never thought he'd feel this way about a woman so he was taking it all in slowly. He had wanted to iron out all the details with Adele and have it a done deal before he told Luke and me. I could respect that. It wasn't any of our business anyway, but Cooper rarely kept big things to himself.

I sat watching the straggle of passengers come and go. My leg bounced in nervous anticipation of meeting Adele. The plan was to pick her up at the airport and bring her to the hotel to meet Cooper. I had offered to let her stay at our house, but she had declined. It made sense. If it were me, I'd want to be wherever Luke was staying.

As more passengers started to swarm the baggage claim area, I reached into my pocket and pulled out my phone. I scanned through Cooper's recent texts until I landed on the photo of Adele. I clicked and enlarged it. Cooper had sent Adele a photo of me as well so we could find each other.

I glanced down at her photo. There was no other way of saying it. Adele was a beautiful woman. Her skin was a deep chocolate brown, her brown eyes were crowned by long thick eyelashes that made me envious, and her hair was braided and twisted on top of her head. From the photo, she was also in great shape with long thin limbs and gentle curves in the right places.

It left me feeling a bit like a pasty potato sack. My hand went straight for my long auburn tresses. I ran my fingers through and tried to tame them down. I tugged down my shirt, which had ridden up in the back, exposing a thin strip of pale skin at the top of my pants. Luke called me thick as a compliment. Hips, breasts, butt – my curves went on for days. Staring at the photo of Adele reminded me how much I needed to get back into the gym. My mother's voice screaming something about carbs echoed in my brain.

"Riley?" a woman said from in front of me, interrupting my self-deprecation.

My eyes scanned up the woman, who was dressed in stylish soft gray pants and a maroon V-neck sleeveless shirt, until I landed on her face. I stood and came nearly eye to eye with Adele. The photo made her seem taller, but she was otherwise everything I thought she'd be. I reached out my hand to shake hers, but she wrapped me in a hug.

"It's so good to meet you. Cooper has told me so much about you." Adele had a laptop bag looped over her shoulder and a purse in her hand.

Cooper hadn't really told me much about her so I couldn't say the same but didn't want to call attention to that. "I'm looking forward to getting to know you. Cooper is at the hotel waiting for you. Do you have luggage?" Of course, she had luggage. I wasn't sure why I was feeling thrown off my game. I stammered, "I just meant do you want me to help you get your luggage or hold your things for you while you grab it?"

"Great, thanks," Adele said and dropped her laptop at my feet and thrust her purse towards me. Adele commanded a presence in the room I hadn't been expecting, but then again, Cooper did say she was a formidable criminal defense attorney. She'd have to be sure of herself and powerful in the courtroom.

A few minutes later, Adele walked towards me pulling a large black suitcase with a smaller one attached to it. She laughed, looking back at her luggage. "I always overpack, but I didn't know how long I'd be here. I'm anxious to see Cooper. Maybe on the drive there you can fill me in on what you know."

I nodded and led the way to my car. We didn't speak on the walk there, but once I put her bags in the back of my SUV and we were strapped in, Adele started to cry. "I keep trying to hold it all together. I know that I need to in front of Cooper, but I feel like I'm on the edge of losing it completely."

I reached my hand out and squeezed her arm. "Lose it all you want around me. I'm feeling the same. I can't believe this happened."

Adele turned to look at me. "I don't want to offend you, but aren't you feeling stuck in the middle? Cooper told me that Luke is the detective on the case. I owe Luke everything for solving my sister's murder. I am so grateful and can never repay that debt, but given your relationship with him, won't helping Cooper complicate things for you?"

She was testing my loyalty. I didn't even need to choose my words carefully. "Luke is doing his job, and I'm going to do mine. I know that Cooper didn't do this. I'm fairly certain Luke feels the same. I'm going to do whatever I can to find Holly's killer and clear Cooper's name. It will help Luke in the long run."

Adele searched my face, probably assessing my credibility and if I was being completely honest with her. When Adele decided I was, she asked, "Are you willing to help me?"

I turned to face her. "Absolutely. I thought that was a given. I already told Cooper I'm on board for anything he needs. But that brings up another point. Cooper really shouldn't be out there investigating his own case. That puts him in the line of fire with law enforcement."

Adele agreed. "It also brings up a lot of legal complications. Do you think he will listen to us?"

"Probably not," I said and started my car. "Cooper is pretty stubborn when he wants to be. He also has a tendency to think he knows best most of the time. Unfortunately, he's usually right so that's never helped my argument the handful of times he's been wrong."

"I've seen some of that stubbornness in him, but so far, as you said it's worked to his advantage. Any idea how we can work around that in this situation?"

"I've been giving it some thought. I think we should probably just be direct with him." I drove the route to downtown Little Rock where Cooper was staying, navigating in and out of traffic, trying to ensure my heavy foot maintained some semblance of the speed limit. I turned briefly to look at Adele. She stared straight ahead, having wiped the tears from her face. She looked determined and strong.

"What you should know is that no matter how much Cooper says he left the police force because he didn't like the confines of the work, all the rules and regulations – Cooper is a stickler for the rules and doing things the right way," I explained. "He doesn't cut corners like some private investigators. He doesn't skirt the law to get information. He doesn't go rogue, and annoyingly pulls me back when I do. We can use that to our advantage. He's not going to want to mess up his own case."

Adele laughed at that. "I wouldn't take you for a rule breaker."

"It's why I'm good at it. I don't look the part."

Adele pulled out her phone and turned it back on. She scanned through the messages. "Cooper has already texted me to make sure I arrived. He thinks I'm just coming here to be supportive and to follow through with the original visit we had planned. But he needs legal counsel. I'm going to do it for as long as I can. If this goes to court, I'll also be a witness so we will need to retain someone else, but my goal is to never let it get that far. What are we up against with the Little Rock police?"

I kept my eyes on the road. "The Little Rock detectives are good, some of the best I've ever worked with. Luke is exceptional. He's dogged and determined. He may not always listen to reason. He may even get tunnel vision sometimes, but he's fair. Cooper and Luke are the same – rule followers, have a keen sense of justice, but both reasonable men. We can use that to our advantage."

"How so?" Adele asked, her interest clearly piqued.

"We zig while they zag," was all I said for now. A plan was starting to form, but I couldn't explain it while making sure I didn't blow through a red light and get into an accident. I was quiet the rest of the trip, formulating how we could go about finding Holly's killer.

CHAPTER 13

Luke sat at his desk making calls, trying to track down some leads on Holly Reed's daily life, the people she knew, and what exactly she had been doing on the last day of her life. Luke had met with her parents when they came to the morgue to identify her body the night before. Her mother was utterly distraught, the sobs wracking her body as the tears ran down her face. Holly's father, in contrast, stood stoic. Luke hadn't been able to get a good read on the man so he wasn't sure if he was as cold and detached as he appeared in that moment or just in shock.

Luke had pulled Holly's father aside and tried to explain some of the details surrounding his daughter's death. The man stood silently as Luke explained where his daughter had been found and the nature of her injuries. The man uttered nothing. He had not called on Luke to arrest Cooper. He didn't scream or yell or even show any grief at all. He had simply looked at Luke and said that he was sure the police would do everything they could to catch his daughter's killer.

Luke had stood in the hallway of the morgue watching them leave. Holly's father had guided her mother by the elbow. When the woman dropped her head and sobbed one last time, the man had leaned down in the woman's ear and said in a harsh whisper that their daughter lived a risky lifestyle and what did she really expect. The woman turned to look up at her husband, the disgust written all over her face, but she pulled herself together and walked out with him.

Luke hadn't been sure what to make of the interaction. In all of his years as a detective, he'd been witness to a range of emotions from people who were summoned to the city morgue to identify the body of a family member or friend. Luke had never heard a father make such a comment.

Before they left, Holly's parents had given Luke permission to access her apartment. Not that he needed it, but it was easier when families were cooperative. They had handed over the key willingly and told him to have free rein in her place. Luke had initially planned to go there earlier in the day right after his morning meeting, but he had waited by his desk for Cooper's lab results. The lab was backed up, and Luke had just been told that it would be another several hours.

Det. Tyler had left earlier to run down some leads on the other case so Luke headed to Holly's apartment in West Little Rock. Stopped at a light, Luke checked his phone, but he still hadn't heard from Riley. Normally, he'd at least get a text midday to see how he was doing. Their relationship had been going so well. He worried what the strain might do to them.

Luke arrived at the address and pulled into the apartment community. He followed the winding road until he found building number five. Holly's building sat in a back corner of the quiet community, shaded by trees on both sides. Luke put his car in park and picked up his bag in the passenger seat. It contained gloves, evidence bags and markers and other items he might need assessing the scene.

Holly lived in apartment 519. Luke made his way into the breezeway on the first floor and quickly found her door. Luke stepped on the simple blue welcome mat and unlocked the door. He nudged it open with his arm and stepped inside. Luke was immediately struck by the mess. Clothes were strewn on the floor of the living room and a plate and silverware with half-eaten, now crusty food sat in the middle of the coffee table. A mug and water glass took up a spot on the end table. Magazines littered the floor, some piled in spots, others tossed haphazardly.

Luke set the bag down on the tiled floor in the foyer. He pulled gloves from a side pocket of his bag and snapped them on. He did a quick walkthrough of the place, carefully scanning each room as he went. Holly's apartment was a basic one-bedroom with a kitchen and small dining room next to it and a bedroom off the hall with an adjacent bathroom.

The mess Luke found in the living room carried throughout. The kitchen sink overflowed with dirty dishes and soiled cups. Some of the dishes had caked on food that looked like they might never get clean again. Clothes were piled so high in the bedroom that it was hard to distinguish where the bed started and stopped.

Luke ran a finger along the top of the dresser and came away with at least an inch of dust. He wiped his hand on his pants and grimaced. It would take longer than he thought to go through Holly's apartment. Overwhelmed, Luke wasn't even sure where to start. It was a stark contrast to the other victim's residence where nothing seemed out of place.

Luke pulled out his phone and snapped a few photos around the apartment and then got down to work. He sifted through the piles of magazines in the living room, picked up each one, tipping it on its side to see if anything was hidden within its pages. He looked under couch cushions and behind the furniture. Finding nothing of value, Luke moved on to the kitchen and bathroom. He scanned Holly's medicine cabinet. Other than a half-used birth control packet and some over-the-counter cold medication, nothing jumped out at him.

In the kitchen, Luke opened a drawer that held matches and menus to local restaurants. Surprised, Luke pulled out a photo of Cooper sitting at a table in Kepler's. He was smiling, but not at the camera. His head was turned toward someone. Luke could only make out the other person's hands in the photo because their face had been scratched out. It was clear to Luke the other person in the photo was Riley. Cooper's face had also been obliterated with a big X in red ink. Someone, Luke assumed Holly, had written on the back of the photo, *You'll pay.* Luke left the photo on the counter for now. He'd take it as evidence.

Luke made his way into Holly's bedroom and spent the next hour going through the piles of clothing, dresser drawers, and the closet. Finally, giving up on the mess, Luke flipped off the closet light and turned to close the door. Before he shut the door all the way, Luke caught sight of a shiny square object that peeked out from behind a pile of shoes. Luke bent down and tugged the object free. It was a cellphone. Holly's phone had been at the scene with her body. The crime techs found it among her pile of clothes next to Cooper's bed. It had been bagged already as evidence. Luke would take this phone as evidence, too.

Luke toyed with the phone in his hands. He thought at first it might just be an old phone that Holly had used previously and never got rid of. On closer inspection, the phone was a newer model that had been released just last year. Luke shut the closet door and carried the phone to the living room, stopping only briefly to grab the photo of Cooper from the kitchen. Back in the foyer, Luke pulled two evidence bags from the same pocket where he had earlier grabbed his gloves. One he used for the phone and the other the photo in the kitchen.

Luke gathered his things and closed and locked the apartment door behind him. As he walked back to his car, Holly's mother's face flashed in his mind. She'd probably be the one responsible for cleaning up the mess in the apartment. His own mother would curse him even in death for leaving such a disaster.

CHAPTER 14

Cooper paced the floor of his hotel suite, waiting for Riley and Adele. He was nervous about Adele being there in the middle of this mess, but he was equally nervous about how Riley and Adele would get along. They were both strong-willed women with big personalities. Cooper assumed they were either going to love each other or the hate would be evident.

Cooper had already texted Luke twice to see if his lab results had come back. But nothing yet. Knowing for sure that he had been drugged wouldn't necessarily make him feel any better, but it would explain the memory loss, which right now was what was driving him mad.

Last night, Cooper had walked to Kepler's from the hotel and went inside. He didn't drink or eat, but rather went to the table he remembered sitting at while he had texted Adele. He hoped something would jog his memory. Nothing did. Cooper inquired at the bar who the bartender on Saturday night had been. He knew some of the staff well but wanted to make sure he got it right given his jagged memory. The girl behind the bar told Cooper that it was Sam, but that he wouldn't be back on a shift until Tuesday, the following night.

Cooper walked back to his condo the same way he assumed he would have walked on that night. He looked for cameras but saw none. He rolled through his memories but only came up with other times he had walked from Kepler's back to his condo. None of the memories he retrieved were from the night in question.

Giving up, Cooper went back to the hotel. He wasn't sure what else he could be doing. He read through his texts to and from Adele over and over again, but they made little sense to him. The only thing that was clear was there was a point where things took a turn. He was clearly interacting with someone other than Adele and told her about it. But his messages didn't make sense enough that he could decipher it.

When Adele finally arrived, the first thing Cooper wanted to do was get a full account from her about what she heard. He had tried to get Adele to talk about it over the phone, but she had brushed him off, assuring him it was a conversation better to be had in person.

Now, every synapse and nerve flamed like it was on fire waiting for her arrival. Cooper paced a line in the carpet until a knock at the door disrupted his march. He moved quickly to it, nearly tripping over himself in his haste. He unlocked it and pulled the door open.

Cooper fell into Adele, wrapping his arms around her and nearly lifting her off the ground. His display of affection caught Riley so off guard she actually stepped back. He looked over at her and gave a weak smile.

With her arms wrapped around his middle, Adele urged, "Let's move into the room. We have cameras watching us."

Cooper didn't care, but he stepped back and gave them space to enter. Riley dropped one of Adele's bags on the floor and then excused herself, telling them she had to go make a call. Cooper knew Riley was just giving them a few minutes alone. Lying or not, he appreciated the gesture.

Once they were alone, Cooper wrapped Adele in his arms again and kissed her deeply. He pulled back and looked into her face. "I'm so sorry to put you through this. I know our relationship is still new. No matter what we talked about before, if you want to walk out that door and have fewer complications in your life, I completely understand. You've already lived a lifetime of stress and grief with your sister's disappearance and murder. It isn't fair to put you through this."

Adele smiled up at him. "You're not getting rid of me that easily. Besides, what happened isn't fair to you. Riley and I talked on the way over. I think she has a plan."

Cooper laughed. "She always has a plan."

Adele pulled back, stepping out of his embrace. "Cooper, I hate even asking this, but can we trust her? I know Luke is your best friend and Riley is your business partner, but they are in a relationship. I know I owe all of you for helping to catch my sister's killer, but you're my focus right now. I have to know, will Riley's loyalty really be with you?"

As sure as Cooper was about how much he loved Adele, he knew Riley's loyalty to the truth. And the truth was, he didn't kill anyone. "The thing about Riley is she's loyal to a fault. Now that's not to say she won't call you out on your behavior or make you be accountable because she will. She's not going to let someone get away with murder just because she's friends with them. Riley is a great judge of character. I've seen her put it on the line for people she didn't even like very much because she believed they were innocent. She will fight for me. I have no doubt about Riley's loyalty."

"And Luke?" Adele asked softly.

Cooper smiled weakly. "Luke is loyal to the truth and to justice. He's struggling right now to wrap his head around what happened. It's not as black and white for him as it is for Riley. This isn't easy for him. I know him well enough to know that right now he's running through every scenario both proving me guilty and looking for the real killer."

Adele's eyes grew wide. "Why on earth would Luke be running through scenarios trying to prove you guilty?"

"That way when he rules it all out, he can be sure that I'm not."

Adele looked at him, confusion blanketing her face. He took her hand and led her over to the couch. Cooper explained, "Luke needs to explore how I could be guilty to see how ridiculous that really is and to see that the evidence doesn't fit. If Luke can work through every possible scenario where I could have killed Holly, he'll come to realize none of the evidence fits. I've known Luke for nearly twenty years. I know how his mind works."

Adele squeezed Cooper's hand. "But what if he does that and hits up against a scenario that the evidence can't disprove?"

"That's where we come in with the evidence we find," Cooper said determinedly.

"I think Riley and I need to talk to you about that."

Cooper nodded. They sat catching up until Riley returned. Cooper got up to let her in, and they quickly got down to work. The three of them sat at the table in the kitchenette area of the suite hashing out a game plan.

Riley reached her hand over and rested it on Cooper's arm. "Adele and I talked on the way over here. We are in agreement that while I want your help and input with investigating, you need to keep a lower profile."

Cooper jerked his arm out of Riley's reach. "That's ridiculous. I can more than handle investigating this murder. In fact, I'd say I'm probably more prepared than anyone since it happened to me. I knew Holly."

Riley raised her eyebrows. "How well did you really know her though, Cooper? Honestly?"

Cooper started to argue but came up short. In truth, he didn't know her well at all. Riley sighed and shot Adele a look that Cooper caught and did not appreciate.

Sternly Riley explained, "Cooper, be reasonable. Witnesses are not going to be straight with you. You're going to be out there stepping on Luke's toes and making him angry, which isn't going to help you. If another investigator came to us in a similar situation, what would you tell them?"

Cooper didn't say anything. He sat back in the chair and folded his hands in his lap.

Adele stressed, "Riley is right. I'm not saying this is going to court, but if it did, evidence that you collect is going to be looked at suspiciously. Consider for a second that you find a witness who has critical information to prove that you're innocent, and they have to get on the stand and say that the defendant interviewed them. That's not going to look very good. It will give the prosecution room to say that you pressured them. Now, if Riley collects the information, she is then free to testify to her investigative process and the evidence she obtained. It's cleaner, which is better for you all the way around."

Cooper capitulated more quickly than he wanted to, but after listening to them both lay it out the way they did, they were right. But he couldn't sit idly by and have his fate rest in someone else's hands. He'd have to find a way to be helpful.

"Fine," Cooper said begrudgingly, "where do we start?"

Riley sat stone-faced and ready to go. "With Adele, the primary witness to it all."

CHAPTER 15

By the time Luke made it back to the station, Det. Tyler had texted him several times, asking when he'd be back so they could go over the evidence and talk through what each had found. When Luke got back, he found Det. Tyler at his desk with his head down buried in a case file. He popped his head up when Luke passed by. "The tox report is on your desk. I didn't look through it yet. I thought I'd let you have first read."

Luke went immediately to his desk and picked up the report. Before he got a chance to read it, Det. Tyler called over to him, "Let's go in the conference room and you can read it there."

Luke didn't want to waste another second but trailed behind Tyler into the conference room. He flipped pages in the report, scanning the information line by line. The tests ruled out every substance but one. It was there in black and white. Cooper had, in fact, tested positive for GHB. He'd been telling the truth about his memory loss.

Luke slapped the report down on the conference table and slid it over to Det. Tyler. "Cooper's positive for GHB. I don't see it often in homicide cases. What does it do to a person?"

Det. Tyler scanned the report, turning through each of the four pages. He finished reading and closed it, looking back up at Luke. "It comes in a colorless, odorless liquid or as a powder that dissolves in liquid so it would be easy to administer into someone's drink without them knowing. It can take effect in as little as fifteen minutes. The symptoms can vary from person to person. Given Cooper's size, but lack of overall drug use, it might hit him fairly hard especially in a higher dose, which is what the report is indicating. It would explain his lack of coordination with texting, confusion, irritability, and memory loss."

"Could Cooper still walk home?"

"Yeah, probably. It might take someone guiding him though. He might appear to others as very drunk or on drugs, but no one is going to immediately assume he was drugged against his will with GHB."

"If Cooper was that unsteady, would he even be able to fire the gun?"

Det. Tyler shrugged. "It's hard to say. I didn't see the state Cooper was in or how much assistance he needed walking. From what you said, it was a pretty clean shot to the head though. I don't know that he'd have the precision for that. There are too many variables to say for sure though."

Luke scanned his memories for the times he'd seen Cooper drunk. Even in college, Luke had never seen Cooper lose control. Sure, they might have had a few drinks together from time to time and enough that Cooper wouldn't have driven, but Luke couldn't recall even one time that Cooper couldn't walk, slurred his words, or needed assistance. It didn't match up for him.

Det. Tyler dragged Luke back to the present. "I called the defense attorney on the other case. Scott Davis is more than willing to get a drug test. The attorney was actually relieved we might have an avenue to free his client. What did you find today?"

Luke detailed the conditions of Holly's apartment and explained about the photo and phone. When he was done, Luke got up and went back to his desk to grab his bag. He carried it back in, pulling out the photo and the phone from the bag. "You've got to look at this photo. It's creepy. This girl was completely obsessed with Cooper."

Tyler looked down at the photo and quickly back up at Luke. "Who is the woman scratched out of the photo?"

"That's Riley. Crazy, right? Holly was clearly jealous of any woman near Cooper." Luke went to the side of the room to the bins they kept with cables and cords and random phone chargers. Luke dug through until he found a match for Holly's phone. He plugged it into the phone and into the wall outlet. He had tried to power up the phone, but it needed a fresh charge. Luke would have to wait.

Det. Tyler watched Luke as he set the phone on a stack of bins. "Should we wait for a tech to come up? I wouldn't want to lose anything on there."

Luke glanced down at the phone and back at his partner. "After seeing the mess in Holly's place, I'm fairly certain Holly isn't that high tech. She had a phone on her at the time. This might be a spare. I think we're safe, but we can always get a tech if we need them. I can't imagine she'd have anything encrypted. Even the phone she had on her wasn't passcode protected."

Det. Tyler looked at the photo again. "She crossed Cooper right out of this photo, too. She either really hated him or was obsessed. Did you see anything else like that at her place?"

Luke sat back down across from Tyler. "Nothing. Her place was a mess. It was hard to find anything. Tell me what you found on Casey."

"Not much. She definitely didn't lead a high-risk lifestyle. She was college-educated, rarely drank, didn't do drugs, and was fairly focused on work. Her co-workers and a few friends that I called said that Casey rarely even went out. A co-worker did tell me that Casey had a crush on a guy. The co-worker said that Casey talked about him a lot, but the woman wasn't sure he and Casey had ever even gone on a date. She didn't even know the guy's name."

"Did you get an alibi for her ex?"

"I've made some calls trying to track him down. Not much yet, but the victim's sister said the breakup was amicable. Everyone I spoke to said they had remained friends. There was no hint of domestic violence or anything like that."

Luke raised his eyebrows. "Did you show anyone Cooper's photo?"

"I did and a few people recognized him from recent news stories, but no one connected him to Casey. I couldn't find any connection between Casey and Holly either. If these cases are connected, I'm not really sure how right now."

"I didn't see much of anything on Holly's end to connect her to Casey either. I'm not really sure if they connect at all. Do you have the evidence boxes from the other two cases?"

Det. Tyler hitched his jaw in the direction of boxes piled against the wall.

"They are all right there for us to go through."

Luke's cellphone buzzed on his hip. He reached for it quickly. "Purvis, what have you got for me?"

"Luke, we were able to get both autopsies underway today. My assistant handled one and I did the other. This is just preliminary information, but I can confirm that both of the women were killed up close. They both had wounds that lead me to believe the gun was pressed against their skin when the shot was fired. Both were killed with one shot with a nine-millimeter bullet. Neither woman had defensive wounds. These victims didn't fight back."

Luke couldn't understand how the women just sat there while someone shot them. Holly was in a sitting position, that much was clear from the scene. Casey could have been asleep. He said as much to Purvis.

"I thought about that, Luke," Purvis started. The sound of flipping pages and clicks of a keyboard were apparent over the phone. "I just pulled it up. Holly had a blood alcohol level of 0.10 percent, and Casey 0.02 percent. I'd guess Casey maybe had one drink but not much more than that. Holly had significantly more. Because you said Cooper had memory loss, I also ran a quick screen for GHB and Rohypnol. Luke, both victims tested positive for GHB."

Luke started to speak, but Purvis interrupted. "Luke, that's not all. I went back and looked at Det. Tyler's other two cases that seemed similar to me. Both of those victims were also shot with the same bullet type, same pattern wound, and both tested positive for GHB. You have to consider these cases are connected to one killer or group of killers."

CHAPTER 16

Luke finished the call with Purvis and backed up against the wall. He let his arms relax down by his sides. He wasn't sure what to make of what Purvis just said to him.

Det. Tyler watched Luke carefully. "Are you okay? You look a bit shaken. What did Purvis say?"

Luke started to speak but his voice was suddenly hoarse. He coughed and cleared his throat. "Purvis said both of the victims were shot with a nine-millimeter and had GHB in their systems. Actually, not just the two – all four cases. Holly also had a 0.10 blood alcohol level. Casey less at 0.02. Given all that, I'm not even sure how Holly would have made it to Cooper's apartment on her own. That's a pretty high BAC. Don't you think she'd have needed some kind of assistance walking?"

Det. Tyler ran a hand through his hair and clicked his tongue. "I don't know. I guess it depends on how heavy of a drinker she was. If she got drunk like that often, she probably handled it better than most. I think that's more than enough now to say all four are connected, right?"

Luke nodded. "I think we have to look at them that way. I'm still not sure what it all means though."

"Well at least for me it probably means Cooper is off the hook as is the poor guy I arrested and had arraigned."

"Let's slow down. We don't even know anything for sure. Get Scott tested and see what comes back. We'll run through this other evidence here before we make any big decisions. Purvis also said there were no signs the victims put up a fight, but given they were drugged, that could make sense. I imagine they'd be pretty out of it. Maybe they didn't even realize what was about to happen to them."

"That happens a lot in sexual assault cases. The victims are no longer in control of themselves mentally. They act in ways they wouldn't normally. I've seen many that have little self-protective instinct while under the effects of GHB."

Luke started to speak but his attention was drawn to the voices approaching in the hallway. Before either of them made it out of the conference room, a uniformed officer stood in the doorway with another man hovering right behind him. The cop hitched his thumb over his shoulder. "This is Brent Adams. He says he knows something about one of your murder cases."

The cop and man stepped back out of the doorway as Luke and Det. Tyler came into the hallway. Luke appraised Brent, who stood shifting his weight from one foot to the next, bouncing almost side to side. His tie was undone at the knot and askew. His shirt was half untucked under his suit and his brown hair, which looked like it had once been perfectly combed, was sticking up in all directions.

"I'm Det. Luke Morgan. How can I help you?"

Brent stuttered over a few words and then calmed himself down. "I saw a news report about a murdered woman down at the Riverstone apartments this morning. I think I know who killed her."

Luke appraised the man, not sure he really heard what Brent had said. Without missing a beat though, Luke extended his hand, "I appreciate you coming in, Brent." Luke turned behind him. "This is Det. Bill Tyler, he's the lead detective on that case. We'd be happy to sit down with you. Follow me into a more private room and we can talk."

Luke led the way with Det. Tyler and Brent following right behind. He didn't bring them to an interrogation room, but rather a witness room down another hallway. The room was still equipped with recording technology, but it was a little more relaxed. Luke wasn't sure what they'd hear, but if the guy was primed to talk, they'd do whatever they could to get him to tell them everything he knew.

They sat around the small conference table, Luke and Det. Tyler on one side and Brent on the other. "Brent, would you like water or coffee or anything before we get started?"

The man shook his head. "I need to just get this out before I chicken out."

Det. Tyler leaned forward on the table. "As Det. Morgan said, we appreciate you being here. We're here to listen whenever you're ready."

Brent swallowed hard. "I work down at an investment firm here in Little Rock. Last week one of my co-workers, Tom Sharpe, came into work, looking completely freaked out and disheveled. He went into his office and closed the door. He spent probably the next three hours on the phone. We could see him through the glass wall of his office. At one point he got up and closed the blinds. That was really odd behavior from him. Tom is normally a really together guy. He's super friendly, a real leader in the office. His door and blinds are always open. I went to his door at one point just to see if he was okay. That's when I heard what he said."

Brent locked eyes with Luke and then Det. Tyler, but he stopped speaking.

Luke urged him, "I know you probably don't want to get someone in trouble, but it's important you tell us. Once you do, you'll feel better, and we can figure out how to help you."

Brent took a deep breath. "I heard Tom say that he was worried that he had killed a woman. He said when he woke up that morning, he couldn't remember what had happened the night before, but that his date was dead in bed next to him. She had been shot is what I think he said. He told whoever he was talking to that he needed to get out of there as quickly as he could."

Luke raised his eyebrows. "He admitted to leaving the scene of a crime? What day was this?"

"Wednesday last week. He came in late, probably around ten in the morning and went right to his office as I said. He couldn't have been in there for more than a few minutes when he called someone from his desk phone. It seemed like he was saying he just left her there. Although, I'm not exactly sure what took place."

"Did you hear him say anything else?" Luke asked, calmly. The guy was credible, and the story was eerily similar to what Cooper experienced. He had Luke's full attention.

73

"No, he just kept repeating that she was dead when he woke up and that he got out of there as fast as he could."

Luke pressed, "Did you try to talk to him later? Maybe tell him what you had heard and ask him what he meant?"

"No, we were never exactly friends at work. Just you know, he was a co-worker. A nice guy, but I didn't feel like it was my place to question him beyond asking if he was okay, which I didn't even get to do."

"Explain that," Det. Tyler demanded. "You said you went to ask Tom if he was okay. When you heard what he was saying, what did you do then?"

"I froze a bit, to be honest. I wasn't sure I was hearing him right. I moved closer to the door and heard it more clearly. I was stunned. I went back to my desk. I wasn't sure what to do. He left the office after that. I haven't seen him since."

Det. Tyler pinned his eyes on Brent. "Is there a reason you're just coming forward now with this information?"

Brent rested his arms on the table and wrung his hands. "I was pretty freaked out, but I also didn't know if he was being serious. He didn't mention the woman's name. He didn't say where she lived. I felt a bit foolish calling and reporting something I had no real details about. It wasn't until I saw the news this morning about the woman found at Riverstone that I connected it all."

Luke eyed him. "What made you think the woman at Riverstone was the woman Tom was talking about, specifically?"

Brent shifted in his seat. He held up his fingers and counted them down as he spoke. "First, what I overheard him say happened on Wednesday morning, and the news report I heard said the woman died either late Tuesday or into Wednesday morning. Second, the news report said that the victim was mid-thirties which is right around Tom's age. The clincher for me though was on that Tuesday, Tom was bragging that he was finally going out with this really attractive woman who wanted him. He said he had her practically begging. He said that Tuesday was the night that he was finally going to give her what she wanted."

CHAPTER 17

I spent the better part of the late afternoon into early evening taking Adele's statement. I asked probably what amounted to two hundred questions, or at least it felt that way. Adele had detailed everything that she had heard the night Cooper was at Kepler's – from the man who approached to the other woman she heard talking.

Cooper remembered nothing. It was like someone had just wiped the slate of his memory clean. Cooper had never met any of Holly's friends so he couldn't even give us a guess who the other woman might have been or even if it was Holly herself. As for the man, Cooper had no idea either. Nothing Adele said seemed to spark a memory.

With all of the information gathered, the plan was for me to head to Kepler's and see if anyone had seen Cooper that night. I'd have to wait to speak to the bartender on duty tomorrow night, but at least I could get a jump on potential witnesses.

As I was getting ready to leave Cooper pulled me aside, wrapped me in a hug, and kissed the top of my head. "Don't mess things up with Luke just to protect me."

I pulled back, unsure of what to say. The fact that Cooper thought my relationship with Luke might not be able to withstand our different views on the case concerned me. I reassured him. "It's okay. Luke and I will be just fine. We have navigated tougher than this."

"He's not going to be happy that you're going to Kepler's looking for witnesses."

I moved closer towards the door. "Let me deal with Luke." It was like

Luke was listening in on us. As I spoke his name, Cooper's phone rang.

He held up the phone to show me the screen. "It's him. Let me grab it."

I waited until Cooper finished the call. Cooper showed no emotion on the call, he just gave a series of yes and no answers. He hung up quickly, and I immediately got a text from Luke asking what time I'd be home. I responded that I'd be back in an hour or two. He said we needed to talk. I didn't disagree with him. We did need to talk about a lot.

Cooper pinned his eyes on me. "What did Luke want?"

"He just wanted to know what time I'd be home. What did Luke want with you?"

"He wants to speak with Adele at nine tomorrow. He asked both of us to be there." Cooper looked over at Adele who was sitting at the small table, typing on her laptop. She looked up at the sound of her name and nodded in agreement that she'd be there.

"Maybe it's good news," I suggested. "Maybe your lab report came back or he's come to his senses."

"Should you wait on Kepler's then?" Cooper asked, hesitantly.

I reached for the doorknob. We were wasting time. "No, it's better I go now and get a jump on this. If Luke clears you tomorrow, then great. But if not, it wouldn't have been a wasted trip. Even if you're not charged criminally, don't you still want to know what happened?"

As I pulled open the door, Cooper put his hand around the door and held it open for me. "Let me know if you find anything."

I told him I'd call him and waved goodbye to Adele. I made my way out of the hotel and walked the few blocks to the River Market district. The city wasn't always the safest at night, especially walking alone, but I wasn't sure I'd even find a closer place to park. I rounded the corner onto President Clinton Avenue, which held a row of bars, restaurants and other shops, and was surprised by the number of people out. It was a nice spring night though with a warm breeze. A perfect night for dinner and drinks on a patio.

I made my way past the Flying Saucer down to Kepler's. I understood why Cooper liked the place. It had a good vibe for relaxing and having a beer without the music and the intense club crowds of the more touristy locations. The enormous flat screens that blanketed the walls made it a popular spot for watching a game.

I could see through the window from the sidewalk that the place was fairly empty. I stepped in anyway. The long oak bar, which took up most of the wall, could seat at least thirty people on the long line of bar stools. Tables, big and small, took up the rest of the space. There were no pool tables or darts or anything else. It was a place to grab a hearty meal, have a few drinks, meet up with friends and catch a game. It was a local favorite. Most tourists probably found the place boring.

I scanned around the room. A couple was having dinner, and there were three single guys sitting at the bar. A group of girls, who all looked to be in their twenties, took up a large table in the middle. Cooper liked the table at the end of the bar in the corner near the front window. Luke and I had been there with him a few times. The spot was currently empty.

I took a seat two barstools down from the group of guys. One of them looked up from his drink and smiled over at me as I sat. I smiled back, but needed a minute before I asked anything. I fumbled for my phone in my bag. Once I grabbed it, I scrolled through until I found a good photo of Cooper. As the young bartender approached, he asked me what I'd like. I ordered a Guinness that I knew I probably wouldn't drink, but a paying customer was more likely to get answers.

After ordering, I held my phone out and asked the bartender, "Did you happen to see this guy in here on Saturday night?"

The guy didn't look up. "I wasn't in here on Saturday."

The guy who had smiled at me looked in my direction. He spoke across his friend. "Who are you looking for, sweetie?"

I let the term of endearment slide and turned my phone to face him. He leaned farther across his friend and squinted down at the phone. "Yeah, I know that guy. He's in here a lot. What do you want with him?"

"Have you talked to him before or just seen him in here?"

The guy hopped down off his barstool and came around his friend to stand near me. The bartender put my Guinness down in front of me. As he did, the short head of foam at the top sloshed over the side. I watched as it slid down the glass and puddled at its base.

The guy rested his arm on the bar and told me his name was Travis. I leaned back so I could get a better look at him. There was nothing distinguishable about him. He was dressed in jeans and collared shirt and looked like nearly every other well-dressed guy in his forties in Little Rock. He probably spent equal time golfing as he did duck hunting.

I leveled a look at him. "As I was saying…do you know him or have you just seen him in here?"

"He's in here a lot." Travis pointed to the table near the window that Cooper liked. "He sits there nearly every time he's in. He's a cop or investigator or something. Good guy. Quiet and minds his own business. The ladies like him though. You're going to have some stiff competition."

I smiled. "That's not what I'm after. Did you happen to be in here Saturday night?"

"Darlin', I'm in here just about every night with those two clowns." Travis hitched his thumb over his shoulder in the direction of his friends.

I peered around him and both of the other men were looking in our direction. One gave a curt nod in agreement with what his friend said. Turning back to Travis, I asked, "Did you see this man then?"

Travis rolled his eyes up toward the ceiling as if thinking. He looked down at me and flashed a smile. "Now that you mention it, I did. It was kind of strange though. He came in and sat down normal-like, but later I didn't see exactly what happened, but a woman followed him out, yelling at him. He didn't seem to want anything to do with her, but he stumbled as he walked. I've never seen him like that in all my time here. He's not a drunk if you know what I mean."

"Do you know the woman who followed him?"

Red rose up the man's face from his neck to his forehead at my direct question, but he didn't say anything.

"You don't have a shot with me anyway. I live with my boyfriend so the truth is probably better," I said, hoping to ease his guilt. I had a feeling he was about to tell me he had a fling or a one-night stand with her.

He hesitated only for a second before admitting it. "Yeah, I've gone home with her a few times, but not worth my trouble. Her name is Holly. Actually, she's harassed more than a few men in here. I haven't seen her in here in a few days though."

I took one sip of my beer and dropped a ten on the bar. "You won't be seeing her anymore. She was murdered. Did you see anyone else leave with them?"

Travis didn't even register shock. "I knew she would anger the wrong man someday," he said almost to himself.

A second later, he added, "I heard them raise their voices and that's what got my attention. There was a man walking behind them as they left, but I didn't see his face. I'm not sure if he was with them or not."

CHAPTER 18

Travis and I grabbed a table to give us more privacy and some space for me to write. I finally told him that I was a private investigator looking into Holly's murder as I pulled my notebook from my bag. I spent the next hour talking to Travis, getting a detailed description of the events he witnessed. I then talked to his two buddies who also confirmed the same story.

The description of the man that followed Cooper and Holly out of the bar didn't yield much. He was about six-foot, medium build and was dressed in jeans, a polo shirt, and a ball cap. No one saw his face, and Kepler's didn't have video surveillance. I also had absolutely no idea if the man even mattered to the case. I had no confirmation that he followed Cooper and Holly down the street. All I know was he walked out behind them and that's it.

By the time I got home, it was nearly eight-thirty. Luke was crashed on the couch watching a baseball game. He looked up as I entered. "Your Red Sox are winning. Tell me again how you're from New York but a Red Sox fan."

"My grandfather was from Massachusetts and was a Red Sox fan," I explained absently as I dropped my things on the chair and went into the kitchen. I called to him, "Did you eat?"

"I grabbed takeout and got you dinner, too. You just need to heat it up."

I snaked my head around the corner and gave him a smile. "You really make it impossible for me to stay mad at you for long."

He laughed and teased, "You were mad at me? I barely noticed."

I moved around my kitchen, pulling out the chicken dish Luke had ordered for me. I grabbed a plate and heated it up. I poured myself some water and joined Luke on the couch, careful to set the plate down on the mat on the coffee table. "Thanks for dinner." I dug in, realizing I was hungrier than I had thought.

Between bites, I said, "You told me earlier you wanted to talk to me. Is this about Cooper?"

Luke muted the television and moved on the couch so he was facing me. "I got the lab report back. Cooper definitely tested positive for GHB so good call on your part suggesting he get tested."

"What does this mean then?"

Luke shrugged. "It means at the very least Cooper was under the influence and has a legitimate reason for not remembering what happened."

He shared so I would, too. "That's going to be backed up by witness statements. I talked to Adele today. There are also a few guys who are regulars at Kepler's that you need to speak with. I have their contact info."

I figured Luke was going to yell at me for going to Kepler's and talking to potential witnesses, but he didn't.

"Do you think you should be telling me this just in case you need to mount a defense?"

"It would all be turned over anyway during discovery if this went to trial. My goal is not to let it ever get to that point. I know you don't believe Cooper killed her."

Luke watched me. I could tell by the pensive expression he had more on his mind. I turned to him. "Listen, if you want to share what's going on like you always do, I'll keep it between us."

He frowned. "You are kind of working for the other side right now. I need you as my sounding board, but I'm walking a fine line here."

I put my fork down and faced him. "Luke, there are no sides. I'm looking for the truth as much as you are."

"Even if that truth leads to Cooper?" Luke asked thoughtfully.

I sighed loudly. "I don't see any scenario where that is likely. Luke, you've known Cooper far longer than I have. Am I missing something? Does

Cooper have some propensity for violence that I'm not aware of?"

Luke shook his head and ran a hand down his face. He glued his eyes on me and moved to the edge of the couch. "No. Cooper has never been violent. But nothing makes sense in this case. Every scenario I run through nothing fits. No one even heard the shots."

I raised my eyebrows. "No one in his building reported a shooting?"

"No, and you've been in that building. Someone would have heard."

"You talk to his neighbor Jenny? She lives directly across the hall."

Luke shook his head. "I didn't talk to any of them. Some of the officers on the scene canvassed them while I took Cooper back to the station to get his statement. I'll have to look for her statement specifically if she gave one."

"Then a silencer was probably used and you know that means it was premeditated, which you know Cooper isn't capable of."

Luke didn't respond. He got up and walked into the kitchen. The cabinet door closest to the sink opened. One of us needed to fix the hinge because it had started squeaking again. Luke called out to me, "Do you want something stronger than your water to drink?"

"No, thanks." Luke rarely drank. He'd maybe have a beer or two if he went out with cops after work or on a weekend with me and Cooper. I couldn't remember the last time he drank at home. I knew we had a bottle of Jameson in the cabinet, which was probably what Luke was trying to find.

Sure enough, Luke came back in carrying a small glass of whiskey over ice. He sat back down on the couch and sipped it slowly. He took another swig and sat the glass in his lap. He laughed and coughed at once. "I don't know how you drink this. It's burning my entire body."

"I don't know why you're drinking it. It isn't going to help."

Luke rolled the whiskey around in his glass. "This case got more complicated today. Cooper isn't the only one who tested positive for GHB. Holly did as well. But that's not all – so did three other victims from similar homicides in the last few weeks. We've got two other men telling the same story as Cooper."

"That lets Cooper off the hook then, right? He didn't drug himself, and he's certainly not going around drugging and killing women. It can't be random that all these cases have a connection."

"That's what Det. Tyler said to me, too. I'll speak to Adele in the morning and get her statement as well as these other guys you found. I need to wait to see if Cooper's prints are on that gun, but he likely isn't our guy."

I was glad he admitted it finally. "Did you ever talk to Cooper's building to check on the surveillance cameras?"

Luke drained what was left of the whiskey in his glass. "Wouldn't you know it, the cameras on Cooper's floor were down. They didn't record a thing that night."

"That can't be a coincidence."

"It's not," Luke admitted. "The security team had no idea their cameras weren't working. They went back to pull the footage from Saturday night and realized they didn't have any for Cooper's floor. I had them back up to their last recording from that floor and on the Thursday night before the murder, there is a guy plain as day walking off the elevator with a small ladder and disabling all three cameras. Problem is, he had a hoodie pulled up, hat on, mask and gloves. The movements and build seem like a man, but it could be a woman. It could even be Cooper, but I doubt it."

"Did you see Cooper going into his apartment that evening before the cameras were disabled?"

"No, he leaves his building around five that night, and I don't see him return so I can't cross him off the list. Do you know where Cooper was that night?"

I took a breath trying to remember his schedule. "He had a couple of later surveillance cases last week, but I don't remember which nights. We don't always trade schedules, especially if it's a case that comes up last minute."

"Well someone disabled the cameras on Cooper's floor before the murder. The rest of the cameras were fine."

"The security team didn't see this person anywhere else coming or going in the building?"

"I have them going through the recordings, but so far no."

I reached out and touched Luke's arm. "You know that means the murder was premeditated. Someone planned this out ahead of time."

"That's how it looks, but even so, we still can't rule out that Cooper pulled the trigger."

CHAPTER 19

Luke arrived early the next morning at the station. He set up the smaller conference room to take a statement from Adele. He waited anxiously at his desk to hear from Det. Tyler who was running down leads on Tom Sharpe. Brent had given a full statement the evening before and now Det. Tyler was trying to confirm everything the man had disclosed about his co-worker and locate Tom.

In some ways, Luke understood why Brent hadn't come forward earlier, but still, he didn't really understand how anyone sat on a confession of that type and not tell a soul. Luke got a weird vibe from Brent but not anything he could explain or connect to anything concrete. It was more a feeling that rose up his spine that indicated something was off. Luke just didn't know what.

At five minutes to nine, Adele and Cooper made their way into the detective's bullpen. Luke glanced up from his laptop and caught sight of them as they rounded the corner walking towards him. Luke wasn't sure what he had been expecting, but Adele had a presence Luke hadn't anticipated and hadn't been clear from the photo he'd seen.

She carried herself with her shoulders squared back, head held high, mouth set in a firm line, like she could take down a room full of men without breaking a sweat. Her black pants and pretty light blue silk blouse fit every slim curve on her perfectly. She wore almost no jewelry except for a simple beaded necklace.

It's not that Luke hadn't imagined Cooper with a black woman, well if he was being honest, he'd never even considered it. Cooper's taste in women even in college ran blonde, fair, petite and vapid. Adele was nearly the opposite in every regard. She wasn't, regardless of her skin color, the kind of woman Luke thought Cooper would date. If the circumstances were different, he would have congratulated Cooper on the spot. He clearly had chosen a woman of substance and grace this time.

Luke stood and reached his hand out to Adele. "I wish we were meeting face to face for the first time under better circumstances."

Adele firmly grasped his hand in return. "I do as well. I owe you a debt of gratitude for solving my sister's murder, Detective. I'm eager to fill you in on everything I heard the other night when Cooper was at Kepler's."

Luke indicated Cooper could sit in the larger conference room and wait while he spoke to Adele privately. Luke added, "I'll speak to you both when we are done."

Cooper barely looked at Luke and didn't utter a word. He went into the conference room and out of Luke's sight. Turning to Adele, Luke said, "I have another space set up for us."

Adele followed in step with Luke. Once in the room, Luke shut the door and sat down opposite Adele. Before Luke could even open his mouth, Adele started with her statement, explaining exactly what she had witnessed the night in question.

Luke scrambled to pull out his pad of paper and pen. He wanted to capture anything critical right then without having to review the videoed interview later. If Luke had ever doubted Adele's prowess as an attorney, he couldn't now. It was on full display in front of him and nothing less than intimidating and impressive. Even though Luke knew Adele had probably told this story at least twice – once to Cooper and to Riley – nothing sounded rehearsed. Adele told it like she was telling it for the very first time. Luke hung on every word.

When she was finished, Adele simply clasped her hands in front of her and sat back. "Something very wrong happened to Cooper at that bar. I think we both know that it's probably the key to solving this case."

Luke didn't acknowledge what Adele said. Although, truthfully, he didn't disagree. He spent the next hour going over her statement again and asking follow-up questions. Getting down to his final questions, Luke asked, "What was the last thing Cooper said to you before you stopped hearing from him?"

"He said that he needed to get out of there. As I said, Detective, when we were on the phone, Cooper was incoherent. I could barely make out what he was saying, but there was a man right next to him speaking to Cooper. It was obvious Cooper's attention was divided between the two of us."

Luke looked down at his notes. "You said this other man was talking about Holly. Is that correct?" Luke was sure she was tired of going over it again, but she indulged him.

"Yes, I don't know exactly when in our communication he approached Cooper, but I think it was probably while we were texting because when Cooper called me the man was already there. He kept asking Cooper why he didn't like Holly and how could he just spend the night with her and dismiss her like that. He also said that men like Cooper make it hard for nice guys to meet nice girls."

Luke tapped his pen on the table. "Did Cooper respond to any of these statements?"

"Yes, he did," Adele said sternly. "He kept apologizing. I can't tell you the number of times Cooper told the guy that he was sorry it didn't work out with Holly but that they weren't right for each other. Of course, everything that came out of his mouth was slurred and hard to understand, but that was the gist of what he said."

"How did the man respond?"

Adele breathed out and shifted in her seat. Luke could tell she was uncomfortable. "He was angry. He just kept saying that Cooper had to make it right. That he couldn't treat a woman like that and get away with it. I told Cooper to leave and get out of there."

Luke looked back down at his notes and then back up. "Is that what Cooper did?"

"I can't know for sure how long after that he left, but he told me he would. Cooper hung up and that's the last I heard from him. I don't know what happened after that. He said he was leaving so I assumed that's what he did."

Luke put his pen down on the table and relaxed his posture. He sat back in the chair and kicked his legs out in front of him. He watched Adele. She was keyed up, nervous, and angry for sure, but she was also credible. She didn't go over the top trying to protect Cooper. She didn't seem to inflate the tension and conflict she heard. Luke believed she gave it to him straight. It made Luke want to do the same.

Luke locked eyes with her. "Adele, you're a criminal defense attorney so I'm sure you've seen all kinds of murder cases. What's your gut on this?"

To say Luke surprised her would be an understatement. Adele's eyes registered shock and then her shoulders dropped. She searched Luke's face. "Knowing Cooper the way I do, I certainly don't think he killed her. Det. Morgan, I ran every situation I could think of. Maybe he killed her in self-defense, but even at that, I can't see Cooper hurting the woman. He's big and strong enough that he could have removed himself from any situation before doing that. Even if he was drugged, I don't believe it would change the nature of who Cooper is. If I were defending him, I'd figure out why he was set up because that's exactly what this looks like to me."

Before Adele got out her last word, the insistent knocking on the door started. Luke excused himself and opened the door.

A crime scene tech who had been at Cooper's apartment thrust the report into Luke's midsection. "You seemed in a serious hurry for this so we put a rush on everything. I just dropped off the report from the other murder to Det. Tyler. You might want to sit down and go over the cases and compare notes."

Luke stepped out into the hallway and let the conference room door close behind him. He got up close to the tech and said quietly, "Did you find a silencer at either scene?"

"No, and there are no prints on the gun. It's been wiped clean, but ballistics match that gun on all four cases."

Luke flipped through the report. He asked, confused, "Four?"

"Holly Reed, Casey Perry and the two cases that Det. Tyler had from the last couple of weekends."

Luke breathed deeply as his gut churned. This was bigger than Cooper. All the evidence was pointing to a connection among the cases. That much was clear.

The crime tech started to walk away but then circled back. "Det. Morgan, there's something else you should know. The watch face you found at the Casey Perry murder scene was similar to one we found under Cooper's bed. We also found watch faces at the two other murder scenes that were similar in nature. I put an evidence box with some of the evidence on your desk."

Luke stepped back, his confusion apparent. "You found similar watch faces at all four scenes?"

"Yeah, no straps attached just the watch face. All four are round with the arms telling time, nothing digital. Not one of them was working telling active time. They were all stopped at a specific time – not the same time though. All look relatively common, nothing expensive. Did Cooper maybe break his watch recently?"

Luke shook his head. "I'll have to check with him. Are watch faces common at murder scenes? It seems like something that could be easily overlooked."

The crime scene tech looked down the hall past Luke and back at him again. Quietly, he said, "I've seen stranger things. A watch is an easy piece of evidence to brush off at one or two scenes but four homicides that have other similarities is a bit odd. What I find most strange is that you have suspects who are missing time and now watch faces at murder scenes. I think you have a killer trying to tell you something or he's just playing games with you – making sure you know they are connected."

CHAPTER 20

I spent the morning in my home office, going through Facebook and other social media to see if I could connect with some of Holly's friends. I was in luck. Holly had never set up any privacy on her Facebook page. Her posts, photos, and friends list were there in the open for the world to see. I scanned through the photos seeing if anyone familiar jumped out at me. I didn't see anyone I knew, but it was quite obvious how much Holly liked the bars and partying. There wasn't one photo where she didn't have a drink in hand.

I scrolled back through her newsfeed. It became obvious fairly quickly that she put everything about her life out there for public consumption. She had gone out with friends and had been in the bar the same night as Cooper. She had checked-in to that location. Three of her friends were tagged in that post. I had their names, now all I had to do was find some addresses.

I printed off photos and was about to drop their names into my database when my doorbell rang. I left my work and went downstairs to open the front door. Emma, my best friend and neighbor, stood on my porch in a tee-shirt that hugged her enormous rounded pregnant belly and leggings that showed off long slender legs.

She bounced slightly up and down while holding her belly. "Let me in, I have to pee!" Emma shrieked.

I stepped back out of the way and let her pass. She scooted through my living room into the downstairs hall to my bathroom. I stood dumbfounded, wondering why she hadn't just gone to the bathroom at her house. Emma was at the end of her last trimester. Every time I saw her, I worried that she'd accidentally just have the baby in front of me. I could handle a lot in my life and line of work, but being part of someone's emergency home delivery was not high on my list of skills. Even the thought of it brought a wave of nausea and broke me out into a cold sweat.

Once Emma was done, she found me sitting on the couch waiting for her. She looked around my living room and decided on the straight-back chair. "I don't think I'll get myself off the couch." She laughed.

"What on Earth are you doing? You couldn't make it home to go to the bathroom?"

"Joe is home. He decided that since Sophie is down for her nap that it would be the perfect time to shut off the water and mess around with a pipe that needed fixing. I swear that man forgets he has a pregnant wife who needs the bathroom every ten minutes."

I smiled but knew Joe was the best husband anyone could ask for. "Can I get you anything?"

Emma looked towards my kitchen. "Just a glass of water if you can."

I got up and went to the kitchen. Calling behind me I asked, "How is Sophie?"

"She's terrible. We made it easily through the terrible twos, which really weren't so terrible, but three, it's a whole new ballgame. It's like she went from two to a sassy twelve year old."

I carried Emma's glass of water into the room and handed it to her. She took a very long sip and breathed a sigh of relief. She rubbed her belly and said absently, "Miss Sophie is also not happy in the slightest to be getting a new baby brother." Emma's hand flew to her mouth at her admission.

I could barely contain my excitement for her. "I thought you were waiting to find out what you were having at birth. I thought you wanted a surprise!"

Emma bit her lip. "We did at first, but then Joe accidentally saw it in my medical file at the doctor, and you know him, he can't keep a secret so he told me. We decided to just wait and tell everyone after."

I snuggled back into my couch and tucked my legs under me. "I can't believe you didn't tell me. We are supposed to be best friends," I teased.

"If I told you, you would have told Luke and then it would have been a whole thing." Emma laughed. "In all seriousness though, if Sophie isn't good, I'm going to be sending her over here so her Auntie Riley can straighten her out."

"I have no idea what to do with a toddler. Sophie and I would be getting in trouble together."

Emma rolled her eyes. "That's probably true."

Getting serious, Emma said, "On another note, Joe told me this morning that he saw a news report that Cooper might be a suspect in a murder case. He didn't catch the whole news segment though. What's he talking about?"

Emma and Cooper knew each other through Luke and me, but they had become friends, too. I had been meaning to tell her before it hit the news, but things were happening faster than I could keep up with.

I leaned forward, resting my arms on my knees and explained in detail everything that had happened over the last few days. I finished by saying, "I'm not really sure how Holly ended up in Cooper's apartment on Saturday night or who killed her, but the one thing I'm certain of is that Cooper didn't do it."

Emma's face registered surprise at the details. "Cooper couldn't have done it. Does Luke have any leads yet?"

"I don't know. He said something last night about other cases that might connect to Cooper's. But if he's suspecting anyone else, he hasn't shared that with me."

Emma groaned. "Are you doing that thing where you take Cooper's side and give Luke a hard time for just doing his job?"

Guilt washed over me. It was how I felt. While Luke and I did have a good conversation last night, I was secretly harboring some anger at him for not protecting Cooper. I looked at Emma sheepishly. "Probably. We did get into it the other night, but I'm trying to do better."

Emma struggled to stand and peered down at me. "Try harder. You and Luke have been through too much and are finally on track in your relationship to let this come between you."

Emma shuffled off to the kitchen with her glass and came back empty-handed. She headed towards the door but turned back to give me one last piece of advice. "Let Luke do his job, Riley. He's never failed you before. He'll put the right guy behind bars."

With that Emma left and I went back to work feeling sufficiently chastised. Emma and Joe had a strong stable marriage. Not that they never fought, they could go at it from time to time, but Emma had a really good head on her shoulders. She kept me grounded and kicked my behind when I needed it.

I sat back down at my desk and finished searching my database for any information I could find on Holly's friends. Between the database and other information that the women left out in the open on social media, I was able to get all three phone numbers. Two I had to leave messages, but the third I connected with fairly quickly. I explained who I was, leaving out my connection to Cooper, and asked to meet her. There was hesitation in her voice, but she agreed. I closed the call by telling her that if her other friends were willing to talk to me that I could meet them at the same time.

It was settled. We'd meet this evening around six at Kepler's, which meant I could kill two birds with one stone because I needed to talk to the bartender who was back on his shift tonight anyway.

With that squared away, I had the unfortunate job of handling Cooper's surveillance case that afternoon on a fraudulent worker's compensation case. There was nothing I hated more than surveillance.

CHAPTER 21

After talking to the crime scene tech, Luke beelined to his desk. He found the box exactly where the crime tech had left it. Luke dug through the bagged evidence until he found what he wanted. He held up the bag containing the small round watch face and peered at it through the plastic. It was a simple Cassio Forester. The casing and numbers were brown against a cream backdrop. The hands black. It looked like it was from a man's watch. Luke could easily imagine it attached to a brown leather or nylon strap.

The time was stopped at 1:17 am. Luke couldn't recall the time from the other watch he'd found. He had no idea if the time itself was significant. Luke set the bag down on his desk and dug through more evidence, but nothing else caught his eye. He opened the file the crime tech had given him and scanned through the contents listed on the inventory. There was nothing out of the ordinary. Luke also confirmed the dates for the two murders that Det. Tyler had been working prior.

Luke grabbed the bagged watch face from his desk along with a formal witness statement sheet and headed back to Adele. He opened the door to find her sitting exactly as he left her.

Luke handed Adele the formal police witness statement page with additional lined sheets attached. "I'd like you to write your statement out for me, and then we can head into the other room and speak with Cooper. I have a few things I need to go over."

Adele took the witness statement sheet from Luke. She grabbed a pen off the table and started writing. A few minutes later, she read it over once and

94

slid the document towards Luke.

Luke read the statement, ensuring all the critical points were included. He thanked her and turned toward the door. Adele got up and followed behind him. Once in the hallway, Luke pointed in the direction of the conference room, and she walked in step with him.

They found Cooper sitting at the far end of the long rectangle conference room table on the opposite side of the door. His head was down as he intently looked at something on his phone.

Luke had forgotten he had written notes on the dry erase board that was positioned mere feet from Cooper's right, but thankfully the side with notes faced away towards the wall, but Luke wondered if Cooper had taken a look. The evidence boxes from the other crime scene and Holly's phone, still plugged in, sat in the corner. It was an oversight on Luke's part that he hoped didn't come back to bite him.

"Cooper, there are a few things I need to go over with you," Luke said, drawing Cooper's attention. Luke handed the bagged evidence over to him. "That watch face was found in your apartment under your bed. Does it belong to you?"

Cooper held the item in his hand and peered down at it. He looked at both sides through the plastic and then back up at Luke. "I haven't owned a watch since I started carrying a cellphone years ago so it's probably not mine. It does look like a watch I might have had a long time ago, but it's nothing I recently owned."

"Would you have saved it maybe? Kept it someplace in your condo?"

"No, the last time I had a watch like this was right when I started doing police work. Mine is long since gone. Where did you say this came from?"

Luke sat down at the table. Adele went to the far side and sat next to Cooper. Luke reached over and took the evidence bag back from him. "Under your bed."

"Definitely not mine. I never keep anything under my bed." Cooper reached over and gave Adele's arm a squeeze as she sat. "Everything okay?"

Adele patted his hand and leaned over and sweetly kissed his cheek. "It's all good." Turning back to Luke, she asked, "Det. Morgan, you said you had some other things to discuss. Was that it?"

Luke, stone-faced, explained evenly, "I got the report back from the lab. Cooper, you tested positive for GHB. You were definitely drugged."

Relief washed over both Cooper and Adele. Her shoulders dropped and she sat less rigidly in her seat.

Cooper breathed a sigh of relief. "Okay, now that it's confirmed, what does that mean?"

Luke didn't answer the question. He had no intention of telling them that Holly had drugs in her system, too. At least not right now. There were things he still wanted to play close to the vest. "Cooper, do you own a suppressor for your gun?"

Cooper shook his head. "I've never needed one. I only ever carry it for work and shooting quietly isn't exactly high on the list of things I'd need to do. Was a silencer used on the gun that killed Holly?"

"We have reason to believe so. Uniformed cops canvassed your neighbors and no one reported hearing a shot. Given the blood splatter on the wall behind your bed, it's conclusive Holly was killed right where she was found."

Adele interrupted, "If a silencer was used, that might be a reason Cooper didn't hear the shot if he were passed out before Holly was killed."

Luke had already thought of that. "I think anything is possible right now."

Luke got up and walked to the end of the room, and Cooper's and Adele's eyes followed. Luke fought his urge to pace so he stood still with his hands on his hips. "I need to check a couple of dates with you." Luke rattled off the dates of the two previous murders.

Cooper checked the calendar on his phone. It turned out that Luke was his alibi on both. They had still been working to track down victims' families in a previous case. They'd both been out of town together.

Luke asked the final date in question. "Where were you last Thursday night near midnight?"

Cooper checked his cellphone again. As he scrolled through, he offered, "I had a lot of surveillance cases last week so each night sort of blends into the next." Cooper finally stopped scrolling and looked up at Luke. "On Thursday night, I had late surveillance. I probably left my place between five and five-thirty because surveillance started at six in West Little Rock. I didn't come back until near three in the morning."

"Did you see anyone suspicious in your hallway or around the area at that time?" Luke pressed.

"Off the top of my head, no, but I can't recall if I saw anyone. While I know some of my neighbors, I don't know them all. I certainly don't know all of their guests. But nothing really stands out to me from that night. Did something happen while I was out?"

Luke explained, "The surveillance cameras in your hallway were disabled Thursday night. We have a person on surveillance footage, but they were covered from head to toe. While I think it's a guy, we can't even confirm the gender. You were seen leaving the building, as you said, a little after five, but we have no video of you coming home."

Adele asked, "What time were the cameras disabled?"

Luke responded, "Around midnight so it makes sense if Cooper's surveillance lasted until three in the morning, that he'd arrive home after the cameras were out. We will need to confirm your whereabouts though, Cooper. I assume since you were doing surveillance, you'd have photos or video time and date stamped."

Cooper nodded and then got quiet as if thinking. When he finally responded, his voice was clear and strong. "I definitely didn't see anyone messing with the cameras or up on a ladder doing work when I got back home. I definitely would have inquired about that, especially at that hour. How were the cameras disabled?"

"The security company is assessing that for us, but from what I can see, it looks like wires were cut on each. There are three cameras on your floor. The person stepped out onto your floor from the elevator carrying a small ladder and disabled each around midnight."

Adele looked to Cooper. "How easily could he have done that? Do you have actual cameras or the dome cameras in the ceiling?"

Cooper raked a hand through his hair and cast his eyes up. "The cameras are the dome kind so it would have taken some time to unscrew it from the ceiling and get in there to cut the wires. You'd have to know what you're working with. I'm not sure what kind of cameras they are exactly but most aren't just as easy as cutting a wire that's out in the open. You'd need time to mess around and take things apart."

Adele looked over at Luke. "You don't have the person anywhere else on surveillance coming or going from the building? I'm sure there's not much foot traffic at that time of night."

"That's the strange thing. No, we don't. The person isn't captured anywhere else."

"That doesn't actually surprise me," Cooper offered. "My building has odd security. They have hallway cameras, but none in the elevator. There are cameras at the front downstairs entrance, but none on the side entrance that goes to the alleyway outside. Maybe they figure someone breaking in wouldn't know about the side entrance. Many residents that live in the building don't even use the side entrance. It's primarily for maintenance and deliveries, but you have to snake around the alleyway to even find it. Right when you walk in the door though, there are supply closets with ladders and other tools that maintenance use. Maintenance is supposed to lock the supply closet doors, but I've never seen them locked or the doors even fully closed. We don't have a doorman keeping watch over the building who would have noticed either."

"Then all someone would need to know is the code to that side entrance, and they could access the building and all the tools to cut those wires. Is that correct?" Luke asked.

"Yes, but you'd have to be familiar with the building to know the ins and outs. No one completely on the outside is going to know the code, where the cameras are, and what's available to them in the supply closet."

Adele palmed the table, making a soft slapping noise as she rested it. "I think it's pretty easy to say at this point that this was premeditated."

"I'd agree with that," Cooper responded slowly. "What I'm left trying to figure out is if the killer was just after Holly, why go through the trouble of drugging me and involving me in it at all. I don't mean to speak ill of the dead, but Holly went home with a lot of men. Surely, there were easier ways to kill her than at my condo."

CHAPTER 22

Luke excused himself from the room and went to find Captain Meadows. He called out for Det. Tyler, who was back at his desk, and pointed to their Captain's office. Tyler followed Luke to the door.

Luke knocked once and pushed open the door without first being given permission to enter. He was sure his boss wouldn't mind. "I have Cooper and Adele here. I think given evidence that's just come in I can safely rule out Cooper. I need to know what information, if any, I can share with them."

Captain Meadows looked over his glasses at Luke and waved them both in. "Close the door."

Once Luke and Tyler shut the door behind them and were seated, Captain Meadows asked, "What evidence do you have?"

Luke methodically detailed all of the evidence including the GHB, the ballistics, watch faces, and the overall similarities among the cases coupled with Adele's statement and Cooper's alibis for the nights in question. Luke finished by saying, "I'm comfortable saying these cases are connected."

Captain Meadows drummed his fingers on the table. "Tell me more about the watches."

"Sunday when I went to the Casey Perry murder scene, I noticed a watch face in the bed next to the body. I didn't think much of it then but told the crime scene tech to bag it. A sweep of the scene at Cooper's also turned up a watch face that isn't his. The crime tech I spoke to said the two other cases had watch faces found at the scene as well."

"What's the significance?" Captain Meadows asked, peering over his glasses.

"I actually didn't connect it at first. It was the crime tech. He said he found it odd that watch faces were found at murder scenes where the potential murder suspects are missing time. It struck me how it might connect more than we realize. I want to look at the other watches to see the times. I didn't notice the time at the scene when I found the first watch."

Det. Tyler interjected, "The one at Casey Perry's is stopped at 12:32 am. I didn't notice the other two, but the crime tech is right. I saw the watch faces in the evidence bags. It didn't occur to me they were significant."

Captain Meadows raised his eyebrows. "It wouldn't have occurred to me either. Do you think the watches are showing the time of the murders perhaps?"

"Anyone's guess at this point, Cap," Luke said. "I'm asking if I can share information with Cooper and Adele because I think these cases are more complex than just killing the women. I think it might also be about revenge on the men with them." Looking to Det. Tyler, Luke asked, "Did Brent's story check out about Tom?"

Captain Meadows added, "Did you bring him in?"

Det. Tyler looked down at his hands. "He's gone. Tom hasn't shown up for work since last Wednesday morning. I've checked Tom's place, and he's not there either. One of his neighbors saw Tom packing his truck last week and said he left in a hurry. His neighbor thought maybe there was a family emergency or something. We've got an APB out on him, but nothing yet."

Luke suggested, "I'm inclined to believe Brent's story. It connects to Cooper's experience and Scott Davis who was arrested for one of the earlier cases, but we still can't rule out Tom as the killer. Cooper's alibis check out. Scott Davis was sitting in jail when Holly and Casey were murdered, but we have no idea where Tom was at the time of Holly's murder or prior to."

Det. Tyler turned his head to Luke. He asked with skepticism in his voice, "You think someone is specifically targeting these couples, killing the women and getting revenge by setting up the men? If that's the case, wouldn't the killer know that once we connect the cases, Cooper wouldn't be a suspect anymore?"

Luke couldn't quite connect all the pieces yet, but he knew he was close. "Maybe it's not about revenge in the sense of sending them to prison. He's traumatizing them."

"Why?" Det. Tyler asked.

Luke looked around his Captain's office, hoping something might click his thought into place. Luke wasn't exactly sure how to explain it, but that warm feeling he got when he knew he was on the right track spread through his gut.

He turned back to Det. Tyler and explained as best he could. "Many serial killers targeted couples. The Zodiac killer is probably the most famous and recent example. I can't think of any that leave the men alive purposefully, but it certainly would cause trauma and terror, especially to live knowing you were that close to death or that you witnessed a murder and couldn't stop it. You have to live the rest of your life not really knowing what happened to you."

Det. Tyler looked at Luke skeptically. "Now you're saying we have a serial killer on our hands? I know that was the case with your sister's murder, but Luke, come on, it's not that common."

Captain Meadows jumped to Luke's defense. "Tyler, it's not that common, you're right. That said, I think Luke may be on to something. We may not have a serial killer in the traditional sense, but there's a pattern here for sure."

Luke moved to the edge of his chair. "Can I have a little leeway then to give Cooper and Adele more information?"

"Some, but let's not give up too much just yet," Captain Meadows cautioned. "I want to get some hard facts first before we make any theory too widely known outside of the three of us. We still don't know who technically pulled the trigger on any of these cases. Even if these men were drugged up on GHB that doesn't mean this guy, whoever he is, couldn't have convinced these men to kill. I highly doubt that, but we can't rule it out."

Luke left Det. Tyler and Captain Meadows to talk while he went back to Cooper and Adele. As he pulled open the conference room door, Adele and

Cooper stopped talking and gave Luke their attention.

Luke sat back down and kicked his long legs out in front of him, crossing his ankles. "Here's the deal. I left so quickly because I wanted to talk to Captain Meadows to get permission to share some information with you." Luke pinned his eyes on Cooper. "You weren't the only one who was drugged with GHB. Holly was as well."

"I don't—" Cooper started.

Luke held his hand up to stop Cooper from speaking. "Let me finish. Casey Perry was also murdered last week. We believe she was killed on Tuesday night into Wednesday morning. I was at the scene of the murder before I was called to your apartment. She was also drugged with GHB as were two victims from previous cases. We had a witness come forward on Casey's case who overheard a man speaking on the phone, explaining to someone that he woke up in bed with a woman who had been shot to death, and he had no memory of the night before. We've not located him. We also have arrested a man from one of the cases a week ago who claims memory loss in a nearly identical kind of case. We are starting to believe these cases are connected."

"Have you ruled me out then as a suspect?" Cooper asked.

"I don't think if you killed Holly you did so intentionally. There are too many variables right now to rule you out completely," Luke said quickly, knowing it wasn't what Cooper wanted to hear.

"I'm not sure I understand you," Adele said angrily. "I assume some of those dates you just checked with Cooper were his alibis for the other murders. If you think these cases are connected, and Cooper has alibis for the others, then how could he be suspected in Holly's still?"

Luke didn't want to say it, but he had to. "We don't know who pulled the trigger. This third person could have goaded these men into killing while they were drugged. It's unlikely, but we just can't take anything off the table right now."

"Surely, you know whose prints are on the gun and whether Cooper tested positive for gunpowder residue," Adele pressed.

"No prints on the gun and Cooper tested negative for gunpowder residue."

"Well, then that seems pretty open and shut to me." Adele sat back in the chair and folded her arms.

"A gun that was used in four murders was found at Cooper's apartment next to the fourth victim. The gun had been wiped clean of prints, and you and I both know that gunpowder residue tests aren't always an indicator, particularly if time has passed or the suspect washed his hands. My point though is no one here thinks Cooper is a suspect, but we need more information to clear him officially."

Adele eyed Luke, clearly unhappy with him, but she patted Cooper's leg. "Take the win." To Luke, she asked, "What do you need from us?"

"I'm hoping Cooper might be able to give me some more insight into Holly's background, really anything he knows. It's likely the killer is connected to one of you to know the building so well."

Cooper didn't respond but handed his phone to Luke instead. "Since you don't think of me as your primary suspect, and are open to exploring other avenues, maybe you should take a look at this."

Luke took his phone. On the screen was a text from a local Little Rock number. The sender asked Cooper if he liked the surprise that he had left him on Sunday morning.

"It's not the first text like that I've received," Cooper explained.

CHAPTER 23

By the time I wrapped up my afternoon surveillance, I rushed to make it to Kepler's on time. Adele had called briefly to update me on the developments at the police department. She also wanted to know if I had been aware of text messages Cooper had been receiving from an unknown source taunting him about Holly's murder. I was in the dark along with everyone else. It's not something Cooper had shared with me. It didn't surprise me that he hadn't. Cooper could sometimes be like Luke, keeping people on a need to know basis until he felt the time was right.

I wasn't sure what the texts meant, but I didn't really have time to think about it. Adele was meeting me at Kepler's. We'd go separately, and she'd interview the bartender while I met with Holly's friends. We'd convene after to compare notes. Even if Luke had decided Cooper wasn't the most viable suspect, it didn't mean the tide couldn't turn later. Solving the case would put the suspicion of Cooper to rest for good.

I smoothed down my hair while standing on the sidewalk outside of the bar and straightened my shirt. Entering the place was much like the other night. There were a handful of people dispersed at various tables, but it was still early. I checked my phone for the time. Holly's friends still had ten minutes. I grabbed Cooper's favorite table and sat watching the entrance and sidewalk outside. A server came over and took my order and left me to my quiet. At five after six, Adele walked in. She nodded in my direction and went to the bar.

Nearly right after that, two women stood feet from the door talking to each other. They were dressed in heeled boots, tight ripped jeans, and shirts that were a little too snug for my taste. Coupled with the big bleached blond hair and abundance of makeup, I had a feeling they were Holly's friends.

I waved to them, and they headed my way. While I had assumed early in the day both women were mid-thirties, close to my age and Holly's, they both had hard lines around their eyes and one had hints of gray at her roots. If I had to guess, I would have put them both in their forties.

"Did the server already come over? I want to order a drink," one of the women asked me. Then she remembered her manners. She reached her hand across the table to shake mine. "I'm Pam. This is Kim."

I shook her hand but pulled it back quickly and stared at my palm now slick and damp. "I ordered, but I'm sure she'll be back soon," I responded off-handedly.

They both sat. Pam held her hands up. "Sorry just put on some lotion."

The lotion explained the sweet heavy scent of strawberries that hung in the air. I rubbed my damp palm across my thighs and hoped my jeans mopped up some of the lotion. The smell made my eyes water.

Pam rolled her eyes at my reaction. "It's just lotion, sweetie," she said dramatically. "What is it you want to know about Holly? It's horrible what happened to her. It could have been any one of us."

"What do you mean?" I asked.

"The guy she went home with that night. Cooper is his name. He was so normal. If someone like him could have killed a woman, who knows who is lurking around here. I'm just glad he's off the streets now."

I corrected her assumption. "Cooper didn't kill Holly. He hasn't been arrested."

"Well that doesn't mean he didn't do it," Kim added indignantly. "Maybe the cops are just looking for more evidence."

I wasn't going to beat around the bush on this. I asked directly, "What do you know about Cooper and Holly's interaction before that night?"

"Holly was absolutely in love," Kim started.

Pam interrupted sarcastically, "Of course, Holly was in love with every guy she slept with."

Kim turned on her friend. "Don't talk about her like that. Cooper was

105

different. She was really into him. She said they had a lot in common, and that he was really sweet to her. That's what makes him killing her all the more tragic. He seemed like a real upstanding guy, and Holly really liked him. I mean look at the lengths she went to get him to have a relationship with her."

That immediately caught my attention. "What exactly did Holly do?"

Kim remained quiet, her face registering surprise that she let a secret slip.

Pam raised her eyebrows at her friend and then turned back to me. "No matter what Kim says, we all knew it was a fling. Holly made far more out of it than it was. Cooper seemed like a nice guy, but clearly not the kind of guy to settle down. I was right about that. He blew Holly off after the one night they spent together. Holly got clingy. I don't know exactly what she did, but she told us that she had a new friend who was helping her."

I leaned forward in my seat. "What does that mean..."

The server chose that exact moment to drop off my beer and take Pam and Kim's order. When she left the table, I asked again, "What does that mean exactly? She found a friend who could help her?"

Pam nudged her friend. "Tell her, Kim. You claim to be Holly's best friend. Well, we're here to make sure Cooper stays in jail forever so spill it."

I wanted to correct them, and remind them again that Cooper wasn't in jail, but for the sake of getting information, I didn't. I played the angle. "I'm just trying to get justice for Holly. She didn't deserve to die like that. If you can help, you should."

Kim turned around in her seat and scanned Kepler's, looking for who or what I had no idea. When she faced me, Kim leaned in quietly and said, "I really don't know much about the guy. I don't even know his name. Holly was super secretive about him. All she told me was that he was going to help her get Cooper back."

"How did they meet?"

Pam shrugged, but Kim explained, "Holly said that he found her. Approached her one night in another bar. She got talking about Cooper, and he offered to help her get him back."

Looking at Pam, Kim asked, "When did Holly start talking about him?

Like a month ago?"

"Sounds about right. I thought it was the most ridiculous thing I'd ever heard. Why waste your time on a guy who clearly isn't interested?"

"You never got a name?" I asked.

Kim shook her head.

"What did Holly call him when she talked about him?"

"Holly rarely talked about him. Maybe twice, but she never said his name even when I pressed her about it."

Pam interrupted, "Holly was secretive about it. She didn't tell us much, probably because we thought it was ridiculous. I encouraged her more than once just to move on."

"What did this guy want in return?" I asked. The story sounded strange, to say the least.

"Nothing apparently. That's the weird part. Holly said he thought she was nice and just wanted to help her," Kim explained.

I wasn't sure what to make of it, but I still needed other information. "Cooper and Holly met about six months ago. They had a brief fling, one night if I understand correctly. I know they saw each other a couple of times after that in passing. Cooper had to travel to Atlanta and then New York for work. My understanding though is once he got back, Cooper hadn't had any more contact with Holly until the other night. Is that your understanding?"

"Yes, that's what happened," Pam confirmed. "She got really angry with Cooper while he was away. I think he blocked her. She got another phone, but I think Cooper might have blocked that too. It enraged her, but it also made her more determined to win him back. Then Holly connected with the guy who said he'd help her and had been trying to get Cooper back ever since."

I rested my arms on the table. "Help me to understand this. Has Holly had recent contact with Cooper or was she just trying, maybe texting and he still had her blocked? I didn't think he'd spent any time with her recently."

Pam shook her head. "He hadn't. I don't know how much Holly was trying exactly. All she told us was that a plan was in the works. Holly said part of that plan was to pull back and let Cooper miss her. He didn't miss her. I'm sure he was glad to be rid of her."

The server dropped off their drinks. Pam had ordered something with vodka and tipped it back, finishing it before the server had even left the table. Pam called her back to order another.

I tried unsuccessfully to wipe the judgmental look off my face so I refocused on the task. "Kim, the night that Holly was murdered, was she in this bar?"

"Yeah, the three of us were together."

"Was she talking to Cooper at all?"

Kim looked at Pam, who shrugged. Kim relented, "Yeah, Holly talked to him, well she tried anyway. She went over to Cooper while he was on the phone and tried to talk to him. He ignored her. Then she went over to another table and talked to a different guy. I assumed that night he was the guy helping her. Probably after about ten minutes, that guy walked up to the bar, stood there for a little bit, and then went over to Cooper's table with a beer. I don't know what he said to Cooper, but after talking for a bit, he waved Holly back over."

"What happened then?"

Pam grunted. "What normally happens when Holly talks to a guy. She messes it up. They weren't talking ten minutes, and she started yelling at Cooper. He got up and walked out of the bar. Sure enough, like a glutton for punishment, Holly followed. I'm sure it made the guy that was helping Holly mad because he followed them out, too. Now Holly is dead."

CHAPTER 24

My face must have registered some kind of shock because Pam snapped her fingers in front of my eyes. "Hey, are you listening to me?" she barked.

I pushed her hands away from my face. "I'm listening," I said indignantly. "I'm just not understanding. Did either of you go over to Cooper's table that night? I heard from another witness that she heard a woman talking to Cooper in addition to the man."

Pam shook her head in disgust. "The person must have heard Holly talking. We didn't want Holly back with Cooper so it wasn't us."

"What Pam is trying to say is that we thought Holly could do better than Cooper. Yes, he seemed like a great guy, but he obviously didn't want a relationship with her so she needed to move on. Neither of us was supportive of the guy who was helping her. I thought he was filling Holly's head with a lot of false hope when she should have just been out there dating someone else."

"We certainly weren't going over to convince Cooper to date Holly," Pam said with finality in her voice. "There were no other women we saw, and we were watching the whole ridiculous scene closely."

"Let's back up a little. This guy that you saw with Holly that night. Have you ever seen him before?"

"I don't think I'd ever seen him before that night, but it's not like I was looking for him either. I can say that I never saw Holly talk to that guy before. That I can say with certainty," Kim said.

Pam echoed the same.

I pulled out a notebook and pen from my bag and laid them on the table. I flipped the notebook open until I landed on a blank page. "Can you describe this guy to me?"

Kim looked around the bar until she landed on a guy. She pointed. "He's about the height of that guy, kind of the weight, too, but maybe a little thinner. He was average, I guess. Nothing really distinct about him. He had a ballcap on, black tee-shirt and jeans."

I jotted down a few notes but it didn't amount to much. A guy a little under six-feet and average build. "Was he a white guy? What color hair?"

The server dropped off Pam's second drink. She immediately took a sip but set it back down. "So many questions you have. Umm…he was white for sure. He had a hat on but his hair was probably dark. He was the kind of guy who looked like he had a tan. Do you know what I mean? Like he was Italian or from the Mediterranean or something."

Kim looked at me skeptically, "Why does this guy matter so much?"

"You said he followed Cooper and Holly out of the bar, right? If Cooper didn't kill her, and that's a big possibility, then we need to explore who else might be a suspect. If not this guy, then who?"

Pam laughed. She laid her hand across my forearm. "Holly angered a lot of men. She ticked off quite a few women as well for stealing their boyfriends if only for a night. If you're telling us that Cooper didn't do it, and it's your job to create a suspect list, we could be here all night."

"Pam, stop. Holly wasn't that bad," Kim started.

Pam insisted, "Don't lie, Kim. She was terrible."

When Kim spoke again, she was hesitant. "I don't want to speak ill of the dead, but Pam, while being totally dramatic, is right. Holly made a lot of enemies. I couldn't even tell you where to start looking."

With that, both women got up from the table and started to leave. Kim turned to look at me, "I really wish we could help you, but if Cooper didn't kill Holly, then I really have no idea who did so it's probably best we don't say any more."

They made their way through the few people that had filled the bar. They stopped every few feet giving air kisses to women and affectionately touching men as they worked the crowd. I wasn't sure what to make of them exactly, but the word barfly popped into my head. It was a word my mother had used to describe women out of their twenties who still trolled the bars on a regular basis, getting drunk and picking up men.

I outgrew the bar scene back in my hometown sometime around the age of twenty-three. I think my sister, Liv, was a little older. If it had gone on any older for either of us, my mother would have probably dragged us out by the hair. She had little tolerance for that kind of lifestyle.

I jotted down a few more notes until Adele made her way over to me. She had a martini in hand and hitched her jaw at my beer. "You ordered but you're not drinking."

"I just wanted to finish talking to Holly's friends." I moved my notebook to the side. "Sit. Tell me what you found out."

Adele sat down, took a sip of her drink and filled me in on her conversation with the bartender. "Everything Cooper had told us panned out. The bartender, Sam, remembers Cooper coming in and ordering a drink. He sat at this table. Sam knew Holly, too. He told me that she approached Cooper, but he brushed her off."

I interrupted, "Her friends said that, too. What else did he say?"

Adele tapped her glass with her manicured fingernail. "Sam said a guy came up to the bar and asked what Cooper was drinking. He said he was an old friend. Sam poured him Cooper's favorite beer and the guy took it over to the table to Cooper. The guy and Cooper talked for a while and then he waved Holly back over. Maybe it was Holly that I heard. It was all very noisy."

Adele described the guy that said he was Cooper's friend.

I grabbed Adele by the arm, excited. "That's exactly what Holly's friends told me. They both described him the same, too."

I explained to Adele the very strange story about Holly and the guy who was giving her advice for getting Cooper back. I slapped my hand on the table. "I think this guy is the missing element to this whole thing. I think he was messing with Holly to set this whole thing up."

"Why though?" Adele wondered. "Do you think it was a grudge against

Cooper or was Holly who he was really after? That's the part that doesn't make sense to me."

The bar was starting to get crowded now. I wished I had a photo of the guy I could show around to figure out who he was, but I didn't have much of anything. I didn't know if I even had enough for Luke to do anything with. I excused myself from Adele and went up to the bar.

I waved Sam over and explained who I was. "I need to know more about the guy who went over to Cooper last Saturday night. Do you know anything?"

Sam laid his forearms on the bar and gave me his full attention. "I wish I did. I really like Cooper. He's one of our regulars. I can't believe he'd kill that girl. I don't know anything about that other guy though. I've seen him here a few times. He pays with cash but doesn't talk to too many people. It didn't surprise me that he might know Cooper. Everyone does."

"Is there anything about him you might have heard from someone else or quirks he has? Really anything at this point might help."

Sam looked back down the bar, which was quickly filling up with customers who needed him. He tapped the bar in front of me. "Nothing I can think of. Let me get back to work, but I'll ask around. If I hear anything or see him in here again, I'll call you. Leave your number for me." With that, Sam went back to work.

There was a pen on the bar from someone who had recently paid their tab. I grabbed it and a napkin and jotted down my name, phone number, email address, and a reminder note of who I was. Sam was cute. I didn't want him to mix my number up with the countless others he probably received from women who were hitting on him. I waved the napkin in his direction, and he caught my eye. I set it down on the bar and shoved it forward.

"Definitely call me. Anything. I don't care how small or insignificant it seems."

CHAPTER 25

Luke stirred in his sleep, some noise far off in the distance calling his attention. He rolled over and snuggled into the covers.

Riley nudged him. "Luke, your phone is ringing."

He grunted in his sleep and burrowed farther into the soft comforter. Riley nudged him again.

"What time is it?" Luke asked groggily after a few seconds.

"It's just after five. This is the third time they are calling. You better grab it."

Luke rolled over onto his back and slapped at the nightstand until he found his phone. He pushed himself upright and rubbed the sleep from his eyes. It was Det. Tyler. Luke sat up. He coughed and cleared his throat and called his partner back.

"Luke, sorry to call you so early. We've got another murder. A 911 call came in at four this morning from a guy who said he woke up to a dead woman next to him."

Luke cursed under his breath. "Where?"

"I'm down here at one of the condo buildings on Rock Street. I'll text you the address. Come up to the second floor number two-twenty-eight. The victim's name is Nikki Eagan. I'll fill you in when you get here."

"All right, I'll be there soon." Luke went to end the call, but Det. Tyler called his name. He put the phone back up to his ear. "I'm here."

"This one, Luke, is worse than before. He used a knife this time. The medics are here with the victim's date Brendan Howe. He's not hurt, but he's completely traumatized. I don't think he killed her. Looks like it's the same kind of situation as the others."

Luke hung up, dropped his phone in his lap and pressed the palms of his hands into his eyes, willing the nightmare to go away. Of course, it didn't. Luke could feel Riley's gaze on him. He knew without looking that she was sitting there waiting for an explanation. Luke reached for her and slipped her soft hand into his. "That was Det. Tyler. He said there's been another murder downtown in one of the condo buildings on Rock Street. Where is Cooper?"

"He's at the hotel as far as I know. Adele is there with him," Riley said hesitantly like she couldn't believe he was asking. "You don't think he had anything to do with this, do you?"

Luke shook his head. "I just want to make sure he's got a solid alibi before I even go to the scene." Luke stood and grabbed a towel that he'd thrown on the back of the chair the night before and headed for the shower. As the hot water ran down his back, Luke tried unsuccessfully to make sense of what was happening. They'd spent the last week running down every lead they could find after Holly's murder to no avail. Now that the weekend had rolled around again, there was another murder.

Returning to the room with just the towel around his waist, Luke found Riley exactly where he had left her, sitting up in bed, staring off into space. Luke pulled boxers and a pair of pants from the armoire. He stepped into them and buttoned his pants, turning to her. "It's going to be okay, Riley. You know there's going to be questions about Cooper. I just want to be prepared. Go back to sleep. I'll text you when I can." Luke went over to the bed and kissed her forehead.

"I know. I just don't understand," she said quietly and rested her head back on the pillow.

Luke had nothing to say to make Riley feel better. He knew exactly what she was feeling because he was feeling it too. He quickly finished getting dressed, grabbed his wallet, gun, keys, and phone and headed for the door.

Even if Luke hadn't had his GPS on to find the exact locations of the condos on Rock Street, he couldn't have missed it. Several police cars with their lights ablaze blocked off streets around its perimeter. A uniformed officer waved to Luke as he approached and moved a barricade so he could drive through. Luke found a spot in the small parking lot in front of the building and made his way into the lobby. The space had a simple clean black and white tiled floor, a concierge desk to the left and a row of mailboxes to the right. A couch was placed haphazardly in the corner, but Luke couldn't imagine anyone sitting there for long.

Luke found Captain Meadows standing in front of the concierge desk, looking down at his phone. The building was full service twenty-four hours a day, seven days a week. Residents paid a premium for the service, but apparently, it didn't do anything to keep them safe.

"What do we have, Cap?" Luke asked as he approached.

Captain Meadows looked up from his phone, put a hand on Luke's shoulder when he got close enough, and expelled a breath. "It's bad, Luke. Whoever this guy is, he's ratcheted up the violence."

"What's the plan?" Luke asked, distracted by the orange numbered crime scene markers that dotted the staircase at the back of the lobby, the floor at the bottom of the stairs, and trailed off to the left down the hall. The markers were positioned one right after the other as if breadcrumbs marking a path. Luke stepped away to go inspect before the man could answer.

"I'm putting you in charge and Det. Tyler second in command. You'll have whatever team you need," Captain Meadows said to Luke's back.

As Luke stood over the spot at the bottom of the stairs, he peered down at the blood drops that had splattered on the floor. One after another, each marked by a crime scene tech. Luke assumed the blood indicated the path the killer had taken. The trail continued down the first-floor hallway, which ended at a side door to the street. Luke followed the blood to the door, which had been left slightly ajar.

Luke pulled gloves from his back pocket and snapped them on. He nudged the door open with his fingers, careful not to touch the handle, pulling only from the door's side until he had enough room to step through. Orange triangle markers continued into the parking lot at the side of the building and then abruptly disappeared. Luke assumed maybe the killer had gotten into a vehicle.

Luke scoped out the door. It was like Cooper's with a keypad instead of a lock and key. He went gently back through the door and rejoined Captain Meadows in the lobby.

"Where is the concierge?"

Captain Meadows pointed to a door behind the desk. "He's back in the office waiting with an officer. Do you want to talk to him? He says he didn't see anything."

"Did he call 911?"

"No, it was the victim's boyfriend or whatever he is. I don't understand relationships today."

"Where did all the blood come from? Did the boyfriend come down here for help?"

"We don't think so. At least he said he didn't. You can talk to Det. Tyler to understand better, but I think the working assumption right now is this might be from the killer leaving."

It made no sense to Luke. How could the concierge not have seen the killer leaving and dropping blood through the lobby? Luke left Captain Meadows and went behind the desk to the backroom. He found the young concierge sitting at the desk with the uniformed cop standing guard over him. Luke waved him off.

When the cop was gone, Luke shut the door behind him. "I'm Det. Luke Morgan. I'm hoping you can tell me what happened here last night?"

The young man turned his face up to Luke with tears streaming down his face. "My supervisor told me that I could sit back here at night and watch television unless someone came in or needed something. It's been quiet all night. I had no idea anything happened until the police showed up. I swear. No one came through that front door or passed by the desk."

CHAPTER 26

Luke made his way to the second floor to the victim's condo. The building had no surveillance video, and the concierge at the desk would be no help whatsoever. Luke couldn't blame the kid. He had only been doing what he was told. But it left no eyes on the side of the building or the stairs.

The upstairs hallway had the same markers as the first floor, indicating the trail of blood. Luke followed the path down to unit two-twenty-eight, which was at the very end of the hallway on the right. The door had been left wide open. The scene knocked Luke back before he ever crossed the threshold.

Brendan was about Luke's age. He sat covered in blood on the floor on top of a clear plastic tarp. His pant legs were so blood-soaked Luke couldn't tell its actual color. Blood streaks crisscrossed his chest from top to bottom and side to side. Brendan's blood-matted hair stuck to his head, and one single streak ran from his jaw to his ear. A crime tech crouched low, swabbing and collecting evidence while it was still fresh.

Seeing Luke enter, the crime tech nodded. "I'm just about done here and then he's all yours, but grab those booties in the box outside near the door and put them on your feet. We have significant evidence scattered throughout the place."

Luke did as he was told, stepping back into the hall and grabbing the blue coverings. Once he was done, Luke moved from the living room down a hallway to the two bedrooms, one to the left and another at the very end. A bathroom sat off to the right. It was a room at the very end of the hall where Det. Tyler's voice could be heard.

Luke called out to his partner. Det. Tyler finished asking the crime tech his question about evidence collection, listened to the response, and stepped into the hall with Luke. He raised his eyebrows and hitched his jaw towards the living room. "From what I understand, Brendan tried to stop the attack. He's got defensive wounds all over him. He wasn't stabbed, but he's got a pretty big knot on the back of his head. Looks like the killer knocked him out. The medics have come and gone."

Luke kept his voice low. "Was he drugged?"

"Looks that way. I didn't fully question him yet. He can't remember all of the night. He doesn't even fully remember fighting off the guy. He said his memory is like a movie that keeps skipping. He's been trying to piece things together for me."

Luke looked back toward the living room. "Are you sure he's not good for it?"

"I don't see how it could be him. Neighbors heard a commotion around two in the morning. It was loud enough to wake a few people. One of the victim's neighbors said she went to her door to listen, but didn't hear anything more. She stood there quietly listening, wondering if she should call the police. A few minutes later, she saw a man walking past. She didn't get a good look at him but didn't see blood or anything that caused immediate alarm. Of course, all she could see was the side of his head, but she assumed there was an argument and went back to bed."

Luke pointed toward the guy in the living room. "Brendan's been in the condo the whole time?"

"Yeah, so he says. He called 911 around four. He said he came to, saw the scene and freaked out completely. Who wouldn't? Look at this horror. He checked the victim for a pulse, didn't find one and called immediately. We found a large butcher knife in the kitchen sink. Looks like it's been scrubbed clean, but there's still blood smears in the sink. It's most likely the murder weapon."

Luke stepped into the bedroom and faltered on his feet. He'd been to a lot of crime scenes in his life, but the sheer violence of this one shook him where he stood. The victim, Nikki, was naked and sprawled sideways across the bed, her right arm bent at an odd angle above her head. Blood covered the victim's body from head to toe, so much so that it was impossible for Luke to tell where the stab wounds were located, although he assumed there had to be many.

He turned back to Det. Tyler and asked, his voice giving away his shock, "Is Purvis on his way?"

"He should be here any minute. I let the crime techs get to work, but left it pretty much undisturbed."

Luke took a cautious step farther into the room, watching the floor as he walked. The crime tech had been right to caution him. Luke feared he might step on something critical. Evidence was everywhere from the victim's clothes that lay in a heap on the ground to a cellphone, wallet and other items. Luke spotted a men's shirt crumpled in a ball on the floor at the end of the bed. It too had blood on it, at least the part that Luke could see. He cursed loudly.

"I know," Det. Tyler said from the doorway. "Shooting the victims apparently wasn't enough of a thrill for the guy."

"No," Luke said quietly almost to himself as he peered down to more closely inspect the body. "It's not the thrill of the kill for him. I don't think that's why he's doing this. It's the terror he's trying to evoke. He's doing it to get a reaction out of the men. It's for show."

Luke wasn't sure what exactly made it finally click for him, but he knew he was right. Sure, the killer probably despised the women, but his main objective was to terrorize the men. Luke even wondered if this time the killer used less GHB on the man to ensure maximum terror.

"What do you mean, Luke?" Det. Tyler asked.

Luke held a finger up for Det. Tyler to hold on a second. Luke was looking for something. He scanned the bed without touching anything but didn't see it. He crouched low and checked under the bed. Nothing but some bins that looked chock full of clothes and other personal items. Luke stood again scanning the space. Call it intuition, but as soon as his eyes landed back on the crumpled men's shirt, he knew.

Looking up at Det. Tyler, he said, "Grab me a crime tech and an evidence bag." He stood in place until Tyler had returned with both.

Luke waved the crime tech over, pointing to the shirt. "I think there's something under there, but I didn't want to lose any potential evidence in the process. Can you take a look for me and bag the shirt?"

The crime tech bent down and carefully unfolded the shirt. There was nothing inside of the balled-up mess, but surprisingly, other than blood on the areas of the shirt that had been exposed, the shirt remained fairly clean of evidence. As the crime tech removed the shirt from the floor and put it in the bag, Luke spotted what he knew would be there – the watch face.

"Leave that there," Luke instructed. "Det. Tyler, we've got another. This must be some sort of signature or something for the killer." Luke reached down and picked it up with his gloved hand. "What time did the witness see the man walking down the hall?"

"Just after two is what she said. A couple of the neighbors we spoke to heard a commotion in approximately the half-hour before that."

Luke held the watch face up for Det. Tyler to see. The hands were set at exactly 1:41 am. "I think he stops the time right before he kills the victim. Maybe the guy fighting back surprised him, threw him off his game."

"He upped the violence but also upped his risk."

"Maybe we just got lucky." Luke handed the watch face to the crime tech for him to bag and stepped around him and out of the bedroom. To Det. Tyler, he said, "Let's go in here to talk privately before Purvis gets here." Luke walked directly into the spare bedroom, which the victim had used as an office.

Det. Tyler followed right behind him and shut the door. "Don't you think it's kind of strange, Luke, that the killer went out of his way to use a silencer on the first four murders, and then makes this mess and all this noise? Does he want to get caught?"

"I can't say for sure, but I think he's evolving or changing how he kills because he's not getting the reaction he wants," Luke explained. Luke knew serial killers could change how they kill, but he wasn't even sure that's what this was. There seemed to be some personal connection he couldn't quite put his finger on. These weren't break-ins or women snatched off the street. These women were killed in the safety of their homes with their male companion present.

Luke quickly walked back to the victim's bedroom and looked back at the position of her body on the bed, and for the first time, wondered if there was a sexual assault component to these crimes. Was the killer not just trying to terrorize the men, but in some way, humiliate them, too?

CHAPTER 27

Cooper read the text again and stumbled back towards the bed, sitting down resting his head in his hands. *Did you enjoy your first kill? You seemed to enjoy this one too. We put on such a little show for you.*

Cooper hadn't admitted it to anyone, but he wondered if Luke was right. Could this guy have convinced him to shoot Holly? Cooper knew he'd never really know for sure because that morning he had acted like a guilty man. Cooper's first instinct had been to scrub himself down to free himself of any gunpowder residue.

Now that one act allowed the niggling doubt to creep up on him in moments of quiet. Because of his own actions, Cooper would never really know the truth. His own decision-making galled him. Even if they found the person ultimately responsible, deep down, Cooper believed he'd never really know the role he played in it all. He hadn't told Riley or Adele he had done that, and he knew it was a secret he'd take to his grave.

But that wasn't his only secret. Cooper hated Holly. Riley would probably tell him he was being dramatic and that hate was too strong of a word for what he felt. No, Cooper truly hated her. Her incessant badgering drove him crazy. He felt boxed in and constantly backed up against a wall. It had been one night of misplaced passion, and he'd paid a price for it for months. Now, he'd pay for the rest of his life.

Because the case had taken a turn, and Luke's focus was elsewhere, Cooper couldn't help but be relieved. Even that caused him guilt. He was free because Holly hadn't been the only one murdered. How could he be happy he was free because other women were dead? Emotions welled up in Cooper like a knot he couldn't untangle. The more he tried, the deeper into despair he sank.

Deep down in a place Cooper didn't even want to acknowledge, he believed that he could have killed Holly. Before her murder, Cooper had even thought about it in his angrier moments. Holly's constant badgering had reached a point where he couldn't even relax and enjoy his time unwinding at Kepler's because the threat of her being there plagued him. Cooper had tried everything – being nice, directly telling her he didn't want to be involved with her and straight up ignoring her. Nothing worked. She dodged and weaved like some prizefighter and kept coming back for more.

Cooper had technically lied to them all. He had seen Holly several times in the months leading up to that night, but he hadn't interacted with her. That much was true. He was embarrassed by the extent that Holly had been stalking him, and more so, his own powerlessness to stop it. A few times, Holly had pushed him hard enough that he'd nearly lost his temper in public, but Cooper had restrained himself and simply left whatever establishment he'd been in when she arrived.

No one deserved to die the way Holly did. It wasn't that Cooper was glad she was dead, but he felt relief. Guilt bubbled up inside of him every time he felt that way. Cooper's own conflicting emotions tugged him in different directions so much that he had chosen to just remain quiet to it all. Cooper's only goal over the last week had been keeping himself out of prison for the rest of his life.

Cooper picked up his phone off the bed and stared down at the text again. He hadn't responded to the previous texts. Luke had told him not to. In a flash, Cooper banged out a response. He admitted his innocence. He told the person texting him that he did not and would not have killed Holly. That nothing would convince him of that. Cooper promised that he'd hunt him down and expose him. Cooper would get his vengeance.

When he was done, his index finger hovered over the send button. But Cooper could not will himself to send the text. He felt powerless even to defend himself. Cooper deleted the draft of his text and threw the phone across the room. It hit the soft sofa and bounced to the floor. Cooper threw himself back on the bed and draped an arm over his eyes.

Normally, not having a family didn't bother Cooper. It was a rare moment where he longed for a life that others lead, but right then and there, Cooper wished he had a warm home to go to and a mom to fix him a hot meal and tell him everything was going to be okay. Cooper allowed himself a few moments of rare pity for being so alone in the world.

But he didn't even get that, because it was at that moment, just when he was sinking under a wave of self-loathing, that Adele and Riley shoved through the door. They had been keeping him in the dark about the progress of the investigation. They had spoken to Holly's friends and the bartender nights ago, but they told him very little. He hadn't been pleased that Adele had kept him in the dark, but she said it was for his own good until they could figure out a few things.

Now here they both were a little out of breath and looking like they'd been caught in a strong wind storm. Riley rushed towards him. "There's been another murder," she said quickly.

Cooper stood, not quite steady on his feet. "Another one? Where?"

Riley tried to catch her breath. "Luke got a call early this morning. The murder happened down at the condos on Rock Street. It's more than that. Luke discovered a pattern, and with what we found, I think we can help him."

"What pattern?" Cooper asked, confusion on his face.

Riley turned away from him and searched the couch. "Where's the remote control?"

Cooper went to the desk and grabbed the remote near his laptop. He handed it to her. "Riley, slow down, and tell me what's going on."

Riley stood in front of the television and flipped through channels until she landed on a local news station. There stood Luke and Captain Meadows at a podium. Det. Tyler stood right behind them. Captain Meadows was finishing his statement. "While information is coming in quickly, we are still processing the scene. What we know is that there is one deceased woman and a man who is a potential witness. He is not a person of interest at this point. We anticipate that we will have more information as the day progresses."

Janelle Brady, a crime reporter for Channel 5 News shouted a question from the crowd. Her cameraman grabbed a close up of her thin heavily made-up face. "Do you have any reason to suspect this murder is connected to the string of murders over the last few weeks?"

Captain Meadows shot a look to Luke who simply nodded his head once. He responded sternly, "We have reason to believe they are connected and will be making a statement later in this regard."

Janelle shouted again. "Does this mean that Scott Davis who had previously been arrested is being let go and that Cooper Deagnan is no longer a suspect in the murder of Holly Reed?"

"That is correct," Captain Meadows said evenly.

"Is there a serial killer on the loose, Captain Meadows?" Janelle shouted once more.

"We will be releasing a statement later providing more details."

The crowd of journalists erupted with more questions as they jockeyed for a position closer to the podium. Neither Captain Meadows nor Luke gave any other statement. They retreated out of the sight of the camera.

Riley clicked off the television and turned to Cooper. "You were definitely set up. We think we might have some idea how he's doing it."

CHAPTER 28

"You have five murders and you're telling me you have absolutely no suspects yet!" Jennings screamed, slamming his fist down on the conference table. "This is absolutely unacceptable."

Luke, Captain Meadows, and Det. Tyler had gathered in the detective's bureau conference room after the press conference to discuss strategy. Luke expected a call from Purvis sometime that afternoon to further go over the autopsies and confirm whether any of the cases looked like a sexual assault. What Luke hadn't anticipated was the assistant prosecutor disrupting their meeting. Apparently, neither had Captain Meadows, whose face grew redder with each passing second.

Captain Meadows looked over the rim of his glasses at the man. "Jennings, I called the prosecutor's office. You have not been assigned to this case. You really don't have any business here right now. As you just said, we have enough to handle. Please see yourself out."

Jennings fumed like a toddler. Luke wouldn't have been surprised if the man threw a temper tantrum right then and there. "I want Cooper arrested right now," he demanded. "Clearly, none of you can see past your personal relationship with him. If you don't handle it, I'll take matters into my own hands. I'll hold a press conference and let the entire community know you aren't doing your jobs."

Luke sprang to his feet and pushed the man back into the wall. He got right up in Jennings' face and jabbed a finger into his chest. "No, you won't unless you want to get sued. Cooper has no connection to four of the victims, and there is no hard evidence to suspect him otherwise. I'm not sure what your issue with Cooper is, but if there's anyone here who can't contain his personal feelings, it's you. Now get out and let us do our jobs. You are wasting our time."

A hand gripped Luke's shoulder. "Luke," Det. Tyler said calmly, "let him go. He's not worth the fight. After the crime scene I saw this morning, there is no way Cooper is connected to this. We all know that."

Luke relaxed his posture and shot Jennings a look of contempt, but he didn't back down. Neither man did. Jennings looked like he might wet himself. Luke was stronger and angrier.

Captain Meadows stood. "All right, you caused the scene you wanted. You've riled up my detectives. Now get out of here before I call your boss. This is still my detective's bureau. When we have something for the prosecutor's office, trust me, we'll let y'all know."

Jennings looked for a second like he might argue, but he relented. He didn't leave though without a parting shot. "If it's the last thing I do, I'll make sure Cooper goes down for this."

After the man left, Det. Tyler closed the conference room door, ensuring it was shut tight and they had the privacy they needed. When he sat back down at the table, he asked, "Why does Jennings have it out for Cooper?"

"I don't know," Luke said, disgust in his voice as he sat back down. "Cooper didn't explain their connection, and Riley didn't know. I've got a long list of things that I need to get done, and it's been getting away from me." He pointed to the phone still plugged into the wall sitting on a stack of bins. "See like that. That's Holly's phone I found at her place. I needed to charge it, and then I forgot all about it."

Captain Meadows twisted his head in the direction of the phone and then refocused his attention at Luke. "It's going to have to wait. Det. Tyler, did Scott Davis test positive for GHB?"

"He did but the prosecutor's office was hesitant to drop the charges until we have something more solid. That and the connection to the other cases alone wasn't enough for them. It took a lot of convincing. There's no way he committed the recent cases sitting in jail."

"Luke, do we know anything about this killer? Anything at all that we can give to the public?" Captain Meadows pressed.

"I think the most important thing we can say is this probably isn't a stranger to them. We have a killer who is familiar enough with the victims to gain their trust to both get close enough to drug them and go back to the victim's residence with them without a fight or struggle. And at least in Cooper's case, he'd been to the residence before. I think there's some familiarity before the night of the murder."

Captain Meadows tapped his finger on the table. "Do we have any viable suspects right now?"

Luke shook his head. "No, we don't. But as we promised, we are going to need to make a stronger statement for the community about these cases. I just have no idea what we say, but we are going to have to give some kind of warning. Most of the couples were down in the River Market before the murders. It's going to send panic through the city."

"What kind of warning are we looking at? Don't have casual sex? Don't go home with women you barely know?" Det. Tyler asked, his eyebrows raised.

Luke knew Det. Tyler's wife. They had been married for longer than Luke could remember. They had been high school sweethearts. Bill Tyler was not the kind of man that went home with strange women, and Luke could see the annoyance for risky behavior written on his face.

"Well, I…" Luke stumbled over his words. "That's probably the gist of it. I don't know the relationship status of all of the victims. Cooper and Holly weren't even involved at the time of the murder. It sounded like a first date for Tom and Casey. We still have to talk more to Brendan about him and Nikki."

Det Tyler explained, "It was a first date for Scott Davis, too. The very first case we have, the victim, Chelsea Gordon, was alone. No one has ever come forward. We know Chelsea was in Kepler's at some point before her death. We have eyewitnesses who saw her there, but no one that remembers who she spoke to or when she left. Chelsea had told friends she was meeting someone for dinner that night, but we have no leads on who that someone is. The strangest part of that case is that her phone and computer turn up nothing. No messages about meeting anyone or any men in her life."

"Maybe they met offline and made a date and didn't communicate beforehand," Captain Meadows offered.

Det. Tyler squinted. "Does anyone do that anymore?"

"We have to at least consider it a possibility," Luke said.

Captain Meadows took his glasses off and rubbed his eyes. "What's most clear to me is we have one killer who is upping his game. He kills up close and personal. He drugs his victims. As Luke said, there seems to be premeditation not only about the murder but victim selection. He's not picking these victims at random. Cooper's building had the surveillance video messed with. Two of the other buildings didn't have surveillance video at all. I assume he knows that ahead of time, which tells me he's picking his victims long before he kills."

"Sounds about right," Det. Tyler agreed.

"The scariest part of this is he walks among our community unnoticed," Captain Meadows said. "It's clear he's blending in enough not to cause alarm but physically strong enough to take on two victims at once, even if they are drugged. Mentally, he's smart, calculating. While this last kill may have been frenzied, he's organized and planned."

"I agree with all of that," Luke said and then detailed for Captain Meadows the theory he had explained to Det. Tyler earlier about his belief that the killer was at least in part doing this to terrorize, and possibly humiliate the men. "I'm waiting for Purvis to let me know if there are any signs of sexual assault prior to the murder."

Captain Meadows nodded along as Luke spoke. In the end, he asked, "Luke, are you saying that you think the woman is just the pawn in all of this? That the real target is the man?"

"It was a theory, but I don't know enough yet to say one way or the other," Luke concluded.

Det. Tyler agreed. "There's a lot of evidence still to uncover. We still need to interview Brendan Howe."

"Where is he now?" Captain Meadows asked.

"The crime techs finished up with him, but he had a mild panic attack.

He's at the hospital now. They admitted him for observation. We gave them permission to let him get cleaned up. The crime techs took his clothes and are drug testing him. We are going down to the hospital later to interview him once he's in a better frame of mind. I couldn't get much out of him in the state he was in."

Captain Meadows picked up a file folder. "The victim, Nikki Eagan, did you notify next of kin?"

"Calls are out, Cap, but so far no one has responded. That's why we didn't mention her name at the news conference," Det. Tyler reminded him.

"Right, right," Captain Meadows said more to himself than them. "I think we need to figure out how he's meeting these victims and identify that early connection."

The conference room door handle turned and the door swung open before Captain Meadows got out his last word. It was Riley. She was rushed and out of breath. "I think I might know the answer to that. I think I found some interesting evidence in Cooper's case that just maybe connects to the rest."

CHAPTER 29

"Riley, you can't just barge into my meeting like this," Luke admonished. He stood to shoo her out of the room, but Riley dodged him, moving to stand at the end of the table.

She looked up at him with big brown doe eyes. "Don't be mad at me, Luke. I've been trying to call you all day. When I couldn't reach you, I came down here. A crime tech told me you were in a meeting talking about the case. I saw the news conference."

Captain Meadows waved him off. "Riley, sit down and tell us what you found."

Riley pulled out her chair. "Last night, I spoke to Holly's two best friends – Kim and Pam. I can write down all their contact info for you. They told me that Holly had been approached by a man who told her that he could help her get Cooper back. She's been friends with this guy for the last couple of months."

"I don't see how this relates," Luke interrupted.

"Let me get to it," Riley snapped. She spoke directly to Captain Meadows. "That night in Kepler's, according to her friends, Holly had gone over to Cooper, but he brushed her off again. She was then seen going to a man's table. After talking to Holly for a bit, that same man got up and went to the bar to get a drink and then sat down at Cooper's table. A short while later, he waves Holly over. That's when Holly and Cooper started arguing, and Cooper left with Holly following after him. The man walked out right behind them. I have that confirmed by Kim and Pam. There are regulars at the bar who also confirmed the argument between Cooper and Holly and

131

saw a man walk out behind them. Now, Kim and Pam can't be sure who the man was that Holly was speaking with, but they had never seen him before. At the time, they both kind of got the vibe he was the one helping her. The friend Holly talked about but no one had ever met."

Captain Meadows tapped the table and looked to Luke and Det. Tyler. "I'm not sure I'm making the connection, Riley. How do you think this is relevant? Sure, he's another guy at the bar that we should probably speak with, but how does it connect to the murder?"

"I think he's the one that drugged Holly and Cooper. He's the unknown factor at play that night. He's also the one that Adele heard on the phone, yelling at Cooper for screwing over Holly. The timing matches up. He was angry that Cooper would have a one-night stand. He told him that he was ruining everything for men like him. He made it personal. He is also the only one we have handing Cooper a drink that didn't come directly from the bar, and he had ample access to Holly."

"Well you do make a good point there," Captain Meadows admitted.

"There's more," Riley offered. "The man who turned off the video surveillance in the hall had to know the code to get into Cooper's building. He also had to have had Cooper's phone number because he's been getting harassing text messages. Holly had both the code and Cooper's phone number so the killer must have some connection to her. Whoever drugged them had to have been in close contact with both of them that night. At least two witnesses can confirm he was and another two, in addition, saw him follow Holly and Cooper out of the bar. Unless there's other evidence I'm not aware of, this is the only guy right now that seems to have had all of those opportunities."

Det. Tyler leaned forward on the table. "You don't have any information about this guy? Name? Photo? Anything?"

"Unfortunately, no, but both Pam and Kim could identify him if you found him. The bartender at Kepler's said the guy wasn't someone he saw regularly, and as you know, that bar is primarily made up of regulars. Everyone kind of knows everyone there."

Det. Tyler caught Luke's eye. "It's worth exploring."

"You can also see what kind of relationship each couple had before the murder," Riley offered.

"We were just talking about that," Luke said. "What are you thinking?"

Riley explained, "In Holly and Cooper's case, Holly wanted a relationship and Cooper didn't. It had just been a one-night thing. I'm wondering if the killer is specifically targeting couples who have more of a casual relationship, punishing men, who in the killer's eyes, aren't respecting these women. As he said himself, making it more difficult for men like him to date. The prior connection would give the killer time to know what men deserved to be punished."

Captain Meadows nudged Luke's arm. "That kind of falls in line with what you were saying about the killer possibly targeting these men. That they are really his intended victims."

Luke smiled at Riley. He hadn't meant to be so annoyed with her when she first showed up. He had just been taken by surprise. Luke had been so preoccupied with other things that he hadn't gone down himself to Kepler's the night before to talk to the bartender. He wanted to be annoyed that Riley had done that as well as talk to Holly's best friends, but Cooper had every right to hire, or in this case, use the resources of his own private investigator firm to defend himself against the speculation.

"You had a theory, Luke?" Riley asked, nudging him out of his head.

"I did," Luke started. "I suggested that maybe these murders are more about terrorizing the men than killing the women. He's killing to instill fear."

"To instill fear or to punish?" Riley asked.

"Tell me what you mean by that?" Captain Meadows asked, shifting in his seat to face her.

"I agree with Luke that it's about the men probably more so than about the women he's killing, but my guess would be more to punish the men as well as instill fear. I'm not too familiar with the other cases, but with Cooper, sure he felt terror and was horrified by what he woke up to, but his life has been tipped upside down. He was nearly arrested for a crime he didn't commit. Even if someone else is arrested and found guilty some level of suspicion could fall on him for the rest of his life. Not to mention, do you think Cooper's ever going to have a fling with a woman again?"

Captain Meadows agreed, "I think both you and Luke are on to something here. Luke, why don't you and Det. Tyler question some of the other victims' friends and see what you can find out about the men they were involved with. Then when you question the men, let's also see their intentions and interactions with these women. We can see if there are other similarities."

"Is there anything I can do to help?" Riley asked.

Luke shook his head. "I think it's probably best—"

Captain Meadows interrupted. "Actually, there is something. Talk to Cooper and find out what if any interaction he's had with Don Jennings. That man seems to have it out for Cooper, and I'd like to understand why. You also used to work for the news, didn't you?"

"I did. I spent a couple of years working for the local newspaper. I was a crime reporter."

"Good, that's exactly what we need. We have a difficult statement we need to craft to give to the media about these cases. Now, we have to get whatever we provide past our public affairs office here, but I'd like to get the message right before we send it to them. Do you think you're up to the task?"

"I'm happy to help however you need me."

Turning to Luke, Captain Meadows said, "Why don't you and Det. Tyler go talk to Brendan Howe, and Riley and I will work on the statement."

CHAPTER 30

After Riley had explained to Cooper what she had discovered, she left quickly for the police department to tell Luke. Adele had watched Cooper carefully, waiting for a reaction, but he wasn't sure what he felt. Hearing the news that he was no longer officially a suspect, a tidal wave of emotion washed over him. All he wanted was fresh air. The hotel room walls closed in on him, and his breathing became labored. Adele had rushed to him asking if it was a panic attack, but Cooper had never had anything close to that so he couldn't be sure. He just needed air.

Cooper walked the streets of downtown Little Rock for nearly an hour. Each person he passed, he wondered if they knew who he was and that he had been, at least for a short time, suspected of killing Holly. No one said a word to him other than polite nods and helloes as people passed.

As he put each foot in front of the other on the cement pavement, Cooper couldn't get out of his mind the image of Holly dead in his bed. He didn't know how he'd ever move back into his condo now, and he was sure he'd have a hard time selling it. Thinking about the future caused Cooper's heart to beat faster until it felt like it was going to leap out of his chest. His chest rattled with each breath. He had to calm down, think of something else. Take a break from his brain.

Cooper found himself on Third Street in front of Dugan's Pub. Not that he wanted to drink in the middle of the day, but his stomach growled from no breakfast or lunch. He texted Adele and asked her to meet him there. The least he could do was buy her lunch. Adele could easily go back to Atlanta and put all of this behind her, but Cooper understood why she hadn't.

When people talked about finding "the one" Cooper often laughed at the notion, not believing there was any one perfect person for the other. When he met Adele, he felt it. All those things people said about just clicking – he clicked, they clicked. It was chemistry, compatibility, friendship, and respect all rolled into one big ball of rightness. Cooper's face grew hot. There was no mirror around, but he was sure his face and neck were red. He could feel the heat against the back of his hand. It embarrassed Cooper to even think such silly romantic thoughts.

Cooper pulled open the door to Dugan's Pub and found a seat at a table positioned along the side of the dining room near a window. When the server arrived, he asked for a soft drink, explained someone else was joining him, and he'd wait to order. Cooper looked over the menu, but was so hungry he couldn't decide. Everything looked good.

Cooper's phone buzzed in his pocket. He gripped the phone in his hand and peered down at the text. Cooper had assumed it would be Adele, maybe letting him know she was just about there or even running late, but the text stopped Cooper cold.

I'd hate to see your pretty new girlfriend end up just like Holly. Are you going to do right by this one?

Cooper dropped his phone on the table with a clang. He scanned around the place, but there was only a handful of people, mostly couples and a few guys having drinks at the bar. No one looked familiar, but then again, Cooper had no memory of the guy who laced his drink. Cooper stared hard at the drink in front of him. Instinctively, he shoved it away.

The phone buzzed again.

How are you going to protect her? You couldn't even protect yourself.

Frantically, Cooper called Adele. When she answered, he blurted, "Be careful, he's watching us. Where are you?"

"Cooper, calm down. What are you talking about?"

Cooper stumbled over his words. He could barely get them out. "The killer just texted me again. He's watching us, Adele. He knows about you. I can't protect you. You have to go back to Atlanta."

Adele expelled a breath on the other end of the phone. The sound of street noise echoed. "Cooper, I'm almost there. Let me call Riley. Don't move. We'll meet you. I'm about a block away."

Cooper had just hung up when he got another text.

You're scared, aren't you? You're going to be afraid for the rest of your life.

Cooper read the text, looking for some kind of clue to the killer's identity. Out of the corner of his eye, movement on the street outside drew his attention. On the corner of Third and Rock Street, a man stared at Cooper. He had a phone in one hand and a baseball cap on his head. Cooper thought, at first, that he was just being paranoid. He turned his head to scan the crowd at Dugan's, but it was still just the same people.

Cooper looked out the window again and jumped back. The man had moved even closer to the window this time. He stood just across the street. Because of the cap on his head, Cooper could only see the man's mouth turned up at the edges in a cruel sarcastic grin. Nothing about the man looked familiar to Cooper, except for that grin. Pieces of Cooper's memory jockeyed in place. All at once, Cooper knew. That had to be him.

Cooper jerked his chair backward, hitting the table and knocking over his drink. He didn't care though. He took off in a run out of the pub, bumping chairs and other patrons as he went. Gasps and a man yelling roared in his wake. Cooper slammed through the two sets of double doors and hit the streets in a sprint. He got to the corner, but the man was gone. Cooper spun in every direction looking for him. Down a block, Cooper caught just the briefest hint of shirttail as it sailed around the corner onto Cumberland Street. Cooper took off after him, running with everything he had. His legs pumping one after the other. Cooper cursed under his breath for not staying in better shape, exercising more frequently. He used to be faster, but still, he was no slouch.

He reached Cumberland and nearly tripped on the sidewalk turning the corner. As soon as Cooper regained his footing, he saw the man up ahead. The man turned once to look behind him to see if Cooper was hot on his heels and then turned back and ran even faster. The man ran across the road and cut down Sixth Street. Cooper knew there were various alleyways and the backs of buildings and parking lots where the man could hide.

Cooper pushed himself harder and crossed the street, running right into oncoming traffic. A car blew its horn and squealed its tires, nearly clipping him. The man cut down an alley, but Cooper was too far away to see which one. He just continued to give chase. When he got several hundred feet down Sixth, Cooper stopped at the alleyway he thought the man might have ducked into. He stopped running, listening instead to see if he could hear him. There was nothing but street noise.

Cooper walked quietly down the alleyway looking behind garbage bins and in between parked cars, but nothing. Cooper gave up, turning on his heels to head back in the direction he came. A car came screeching to a stop blocking off the alley. The passenger side window came down. Cooper barely had a chance to react before the first shot was fired. By the second, Cooper had already dived to the ground behind a dumpster for cover. A third shot ricocheted off its metal.

The car sped away, but Cooper stayed on the ground huddled in place. Fear that the man would return coursed through his veins. After a few minutes of heavy breathing, Cooper realized the man wasn't coming back. He relaxed his legs under him and slid back against the brick wall. Hot tears spilled down his face.

CHAPTER 31

L uke drove through the streets of Little Rock in the direction of the University of Arkansas for Medical Sciences. He and Det. Tyler were headed to the hospital to speak to Brendan. Before they left the police station, Luke had grabbed Holly's cellphone. Once they were in the car, he handed it to Det. Tyler to go through.

Det. Tyler scanned through the phone for several minutes. When he was done, he told Luke, "It doesn't look like this phone was used for much other than to email two people – Cooper and some other person, Johnny Smith, which sounds as close to an alias as you're ever going to get."

Luke navigated the streets but turned his head slightly to look down at the phone. "What's in those emails?"

Det. Tyler scanned through the emails, occasionally reading a few aloud. The witnesses that Riley had interviewed had been correct. Luke was glad that she had spoken to them first, otherwise, the emails might not have made a whole lot of sense, but Holly definitely had communication with a man who was giving her advice on how to get Cooper's attention.

Luke assumed that the sender used a fake name, and if they ran the IP address, they'd come up someplace other than Johnny Smith's home address or workplace. Luke considered this the first real lead on the killer though. They now had physical evidence to back up witness statements.

"I'm sending the IP address to our crime techs. Let's at least see what they get back," Det. Tyler said.

Luke navigated the car into a parking space at the hospital. As they navigated the length of the parking lot and its maze-like halls, they ran through questions for Brendan. Det. Tyler encouraged Luke to take the interviewing lead.

They stopped at the nurses' station on the floor where Brendan had been admitted. Once they got the all-clear, they headed to his room. Luke found Brendan resting with his eyes fixed on the television. The blood that had soaked the man earlier that morning had been washed off and he had on fresh pajamas.

As Luke and Det. Tyler entered the room, Brendan clicked off the television and sat up. "I'm sorry I couldn't speak with you earlier. It was such a shock at what had happened that I just lost it," Brendan explained, clearly embarrassed.

"No need to apologize, it happens," Det. Tyler said. "Had I dealt with what you did, I might have reacted the very same way."

"Before we go any further, I swear that I didn't kill Nikki. I hope you believe that." Brendan's eyebrows knitted together in a worried line. "As I started to say this morning, I regained consciousness at one point, and there was a guy next to me, stabbing her." Brendan barely got out the last words, his voice breaking.

"We believe you," Luke assured. "We'd like to ask you a few questions if you're up for it. Time is of the essence."

"Sure, I'll tell you whatever I can remember. Do they know why I can't remember?"

Luke took a seat across from his bed, propping his ankle on his other knee. "We think what happened to you is connected to other cases. We don't have your lab report back yet, but the two other cases the male victims were drugged with GHB."

Brendan got a far off look on his face, seeming to think through the night before. His face registered surprise. "I wonder if it was the guy who was a friend of Nikki's. He brought drinks over to our table when he said hello. He said he was glad we were spending time together. I didn't think anything of it at the time, but that's some of the last clear memories I have. It gets really foggy after that."

"Do you have a name or description of what he looks like?" Luke asked and wrote down what Brendan said.

"He said his name was Johnny Smith, which is a fairly common name around here. There was nothing distinct about him. I'd say he was just under six-foot, dark hair a bit longish, although he had on a baseball cap. Nothing real distinct about his face that I can remember."

Luke scribbled down more notes in the case file, not showing any visible reaction to the man's name. "Where were you when you saw him?"

"We had gone to dinner and then had drinks at the Flying Saucer in the River Market. That's where we saw him. Nikki saw him first and waved to him. She said he was her friend. I didn't really think anything of it."

Luke shared a look with Det. Tyler. "Let's back up a little if we can, Brendan. Can you tell us more background information about how you know Nikki? Were you two dating?"

Brendan raised his eyebrows at them but didn't say anything.

"We've heard it all, Brendan. You don't have to be embarrassed, but it's really important that we know the truth," Luke coaxed.

Brendan expelled a breath and raked his hand through his hair. "Nikki and I met a few months ago through some mutual friends. We would see each other occasionally in a group of people. I knew she liked me, but I just wasn't feeling it. She was persistent though and asked me out a few times. I'd always try to make it a group thing with all of our friends. She was nice, don't get me wrong. I just wasn't that attracted to her. Last night, I finally agreed to meet her for dinner. We had a good enough time that it turned into a few drinks after. I don't even remember going home with her. It wasn't even my intention to go home with her."

Det. Tyler shifted in his seat. He leaned forward. "How did Nikki seem last night?"

"She seemed okay to me," Brendan recalled. He rubbed at the side of his face where a bruise had formed. "We both had fun, but I still didn't think we had much of a connection. I started to get the sense the more we talked last night that she felt it, too. Friends, definitely, but nothing more."

"Was it the chemistry?" Luke asked.

"That and we also didn't have a lot in common," Brendan explained. "Once her friend Johnny came over to the table last night, I had hoped to leave. I figured they might start talking, and I could slip out, but it didn't happen that way. He insisted we have a drink with him. The one he brought over. Then he stayed a few minutes and left. I tried to figure out a polite exit, but the next thing I knew, I woke up to find a man on top of Nikki stabbing her."

Luke tapped his pen against the pad of paper. Brendan's story so far seemed like it could fit. It wasn't exactly like Cooper's, but it was another story of a man not really interested in a woman. The circumstance was different but similar enough.

Luke pressed, "Let's talk about that. You said you don't remember leaving the bar or getting back to her place. When you woke up where were you? Walk us through that?"

"Let me back up some," Brendan started, rubbing his eyes. "Nikki being stabbed isn't the first thing I remember. I don't know if this is real or just something I've made up. I only just remembered this about an hour ago. The first time I woke up Nikki and Johnny were in the living room having sex. I was on the couch. I opened my eyes and saw them across the room, but must have passed out again."

"Was it consensual sex?" Luke asked what he knew was a tricky question, but he wasn't sure how else to phrase it. If Nikki was found to have GHB in her system, it was still rape, but Luke needed context.

"I don't remember Nikki screaming or fighting him off or anything if that's what you're implying. I guess at the time I figured Johnny came back with us, and they hooked up. I couldn't have been awake for more than thirty seconds. It's only a flash of memory, and I'm not even sure it's real," Brendan said, his voice strained.

"I understand," Luke assured. "Let's talk about the second time you woke up."

Brendan swallowed hard and expelled a breath. "I was in a bed this time. I was next to a man who had straddled Nikki and kept stabbing her. I remember his arm with the knife going up and down. It felt like a dream. If I had not come to later covered in blood with Nikki on the bed, it could have very easily just been a bad nightmare. Everything seemed foggy to me, unreal almost. I was weak, but I lunged for him. My limbs didn't feel like my own. I didn't seem to have control over them. I know that's a weird thing to say, but it's how it felt."

"GHB can do that to you. It's a pretty normal feeling," Det. Tyler said. "What happened next?"

"I lunged toward him and knocked him off of her. We fell to the floor. I kept swinging my fist at him, but I don't even know if it connected. That's all I remember. I must have passed out again because when I came to later, I was in the same spot on the floor. He was gone. Nikki was dead. That's when I called 911."

"Brendan, is there any chance that the man on top of Nikki stabbing her was Johnny?"

Brendan looked between Det. Tyler and Luke. "That would make sense, right? If I really saw them having sex, if that was real, it might be him. I can't recall the face of the man stabbing her though. He's just a black mass for me, no face or anything."

Luke understood. They stood and thanked Brendan for his time. Luke told him they'd be in touch as they learned more. As they turned and headed for the door, Brendan called them back.

"There's something I don't understand, Det. Morgan."

"What is that?"

"Why didn't he kill me?"

CHAPTER 32

Luke dropped Det. Tyler back off at the station. Tyler wanted to interview Casey Perry's friends and co-workers to see if she had a new male friend in her life or knew anyone that went by Johnny Smith.

Luke had other leads to run down. He aimed his car back towards the River Market and called the phone numbers Riley had given him for Kim and Pam. He wanted both of them in front of a sketch artist. He left a message for Pam and reached Kim. She balked at his request, but Luke pushed harder until she finally relented. The sketch artist would be visiting Brendan as well.

Luke kept thinking about what Brendan asked before they left his hospital room. Luke didn't have an answer but knew that Brendan would probably suffer from survivor's guilt, if not now, then down the road. He'd never forget what he had witnessed. Maybe Riley was right when she said that this went beyond terror to punishment.

Luke's phone rang. He clicked the button on the steering column to answer.

Riley's voice rushed and stressed, boomed through his car speakers. "Luke, you need to come to Dugan's Pub. It's all too much to explain, but Cooper had a run-in with who he believes is the killer. Cooper gave chase, and the man shot at him. He's already called 911. I figured you'd want to check-in at the scene first. We are in the backroom of Dugan's right now though."

It took Luke a second to process what he just heard. "Is Cooper okay? Why are you at Dugan's? Just go back to the hotel."

"The killer threatened Adele. Cooper assumes the killer saw them at the hotel."

"Got it, okay," Luke said slowly, not really getting it at all. "I'll be there soon. I'm heading back downtown now and will go to the scene first. I'll be there right after." Riley gave him the cross streets where Cooper had been shot at.

Luke checked traffic in both directions before making a U-turn and heading back towards the city. He made it to the scene in record time, after getting green lights all the way. Luke couldn't make it far down Sixth Street though because of the crowd. He found a place to park behind a row of three cop cars and set off on foot.

Luke walked the distance and found Captain Meadows standing halfway down the alley. Crime scene techs crouched low and sifted through potential evidence.

"I just talked to Riley. She told me what happened," Luke said as he approached.

Captain Meadows shook his head in disgust. "This guy is just walking the streets, and we can't seem to get the jump on him. He's thumbing his nose right at us."

"We talked to Brendan. He told a similar tale as Cooper's, although nothing quite as dramatic on the lead-up. Brendan said he and Nikki were just friends. She liked him more than that, but he just wasn't into her. He went out with her to be nice. On their date, they ran into one of her male friends, Johnny Smith, who brought them over drinks. I assume when their labs come back, we will find GHB. We also found emails to and from Holly to Johnny Smith. We've got a name at least. Although I'm pretty sure that's an alias."

"Does he remember anything about the killer? Det. Tyler said Brendan woke up and tried to fight him off. Did he confirm that?"

Luke ran a hand over his bald head. "That happened and more. Brendan said he woke up twice. Once in the living room and Nikki and Johnny were having sex. The second time in the bedroom and a man was stabbing Nikki. Brendan said Nikki wasn't fighting or yelling during sex, but you know if she was drugged it wasn't consensual anyway. But it adds another dimension to the case. I'm sending a sketch artist to see if we can get a composite of Johnny Smith. Holly's friends are going to do the same. Cooper, I'm sure, will do the same for us on the guy today."

"At least we are making progress."

"I just hope it leads to someplace. This guy isn't taking much time between murders."

"This may seem like a crazy idea," Captain Meadows started, "but do you think since Brendan is remembering bits of the night, he'd be open to talking to a hypnotist? Maybe if he can relax his mind enough, he might remember more during the times he was lucid."

Luke considered it. He didn't know much about how hypnotists worked. "I don't think it can hurt. I'll give Brendan a call later. If everything is handled here, I'm going to talk to Cooper." Captain Meadows waved Luke off.

Ten minutes later, Luke pulled open the door to Dugan's Pub, waved hello to some of the staff he knew since he and Riley frequented the place so often. Luke ducked down a small hallway off to the left and found Riley, Cooper, and Adele sitting at a long table in the pub's back room. The three were eating.

"What happened, Cooper? Are you all right?" Luke asked as he took a seat at the table across from Cooper and next to Riley. He reached his arm over and gave Riley's thigh a pat. She returned a sad smile.

Cooper went through the entire story in detail from the text messages he'd received to spotting the man on the street. "It was something in the sinister way he grinned. It was discomforting and familiar. I can't explain it. I just knew it was him."

"You shouldn't have chased him unarmed like that," Luke admonished. Then his voice became softer. "But honestly, I would have done the same thing. If someone was threatening Riley, I'd have gone after him in a heartbeat."

"It was still foolish," Adele agreed. "He could have killed you. I don't want you to take a chance like that again. You didn't even have any backup. His whole goal could have been for you to chase him and then he could have ambushed you."

"I know. I just saw him and I took off. I didn't even really think about it." Cooper reached over and laced his fingers through Adele's on the table. "Luke, what do you want to know?"

"We need to analyze those texts and see what name and address they come back to and ping locations."

"I'm already ahead of you on that. I used my database a few days ago and just got the report in my email about an hour ago. You're not going to get much from the phone records."

"Burner phone?" Luke interrupted.

"No, that's the funny thing. The name on the account is listed as Johnny Smith and ties back to a real address in midtown. I've sat here trying to pull up some information. That address is owned by a John Smith, but he's ninety years old."

"Do you think it could be a relative – a grandson maybe?" Riley asked.

"I don't know. It could be that," Cooper said, rubbing the back of his head.

Luke raised his eyebrows. "You okay?"

"Just a pounding headache. I'll call my cell provider and authorize anything you need. I can get a printout of every text he sent, too."

"Are you responding to any of them?"

"No, you asked me not to so I haven't. My worry is this guy has seen Adele. He drugged me before and killed a woman I wasn't even with that night. How do I stop him from doing it again?"

Before Luke could answer, Riley suggested, "You have that camp on Lake Catherine. You and Adele could go there until this guy is caught."

"I've thought about that, but that leaves us more isolated," Cooper explained. "I wanted Adele to go back to Atlanta, but the more I thought about it, I want her here. If he knows anything about her, he could already know she's from Atlanta. Adele would be more at risk alone."

Adele expelled a breath. "Cooper, I'm not helpless, but I'm staying here. Luke, can you assign us some protection at the hotel?"

"I can get some protection over there for sure. Cooper, I'm also going to connect you with a sketch artist." Luke's phone buzzed on his hip. He checked but didn't recognize the number. It went to voicemail. "There's something I need to ask before I go. What's your connection to Don Jennings? You didn't say the other day, but clearly, you know each other, and he's got it out for you."

Cooper laughed sarcastically. "Doesn't surprise me. I made sure his pedophile brother went to jail for twenty years. The whole family, Don included, are a bunch of psychopaths."

CHAPTER 33

Parking had been horrible when I had arrived earlier at Dugan's in a rush to meet Cooper and Adele. Now, Luke walked me back to my car a few blocks over. He walked right by my side as if he were afraid that terror might strike at any moment.

"You okay, Luke?" I asked squeezing his hand.

"Not really. I didn't want to say anything in front of Cooper and Adele, but as we were getting ready to leave, I listened to my messages. Janelle Brady, that reporter with Channel 5 News, called me. She wants to meet. She received a letter from someone claiming to be the killer. He wants what he's calling his manifesto to be printed in the newspaper. He said if they didn't, he'd kill again."

"Are they going to print it?"

"Probably, but Janelle wants me to see it first. I know you're busy, but any chance you want to come to the news station with me?"

I readily agreed and so we headed back towards Dugan's to grab Luke's car and went together. Luke drove a few blocks into the heart of downtown and parked right behind one of the big news vans in front of the station. The woman at the desk buzzed us up to Janelle's office.

As we stepped out of the elevator, we didn't have to wait. Janelle clicked her designer heels in a fast-paced march towards us, her face registering shock that Luke wasn't alone.

Janelle reached her manicured hand to me first and looked down at my jeans and tee-shirt with disdain. "Riley, it's been a while since I've seen you. You look exactly the same."

Janelle and I did not run in the same circles. I had met her on a case more than a year ago when she had been getting anonymous tips from the killer. She hadn't liked me on sight back then. Nothing's apparently changed.

I returned the same fake smile. "It seems these killers love to keep you in the loop. If I were you, I'd want some extra protection. You're a real favorite with the murdery crowd."

Luke's hand shot out from his hip and smacked mine, but I didn't budge. The fake smile remained plastered on my face as Janelle stumbled over her words. I didn't need to see Luke's face to know his scowl of disapproval.

"Janelle, you said the killer sent you a letter or some kind of writing," Luke said, redirecting the conversation away from my snark.

"He did, follow me," Janelle said and turned on her heels. Over her shoulder, she tossed a bomb. "That is if you can keep up, Riley."

"Can I trip her?" I whispered under my breath.

Luke shot me a warning look and nudged me forward. Truth be known, I could keep up, but I'd never been able to do it in those heels. How Janelle clicked around like that all day was beyond any ability I had. The balancing act required on tiny little stems wasn't in my skill set. Neither was being good at making fake polite conversation with someone I didn't like.

Luke stepped into Janelle's spacious, perfectly decorated office. She had a plush cream high-back chair behind her desk and not a picture frame or paper out of place. Janelle pulled open a drawer and grabbed a file folder. She directed us to a round table at the far end of her office. Once seated, she pulled out several pages and handed them to Luke.

He scanned it, flipping to a second page and then a third. Luke didn't say a word as he read it nor did his face register any emotion. Janelle tapped her foot as she waited for him. The tapping annoyed me to no end, but Luke asked me to be here, so I could behave for a few minutes at least.

When he was done, Luke set the pages on the table. "This lays out all his grievances against men and women and the current state of dating. He's angry, blaming society for their relationship failings. He's blaming women for being superficial in their relationship choices and not choosing the right men. But he's talking out both sides of his mouth. He's blaming women for being sluts and whores, but he's also indicating that women owe him sex and that's all women are good for. But he blames men like Cooper who he feels has ruined women before this guy has had a chance to. He makes a complicated argument that doesn't make a whole lot of sense."

"He sounds like an incel," I blurted, not really meaning to.

Janelle raised her eyebrows at me. "I know the term, but what makes you think so?"

"The anger over his own failed relationship. The fact that he thinks women are superficial in their choices and owe him sex. He's frustrated and taking it out on women while punishing the men he sees as standing in his way."

"Care to elaborate more on the details of these crimes?" Janelle asked me.

"I don't think I should say much more." I stopped myself because I couldn't remember what Luke had already made public versus what I had helped Captain Meadows craft in the media statement earlier that afternoon. I nudged him.

Luke wasn't expecting my elbow in his rib so he lurched forward ever so slightly, but he got the hint. Stone-faced, Luke said, "We are planning to make a more detailed statement to the media later today. I think what Riley said brings up an interesting angle, but I don't think we can say with any certainty the killer comes from the incel community. While characteristics could be similar, it's probably best not to speculate."

Janelle reached over and picked up the killer's manifesto from the table. "What do you want us to do with this? He says he's going to kill again if it's not published immediately."

Luke reached for it back. Janelle didn't seem to want to give it to him, but he tugged on it until she let it go. "I'll need a copy of this, but right now I want Riley to read it."

Luke handed me the document. I scanned the words, reading quickly. I tried to keep my face even and not register the surprise, shock and disgust I felt as I took in the killer's words. It was a justification of his actions. Not only did he defend himself and explain why he killed, but he blamed the victims entirely for their fate. I felt Janelle's eyes on me as I read. When I

151

finished, I handed the document back to Luke. "I really don't know that you should publish that."

"Of course, I'm publishing it," Janelle said, clearly taken aback. "I didn't call Det. Morgan here to ask permission. I certainly don't need it from you, Riley. I called to give you a head's up. My editor thought it best we play nicely on this."

"I can't stop you from printing that," Luke said evenly. "We shouldn't give him a platform, and I believe he will kill again regardless if it's published or not. In the interest of playing nicely though, I hope you could wait until the police department makes a statement first. We'd like to get in front of this."

Janelle crossed her arms. "You have about two hours. We are going to run this during the evening news at six. I can bring a camera crew up here right now and you can go live, giving us the exclusive, if you'd like."

Luke smiled. "That's not going to happen. Let me step outside and call my Captain and public affairs office." He got up, pushing buttons on his phone already calling someone and stepped out of Janelle's office, closing the door behind him.

"Tell me, Riley, do you enjoy this sort of work – tagging along with your boyfriend?" Janelle asked sarcastically, as soon as Luke was out of earshot. "You used to be a decent journalist from what I hear. Now you're what – Det. Morgan's apprentice?"

Janelle knew full well that I was a private investigator. "I'm hardly an apprentice. As you know, I'm co-owner of a private investigator firm."

"Oh, that's right." Janelle laughed. "You run around town catching men cheating on their wives. That must be such a hard job."

"It's a bit more than that," I responded quickly, but then didn't keep my mouth shut even when I knew I should have. I leaned forward and pinned my eyes on her. "You know, Janelle, you're not married. You probably need to be careful going home with random men or you could be next on the killer's list. Seems he targets women just like you – superficial, desperate, and fake."

"Riley! Let's go!" Luke's voice boomed from the doorway. "Janelle, I'll expect those pages faxed over to me by the time I get back to the station."

CHAPTER 34

"She started it," I said as I stepped out into the hall with Luke. I assumed he was going to scold me, as he probably should have.

Luke laughed instead. "You didn't have to take the bait so easily. Why don't you like her?"

"I'm not sure exactly," I responded truthfully and slowed my pace behind Luke as I thought about it. I really wasn't sure why I disliked Janelle so much. She hadn't been nice to me since the moment she met me, but it was more than that. Part of me wondered if I was jealous of her looks or designer wardrobe. That didn't feel right though. I think I just didn't like how fake she was all the time. Her icy veneer remained impenetrable.

Once we reached the ground floor, Luke booked it out of the news station. His long legs making mine work overtime to keep up. He called to me over his shoulder. "We have to get to the police station. The public affairs office is calling the media now. As soon as I get back, I need to make the statement."

"Why didn't you tell Janelle that when we were up there?"

Luke gave me a grin. "I don't like her either." He threw his arm around my shoulders and gave me a squeeze. "On the way over there I want you to tell me more about this incel community you mentioned. I don't know much about it all, but the more I know about this killer, the more I can get into his mindset and hopefully trip him up."

We walked quickly back to Luke's car, and I filled him in on the details I knew about the incel community, which wasn't all that much. I knew they were known as involuntarily celibate and blamed women for their inability to secure romantic partners. What had started in chat rooms in the late nineties turned into a subculture of young men fueled by rage and hate. Rape was a common resolution discussed to counter their frustration. If women wouldn't give it willingly, they should be able to take it.

The incel community ranged in the tens of thousands by all reports I'd read. It's run in online forums and dark corners of the internet. The biggest common thread is that the members of this community generally reject women's sexual freedom and are sexist in their thinking, labeling women shallow and cruel who nearly always chose only the most attractive men.

Most who identify as incels are young men with a history of isolation who have faced rejection by the women they want. They have turned to the internet for connection and to make sense of their pain. They also feel a sense of social entitlement, believing that women owe them sex and that there is something wrong with a society in which women don't have to give it to them.

Not all resort to violence, but it has happened. In Toronto and Santa Barbara mass killings have been carried out by those identifying as incels.

As I finished telling Luke, I stressed my main point. "There is a subculture within incels who think rape is okay. Members talk about the sexual assaults they have carried out and violence they have committed in communities that no one has ever reported or identified. When you take any group and put them together like that, the rage is intensified. They feed off one another. They try to one-up each other, too."

"Do you really think our killer is among this group?" Luke asked, navigating his car into the police station parking lot.

"I have no reason to believe he is, but I also don't think I'd rule it out completely. It's the violence toward the women and the punishment toward the men that really drove home for me that there could be this connection. Are the other men as attractive as Cooper?"

Luke gave me a sideways glance. "You think Cooper is attractive?"

"Stay on track," I said, reaching over and rubbing his arm. "Cooper's not you, but he does okay."

Luke laughed. "I knew what you meant, and yes, I'd say that along with

154

Cooper, the other men are conventionally attractive, at least the ones I've seen."

"The man that Holly's friends described in the bar wasn't described as attractive. They basically said in so many words that he was plain, that he blended in. Attractive certainly is subjective, but neither of those women was falling all over themselves to talk to him."

"I'm just confused about one thing," Luke said. "You said that incels hate that women only pick the most attractive men. Why then would he want to help Holly get Cooper back?"

"I think that's all part of the game. He showed he could control Holly. He messed with her head. And really, all he did was help Holly harass Cooper and annoy him more. Either he directed her to do that on purpose or he's really clueless about how relationships work, which would give hints at his own ineptness."

Once Luke shut the car off, I stepped out into the parking lot. News vans already lined the side of the police station where most of the press conferences were held.

Luke stood at the driver's side of the car. He held up his phone. "I just got a message from Purvis. He wants to meet us here and go over the autopsies with us. Stick around after the press conference if you want."

I trailed behind and mingled my way into the sea of reporters while Luke went up to the podium to join Det. Tyler and Captain Meadows. I stood back scanning the area. Not that I thought the killer was going to show up, but it's happened before.

Luke took his place behind the podium and quieted the crowd. He gave an overview of each case, explaining that they had every reason to believe the killings were connected. He gave far more information than I thought he might, but at the same time, he left out some key specifics. Luke even touched on Cooper's chase earlier in the day, informing the media that man was now a person of interest. Luke promised a composite sketch of the killer in the days to follow.

Luke wrapped his statement. "We need the public to take extreme caution at this time. The killer is targeting couples who are enjoying a night out at one of our local River Market bars. All of these couples were involved in a casual relationship with each other. While we cannot tell the public not to engage in a one-night stand or not to go home with someone they don't know, what we can stress is to watch your drinks and do not consume anything you haven't been served directly by bar staff that you watch being made yourself. The killer is drugging both the man and woman, going back to one of their residences, and then killing the woman. We have evidence that leads us to believe that the killer knows the women before the murders are committed. We believe he may be using this friendship as a means to facilitate these heinous crimes."

Reporters erupted with questions all at the same time. Luke took them one by one giving more details where he could and telling the media he couldn't share other details. It was the way these things went. Thankfully, there were no surprises. Luke hadn't disclosed that the killer had written a manifesto that Channel 5 would run later that night.

I wasn't sure why he held back that information. I figured he'd want to address it. But Luke stepped back from the podium without saying another word, leaving the reporters wanting more and waving for me to join them. I figured Luke had his reasons for what he did. I headed toward the podium to join Luke at the side entrance of the police department. I was about halfway to the door when Janelle shoved past me, bitterly complaining that the cops couldn't shut down her story.

CHAPTER 35

Coming back to the hotel, Cooper's guard was up. He checked out the lobby, his eyes darting from left to right while he held Adele's hand tightly. She had tried to loosen Cooper's grip, but he squeezed her hand even tighter. Cooper was responsible for her now. If Adele insisted on staying in the city, Cooper had only one job – to keep both of them alive and find the killer.

He didn't see the two as mutually exclusive. Finding the killer would put them at added risk, but not finding the person taunting Cooper and trying to destroy his life wasn't even an option. Cooper knew only one thing for sure. He had to stay and fight rather than run and hide.

If Cooper had any doubt, it was erased fifteen minutes after getting back to the hotel. While Adele stripped off her clothes and headed to shower, and Cooper waited for the police sketch artist to arrive, Cooper received another text.

I could have killed you earlier, but what would have been the fun in that. I'm going to enjoy watching you squirm for the rest of your life.

Cooper resisted responding, but it wasn't easy. The phone chimed again, and he braced himself for another, but it was just the sketch artist letting him know that she would be at the hotel soon. They made a plan to meet in a downstairs conference room.

Cooper rapped once on the bathroom door and pushed it open. The glass shower doors did nothing to hide Adele's naked form, but Cooper knew she didn't mind. His eyes took in her every curve, and she flashed him a grin.

"Joining me?" she asked seductively, as she let the water run down her back.

"I wish." Cooper chuckled. "There's no time. The sketch artist will be here in a few minutes, but I didn't want to leave until you were out of the shower and could lock the door behind me."

Adele rolled her eyes. "Cooper, you can't hover over me forever. I appreciate it, but we are in this together. I'm more worried about your safety than mine. He's not after me."

Cooper protested. "He will go after you to get to me. I don't know if he knows where we're staying, but you can't trust anyone. Even if it's someone in a hotel uniform or a cop approaches you, no one is to be trusted. No one. Promise me."

"I promise you," Adele said and turned her back to him. She finished her shower, and Cooper handed her a towel. She dried off and then wrapped the towel around her, tucking it together above her breasts.

Adele stepped out of the shower and leaned into Cooper, giving him a sweet kiss. "I promise I won't trust anyone, but please remember, I'm a defense attorney and have worked with criminals every day of my career. I have some instincts."

"I don't doubt it. I know I'm being overprotective." Cooper kissed her again but pulled back. He furrowed his brow. "There's been something I've wanted to ask you, but I don't want you to think I'm being immature."

"Go on," she urged cautiously.

Cooper leaned back against the counter. "Why doesn't it bother you that I went home with Holly the other night? I mean I know nothing happened, but you're really calm about it all. Most women would be flipping out. You have barely reacted to it."

Adele exhaled and stepped around him. She wouldn't look at Cooper but instead focused on her reflection in the mirror. When Adele spoke, her voice was flat and even. "If I'm going to be honest, it bothers me a lot, but there's no point getting angry with you. Cooper, the whole thing bothers me. Not just you going home with Holly. I wish there had never been a Holly. She's the woman you were with right before me, and it does bother me more than I've let on. I can get jealous and possessive when I'm in love.

It's not a trait that I'm proud of so I've been trying to just rise above it. But yes, the thought of you with her that night bothers me. The thought of her in your bed makes me crazy. The only solace I have is that you weren't you. If you were fully making decisions and in a sound mind that night, it wouldn't have happened. That's what I have to focus on."

Cooper reached out and put his hand around Adele's waist. He pulled her into an embrace and kissed her forehead. "Thank you for telling me that. I know this is going to sound stupid, but I was worried that you weren't acting at least a little jealous. I took it as a sign that maybe you weren't as into this as I am."

Adele laughed into his chest. "I didn't want to scare you off too soon. I was just trying to hide the crazy for a little while. No one would ever accuse me of being high-maintenance, but I'm not the kind of woman who shares. I've been single for a long time because I don't like drama. I don't like situations that make me feel insecure. I'm more likely to just walk away than throw a fit."

"You don't have to," Cooper said, kissing her again. "I'll never play games with you. I promise you that. I love that you have this professional demeanor, but you can be real with me. I'm very serious when I tell you that I want you in my life forever. I'm fully prepared to show you that as soon as life settles down."

"I don't have any doubt of that," Adele said and then stopped.

"You seem like you want to say something else," Cooper nudged.

Adele watched his face carefully. "I do. I've been wanting to say it for a while. You're amazing at telling me how you feel about me, but sometimes I feel like there's little else I know about you or your life. You have to let me all the way in if this is going to work."

Cooper nodded. He knew she was right. "It's going to take me a little while to let down my guard, but I will…" Cooper's phone buzzed again. He pulled it out of his pocket. "I need to go. I'll be back up when I'm done."

Cooper kissed Adele and left her standing there in the bathroom. He wished their timing was better. He didn't want to leave, but he didn't have much of a choice. Cooper went down to the lobby and through a hallway to find the conference room that Luke had scheduled for them. Cooper had never been through this process before, but he hoped that he'd be able to provide enough detail to allow the sketch artist to draw an accurate picture.

She was already waiting for him. Cooper greeted the woman who was a bit older than he expected, but she had a pleasant smile and a warmth that he liked. Cooper sat down, introduced himself and spent the next ninety minutes providing details as the woman sketched.

She'd ask about a facial feature, and Cooper would explain as best as he could. This went on with each feature until the woman stopped drawing. Cooper held his breath as she finished. Once she was done, she held up the image. Cooper was taken aback.

The sketch she drew looked exactly like the man that Cooper saw outside of Dugan's Pub. Strangely though, as Cooper stared at his face, the man looked eerily familiar, but no matter how hard Cooper tried, he couldn't quite place him.

CHAPTER 36

L uke, Riley, Captain Meadows, and Det. Tyler waited patiently after the press conference for Purvis to arrive. Riley messed around on her phone and then announced she was going to pick up dinner for the four of them.

Luke used the time to run down leads. He secured Cooper's and Holly's cellphone records and confirmed what Cooper already found – that the phone texting him belonged to Johnny Smith. Luke explored more about Johnny Smith in the databases that law enforcement used but again found exactly what Cooper had said. The man was in his nineties. There were no sons or grandsons with that name, at least in any of the records that Luke came across. The man had no prior arrests or convictions, not even any old traffic tickets.

Frustrated, Luke leaned back in his chair and ran a hand over his head and down his face. Riley's words about the incel community rolled around in his brain. It wasn't that Luke had never heard of them before. He was sure that at one police training within the last year, the subject had come up. Compared to other more pressing issues, the incel community hadn't been a top priority.

Luke leaned forward and typed a few words into an internet search. Shocked by how much came back, he scrolled through some mainstream articles that indicated the group mostly spoke on Reddit and some subreddit forums. It didn't take Luke very long to discover that what Riley had told him was in fact not only true about the incel community but far more serious and dangerous than he had initially believed. Luke's anger rose with each thread he read. He had absolutely no idea if the killer was part of this community or not, but Luke wouldn't have been surprised.

"I found Tom Sharpe," Det. Tyler said, a tinge of excitement in the man's voice, drawing Luke's attention away from his screen.

"Tom Sharpe?" Luke asked, distracted.

"The missing guy in the Casey Perry case," Det. Tyler reminded him.

Luke gave a nod in understanding. "I knew the name sounded familiar, but too much to keep track of lately."

Det. Tyler sat down across from Luke's desk. "He's holed up at his parents' house in Vermont. He left the morning after the murder. He sent me hotel and gas receipts from his travels. He's refusing to return until the killer is caught."

"Did you at least get to question him?"

"He was cooperative. Everything Tom said matches up to the other cases. He and Casey initially met months ago online, some app or another. They had one date. He wasn't very interested in her and they went their separate ways or so he thought. Casey pursued, not aggressively like Holly, but she kept trying to get him to do things with her…movies, dinner and the like. Finally, Tom said they went out again. They listened to some band in the River Market, then headed over to Kepler's for a few more drinks. The next thing he remembers is waking up in Casey's bed covered in her blood."

"Same story then. Did he say anything about another guy that night? A friend of Casey's or anything like that?"

"Tom said Casey knew a few people in the place where they saw the band. He didn't remember anyone at Kepler's, but did say Casey had gone up to the bar to grab the second drink while he went to the bathroom. Tom said it was shortly after that he had memory loss."

"Why did he run?" Luke asked although he knew it was a stupid question.

"Terrified, mostly. Tom also figured we'd suspect him of killing Casey. The guy's not the most sensitive. He clearly didn't care all that much for her. He didn't even ask me anything. If his story didn't line up with the others, I might suspect him more. His parents confirm he's been there since Thursday afternoon, which makes sense if he left here on Wednesday and spent the night in Virginia, which is where his hotel receipt is from. I've connected with the Vermont State Police. I'm sending over a detective to question him again. If we have to extradite him back here, we will."

"Did Tom ask how we found him?"

"He did," Det. Tyler confirmed, craning his neck at the sound of Riley's voice announcing dinner would be in the conference room. Looking back at Luke, he added, "I just told him people at work overheard him that morning. Tom immediately suspected Brent Adams. He said the guy has always been jealous of him. Tom said Brent didn't have a girlfriend and hadn't had one the entire five years he's known him. He called him an odd duck. The two clearly didn't have a good relationship."

Luke tapped the pen on the table. He hadn't thought much of Brent when he had come into the station. His story was a little strange. Luke wasn't sure how you overheard a co-worker's confession of waking up with a dead woman and not confront the guy or call the cops immediately. Luke tucked away that information about the dynamic between Tom and Brent for later.

"You know this murder is a little outside of the killer's strike zone," Luke said. "He's clearly drugging them in the River Market, twice now at Kepler's, but the other victims were found within walking distance. Someone had to have driven Casey and Tom back to her condo in Riverdale."

"I asked that," Det. Tyler responded with a sly smile. "Tom said that he had been driving that night. When he woke up that morning, he had to take an Uber back downtown to grab his car. The killer must have driven them. Something struck me as odd about these cases though."

Luke raised his eyebrows. "What's that?"

"In all of the cases, the women were killed in their own beds. Holly was killed at Cooper's."

"That's a good point. Holly lives way out in West Little Rock. Maybe the killer doesn't know the area as well," Luke theorized.

"Maybe the killer lives downtown. He seems to know the River Market and Riverdale well enough he's comfortable killing undetected. Then again, Cooper is a smart guy. Maybe he just couldn't get Cooper in his car that night."

"That's true, too. I'm concerned about the escalating violence. The victims were asleep in the two earlier cases. Casey seemed to be asleep as well when she was killed. Holly was sitting up and possibly awake. The last one with Nikki was just sheer carnage. He's upping it each time."

"Short period between each kill, too. You think there will be more?"

Luke exhaled loudly. "I'm afraid so. We were able to stop Channel 5 from running the killer's manifesto for the five o'clock news, but I'm sure Janelle is going to run it at ten. I think he's going to kill regardless, and there's no point giving him a platform like that."

"I agree with that. Any way to stall them longer?" Det. Tyler stood and stretched.

"No, Captain Meadows talked to the news station manager and said we had more information coming from the medical examiner's office. He asked for more time as a courtesy. He had hoped the mayor would get involved, preventing the publication. After speaking to the mayor's office, the mayor wanted it run. He said if the guy is threatening to kill if it's not published, then to publish it."

Riley waved them over to the conference room for dinner. Luke appreciated that she had thought of grabbing them food. He hadn't eaten since breakfast, and his stomach had started growling more than an hour ago.

Captain Meadows was already seated at the end of the table, digging into baked ziti and salad. He picked his head up from the food at the same time he clicked on a television in the corner of the room.

The screen jumped to life with an image of Janelle and "Special Breaking News" written below her. "Channel 5 wouldn't wait until ten. We were outvoted," Captain Meadows said with disgust in his voice.

CHAPTER 37

"The mayor's office?" Luke asked as he grabbed a plate and a can of soda.

Captain Meadows shrugged. "It must be because I certainly didn't give the go-ahead for this. Janelle is reporting from right outside the Rock Street crime scene. She has even brought in some quack psychologist to give insight into the killer's mindset. They are getting to that segment next."

Det. Tyler joined them and took the plate Riley handed him. He leaned over the table and scooped a helping of ziti and then dropped a little salad on his plate. "Thanks for dinner, Riley. We've been at this since before dawn. I don't even know how I'm still standing."

The four of them ate in near silence, eyes glued to Janelle's news report. The segment with the psychologist clearly wasn't a live feed. Janelle had recorded it in her office earlier in the day. Luke wondered if Janelle had spoken to the psychologist before she had even spoken to him about the release of the killer's manifesto.

The psychologist noted that the killer probably wasn't working alone. He noted that the man wasn't an organized killer and these were probably random and frenzied. He gave his "expert" opinion based on the small amount of evidence that had been released on the news.

"This guy couldn't get this more wrong if he tried," Riley said through a bite of salad. "Nothing he's saying is accurate. There is nothing random about this. He's premeditated and carefully planned. I even think the escalation of violence is planned, too. He realized early on that he wasn't

165

punishing the men enough. He had to up the terror."

Luke agreed with her. Of course, the psychologist didn't have access to the information that law enforcement had that would quickly disprove all the man had said. Even so, Luke thought it was pretty dangerous to present this like an expert opinion on the case when he clearly knew nothing.

Janelle wrapped the segment indicating that the news had set up a tip line in case anyone wished to share information. Never mind the fact that Luke had provided the Little Rock Police Department's dedicated tip line for this case in earlier segments. The last thing Luke needed was Channel 5 sorting out credible tips. He'd need to find a way to redirect that line or shut it down altogether.

"Did y'all think eating was really the best plan right before reading autopsy reports?" Purvis joked from the doorway.

Captain Meadows wiped his mouth and waved him in. "We've all got strong stomachs at this point. Want some supper?"

"No, thanks. The wife has some waiting for me when I get home. You're my last stop for the night. I've got some staff on call for tonight. I've been without sleep now for nearing thirty hours."

Luke pulled out a chair for Purvis. "We appreciate how quickly you and your team have been working on these cases."

"Had to be done," Purvis said seriously. He dropped thick file folders on the table. "I think it goes without saying, all five of these cases have been ruled homicides by my office. You have the four shootings to the head and the stabbing. Now from what you told me, Luke, you believe the killer in all five is the same. With the presence of GHB for all and similar kill shots, I'd agree. What you told me about the surrounding evidence, it backs up that theory even more."

Purvis grabbed one file folder and flipped it open. "Now the Nikki Eagan case. She had more GHB in her system than any of the other victims. Maybe she metabolized it differently than the other women or it was given to her in a closer time to her death, but either way, she didn't put up a fight when she was being stabbed because she couldn't. She had been heavily drugged. I could even venture to say she might have died regardless."

"Would you say she was rendered completely helpless by the drug?" Captain Meadows asked.

"I think all of them were, but the other women wouldn't have died from the dosage of GHB they were given. Nikki most certainly could have."

"Overkill then?" Luke asked, finishing his food and picking up his plate. He stood and started to clear the table, but Riley stopped him. She took the plate from his hand and began picking up. He leaned over and gave her a discreet kiss on the cheek.

"Yes, most definitely overkill. I can't say for certain the killer knows what he's doing with the drug or if it was an accidental overdose. I don't know his reasoning or thinking. I just know what I'm reading in these levels. Regardless of the GHB, it was overkill for sure. The victim suffered fifteen stab wounds."

"Can you say if the killer is right or left-handed?" Det. Tyler asked.

"Given most of the wounds are from the top coming down at the victim, it's not quite as easy to tell, but I'd say you're probably looking at a right-handed assailant."

"Any signs of sexual assault?" Luke asked, sitting back in his chair. The promotion of rape on the incel community pages was right at the forefront of Luke's mind.

"No presence of semen with any of the victims. But I did see some trauma that might indicate rape so it can't be ruled out completely. That's not why I wanted to meet though. I found something in the Nikki Eagan case I wanted you to see. She had a bite mark above her left breast."

Purvis handed the file folder to Luke. "Now finding that bite mark, I went over the finalized autopsy reports from earlier cases but no bite marks found. Just on the Eagan case. With the increased violence in that case, maybe he knew that victim or had reason to be angrier with her. Shooting someone is a more detached way to kill someone. Stabbing is up close and personal. The bite mark is intensely personal or his anger was just more ramped up that night."

Luke studied the blown-up photo of the bite mark. There was no mistaking what it was. The killer had sunk his teeth into the victim's flesh enough to leave a red, distinct impression. Luke passed the file to Det. Tyler, who studied it carefully before passing it on.

"Does this mean we have a DNA sample from his saliva?" Luke asked hopefully.

"No, we don't," Purvis explained. "We swabbed the area. The bite mark was covered in the victim's blood so there was contamination there."

Luke leaned back in his chair and stared at the ceiling before locking eyes with Purvis. "We believe that the killer had sex with Nikki prior to the murder. Brendan, who is the male victim in that case, said he woke at one point to see Nikki having sex with a man. He wasn't conscious long. In fact, he thought he might have dreamed it. Later, he woke to the killer stabbing her. Given that we know there was sex, which given the levels of GHB present there's no way she could give consent, but I assume we don't know when the bite mark was made – during the rape or during the murder?"

"I can't be certain of the timing. It was made while the victim was alive. It wasn't done post-mortem. But this wasn't a little nibble, Luke. This is a deep bite. If it happened during the rape, even with the GHB, the victim would have had serious pain."

"At least now, even without DNA, you have bite mark evidence," Riley said.

Purvis nodded. "Once you find the killer, you can match his dental impressions with the bite mark. I'd say for the first time, the killer has left behind some viable evidence. Bite mark evidence is somewhat controversial, but it's better than nothing."

Captain Meadows asked, "Do we believe he's sexually assaulting all of the victims?"

"I can't say for sure. I saw some trauma that could be from rough sex or rape. It could have happened before the night of the murder or during. There isn't enough to say with certainty."

Luke added, "I don't think given Purvis' assessment and the information we have, we can say for certain. The Eagan case, while I think is connected, has variables not seen in the other cases."

Standing at the end of the table, Riley said, "He's expressing sexual frustration in his manifesto. He's angry at these women for not giving him what he wants, and he's angry with these men for taking what they want and messing it up for him. It's completely twisted, but what if he's raping these women in front of their partners, taking what he wants from these women while the men are too incapacitated to stop him. In his mind, even if the men don't remember, he's humiliating them even more."

CHAPTER 38

After the meeting with Purvis the night before, Captain Meadows shooed us all out to go home and get some rest. I had stripped off my clothes and climbed into bed, waiting for Luke to take a shower. When he was done, he climbed into bed, pulled me close, and we were both fast asleep before we even said goodnight.

This morning Luke had roused me from sleep before he left for work and asked me if I could find him an expert on incels. He also wanted me to search the online chat forums to see if there was any chatter about the cases. Luke told me he'd request more help at the station today, but he had no idea if he'd get it. The Little Rock Police Department just didn't have the manpower to cover everything. For the first time, he seemed to be happy that Cooper and I had been given special consultant status from Captain Meadows. For me, it felt like we were a team finally and that I wasn't just stepping on his toes.

Luke also asked me to review all of the comments left on Channel 5's social media pages, too. The story had blown up overnight. Calls were coming into the station tip line. Frantic residents worried there was a serial killer on the loose. The mayor's office worried what the cases would do to the little bit of tourism the city had.

I assured Luke I'd do it all. Not much else to do otherwise. I still had some private cases to handle for Cooper, but nothing too pressing.

Two hours after waking though, all I had managed to do was shower and watch the news. I sat at my kitchen table completely exhausted. My oatmeal hardened in my bowl because lifting the spoon to my mouth required more energy than I had. If I could have stuck my face into my coffee mug and slurped it up like a dog with water, I might have. I had no idea how Luke was hanging on.

A knock on the front door jolted me upright. I left my cold coffee and pathetic oatmeal and went to answer the door. Emma stood on the steps, a worried expression blanketing her face.

"Are you in labor?" I asked nervously.

"No, of course not. You ask me every time you see me. Trust me, you'll know." Emma laughed, moving past me into the living room. She made her way back to my kitchen and took a seat.

As I followed behind her into the kitchen, Emma said, "I wanted the gossip about these cases. I knew Cooper didn't do anything. The news is crazy though. It's even made the national news."

"Luke will love that," I responded sarcastically. The news just added more conjecture and speculation and far more pressure to get the cases solved – like he didn't already have enough.

Emma waved at me to get on with it. I took a seat next to her. I wasn't sure what she wanted to know. These cases had been covered so thoroughly by the news. "Start with questions. It's too much to just launch into."

"Any viable suspects?" Emma asked.

"Just the sketch they showed on the news this morning. Cooper got a fairly good look at him and so did one of the victim's friends. Luke had them all work with the sketch artist. It surprised me how closely the sketches aligned with one another."

"Yeah, but the guy looked like he could be anyone. Heck, it could be Joe. I've never seen a face more bland and common. The hat pulled low on his head also didn't help."

Emma was right. No one had seen the man without a hat on. He also had a fairly common face. I had even thought the guy looked familiar but couldn't place him. "It's all they have to work with. They have a name and an address, but they think the killer is using an alias."

I debated telling Emma about incels but wondered if she might know a little. She's a voracious reader of nearly everything. "Have you heard the term incel?"

Emma nodded. "Wasn't there a case in Toronto where a guy drove a van into some people? Didn't he identify as an incel?"

"Yeah, that's one of the cases. I wondered if this killer is an incel. I find the whole dynamic of punishing the men and committing such violence on the women kind of telling. I think there's something there to give some hints to this guy's psyche."

Emma narrowed her eyes at me. "You mean other than him just being stark raving mad?"

"Well, there's that." I shrugged. "I'm looking on some chat threads today to see if there is any chatter about the cases in the incel community."

"Have you and Luke stopped fighting?" Emma moved in her seat from side to side, her face giving away her discomfort.

"Now that Cooper isn't a suspect, yes. I still don't understand how he could have suspected him like that."

"Don't be stubborn. Luke was just doing his job." Emma rubbed her belly and groaned. She caught sight of my horrified look. "Stop making that face. I'm not in labor. I just cannot wait for him to be born. I can't get comfortable no matter how I move."

"How much longer left until your due date?" I asked.

"Ten days, but I'm hoping to go sooner. Give me your phone."

I handed my phone to Emma and she typed in a name and number. Handing it back to me, she explained, "My friend Moriah Winter. She's a psychology professor at the University of Arkansas Little Rock. She was doing some research on incels awhile back. I don't know if she has anything useful for you."

Emma always had something for me. It's why I shared more than I should. Any lead would help at this point. I offered Emma my hand and pulled her up from the chair. She kissed my cheek as she left. As soon as I closed and locked the front door, I ran up the steps to my office and sat down at my desk to get to work.

Before I did anything else, I pulled up Dr. Moriah Winter's profile on the university website. She certainly had impressive credentials and background. She had a specialty in hate crimes and domestic terrorism and had done work inside two federal prisons before teaching. I placed a call to her immediately but had to leave a message.

I grabbed my notebook where Luke had written down some addresses for websites and chat forums that he wanted me to review. I typed in the first address and steadied myself for the information I was about to review. Normally, I have a tendency for exaggeration, making more of something than it might really be. This though was truly worse than I could have expected.

The forums detailed a diatribe of hate against women and men. I lost nearly two hours going down a rabbit hole of the forums and subgroups. All I was left with was a desire to take a hot shower and wash away the hate. It frightened me that these men were wandering around society with such rage and anger building and forums like this to feed it.

What I didn't see was anything connected to the murders in Little Rock. No one claimed credit. Nobody even talked about it. Maybe my lead wasn't such a good one after all. My cellphone ring snapped me back to the present. It was Dr. Moriah Winter.

I explained to Dr. Winter my connection to Emma and the information I needed. She said she'd be more than happy to speak to me and the sooner the better. I checked the time and told her I could be there in thirty minutes.

CHAPTER 39

After a morning of running down dead-end leads, Luke geared himself up for action. He pulled the bulletproof vest over his head and strapped it in place. His gun ready and holstered at his side. Det. Tyler completed the same ritual. They had decided it was time to pay Johnny Smith a visit. Luke had done enough research to say with a fair degree of certainty that Johnny Smith who was living at the address where they were headed was ninety and not the killer, but they weren't taking any chances.

Luke knew whoever the suspect turned out to be, he would be armed and dangerous and not come willingly. He had already shot at Cooper during the middle of the day. Luke expected the same or worse should the day come where he was identified, and Luke went to bring him in.

Standing by the side of his car in the police department parking lot, Luke gave last-minute instructions to the four uniformed cops who would be joining them. He needed them to fall back and only go on his signal. The goal was to approach the man with caution, but if trouble rang out, to be ready. When Luke was done with his instruction, two-by-two they got into vehicles and drove away from the police station toward Little Rock's Midtown neighborhood.

Luke double-checked the address. The 4000 block of N. Hughes Street. Right behind Cantrell Road. Luke had planned it so they'd be there in the middle of the day, hopefully with fewer people around.

Adrenaline rushed through Luke's body. Warm prickly heat rose up his back, but his hands remained steady at the wheel. His mind stayed laser-focused on the task at hand.

Pulling onto N. Hughes, Luke knew they picked the right time. The streets were empty except for a mail truck. The postman, with his heavy mailbag slung over his shoulder, delivered three houses away from Johnny Smith. Luke parked back a few houses and stepped out of his vehicle. He didn't want the man to get hurt. Luke waved to the postman, who stood on the edge of a driveway looking back at the police cars. He slid a stack of mail into the mailbox that sat atop a post at the end of the driveway and then cut across the lawn toward Luke.

When he approached, Luke asked, "Is this your regular route?"

"No," the man said, "but I've covered it before."

"Do you know Johnny Smith?" Luke said, pointing at the house in question.

The postman groaned. "We all know him. He's old and waits by the door for his mail each day. I think it's the only thing he's got going on. He complains if we walk across his lawn, too."

"Have you ever seen anyone else at the house?"

"No, sir," the postman said. "I think he lives alone. Never any mail for anyone else that I recall."

Luke thanked him and gathered his team, leaving the postman standing on the side of the road. The uniformed cops took up position on the sides of the house, out of sight from the front door. Det. Tyler had his gun drawn at his side and watched Luke's back. Luke walked up the driveway and stepped on the porch.

A small frail old man immediately appeared behind the screen. His back hunched over and a cane steadied his walk. He griped, "You're late today…" but then he got a look at Luke. "You don't have my mail. What can I help you with?"

Luke held up his badge and confirmed the man was Johnny Smith. "I'm Det. Luke Morgan with the Little Rock Police Department. Are you alone, sir?"

"Yeah, you still didn't answer my question though. What do you want? We don't have no trouble in this neighborhood."

"I need to speak with you about a criminal case that you might be able to shed some light on."

Johnny nodded once and stepped out of the way so Luke could open the door and step inside. Det. Tyler followed. Johnny led Luke and Det. Tyler into the orderly, nearly spotless living room, which had been well-decorated and had plush new furniture. Johnny sat down in a chair positioned not far from the television. Luke sat on a nearby couch.

Det. Tyler stood at the edge of the room. "Mind if I just walk through the house and make sure we are alone?"

Johnny shrugged. "I don't care. Waste of time, but it's your time to waste."

As Det. Tyler left the room to start his search, Luke leaned forward. "Do you have children or grandchildren who come to see you?"

"I've got three daughters, only one lives here in Little Rock. The rest are out of state, but they visit. I have grandchildren and even a few great-grandchildren. They are good kids though. Why?"

"Do any of your grandchildren share a name with you?"

"Nope," Johnny said definitively. "It's mostly girls." He pushed himself off the chair, steadied himself on his feet, and gripped his cane firmly as he shuffled to the side of the room. There on the mantle of the fireplace sat a line of photos. He waved Luke over. "Here, you can see here, nearly all girls. I have two grandsons, but neither named after me. One is a lawyer in California. The other is in the Navy. He lives in Virginia when he's not deployed. Can't remember the last time they were back here."

Luke scanned the photos, searching them for some clue. He asked a few more questions about Johnny's family and friends that yielded nothing of interest. The feeling settled over Luke that they were barking up the wrong tree.

Sitting back down, Luke asked, "Have you had any issue with identity theft?"

"You mean like someone pretending to be me and taking out credit cards and such?"

"Yes, anything like that?"

"No, my credit score is good. Nothing on my report. I don't trust anyone calling asking me for anything. My daughter who just retired from the bank keeps up on all that." The man leveled a look at Luke. "I've answered your questions now can you tell me what's going on?"

Luke wasn't sure how much to tell him, but it was clear the man was sharp. "Have you seen the news recently with those murders downtown?"

"Yes," Johnny said hesitantly. "But what's that got to do with me? I can't even make it upstairs. I'm not out there killing anyone."

Luke smiled. "I didn't think you were, but I wondered if it was maybe a son or grandson or someone using your identity. We have a cellphone that comes back to this address and reason to believe this killer is using your identity."

Johnny leaned forward in his chair. "You going to catch him?"

"I'm trying, sir."

"Good, when you do, you bring him here. My family has been upstanding members of this community for more than one hundred years. Nobody drags my name through the mud and gets away with it." Johnny stomped his cane on the floor for good measure.

Det. Tyler returned to the room and caught Luke's eye. He shook his head.

"I told you there wasn't anyone else here."

"We just needed to be sure," Det. Tyler explained.

Johnny stood, wobbling on his feet a second before gaining his balance. "Are we done? That postman is late, and I'm waiting for something."

Luke followed the man to the door. "Don't blame him this time. I asked him to wait until I spoke to you."

Johnny grunted. "Well, maybe I'll cut him some slack today. I meant what I said, you bring that bum back here when you catch him. People think when you're up in years, they can mess with you. Not on my watch. The kids in the neighborhood are on their best behavior because they know I'll call their parents. Nothing much gets past me, and it bothers me this time it did. It means I'm getting old."

As they left, Luke assured Johnny he'd update him when he knew more. As they got down to the sidewalk, Luke asked, "You find anything when you searched?"

"Nothing. He's alone in there. Just his clothes in the closet. Barely anything upstairs."

Luke took a breath. "It's got to be identity theft then. We're no closer to catching this guy than we were earlier."

"Eventually when we rule out enough, we'll find him," Det. Tyler said absently as they walked back to the car.

CHAPTER 40

Cooper spent the morning calling around to find a therapist that did hypnosis. Luke had mentioned to Riley that he was looking for a hypnotist to work with the victim from the recent murder case who was still in the hospital. Riley had asked Cooper if he'd consider it, too. At first, Cooper had balked at the idea of any kind of therapy, but then at the prospect of recovering some memories, he ran full steam ahead with the idea.

Adele adamantly opposed it. She worried that the therapist might say something to suggest a memory and that it might just confuse Cooper more. Cooper debated back and forth with her for more than an hour. He wouldn't relent. She wanted to go with him and listen in to make sure the therapist didn't suggest something. Cooper had denied her on that, too. He would go alone.

What Cooper hadn't told Adele was that he worried he might have had sex with Holly that night. He had no idea what he'd say, but he wasn't going to take the chance that it would ruin his relationship with Adele. Cooper just wouldn't take the chance.

At noon, Cooper had finally tracked down a therapist who took his insurance and even had an opening that afternoon. The man was hesitant to do any sort of hypnosis on the first meeting, but after explaining the critical nature of the situation, the therapist agreed.

Later that afternoon, Cooper relaxed in a chair in Dr. Jonathan Tindell's office worried that he couldn't be hypnotized. Cooper knew nothing about the process but felt so keyed up and anxious that it couldn't be done, he wondered if he was psyching himself up for failure.

Dr. Tindell's voice, soft and melodic, calmed Cooper nearly immediately. "Everything here is safe, calm, and peaceful. Feel every muscle relax down from your neck, into your shoulders...just relax and listen to my voice. Focus on your breathing...in and out slowly. Focus on your breath and my voice. You're comfortable, relaxed and safe."

The doctor repeated the words over and over again as Cooper's entire body gave way into relaxation. The stress left his shoulders. His arms relaxed, and his back sank into the chair. Cooper's eyes closed once, opened and then closed again. Peace was the only word that came to Cooper's mind. He could hear Dr. Tindell, but his voice sounded far off like in a dream.

"Cooper, let's start with the Saturday night you were in Kepler's after the event you attended. How were you feeling?"

"Happy at first," Cooper said, not even recognizing his own voice. "I was talking to my girlfriend. Life was good."

"What happened after that?" Dr. Tindell said softly.

It felt like a dream, everything was hazy around the edges. Cooper tried to get the scene in focus. He saw himself sitting at the table texting with Adele, half of a beer in front of him. Kepler's had been fairly crowded, but he was in his own little world. Until he wasn't.

"Holly wanted to talk to me. She had been harassing me in the months leading up – texts, phone calls, and emails. She wouldn't stop. I couldn't get her to stop. I didn't want to talk to her so I ignored her. She sat down and kept asking me to talk to her. I ignored her. I kept my eyes focused on my phone."

"You're doing great, Cooper. What happened next?"

Cooper strained to remember and the picture in front of him faded. His breathing became rapid.

"Just focus on your breathing, Cooper. Let your mind relax. No need to try so hard. The memories are there. They will come back in their own time. Breathe slowly in and out. All you need to focus on is your breathing," Dr. Tindell coached.

Cooper did just that. He took a breath and let it out slowly. Breathing was his only focus, and then eventually, Cooper's mind guided him right back to Kepler's. He could see the scene clearly again.

Cooper said slowly, "Holly got angry with me and got up and left. I finished my beer and kept texting my girlfriend. But I got interrupted. A guy came over. He knew my name. He said he was so glad he ran into me. He set down a beer for me. I thought it was weird a guy bought me a beer, but he knew me by name. I thought maybe it was someone I had known. He looked familiar. I was embarrassed I didn't remember him. He made a toast to old friends."

"It's okay, Cooper. You're doing great. Can you remember what this man looked like?"

Cooper tried to study the man's face in his mind's eye, but all he saw was the same man who he saw on the corner near Dugan's. The one who had shot at him. It was definitely the same man, but his face remained unclear, fuzzy around the edges. Cooper described him to Dr. Tindell as best he could. "There was nothing distinct about him. He could be any guy."

Cooper focused more on the man – took in his face and his clothes, but nothing stood out. Thinking back not to Kepler's, but when he stood across from Dugan's, Cooper scanned down the man's body until he got to his shoes. "He wore black shoes or sneakers. You know like the kind you wear to work in a restaurant."

"Good, Cooper. I know what you mean. Let's go back to the conversation you had with him," Dr. Tindell prodded.

"He kept talking to me about softball. I used to play on Kepler's team in pub league softball. He said we had played in the same league. He knew I played third base. I assumed I had known him. We sat there talking while he drank his beer, and I drank the one he gave me. I kept texting Adele. I don't know how long we sat there like that. But then he brought up Holly. He said she was a nice girl. I remember I told him he should date her. He told me she really liked me."

Cooper tried to recall what happened after that, but it was like the movie reel ran out and faded to black. Nothing but a void. Cooper's breathing became agitated. Dr. Tindell slowly brought Cooper back to the present.

Cooper woke up almost like waking up from a vivid dream that he couldn't quite remember. The sensations still tingled through his body. Cooper reacquainted himself with his surroundings and sat up straighter in his chair. "I feel tired, Doc. Is that normal? Did I remember anything?"

Dr. Tindell set his notepad aside and shut off the digital recorder on the table in front of him. "I think you remembered quite a bit, but it seemed before the GHB took full effect. The drug can do that to you, make you lose time before the drug takes full effect. That's usually the easiest memories to recall. I think you did great today. I'll send you the audio recording so you can listen for yourself and see what's new memory for you. I think you might be surprised by some detail."

Cooper sat ready, anxious to hear it. He recalled talking about softball and sneakers and wanted to know more of what he said specifically. "Will I ever remember all of it?"

"I don't know that you'll ever fully recover your memory, Cooper. That isn't a promise I can make," Dr. Tindell said honestly. "If you're open, I'd like you to practice the same meditation exercises again. Don't go overboard with it. The more you try to force it, the less likely you'll recover anything. When you're at home and relaxed, meditate and see where your mind takes you. I'd also like to schedule with you again."

Cooper agreed to it all. Anything he could do to remember more of that night, he was in. If the doctor had told him to go outside under a full moon and hop on one leg, Cooper would have readily agreed. Anything to fill the missing spaces in his memory. Cooper had no idea how he'd live the rest of his life not knowing.

Cooper made the next appointment for Monday of the following week and left, excited that he felt at least some progress was made. By the time Cooper was back in his hotel room, Dr. Tindell's email with the audio file came through to his phone. Cooper listened to himself talk about that night. Shocked by what he heard and had remembered, Cooper left again to go see Luke.

CHAPTER 41

I sat in the parking lot right outside of the social sciences building at the University of Arkansas at Little Rock, waiting for Adele. She had called me just as I had started my drive to the campus. Adele had explained in rushed annoyance that Cooper had left to see the therapist and that she was going crazy waiting for him to come back. I explained my meeting with Dr. Moriah Winter and asked her to meet me.

I didn't have to wait long. Adele pulled Cooper's truck right next to my SUV. We met on the walking path in front of the building. Adele had on light-weight cuffed jeans and a simple purple scooped neck shirt with a long beaded necklace. The wedges on her feet were more than I'd ever be able to walk in but accented the outfit perfectly. It was the first time I saw Adele dressed down.

"You look like you're settling in nicely," I commented, smiling at her.

"I am. There's a vibe here that's a bit more relaxing than Atlanta, even in the midst of all this craziness."

We walked to the building, and once inside, navigated long hallways until we found our way to Dr. Winter's office. I knocked once, and a woman yelled for me to enter.

We found Dr. Winter sitting behind her desk, which was consumed by piles of books and papers. I introduced Adele and myself and explained why we had wanted to speak with her.

She waved us in. "Please just call me Moriah and have a seat so we can talk."

I moved a pile of books and sat down on one of the chairs across from the desk. Adele took the other. I gave a short overview of what had been made public about the cases and the information Luke had authorized for me to share with whatever expert I happened to find.

In closing, I explained, "We have no idea if the perpetrator of these cases is connected to the incel community or not, but given some of the particulars of the cases, I thought there might be a connection. My hope was to speak to an expert and learn how credible that theory might be."

Moriah sat back and bit at her lip. Her messy brown hair fell around her face. She picked up a pair of glasses that had been sitting on her desk and slid them on. "I only know a little about the incel community, but that's all most people know. There haven't been any large studies done as there have been for some other radicalized groups. We know just enough to have identified and understand their reasoning and how they operate. It's all surface really though. I've been fortunate to have spoken to some members that have left the community to get some additional insight, but it's all rather new. A few journalists have written some good articles as well, but I wouldn't say there are any experts on incels, not yet anyway."

"Can you share with us what you do know?" Adele asked.

Moriah folded her hands on her desk and peered over at us. "I think above and beyond anything there is extreme loneliness in this group. They feel isolated from having real relationships. There is a fixation on physical appearance, but a general lack of understanding of how attraction and dating work. They feel men are entitled to sex and women should be required to provide it. To not provide it is a crime against nature, at least in their minds. They don't often see women as fully autonomous human beings. Not all who identify as incels commit violence against women, but the misogyny online in the forums is pervasive."

Moriah wasn't saying anything that I hadn't already read. There were a few things holding me back from fully saying the perp identified as an incel, and I needed that insight the most. "The killer in at least one case connected with the victim and convinced her that he could help her have a relationship with the man she wanted. The tactics only seemed to drive him away. But it was the ruse the killer utilized to get close to the victim.

The two incel attacks I read about were mass casualty. Could someone in the incel community have enough sophistication with women to pull off a ruse like this?"

Moriah folded her hands in front of her and seemed to give it some thought. "I don't think you can rule out that this killer might have the same mindset as an incel, but he's probably older than the average age in the community and probably has more advanced social skills to pull off what you're describing."

I hadn't thought of the age factor. Most of the incels I read about were under thirty. The man the witnesses described was probably closer to Luke's age, nearing forty. I suddenly felt like I was heading in the wrong direction with all of this, but I didn't want to waste Moriah's time. "Do you happen to have any experience dealing with a killer like this?"

Moriah dug through a stack of papers on her desk until she found a thick stack of articles clipped together. She handed them to me over her desk. "Take these and give them a read. You can return them later. This is about all I know about serial killers, which is probably more than likely what you're dealing with. I'd read up on some research by Roy Hazelwood, one of the original FBI profilers. He had a focus on sex crimes. I think whether this perp is sexually assaulting these women or not before he kills them, there is probably a sexual component given the use of a date rape drug and killing the woman in the bedroom."

I had not told Moriah about the bite mark or what Luke had said about Nikki Eagan being raped. What Moriah said drove home the point even more. I think it was fairly clear we were dealing with a serial killer, but Luke hadn't used the term yet. The media had, but it hadn't crossed his lips publicly.

I flipped through some of the articles that Moriah had handed me to make sure I didn't have any follow up questions. Adele did the same. When we were done, we thanked Moriah for her time and started to leave.

As we crossed the threshold of her door and stepped into the hall, she called to me. "You know I spend my days teaching and researching domestic terrorism and the evil people who commit those crimes. This case though.

It's shaken me in a way that nothing else has. My colleagues who are still on campus for the summer have been talking about this a lot. I don't date often. I'm in my late forties and divorced. These murders have made me think twice about getting back out there again. The safety of my home looks more and more appealing. I hope they catch the killer soon."

Adele and I walked the halls back out of the building in silence. When we reached the door, Adele sighed. "I don't think we are any closer to figuring this out. Being an attorney, I get the cases when it's solved or they think it's solved – does every investigation always feel like you're standing in a maze with no way out?"

"Generally, until the pieces start fitting together, and it starts making sense." I opened the door, and we stepped out into the sunshine. I shielded my eyes from the glare. "Don't get overwhelmed. All we need to find is one thread and pull it. The whole case will reveal itself in time."

"I'm just worried that more women will have to die before we find that one thread," Adele said sadly.

CHAPTER 42

Frustrated that Luke wasn't at the police station and not answering his phone, Cooper grabbed an Uber out of downtown to Luke and Riley's house. Cooper had texted Riley and found that she and Adele were at the house, having finished talking to a professor at the University of Little Rock. Cooper couldn't wait to share what he had learned during his hypnosis session.

Cooper arrived at the house to find Luke's car in the driveway. He knocked on the door before entering. When he saw Luke and Det. Tyler, he pulled up short. "Is it okay that I'm here?"

"Yeah, of course." Riley waved him in. "Luke and Det. Tyler were running down some leads and wanted to hear what I found out today."

Cooper sat down in the chair across from Riley. Adele, Luke, and Det. Tyler sat on the couch. "That's good. I wanted to talk to Luke anyway about what I remembered today. We might have some more leads."

Riley spoke first, going over in detail everything she had learned from Dr. Moriah Winter. She explained why she thought now that the perpetrator probably wasn't part of the incel community. In closing, Riley apologized. "I didn't mean to get us off track, but I thought we were onto something there. I think the perp is probably too old and too sophisticated in his relationships with women to be an incel. That's not to say he might not hold some of the same kind of views about women that incels have. I think we are probably dealing with a serial killer from everything I've read."

Luke nodded. "No need to apologize. I think anything we can rule out the better. Det. Tyler and I ruled out Johnny Smith today, too. Cooper, everything you found checked out about him. That's definitely a case of identity theft. I can't see any way that the killer is connected to that man. Actually, Mr. Smith was quite angry that someone would steal his identity in that way."

Det. Tyler agreed. "When we get back to the station, we'll pull in one of the other detectives who is more experienced in identity theft, and maybe he can drum up some potential leads on that."

All the information everyone had found intrigued Cooper, but he sat on the edge of his seat wanting to tell them all that he had learned today. He sat wide-eyed and antsy to speak.

Luke noticed and smiled his way. "I'm surprised you'd be willing to speak to a hypnotist, Cooper. I have one who is going to meet with Brendan Howe tomorrow. I would have asked you, too, but I figured you'd say no."

Cooper sat forward in the chair, resting his hands on his knees. "If someone told me to go see a therapist a month ago, I probably wouldn't have gone. I have to remember though. It's causing me serious stress and anxiety not knowing. The doctor I saw, Dr. Tindell, said that sometimes with GHB a person can even forget what was happening right before the drug took hold, and that's what I remembered today. He said it's some of the easiest memories to recover, but he was happy with the progress and so was I."

"Well, don't keep us in suspense," Adele nudged. "What did you remember?"

"I'm sure that the man I saw on the street outside of Dugan's was the same man in the bar. I'm sure of it. I can remember a little now what he looked like that night at Kepler's. More than that, I remember that when he first came over to my table, he acted like we knew each other. Maybe we have met before. I'm not sure, but he does seem familiar to me. I thought that even the other day when I saw him at Dugan's. I just can't place where."

"Where did he say he knew you from?" Riley asked.

"Softball. Luke, remember a few years ago I played pub league softball on Kepler's team. He said he knew me from there. He said he played on one of the other teams. He even knew I played third base." Cooper had played baseball in high school and even later in college. When he had found a chance to get back out on the field, he took it. Police work had interrupted though because Cooper wasn't always available for games because of his erratic schedule.

Luke shrugged. "I remember, but I don't remember barely anyone even on your team let alone any of the other teams. Do you think he really knew you? I mean he could have been a spectator at a game to know you played third base."

"Yeah, definitely that's true. I can't really say for sure," Cooper admitted.

"Do you have any team photos or anything like that from back then?" Det. Tyler asked.

Cooper did, but it meant he'd have to go back into his condo, and he wasn't ready for that. "I do, but it's at my place in my closet."

Luke gave a sympathetic nod. "We are done processing the scene, Cooper. You can go back in. Let me make a call this afternoon to a cleaning company that cleans up crime scenes. They handle everything, especially biohazard materials like blood. They can get the place back to looking normal and then you can go in."

"I'll go with you," Adele said quickly.

"Me too," Riley chimed in.

Cooper nodded. "There's more though. I remembered the man's shoes. He had on black sneakers or shoes like you wear when you're working in a restaurant or the service industry. Not just like normal black dress shoes or even running sneakers. They are the kind many people wear for work. Do you know what I mean?"

"I do," Riley said. "But anyone can buy those. Do you think he maybe works in one of the bars or restaurants that might have had a team when you played softball?"

Cooper got wide-eyed. "I hadn't thought of that. Maybe, but I played softball years ago. Not anytime recently." Turning to Luke, he asked, "Can we take the composite sketch and canvass some of the bars down in the River Market, checking out their staff?"

"We need to do that anyway," Luke agreed. "I wish we had just one sketch of him without a hat on. It would be easier to recognize him. The hat obscures a bit of his face, which was probably intentional. We believe he has darker hair, but even at that, no idea if he's balding or has a full head of hair on top. There's not much variation among the witnesses. Each sketch looked about the same."

Adele looked at Luke. "Do you have any plans for any undercover surveillance down in the River Market, especially next weekend? He seems to hit most on the weekends."

Det. Tyler responded, "We'll have extra uniformed cops down there as well as a few officers working undercover. If this guy blends in as well as everyone says, I don't know how we are going to stop him even if we are staring right at him."

"Luke, have you tried exploring the drug angle yet?" Riley asked.

"I've talked to some of the other detectives. They are exploring some potential leads for us, but I don't know if it's going to turn up anything. I don't know what any of their sources on the street can tell us."

"We do have a source we can ask," Riley said cautiously, not explaining more.

"No," Luke said adamantly, raising his voice. "You are not going down there and talking to Orlando Knight. Absolutely not."

"Who is Orlando Knight?" Adele asked, clearly confused.

"He's a drug dealer and gang member in the southeast part of the city," Cooper explained, giving Riley a side glance. He thought she was crazy. "Riley met him working on another case. He's dangerous though. Unpredictable. Not someone she should have any contact with."

Riley cleared her throat. "He may be all of those things, but when Luke needed information to help save my life, Knight gave it no questions asked. He might help us again. I'd be more than happy to go and speak to him."

Luke stood. His voice was loud and stern. "You'll do nothing of the sort. I completely forbid you from going anywhere near Orlando Knight."

CHAPTER 43

"You know you can't forbid me from doing anything," I stressed for probably the tenth time that night as Luke and I climbed into bed. After I insisted on speaking to Orlando Knight, Luke had ended our impromptu meeting that afternoon. Cooper and Adele had left to go back to the hotel, and Luke and Det. Tyler went back to the police station.

As he walked out the door, Cooper had mouthed, "Don't argue with him. Let it go, Riley."

I didn't argue. Luke wasn't home to argue with anyway so I stewed instead and tried to do some work on a few of the cases that Cooper and I had pending.

Luke arrived home late again. I had saved him dinner and tried to talk to Luke then, but he brushed me off. Now, it was bedtime, and I was itching for more than a grunt and dismissal of my idea.

As I made myself comfortable, I said it again for emphasis. "Luke, you can't forbid me from doing things – not with work and not in our personal lives. This isn't how this relationship is going to work."

Luke propped a pillow behind his back. "Riley, I'm tired of this. I can absolutely forbid you from talking to anyone as part of this case."

"We don't even know if Orlando Knight is part of this case," I reminded him. "Besides, I don't like you telling me what to do. You do this all the time. You knew I was an investigator when we got together so you knew what you were getting into."

"You were a journalist when we first started dating," Luke corrected me. "Did I know you were an absolute pain in my backside though? Yes, absolutely. I knew what I signed up for. However, I didn't realize you'd be running around with a gun talking to dangerous drug dealers."

"Would that have been a dealbreaker?" I worried we might be getting into dangerous territory. I knew Luke worried for my safety, but I hadn't realized that maybe he wasn't on board with my career choice.

Luke reached his hand across the bed and laced his fingers through mine. He turned to face me, his eyes soft. "Babe, it's not so much that you're an investigator. I don't love it, but I can deal with it. What I don't like and don't understand is why you insist on putting yourself in harm's way unnecessarily. I can send an officer down to speak with Knight. You don't have to put yourself in danger."

I squeezed Luke's hand, trying to find the words to deescalate. Five minutes ago, I was itching for a fight, but now I worried if I pushed too hard, my entire career might be up for discussion and that was too much right now in the middle of this case so late at night.

I summoned a more diplomatic tone. "I can appreciate that you don't want me to get hurt. I know you worry about me, and I probably do take more risks than you'd like. You and I both know that an officer going down there isn't going to get the information you need. Knight is going to get one look at the cop and clam up. He's not going to talk in front of his crew. They protect their own and nobody snitches. You know this. I don't know that he'll talk to me, but I think I have a better shot at it. I don't even know if Knight will have the info, but this perp seems to be accessing a good quantity of GHB and who better to have some info than a gang leader running large amounts of drugs in the city."

Luke sighed loudly. "I'm not disputing your point. Talking to Knight might very well be a good idea. But he's dangerous, Riley. I don't want to see you get hurt, especially when we don't even know if he knows anything. That's a rough part of town. Knight is not only dangerous, but he's also unpredictable."

"I promise I'll be safe," I tried to reassure him. "I'll take my Glock. Besides, if I get into any trouble, I have friends in the neighborhood. No one is going to mess with Cecelia and Bishop Moore."

I met Cecelia Baltazar when I was a reporter. Her young grandson, Alexander, had been shot and killed by a group of teens randomly shooting in the neighborhood. Alexander had been playing in the front yard one minute and dead the next. It nearly broke the city, but justice had been served. It was also the case where Luke and I met.

Since moving back to Little Rock, I'd see Cecelia occasionally, taking her to lunch and spending time with her when she wasn't visiting her son out of state. No one messed with Bishop Moore. He ran the local church and youth group.

Luke stayed silent for several more minutes, and I didn't press the issue further.

Finally, right when I figured I had lost the argument, Luke relented, "I'm not agreeing, but you're right, I can't stop you either. Promise me you'll call me on your way and when you're done."

"I'll even call you when I'm there to check in if that's what it takes."

Luke fixed the pillow behind him and looked like he wanted to say something further, but he clammed up.

"Something else?" I asked with my eyebrows raised.

Luke started and stopped and seemed to choose his words carefully. "Riley, you know I want us to get married. When we do, I don't want a wife who is out there putting herself in danger so we need to talk about this further, but not tonight."

I started to protest, but he shushed me.

"Listen to me, please. I make a decent salary. I'm not saying that I want you to stop being an investigator. You're great at it and you love it. I'd never ask you to stop. If we are going to have children though, then we both can't be out there in harm's way. We have to find a happy medium someplace."

While there was a lot I wanted to say in my defense, Luke wasn't wrong. I had thought about it, too. Most importantly though, for probably the first time, it excited me that Luke thought about the future like that. "I think we need to take things one step at a time. We aren't even engaged yet. When we are ready for kids, we'll both need to look at our schedules and work and make adjustments."

Before Luke could say another word, I let go of his hand, kicked my legs free of the covers, and moved to straddle his lap. I put a knee on each side of his thighs, steadied myself and leaned down to kiss him sweetly on the lips. When Luke went to say something, I kissed him deeper until he shifted under the covers. I could tell my kiss was having the effect I wanted. He gripped my hips with his hands.

I pulled back eventually and he looked back at me laughing. "You can't just kiss your way out of every argument."

I fake pouted. "I didn't know we were arguing. I thought you were unsuccessfully trying to tell me what to do."

Luke reached up, pulled my head down and kissed me again. He murmured against my lips, "I think I was winning."

I rubbed him again through the blanket. "I'm pretty sure I'm winning."

In nearly one fluid motion, Luke rolled us over until he was on top of me, my legs wrapped around him. He leaned down and kissed me again. "We definitely aren't done with this conversation, but let's call it a tie for now. I'm suddenly much more interested in something else." Luke put his full weight on me, and I lost myself in the scent, sight, and touch of him.

Later, I laid there listening to his soft snores, wondering exactly when he would propose. I'd never been one of those women who thought longingly about the fairytale proposal and wedding. I'd been married in my twenties, and even then, the proposal had been unromantic during a discussion about the future. It was the next step in our relationship. Looking back, it was a precursor of things to come and why it was not the relationship for me.

Now, with Luke, I wanted to experience a romantic proposal. I wanted it to be a reflection of how much we loved each other. I knew he'd do something special. He was far more romantic than I'd ever been. My tummy fluttered just thinking about it.

I hadn't told anyone else this either, but I had already started planning our wedding. Unlike the first time, where my wedding seemed all about everyone else, I wanted quiet, intimate and small. I wanted to get married back home in New York. Maybe during the fall or even winter in Lake Placid. A roaring fire and a cozy setting. I had no idea if Luke would be on board with that, but I'm pretty sure he'd readily agree. I fell asleep thinking about marrying Luke and slept soundly until morning.

CHAPTER 44

L uke drove to the station with an air of confidence. He had mentioned marriage and babies to Riley the night before, and she hadn't balked at the idea. There was a time when she would have shut him down completely, assuring him that as much as he wanted to marry her, she wasn't the marrying type.

It wasn't Riley's previous marriage that had turned her off the whole idea, but rather, a relationship she had on the heels of her divorce. The guy had lied, cheated and was pretty much the scum of the earth. That had been a chapter Riley worked hard to put behind her. Luke could tell that over the last year, she had been really trying. In turn, Luke had made sure he gave Riley every reason to trust him and rely on him. He hadn't pushed for any deeper commitment than living together in months.

Luke's parents had brought up marriage at the event for victims' families. His father had even stated it publicly while Luke silently cringed, worrying that Riley might get spooked. She hadn't, and Luke knew it was time to propose. Luke already had the ring. It was what Cooper had been keeping in his safe. Luke just couldn't do anything about it right now in the middle of this case or at least until they made some headway. Luke had never been able to multitask romance and homicidal maniac at the same time, especially a case that targeted couples. He didn't have a proposal planned, but Luke assumed he'd just know when the time was right.

As Luke turned the corner onto the street with the police department parking lot, his mood quickly soured. Hordes of people stood in the parking lot and on the sidewalk, spilling into the road. News vans lined both sides of the street as well.

Luke edged his car through the throngs of people, most of them shouting at him and holding up signs protesting that the cops weren't doing enough to protect the community. Luke tried not to make eye contact with any of them as he inched his car forward, but they slapped at the hood of his car, called him vile names, and blocked his path.

Journalists rushed the side of his car, their cameras pointed at the driver's side window. Janelle stood to the side of one cameraman, giving Luke a smug and satisfied grin. The news reports hadn't been enough for her. She published the killer's manifesto, whipping the community into a frenzy.

Yesterday had been quiet — too quiet. Luke knew it was only a matter of time before the community erupted, and now here it was. The community was incensed, and they should be. Luke couldn't deny them that, but he was doing everything he could to solve this case.

Luckily, as far as they knew, there hadn't been another murder – yet. Luke knew it would happen again. He just didn't know where or who or even how they could stop him. The only thing Luke knew for sure was giving the killer his own media platform wasn't going to slow him down. It would serve to do just what was happening – inflame the public and distract the police.

Luke edged forward, keeping his foot light on the gas, but he wasn't going to stop. He'd force the crowd out of his way. Up ahead, a uniformed cop waved to him, and Luke turned slightly toward the left. A makeshift barricade had been set up. The cop quickly moved the barricade out of Luke's way and let him pass, freeing himself from the angry crowd.

Luke found a spot and gathered his files and coffee mug before stepping out of his car. The crowd continued to form rapidly. More and more people arrived.

"It started about thirty minutes ago with just a handful of people and has grown to this," the officer who let Luke behind the barricade called out to him. "They are demanding answers about the Missing Time Murders."

Luke turned to the man, squinting from the sun directly hitting his eyes. "What did you say?"

"The Missing Time Murders. That's what the reporter from Channel 5 has dubbed the cases," the officer called back to him.

That's all Luke needed – a moniker. It happened a lot with serial killer cases when the perp was still unknown. It was the media and even sometimes law enforcement's shorthand for talking about the case. But it sensationalized the cases and drew more media attention.

Luke made his way up the stairs and into the backdoor of the police department. A buzz of activity swarmed the department's first floor. People on phones scurried from one end of the lobby to the other. Everyone seemed to be in a panic.

Luke climbed the stairs to the detectives' floor and found Det. Tyler sitting at his desk talking to Captain Meadows. As Luke approached, Captain Meadows barked, "The mayor has already called three times. Don Jennings was already here calling for Cooper's arrest again. I spoke to our elected lead prosecutor, Matthew Inslee, on the phone, too. I didn't know that man did any work other than mugging for the cameras. The bottom line is the prosecutor's office is angry the manifesto got out. The mayor's office is covering their butts and blaming us – even though they gave the media the go-ahead."

Luke put his belongings down on his desk. "Did you hear they are calling this the Missing Time Murders?"

"We heard," Det. Tyler said dryly. "Let's hope they get someone good looking to play me in the movie."

"Let's hope they don't roast us on some national news program first," Captain Meadows said. He shifted in his seat. "Are we any further along than we were yesterday?"

"No, we aren't," Luke said frustrated. He took a seat next to Captain Meadows. "We have no DNA evidence, no fingerprints, a handful of witnesses who might have seen someone who might be our guy, which has lent itself to a composite sketch of a white man in his late thirties, early forties that could fit the description of half the men in the city. We have four witnesses who had a front-row seat to the murders who don't remember a thing. I don't know if we've ever had a murder spree like this. I mean, we have nothing to go on."

"We've also got another problem. Tom Sharpe is now missing again," Det Tyler interrupted. "I got a call this morning from a Vermont State Police detective I had asked to go to Tom's parents' house and question him. His father told them that Tom took off late last night. We have the make and model of his rental car so an APB has already been issued. His face was already plastered all over local news in Vermont, but we are going to need to make that national."

"What about another search of his place?" Luke suggested.

"Already in the works. We already had a search warrant in place for his apartment, and I'll go back over everything again. We have one now for his office, too. The judge issued it this morning. I still don't think Tom Sharpe has anything to do with these murders. He wasn't even here for the last one, but we need eyes on him either way."

"Agreed. Victim or not, we need more from him," Captain Meadows said. "Johnny Smith didn't yield anything yesterday?"

Luke explained, "It's identity theft for sure. Yesterday afternoon when I got back to the station, I asked one of the detectives who specializes in those kinds of crimes to explore it for some potential leads. Otherwise, a dead end."

"Well, we have to give them something other than our heads on a platter," Captain Meadows said sternly. "The weekend is nearly here. The bars will be crowded, and it's this killer's hunting ground. What's the plan?"

The three sat at Det. Tyler's desk making an action plan for the weekend with the din of protestors growing louder outside. They'd have to address the media again but needed a plan in place first. They needed a break in the case and needed it yesterday.

CHAPTER 45

To say that Luke and the rest of the Little Rock Police Department were getting roasted by the media would be the understatement of the century. I scanned through radio stations as I drove to the southeast part of the city, looking for any station that wasn't talking about what a poor job law enforcement was doing. I never found one. Every station had a commentator speculating about the cases, the background of the killer, and wondering if Little Rock would ever be safe again.

The killer's manifesto, full of misogyny and hate, had been exploited by Channel 5 for ratings. They had provided the full news feature on television and were now doing hourly updates, interviewing people outside of the police station, doing interviews with experts and picking apart the killer's statement.

As a result, the national broadcast news had descended on the city. The big three – CNN, Fox, and MSNBC – all had anchors who were broadcasting live outside of the police department. Luke had snapped a photo from the station window and sent it to me via text. He let me know they were formulating a plan for the weekend and wanted an update immediately if Orlando Knight yielded any clues.

I had called Cecelia that morning and asked if she wanted some company for lunch. She had immediately started telling me what she planned to cook. I tried slowing her down, but Cecelia was far too excited to listen to me. I'd be well-fed within an hour of walking into her house.

Pulling into her driveway, Cecelia peeked out from behind her living room curtain. As soon as she saw it was me, Cecelia had the door open and waved to me before I even put my foot on the pavement. I rushed up the driveway as she stepped out. I wrapped her in a huge hug, which caused me to bend down considerably. I towered over her, and her petite frame was small and delicate in my embrace.

Cecelia patted me on my hip. "You look good, kid. Love looks good on you." She reached for my left hand and tsked. "No ring though. Luke is taking too long. He'd better get a move on before you get scooped up by someone else."

Cecelia ushered me into her house. I was surprised to see Bishop Moore already seated at her kitchen table. I had long suspected that he had a romantic interest in Cecelia, but she wasn't having any of it. They both had lost their spouses years ago and were around the same age. Although I didn't know what age that was exactly. Neither had offered it up, and I'd never ask. It could be anywhere from seventy to ninety for all I knew.

I had asked Cecelia once if she knew how much Bishop Moore liked her. I had even teased her a few times about having a relationship with him. She had given me a disapproving look and told me that she'd live longer if she didn't have to take care of a man. She said this while also encouraging me to work on my relationship with Luke.

Cecelia had simply said, "When you're old like me, then you can be alone if you want. You're too young now. Go be happy and find some romance." And that was the end of the discussion.

Bishop Moore stood when I entered the kitchen and gave me a hug. "Glad you could visit."

"I'm always glad to visit. This time is partly professional," I admitted. I hadn't told Cecelia yet that I was there to track down Orlando Knight.

Sitting down at the table, Bishop Moore asked, "One of your cases brings you down here?"

"Not so much the case itself, but possibly a drug connection…"

Cecelia interrupted, shaking a spoon at me. "Don't tell me you're down here to talk to Orlando Knight, young lady. Don't tell me that."

I gave her a sheepish smile. "It's work. I need to ask him a quick question. Have you seen him recently?"

Bishop Moore cleared his throat. "Of course, we've seen him and not in church either. Knight's on the same corner you found him the last time, running drugs and guns and causing us all grief."

Taking a bite of Cecelia's potato salad, I mumbled, "Good, then he won't be hard to find."

Cecelia and Bishop Moore were kind enough not to lecture me further. We kept the conversation to lighter topics with Cecelia telling me about her kids and grandkids and her travels to visit them. She regaled us with funny stories as did Bishop Moore about the children's choir at church and the little ones who never quite behaved the way they were supposed to during church services.

After lunch, they both stood on the porch and watched me as I made my way farther into the neighborhood in search of Orlando Knight. Sure enough, he wasn't hard to find. Knight stood in the middle of his crew at the corner two blocks away from Cecelia's house. His jeans drooped low on his narrow hips and his gray tee-shirt sported a music artist I'd never heard of. Knight stood only an inch or two taller than I was, but he walked with such swagger and confidence, you'd think he was seven feet tall. Knight had more muscle on him than the last time I'd encountered him. His thick biceps strained the fabric of his shirt.

His eyes locked mine well before I reached him. Knight stared, and I stared back, unflinching. I knew I looked out of place in the predominately black neighborhood. He or any one of his crew could shoot me dead in the street without thinking much of it. I had worked hard the last time I had spoken to Knight to earn his respect by offering mine. I hoped that carried over to now.

"You're alive," he called out from the middle of the pack.

It caught me off guard. "I am," I stammered. "I didn't know you cared."

The corners of his lips turned up in a devilish grin. "I hate seeing anything bad happen to cute little girls like you." His entire crew of at least ten men turned to check me out.

I stood across the street not moving. He could come to me. "I was hoping you could help me with something."

"We don't snitch, you know that," Knight reminded me defiantly.

"You wouldn't be snitching. I just need to understand a few things. Consider it research."

Knight laughed. "I'm like what, a source for you now? You're going to be comin' down here visitin' with me?"

I didn't smile even though I wanted to. I knew I should be afraid, but I just couldn't summon it up. Knight had a charm about him. It made sense why he was the leader of his crew. "Not exactly, but I think you can help me out this time."

Knight said something to the guys standing around him. His voice remained quiet and low enough that I couldn't make out what he said, but a few seconds later, they moved off the corner and into a house behind them. Knight swaggered his way over to me.

He reached a hand out to me, and I shook it. "I'm really glad you're not dead. I was serious about that. That cop came down here asking for information. I gave it because he said you were in trouble. We never heard anything more. I didn't know if he had gotten to you in time."

"Det. Luke Morgan. Yeah, he got to me in time. I'm okay as you can see." It was the wrong thing to have said. I knew it as soon as the words left my mouth.

Knight backed up dramatically and looked me up and down seductively. "I'd say that you're more than okay."

I ignored it. "Thanks for helping Det. Morgan when you had the chance. Today, I'm hoping you know something about the GHB market here in Little Rock."

"GHB is a white people party drug. I don't get too many people asking about that down here," Knight said.

"Have you heard about the murders happening in downtown?" I asked.

"Yeah, couples – something like the woman gets killed, and the man was drugged. I watch the news."

"That's the case—"

Knight interrupted. "You know those were white boys that woke up with those dead girls because if that was a black guy, he'd already been arrested or dead."

I didn't disagree with him, but it wasn't a topic I was diving into. "Both the men and the women were drugged with GHB. We think the killer is drugging them and going home with them, possibly sexually assaulting the women before killing them while the men are unconscious. I'm trying to trace the drugs."

"That's messed up." Knight grimaced. "Y'all white people do some crazy stuff to each other. I only know one guy up your way that supplies GHB. I don't even know his name. He goes by Ghost. He gets the club drugs – GHB, molly, special k."

"You know where to find him?"

"Give me your phone number?" Knight demanded.

I stepped back. "No."

"Naw, it ain't like that," Knight said, laughing at me. "I'll text you the info I have. Not like you got anything to write it down anyway. Besides, I don't want nobody seein' you write it down. They'll be asking me too many questions."

If Luke knew he'd probably disown me on the spot, but it was a potential lead. I hesitantly rattled off my digits to Knight. He didn't write it down or put it in his phone.

"Will you remember that?"

Knight locked eyes with me and tapped his head. "You wouldn't believe the things I remember," he said before sauntering away.

I hadn't even made it back to Cecelia's house when my phone chimed with a text. It was from a number I didn't recognize with Ghost's info. Knight signed off with a heart emoji and a laughing one right after.

.

CHAPTER 46

At close to two that afternoon, Luke readied himself for a sit-down interview with Janelle from Channel 5. He had spent the morning listening to the chants of protesters, creating a plan for safety and added surveillance for the weekend, and running down more leads that didn't pan out.

Luke had absolutely no desire to do a sit-down interview, especially with Janelle who had created most of the uproar, but Captain Meadows said they had to do something to calm the panic in the city. A strong police presence at the time of crisis was needed. Luke relented against his better judgment. Of course, he wanted to calm the panic in the city, but Janelle was after ratings. Luke couldn't imagine that an interview with her would do much of anything other than inflame already heated tempers.

Luke had been checking his phone obsessively all day, getting first a text from Riley that she had arrived at Cecelia's and now waiting for a text that she was on her way home. He picked up his phone again and was relieved to see that Riley finally texted to say that she was headed back. Luke was surprised by the rest of the text. It included the nickname Ghost and a phone number with the note that he was the biggest supplier of club drugs in Little Rock. The number was only good for texting and it changed frequently. Luke had no idea how she did it, but she convinced Orlando Knight to talk again.

Luke jotted down the information and placed a call to Det. Romero's cellphone; the man was never at his desk. Luke hoped he could run down some leads on Ghost if he didn't already have the info on hand. Det. Romero ran most of the drug cases for the detective bureau.

When he answered, Luke explained the reason for the call and the information Riley had gathered. Luke even explained where the tip came from.

"Luke, we are going to owe Riley big if this is the guy who we have been trying to get a handle on for months now," Det. Romero said, excitedly.

"What do you mean?" Luke asked

Det. Romero expelled a breath. "We've known there was a big supplier in the city, but every dealer this guy has working for him claims to not know who he is. We've tried to cut deals for lighter sentences, tried to get someone on the inside and nothing. The dealers get their product in a series of dead drops. And the supplier won't work with just anyone. It's really covert, the likes of which we have never seen. I don't know if I can get you much, but even this nickname and a number are more than we've had."

"Anything you can do will be a help," Luke said and went to end the call. He stopped himself. On a hunch, Luke asked, "Are you still tracking hate groups in the city?"

"Yeah, me and Det. Jenkins mostly. What do you need?"

"Riley wondered if maybe our killer might be an incel. I think we've mostly ruled that out, but I didn't know if there were any groups active in the city."

"We've got them all right. Actually, we had an arrest a couple of weekends ago down at the River Market. A couple of guys who identify as such were arrested on public drunkenness charges and misdemeanor charges for harassing women one Friday night. Both were released on bond. Your killer's manifesto has been rumbling through some local chat rooms, getting some praise from some of them locally, but I'd doubt if your killer is among this group."

"Yeah, the more we explored, we ruled it out as a probability, but keep an eye out for anything relating to this case that might seem of interest. Definitely call me if you get a lead on Ghost."

Det. Romero assured Luke he had his back. Luke hung up just as Det. Tyler sat down at his desk, a smug smile plastered across his face. He slapped down a thick police file on Luke's desk and jabbed at the file with his finger. "Brent Adams. You said there was something off about him, and you were right."

Luke opened the file and near the top was a conviction for domestic battery five years earlier in Florida. Luke flipped through more pages and found more of the same. It seemed Brent engaged in domestic violence across several relationships. Luke read six different women's names all with the same story to tell. After a few months into the relationship, Brent would get violent.

Brent had one incident where he had held the woman for three hours driving around screaming at her that he was going to kill her. When the victim was finally released, she called her father, who forced her to make a police report. But by the time they arrested and dragged Brent into the police station, the victim had refused to cooperate so they never filed charges. Luke had the arrest report. The arresting officer, who saw a pattern of similar charges in the system, made sure to log the info in that national database with a note as to why the charges were dropped.

Luke finished reading and closed the file.

Det. Tyler asked, "What do you think? We never asked his alibi for any of the murders."

Luke had no idea if Brent could be a suspect or not. The escalating violence certainly was a red flag. "Can't hurt to bring him in. He was slow to report his co-worker, but he didn't have to come in at all. I wonder why he did."

"You know sometimes these killers like to get involved with the investigation. Could be that."

"Could be," Luke said.

"I'll go pick him up." Det. Tyler got up to leave.

"Wait until I get this interview with Janelle out of the way, and I'll come with you." Luke stood and stretched. The time he had been dreading arrived. Janelle's camera crew would already be set up in a downstairs conference room waiting for Luke to arrive.

Luke walked to the interview like a man taking his final walk on death row. Luke knew the interview had to go well. His head was on the proverbial chopping block if it didn't.

Janelle was waiting for him in the conference room on the first floor. She stood when he entered and reached her hand out to shake his. "Glad you agreed to the interview."

"Not like I had a choice," Luke mumbled low enough that she hadn't heard him. When Janelle asked what Luke had said, he simply responded, "Nothing, let's just get on with this."

Luke sat down on the chair Janelle had positioned to face her. One of her staff wired him for audio, and they tested the lights. The interview would be streamed live and not pre-recorded. Luke wiped his sweaty palms down the front of his thighs. He wished he had a glass of water at least before they started.

Janelle didn't give him the chance. Luke sat under the hot glow of the lights while Janelle lobbed a few easy questions about the cases to start. Luke handled them with ease, settling into the rhythm of the interview. The questions became progressively more difficult to answer. Luke had to bob and weave in his responses to avoid saying anything about the evidence they hadn't and wouldn't release to the public. Towards the end of the interview, Janelle's claws came out.

"Do you think law enforcement, and you, in particular, are equipped to handle these cases?" Janelle asked, leaning forward in her chair.

The question put Luke back. It was personal, but Luke wasn't sure why. He sidestepped. "The Little Rock Police Department is fully equipped to handle these cases. All hands are on deck, and we are using every resource at our disposal." Luke started to explain some of the safety measures they had planned for the weekend and wanted to issue another warning to the public, but Janelle cut him off.

She pressed harder. "Let's back up. You didn't answer my previous question. I meant you personally, Det. Morgan. Do you think you can handle this case? You've just solved your sister's murder. I would think this would still be an emotional time for you. Are you really in the right frame of mind to lead this investigation? Might there not be someone better to take charge of the investigation?"

CHAPTER 47

L uke wanted to get up out of his chair, rip off his mic, and tell Janelle exactly what he thought of her, but he didn't. He kept his temper in check and projected the cool demeanor he was known for professionally.

Calmly Luke addressed her. "I appreciate that you might be wondering how I'm doing since the success we've had solving several cold case homicides that the public and even other law enforcement agencies didn't even know were connected. I can assure you though, that was a win for us, and we are pleased so many families, including my own, finally have justice. Given that success, I think my fellow detectives and I are perfectly prepared to handle a case such as this. As I said, we are working around the clock to solve this case."

Janelle started to press further, but Luke interrupted her this time to drive home a point he'd made before. Luke didn't think he could say it enough. "I think the most important information we can share with the public right now is to not trust anyone. I know that's a harsh thing to say, but if they are out at the bars and restaurants in the River Market, or really anywhere in the city, don't accept drinks from anyone – even people they know. Take the time to watch the drinks being made and watch them the entire time. This killer has made a prior connection with these women. He's become their friend in some cases. He's taking advantage of all the knowledge he's gained about the victim. He's using that to gain her trust, drug her and her date, and murder her. It's going to take the public's involvement to help us solve this case. People should call tips directly into the police station at the number we have set up."

"We also have a tip line at the news station," Janelle began.

Luke interrupted again. "We want the public to call the police not the news station. At no point should crime tips be filtered through those untrained to handle such information." Luke enjoyed that Janelle was physically taken aback by his statement.

She changed tactics quickly. "What do you think of the killer's manifesto?"

"I think the news station was foolish to have given him a platform to expose such a misogynistic viewpoint. It was a platform he didn't need."

"Let me remind you, Detective, the killer said he'd kill again if we didn't publish it," Janelle said smugly.

Luke turned and looked directly at the camera. "Whether the killer was given this platform to promote his misogyny or not, he will kill again. I can assure the public of that. It's just a matter of time. All the news station has done by publishing the killer's manifesto is feed into his power trip by allowing him to terrorize the public."

Turning back to Janelle, Luke asked, "How does it feel to have helped this killer facilitate his crimes?"

Janelle fumbled for a response while she glared at Luke, looking at him like she could kill him right there on live television. She regained her composure long enough to thank the audience for viewing and encourage them to call in anything suspicious.

When the interview ended, Janelle stood abruptly. "How could you do that?" she shrieked.

Luke stood calmly, unhooking the microphone from his shirt and detaching the audio equipment that had been hooked on the back of his pants. He didn't answer Janelle who continued to shriek the same question.

Finally, Luke looked down at her. "I think you got what you came for. Please leave the station as quickly and quietly as you can. We are finished here."

Luke walked out of the room without looking back. His phone buzzed incessantly against his side, but Luke didn't bother looking, yet. He took the stairs two at a time back up to the detective's bureau bullpen. Part of him wondered if Captain Meadows would be angry. Mostly, he didn't care.

As Luke reached the landing of the detective's bureau, a handful of detectives at their desks stood and clapped for him. Luke laughed, taking the unexpected win.

Captain Meadows stepped out of his office and waved him over. "You knocked that one out of the park." Captain Meadows slapped Luke on the back. "Janelle looked like she was going to crap her pants on live television. I don't think she'll be taking any more cracks at my detectives now on this case or any other."

"Oh, they will get us back for that one. You can be assured of that, but probably not for a while." Luke looked around the bullpen. "Where's Det. Tyler? He was going to wait for me."

"He went without you. I need you to interview a woman who came in while you were in the interview. The conference room was in use so I put her in one of the interrogation rooms, but do your best to make her comfortable. She's got an interesting story to tell. I think she might be in direct communication with the killer."

Luke raised his eyebrows. "Should I ask more or just go talk to her?"

"Go talk to her. I only got part of the story." Captain Meadows slapped Luke on his back again as he stepped out of the office.

Luke made his way down the hall to a row of small witness and interrogation rooms. The third on the left had the door slightly ajar and a petite dark-haired woman sat at the table on the far side of the room. She picked her head up when Luke entered. Luke sat down across the table from her and introduced himself. She told him her name was Leslie Reid.

"Captain Meadows said you might have some information for us related to the recent homicide cases."

"I do," Leslie said quietly. "I don't know if the person I met is the same man, but the story on the news about how he's meeting these women is familiar. I saw what you had said on the news conference yesterday. He's still texting me so I don't really know what to do."

"I think just start at the beginning if you can," Luke encouraged.

Leslie barely made eye contact with him. She was attractive in an unassuming way but seemed unsure of herself and quiet. Luke didn't want to press her too hard for fear she might shut down.

"Please don't think less of me, but there was a man I had been friends with for a while, and we went out a few times…" Leslie trailed off, looking down at the table.

Luke smiled at her. It was obvious she was embarrassed. "Leslie, I know it's probably uncomfortable to talk about, but really I've heard it all. There's nothing you can tell me I haven't heard. I'm not here to judge you. In fact, coming to talk to me tells me how brave and strong you are."

Leslie finally lifted her head and made eye contact with Luke. She nodded once and continued her story, her voice a little bit stronger. "We had gone out a few times and hooked up, which I guess is the best way to describe it. I wanted more of a relationship and had been talking to one of my friends at EJ's Bar one night. The guy must have overheard me because he came over and told me that he could help me. I brushed him off, kind of annoyed actually that he had been eavesdropping, but he wouldn't go away. I think my friend found him kind of funny so she gave him my number."

"Did he help?" Luke asked, not surprised by the similar story, but concerned at how many more women were out there that the killer had done this with.

"Not really. He was awkward and kept suggesting really annoying pushy things for me to do. It just wasn't what I was interested in doing. He'd get really annoyed with me when I wouldn't take his suggestions. He wanted me to invite the guy I was dating out to Kepler's one night so he could watch us interact. He said he'd come over and flirt and try to make him jealous. I refused. The guy kind of creeped me out. I really wished my friend hadn't given him my number."

"What happened when you refused to meet him at Kepler's?"

"He got really angry. He wanted to know where I lived. He said if I wanted the help, I had to do things his way. I told him I never asked him for help, and that I didn't want to talk to him anymore."

"How did he respond to that?" Luke asked.

Leslie took her phone out of her purse, pushed a few buttons and set the phone down in the middle of the table. A man's voice sprung to life from the phone. He didn't start slow and coaxing. He raged at Leslie in a way Luke had never heard a man scream at a woman on their voicemail. He called her vile names – words Luke would never say especially directed at a woman. He threatened her by exposing her to the man she was dating, and he threatened to kill her for disobeying him.

Luke was sure they had the killer's voice on that recording. "When did he send you that?"

"Last night, which is why I'm here. He wants to meet Friday night. I'm afraid I'm going to be next."

Luke was sure Leslie was right. If she met him, she wouldn't live long enough to see Saturday morning.

CHAPTER 48

E arly in the evening, after I made dinner for Cooper and Adele, we talked in the living room. I sat in my favorite chair watching Cooper wear a path in my living room throw rug. Adele sat on the couch doing the same. Cooper paced back and forth mostly muttering to himself.

"Cooper, you are doing exactly what the therapist told you not to do," Adele reminded him.

Cooper stopped and raked a hand through his hair. "I know. I just know that I know him. When I saw the man standing across from Dugan's I knew instantly that it was him. I know that I've seen him before."

"Maybe you just have memory fragments from that night. I mean he came over to you before you were drugged so he's in your brain someplace," I suggested, tucking my feet under me in the chair.

"It's more than that, Riley. I know him and not from softball several years ago. He's someone I've seen more recently than that. It's like when you see the same faces at the grocery store or at Starbucks. Maybe you never talk to them and you don't even know their names, but they are familiar to you. It's like that, but I cannot place him. I'm wracking my brain trying to figure out where I know him from, and it's driving me crazy."

"Just sit down, and we'll figure it out," Adele urged.

Cooper's face grew redder by the second. I got up and went to the kitchen and poured Cooper a drink of sweet tea from the pitcher that I had made earlier. I walked back into the living room with a glass and a pitcher. I handed Cooper his and topped off my glass and Adele's.

After putting the pitcher back in the fridge, I sat curled back up in my chair. "Cooper, listen, stressing about it isn't going to help. Why don't you sit down and make a list of all the places you go frequently? Maybe as you're making the list and thinking about each place, something will jog your memory."

"That's a really good idea," Adele encouraged. She dug through her purse and grabbed her phone. "I'll keep a running note. Let's just talk it through. No pressure. Start with the places you go most frequently."

Cooper sipped his tea. "There aren't that many places that I go to so it's not a long list." Cooper spent the next fifteen minutes going through every place he goes frequently from his favorite coffee shop to the grocery store, dry cleaners, and bank. He's been a member of the Little Rock Country Club and spends a fair amount of time there, networking with potential clients. He rounded out his list with a few restaurants and Kepler's when he wants to relax and have a drink.

Adele finished typing the last of it. "You said the guy had on shoes or sneakers as if he worked in a restaurant maybe. Any chance he could be at one of the restaurants you go to? Maybe he's a cook or server. Maybe he rings you out when you pick up food to-go."

Cooper dropped his head into his hands. "I just don't know."

"When is the cleaning company scheduled to come to your place?" I asked.

Cooper's head remained down. He spoke to the floor. "Friday morning."

"Okay, so Friday afternoon we go look through those softball photos you said you might have and then we stop by the places you frequent and you see if anyone stands out to you. You're just driving yourself crazy right now, and it's not going to help you. We can use the list Adele has and go from there. We have a composite sketch from Luke. We can start canvassing, just like we'd do in any other case."

Cooper finally looked relieved. "I don't know why I'm not thinking normally. If this were happening to someone else, I'd know exactly what to do."

Adele reached over and rubbed his back. "It's different when it's personal."

Cooper's phone rang, and he fumbled to grab it from his pocket in time.

He said hello and listened. Then he said, "I'm at your house with Riley and Adele." Cooper listened again and nodded along to whatever Luke said.

When Cooper was done, he explained to us. "Luke is on his way here. He said there might be a small break in the case."

"Did he say what it was?" I asked, wondering if it had anything to do with the information that I had passed him earlier about the drug supplier.

"No, he just said to sit tight and that he's on his way."

Sure enough, about twenty minutes later, Luke walked through the front door. He made a beeline towards me and kissed me full on the lips right in front of Cooper and Adele. He pulled back, dropped a kiss on the bridge of my nose. "I owe you."

"For? Did the info on the drug dealer come through?"

"Not yet, but I talked to another detective who said they have been searching for the main supplier of club drugs in the city, but no one knows the guy's identity. They have been scrambling for a lead, which you got." Luke pulled out his phone and waved everyone close to him. He hit a button. "Just listen to this. I believe the killer left this woman, Leslie, a message. He met her under the guise of helping her get the guy she wanted."

About five seconds into the recording my mouth hung open in horror at the recording. The man called Leslie names and threatened her. What shocked me the most was the rage. I'd been angry and had confrontations before, particularly in my line of work, but never had I heard the kind of rage that came blaring through Luke's phone at that moment. I imagined that's what the victims experienced that night. All of that pent-up rage spilled over in physical form. A shiver ran down my back, and I wrapped my arms around myself.

Luke shut off the recording and sat back in his chair. "I have every reason to believe that is the killer. We now have his voice, several witnesses who have seen him and provided a composite sketch and bite mark evidence. But he's still a step ahead of us."

"Is there anything you can do with the bite mark evidence?" Adele asked.

"Not really until we catch a suspect. We have nothing to match it to until we get a suspect and get a warrant for his bite mark impressions. Once we have that, we can connect with a forensic odontologist to make the comparison. It's great evidence to have. They used bite marks to convict Ted Bundy. We can certainly use it in this case once we have a suspect and especially if we go to trial, but it's useless to us right now."

Cooper stood and started pacing again. "Even his voice is so familiar to me, but I just can't connect the dots in my brain." Cooper explained to Luke the plan for Friday. "I just need to start ruling places out. I'm hoping something will start falling into place, and I'll remember him. I'm just waiting for that one thing that sparks the right memory."

"What are you going to do to keep Leslie safe?" I asked. I'm sure the woman was terrified.

Luke cast his eyes towards Cooper, who threw his hands in the air. "I don't want to know where she is. This way I can't be accused of anything."

"Cooper, no one thinks you're guilty of anything, except maybe Don Jennings," Luke explained. "I just don't want anyone to know where Leslie is."

"I didn't think you meant anything by it. I'm just frustrated," Cooper explained, sitting back down next to Adele.

Luke offered a sad smile. "I felt bad for Leslie. We had to call the guy she was seeing and bring him down to the station and explain what was happening. We recommended some safety precautions for him, too. Learning Leslie might be in danger, he insisted that he go with her. As weird as this sounds, they might have a real shot at a relationship after all."

I was glad something good might come of all of this. It would be a long time before the city recovered once the perp was caught. There was no question that Luke would catch him.

"Speaking of Don Jennings," Cooper said changing the subject. "After you asked me about him the other day, it occurred to me that he has another brother, besides the one whose case I was involved with. He did time in a state prison in Texas for sexual assault. We should see if he's still in prison. If I remember correctly, it was a brutal assault, marked with the same kind of violence and rage in these cases."

Luke shook his head. "I can't just go digging around like that. I have no reason to suspect his brother right now so if you can do that it would be better. I don't want Jennings catching onto it, and you know Captain Meadows can see searches I do in the database."

"Consider it handled," Cooper said.

"There's one more thing," Luke said, locking eyes with Cooper. "I don't want you alone anywhere. I want you always with someone both for your safety and so we always have an alibi for you. I know you haven't done anything wrong, and you're cleared as far as I'm concerned, but I'd rather be safe than sorry in this situation."

Cooper gave no argument, and I was glad. I agreed with Luke. I was also concerned about Cooper's mental state. The case was taking its toll. He put far too much pressure on himself to remember. I worried what the case would do to him long-term.

CHAPTER 49

Cooper hesitated on the sidewalk outside of the front of his condo building at four in the afternoon on Friday. Two hours before, he had received the call from the cleaning company that they had finished their work.

Cooper's feet were firmly rooted to the spot. He worried he might not have the nerve to go in. It was why he went to the front door. He almost never came in this way, instead usually choosing to enter through the side entrance. Knowing that's the way he probably let in Holly and the killer that night, Cooper couldn't will himself to walk down the short alleyway and use that door. Riley and Adele stood next to him, waiting for him to summon the courage. They both offered soothing words of encouragement.

Eventually, disgusted with himself, Cooper had enough of his fear and finally yanked open the door. The lobby, with its harsh fluorescent lights, looked exactly the same. The building had a front concierge desk, but it wasn't used as such. It was extra space for building management, and they were rarely around.

Cooper walked across the lobby to a row of mailboxes near the elevator and unlocked his. The small rectangle space overflowed with flyers and junk mail. He sorted it quickly and threw most of it in the recycle bin. There was a letter from his insurance company but that was the only thing of importance.

Riley and Adele followed him into the elevator as they rode silently to Cooper's condo. Stepping into the hallway, Cooper stopped and assessed the long corridor in front of him. Unfortunately, the only memory that came to mind was leaving the following morning, escorted by Luke. Cooper jingled the keys in his hand as he approached his front door, the sound cutting through the silence. Cooper was glad to see the crime scene tape that he was sure had been across the front of his door had been removed. He put the key in the lock but hesitated.

"You can do it, Cooper. We are right here with you," Adele said soothingly, with her hand on his back.

Cooper turned to Adele. "You know it's funny. There's a part of me terrified memories will come flooding back, and then at the same time, I'm anxious I'll never remember. I don't know which feeling is worse." Cooper turned the lock and pushed open the door. The antiseptic smell knocked him back.

Riley coughed. "That smell certainly removes any question if the cleaning crew had been here or not."

The three of them crossed the threshold and stepped into Cooper's condo. He was surprised that the place looked exactly the same. Riley tossed her bag on his kitchen counter, and Adele walked through the living room. It wasn't her first time in his place, but her second.

This should have been the week Adele moved her things in, but Cooper knew they had some decisions to make now whether to actually live there or not. Cooper couldn't imagine sleeping in the same room where a murder had taken place, particularly when he and Adele should be happy starting their lives together. Cooper didn't want Adele to be constantly reminded of the life he had lived before her, and the mistakes he had made. But Cooper knew selling the condo now would be nearly impossible.

"You look lost in thought. You okay?" Adele asked.

Cooper hadn't realized that Adele had been watching him. "I'm fine, just a lot running through my mind, most of which can't be dealt with right now."

Riley stepped towards him. "Do you want us to go into your room with you or give you space while you do that alone?"

Riley always knew what to say. Cooper admired that about her. If the situation were different and he was there helping Riley, he would have already gone in her bedroom to show her it was okay. Riley had a way of knowing what people needed, and right now, Cooper needed to do this alone.

"I got it," Cooper assured them both and made his way down the short hallway. The bedroom door had been left open by the cleaners. Cooper wasn't sure what he had been expecting when he crossed the threshold, but the room didn't feel any different to him. Other than his missing bed, nothing looked that different either. No memories came flooding back.

He was glad the cleaning company had removed his bed as he had requested. The blood-soaked mattress had been photographed and samples were taken by the crime scene techs so Cooper had been free to dispose of it. Other than having to get a new bed and the walls, particularly the one behind where his bed had been that needed a fresh coat of paint, the space felt like his own. It was like the murder had never happened. A wave of guilt washed over Cooper for even feeling that way.

Cooper stood for another minute, closing his eyes and waiting to see if anything came back to him. Nothing, not even a sliver of a memory. He exhaled and went into his closet where he kept a bin of old photographs. Cooper was old enough that not all his photos were digital. He found the blue bin in the back against the wall, sneakers and boots stacked in front of it. Freeing it from its space, he pulled off the lid and started his search among photo albums and loose pictures.

Cooper had made it halfway through the bin, working in solitude, when Riley called out for him. Her voice faint and muffled, he couldn't quite make out what she was saying. He dropped a photo album on the floor and retreated back to the living room. Riley sat at one end of the couch talking to his neighbor Jenny Pike. They both stood when Cooper entered the room.

Jenny rushed to him and threw her arms around him. "I'm so glad you're okay. I've been out of town. I had no idea that anything had happened. Yesterday I got a call from Det. Morgan about a murder in your apartment. I haven't had a chance to speak to him. I keep getting his voicemail. I thought something had happened to you."

Jenny had been a friendly but quiet neighbor for the several years Cooper had lived in the building. She was a nurse at a local hospital. Cooper rarely saw her other than occasionally passing each other in the hall. He had no idea Jenny cared this much about him, but it tugged at his heart.

Cooper hugged her back. "I'm okay, but something did happen here."

Jenny pulled back. "Was it the weekend when you had that noisy company?"

Cooper squinted. "You heard people here?"

Jenny stepped back from him and leaned against his kitchen counter. "I had just arrived home from an evening shift at the hospital. I heard your voice and two others – a man and a woman. They were loud and you kept asking them to quiet down. I laughed because even though you sounded drunk, you were worried about waking your neighbors. You rarely make much noise at all."

Riley, Adele, and Cooper looked at each other in surprise.

Excitement in his voice, Cooper explained, "Jenny, that woman was murdered by that man in my apartment. I had been drugged. I don't remember any of that. Please tell me anything you can remember about that night."

Jenny's hand went to her throat. "Cooper, I had no idea. I left the next morning for a trip. I'm just getting back. It was probably somewhere between eleven-thirty and a quarter to midnight. You were annoyed that they had followed you home. You sounded upset, but the other guy insisted they'd just have one drink and leave. He kept saying he wanted to move into the building and wanted to see your place."

Cooper shook his head in disbelief. "I don't remember any of that. What happened next?"

Jenny's face grew red. "Please don't think I'm a nosy neighbor, but you sounded so annoyed I looked out the door to make sure you were okay. I've seen a girl here waiting for you a few times. I wondered if it was her. I didn't see anyone except the man close your door."

"Did you get a good look at him?"

"He had a hat on and was looking down. He caught my eye as he closed the door but with the hat pulled so low, I didn't really see much of his face.

It was really dark in your place, too. Plus, I was embarrassed I had been caught watching so I quickly shut my door. His voice sounded familiar to me, but I still can't place it."

Cooper smiled. Turning to Riley and Adele, he said, "See I'm not the only one."

"I wonder if it's someone who works in the building," Riley suggested.

"It could be," Jenny said. "There's been a lot of construction in the building, which is why this floor is so empty. No one else lives up here right now except Cooper and me. All of the units are empty. Many people have sold and the condo association is doing some major updates."

"I had no idea," Cooper said, dumbstruck. "I knew it had gotten quieter up here, but I work so much, I didn't realize. If you think you hear this man again or figure out where you might have heard him from, let me know. Actually, you should probably try Det. Morgan again and give him your statement."

"I'll call him," Jenny said and went to the front door to leave. Turning back to Cooper, she asked, "You might not even know yet, but are you going to be moving too? I know it will probably be hard to live here after what happened, but I'd hate to lose you as a neighbor."

"I don't know. I've been just trying to take things day by day, but I don't know who would buy the place now even if I sold it," Cooper said honestly.

They finished their conversation, and after Jenny left, Cooper went back to finish his photo search, but it never yielded what he hoped. If Cooper knew the man from softball as he had said, there was no photo evidence, at least that he had.

CHAPTER 50

L uke and Det. Tyler walked the streets of the River Market late on Friday night. Given Luke's heavy media presence over the last few days, there was no way he could do undercover work, but still, they aimed to blend into the crowds enjoying the River Market bars and restaurants on that warm spring evening.

Earlier in the day, Luke had taken Leslie's phone and texted the killer that she was sorry and that she'd be happy to meet up as he wanted at Kepler's later that night. Luke hoped to draw the killer out and into the open in the view of waiting law enforcement. The killer responded to Leslie only that he was glad she had come around in her thinking. He gave no confirmation that he'd show, but Luke remained hopeful. They had a female undercover cop waiting at Kepler's. She had a wig on to match Leslie's hair and looked enough like her to pass in the dark bar lighting. The killer would have to be up close enough to see the difference, and by then, they'd have him.

There were other undercover cops in Kepler's and positioned around the River Market assessing the scene as well. Most of the patrol units who would have been in West Little Rock for the night had been stationed in downtown. The Little Rock Police Department couldn't do any more than they were doing right now.

Cooper and Adele were with Riley at the house so Luke felt some relief knowing they were in for the night and together. Riley had called Luke after leaving Cooper's to let him know they had connected with Jenny Pike and that she'd been trying to reach Luke to give him a statement. Luke had been surprised to learn that the killer's voice had sounded familiar to

Jenny. Luke assumed Cooper must be on the right track that he'd met the perpetrator before. Presently, they were fresh out of leads so exploring a possible connection to someone working or even living in Cooper's building would definitely be the next step.

Luke scanned every face as they walked through the River Market. They'd stop for a few minutes outside of a few bars and assess who was coming and going. They kept their voices low and out of earshot of others when talking about the killer.

Standing on the corner of La Harpe Boulevard and President Clinton Avenue, right in front of Big Whiskey's Bar & Grille, Luke positioned himself to scan the crowd over Det. Tyler's shoulder in the direction they had just come down the main strip of the River Market. It was nearing nine and the killer still hadn't shown his face at Kepler's. Luke and Det. Tyler had already walked by the place twice and now stood a few bars down.

"Do you really think that he's dumb enough to be out here tonight?" Det. Tyler asked.

"I don't know. I think his compulsion to kill might be stronger than his common sense. He had to know as soon as the bodies started piling up that we'd figure out what he was doing. He's been taking risks all along including sending his manifesto to the media. He didn't show much fear of getting caught when he showed himself to Cooper either. Who knows what the guy will do?"

"True enough."

"Let's head back…" Luke started to say when his phone chimed. It was a text from Riley. Luke read the words carefully and read them again. Don Jennings' brother Jim had been released from the state prison in Texas, three months ago. By all accounts Riley and Cooper could uncover, Jim Jennings was in Little Rock now, living on Third Street in downtown Little Rock, not far from where the victim was killed on Rock Street and where Cooper saw the man standing outside of Dugan's.

Luke showed the photo to Tyler. "What do you think? You think he's a close match to the sketch?"

Det. Tyler took Luke's phone and held it close to his face and assessed it.

"Looks close. Who is it?"

"It's Don Jennings' brother Jim who got out of state prison in Texas a few months back and now lives in Little Rock." Luke scanned the other document that Riley had sent. It was Jim's rap sheet, which included breaking and entering, assault, a weapons charge, two violent sexual assaults including the use of date rape drugs, and a kidnapping. Luke detailed the findings to Tyler. "Sounds like he could be a viable lead at least. He's around the right age, too."

"We are going to need something more than that to bring him in for questioning, don't you think? He's an assistant prosecutor's brother. It's not going to sit well if we anger their office," Det. Tyler speculated.

"We'll figure something out," Luke reassured him. He was sitting watching the people as they came and went from bars in the River Market. "Come on, let's go grab a table on the patio of the Flying Saucer. We can watch the crowd come and go from Kepler's and you can tell me what happened with Brent earlier today."

After grabbing a seat at an outdoor table, Luke positioned himself so he could look down President Clinton Avenue towards the library and Kepler's. Det. Tyler watched the opposite direction. They ordered burgers and sodas when the server came and continued surveilling the scene when she left.

Det. Tyler rested his forearms on the table and watched the crowd over Luke's shoulder. He explained, "Brent didn't really have all that much to say. He admitted his past misdeeds with women and said that he had reformed his ways. When I asked for his alibi for the nights of the murders, he claimed to be with his girlfriend who lives in the Heights. I've left a message with her to confirm, but haven't heard back yet."

"Didn't Tom tell you Brent has never had a girlfriend for as long as he's known him?" Luke asked. Not that men shared such things with colleagues, Luke knew, but still, it was curious.

"Yeah, Brent said that he kept the relationship a secret because they had met at work."

Luke raised his eyebrows. "They all work together at the same office?"

"Yeah, apparently they do."

"Did Brent let you search his place?" Luke asked.

"After we spoke in his living room, I asked if I could take a walkthrough. He didn't seem to have much to hide. I did a cursory search in closets, pulled out a few drawers even and nothing suspicious."

"What did Brent say when you asked him again about calling the cops when he first heard Tom disclose what had happened?" Luke asked absently. He was focused on a guy lurking in front of Kepler's. The guy, who fit the description of the perpetrator in height and facial features, peered into the bar and then stepped away. He looked left and right and then peered into the window again. Luke hitched his jaw in the direction and Det. Tyler turned in his seat.

"What's he doing?"

"I don't know," Luke said. "Maybe he's waiting for someone, but he's been standing there a few minutes like that. I'll keep watching."

Det. Tyler turned around to face Luke. "Brent said to me that he hesitated calling the cops because of his past. It doesn't make sense to me. You hear someone say they woke up with a dead woman and they skipped out, you do something with that information."

"Agreed," Luke said, suddenly standing. The man in front of Kepler's had locked eyes with Luke. He didn't move, just kept staring. Luke didn't move either. He stood poised ready to give chase if needed. A moment later, a group of two men and three women joined the man. They walked down the street away from Kepler's together.

"He must have been waiting for people," Luke said with an edge of frustration in his voice. Turning to Det. Tyler, "What were you saying?"

"I'm anxious to hear back from his girlfriend because there's definitely something squirrely about the guy. I was surprised he had a girlfriend, but I think we should keep our eye on him."

Luke nodded in agreement. The server brought their food, and they dug in.

After they ate, Luke checked in with the rest of the team. Everything was quiet. He and Det. Tyler stayed out there on the sidewalk for another two hours, but nothing had happened. It was, as far as Luke could tell, an uneventful night of surveillance.

CHAPTER 51

At a quarter to two Saturday morning, Luke's work cellphone rang on the nightstand and woke me from my sleep. I nudged him once and then twice, calling his name at the same time. He didn't move. Luke had only arrived home and climbed into bed an hour before. I reached over Luke and answered the phone for him.

It was Det. Tyler. Another body had been found. Two bodies actually. This time, the male had fought back and was killed in the process. It was another stabbing and looked to Det. Tyler like it was the same killer. Only this time it was far outside of his normal kill zone. He had killed in our neighborhood mere blocks from us.

I assured Det. Tyler that Luke would be there immediately. I shook Luke and explained what had happened. Luke's eyes flew open and his feet hit the hardwood floor before he was even fully awake.

"Did Tyler say where they were?" Luke asked, rushing around the room to find clothes.

"In a rental house a few blocks from here. Right in that stretch of Cantrell before it intersects with Kavanaugh. Tyler didn't know much more. He wasn't on the scene yet. He got the call from a uniformed officer who was on the scene. You could probably walk over there faster than driving."

Luke dug through the closet for a clean shirt. I had picked up several from the dry cleaners the day before. He found one, pulled it off the hanger and slipped it on, buttoning it up the front and shoving the bottom into his pants haphazardly. He dashed out of the bedroom, and a few seconds later, the water in the bathroom ran at full blast.

"Make sure every door is locked tight behind me," Luke said coming back into the bedroom to grab his badge and gun and then he was gone, running down the steps to the first floor. He opened and then closed the front door, slamming it shut. I trailed behind him, making sure the door was locked. I put on our front porch light, too. I double-checked the back door for good measure and turned on a living room light before going back to bed.

I hoped the killer hadn't been in the River Market area where Luke had been surveilling. I knew how upset Luke would be. It was bad enough the murder happened right under his nose. It would be worse still if the killer had selected his victims where the Little Rock Police Department had been out in force.

I crawled back into bed and pulled the comforter up around me. I couldn't keep my eyes open any longer. Even as worry for Luke fought my brain to stay awake, sleep pulled me under.

At close to eight-thirty, Luke was back home. He found me in the same place he had left me. I woke as he dropped his shirt in the hamper and headed for a shower.

"Are you okay?" I called after him.

"Not really," Luke said, turning on the tap.

There was a bitter tone in his voice. I pulled myself together quickly and went downstairs to make Luke some breakfast and coffee. I knew as soon as he showered and changed, he'd be heading back to the station. The least I could do was send Luke off with a full stomach.

About twenty minutes later, showered and dressed, Luke rounded the corner to the kitchen and gave me a sad smile. He saw the full plate of bacon, eggs, and toast on the kitchen table and steaming mug of coffee. He gave me a hug and nuzzled my neck. "I don't know what I'd do without you."

"Eat a crappy breakfast from a fast food place on the way back to the station," I said, sitting down next to him. "Do you want to talk about it?"

Luke dug into his food. He'd been to so many horrific crime scenes over the years that he had trained himself to push it all aside so that nothing got in the way when it was time to eat or sleep. Otherwise, he'd never be able to do his job.

Biting off a piece of crispy bacon, exactly the way he liked it, Luke explained, "I already cleared it with Captain Meadows. I'm going to need to brief you fully on this one because I need your help."

"With?" I asked with eyebrows raised. Since Cooper and I received our special unpaid consultant status from Captain Meadows, Luke hadn't really needed anything from us. I thought Captain Meadows had just given us the title because he knew Luke shared information with me anyway, and sometimes, we got involved when we shouldn't. In this case, though, Luke was actually relying on me, and I felt closer to him than ever before.

Luke continued eating. "The victim's sister was with her last night and she's overcome with grief and blaming herself. She won't talk to me. She won't talk to the victim advocates. In fact, she threw them out of her house this morning. I thought maybe you'd be able to get through to her. You have a way with people that might be needed here."

"I can try. Where am I meeting her?"

"I think her house would be best. I feel like if I bring her down to the station, she might be more defensive than she is now."

There was something Luke wasn't telling me. I cleared my throat, and he stopped eating long enough to look at me. "Why would the victim's sister be defensive?"

Luke took a sip of his coffee. "I don't know. That's part of what we need to figure out."

"Did the killer befriend the victim ahead of time like the other cases?"

"No idea. The sister, Madison Kane, stopped to see her sister, Haley, on her way home from a bar. Haley hadn't checked in to let Madison know she had gotten home okay. Madison is the one that found the bodies. She's devastated and angry as you can expect, but there's more. I can feel it. There's something she's not telling us."

I grabbed the coffee pot and poured Luke some more. "Are you sure this case is connected?"

"The same kind of watch face was found at the scene. The watch was stopped only about an hour before the first unit arrived. He had to have been covered in blood when he left. There was a trail leading down the front walkway and then across the grass to the driveway to what we assume was his car. There was more blood in the driveway, too. He's getting sloppy."

"It seems like he's getting disorganized and frenzied as he goes. Probably his compulsion to kill is outweighing any sense," I offered. I had been reading up a lot on killers like this. Understanding the psychology behind what made them tick had always fascinated me, even back when I had been a journalist.

Luke finished off his breakfast and carried his dish to the sink. He leaned against the counter and peered down at me. "Frenzied is a good word to use. That scene was a mess. It looked like the violence started in the bedroom and carried over to the living room. I don't know if the killer didn't drug them this time or miscalculated when it would take effect, but that male victim fought with everything he had. He was no small guy either. He had defensive wounds all over him. The killer has to be pretty beat up right about now as well. This is the second time though. He's changed something. The GHB isn't having the same effect on the men as it did before."

"He might be giving them less to up the risk and the terror. Where were the victims earlier in the evening?"

"I think right here in the Heights at Mickey's Bar & Grille on Kavanaugh," Luke said, shaking his head. "But it's all still leads we need to run down. The male victim had a receipt in his wallet time-stamped for ten-forty at Mickey's so I assume that was their last spot."

"Anything else you think I should know or you want to know from the victim?"

Luke shook his head. "I need any information on the killer and how the victim might have connected to him. We need to know whatever Madison knows. She's being defensive for a reason, and we need to know why. If she saw something, we need to know."

CHAPTER 52

I arrived at Madison Kane's house just before noon. She had initially refused to speak to me, but several phone calls later, Luke hadn't given her much choice. She either spoke to me or be dragged down to the police department for formal questioning. She didn't have to comply with either, but it was in her best interest if she did. Finally, she had relented.

Madison's house was a small bungalow over on N. Grant Street. When I arrived, she invited me into her kitchen and asked if I wanted anything to drink. I declined. It was obvious Madison had been crying. She was dressed in leggings and a long tee-shirt. Her bare feet slapped on the kitchen tile as she moved across the kitchen. Her blonde hair, pulled back from her face, highlighted her thin angular features.

"I'm sorry, I'm a mess," Madison said holding her arms out to her sides. "I tried to sleep a little when I got back this morning, but I can't get the images of what I saw out of my head."

"That's pretty normal," I assured her. "You've been through a trauma, and you've lost your sister. Nothing is going to seem right with the world for a long time."

Madison leaned against her kitchen counter, but she didn't say anything for several minutes. Her eyes darted around the kitchen. I waited, knowing I couldn't push her. Finally, she looked at me and said, "Are you a cop? Det. Morgan explained who you are, but I wasn't paying attention. I really didn't want to talk to anyone."

"I'm not a cop. I'm a licensed private investigator, and my partner used to be a detective. Sometimes our work crosses paths with law enforcement, and we help out from time to time. For transparency's sake, you should also know Det. Morgan is my boyfriend."

"Have you ever had to talk to someone like me?" Madison asked, folding her arms across her chest. She shivered.

"I have a few times. Every person is different. Det. Morgan thought you might be more comfortable speaking with me."

"You seem nicer than him," Madison said, assessing me.

I smiled. "He's actually very nice. He can come across gruff and unfeeling sometimes while he's working. He's just doing what he needs to do to get the job done. He can forget people's feelings sometimes in the process, but he's actually a very caring man. He wouldn't have sent me over here otherwise."

Madison pinned her eyes on me. "If he had gotten the job done, my sister wouldn't be dead."

I held my hands up in surrender. "Fair point. I didn't mean anything by that. This has been a hard killer to catch. Please know that Det. Morgan really is doing everything he can. That's why he wanted me to talk to you. Every witness is important. You may know things you don't even realize you know. Can you walk me through last night?"

Madison watched me for a few more minutes, and I didn't press. Eventually, she shoved herself off the counter quite dramatically and sat down in the chair across from me. "I introduced my sister, Haley, to her boyfriend, Noah. I used to work with him at an insurance company. I've known him awhile. They were good together. My boyfriend and I met Haley and Noah out last night for dinner and drinks at Mickey's Bar & Grille. Everything seemed normal."

"Did Haley and Noah have any relationship trouble?" I asked.

"Not that I'm aware of. I saw something on the news about the killer offering relationship advice and befriending a victim, but I don't know of any trouble Haley and Noah had. Besides, my sister wouldn't have asked for advice like that from someone she didn't know. Haley never had any trouble getting any man she wanted. She's smart and pretty and one of the nicest people you could ever meet. But if there were trouble, I'd have known it."

It didn't surprise me that the killer might have changed how he approached victims after the public was made aware, but finding the connection might prove harder now. "Did you see anyone watching them last night or interacting with them that you didn't know?"

Madison shook her head. She looked down at the table. I knew she wasn't telling the truth or she was hiding something.

I pressed gently. "Is there something you know about who your sister and her boyfriend were with last night that you don't want to tell us? It really is important that we know."

Madison sighed. "While we were with them last night, no, I didn't see anyone talk to Haley or Noah or approach them that I didn't know. I didn't stay with them the whole night as I had said. My boyfriend and I got into a huge fight. He left the bar, and I went after him shortly after that. If I had just stayed the whole time as we planned, this wouldn't have happened. My sister and Noah would still be alive." Madison started to cry, tears streaming down her face.

I got up and grabbed her a tissue from a box on the kitchen counter. I handed it to her. "I know it's easy to blame yourself and think you could have prevented this, but the reality is this perpetrator is smart and cagey and could have done the very same thing even if you had been there the whole night."

Madison wiped her tears and blew her nose. "You think so?"

"If there's one thing I know about killers like this it's that they don't let anything stand in their way. Do you have any idea if there was anyone new in her life she talked about? Someone maybe Haley met recently? Maybe someone that hit on her or asked her out? A new guy friend? Anything."

Madison blew her nose again. She sniffled back more tears. "No. Haley kept her circle of friends small. She was much more social in her twenties, but at thirty-four, she was all about work, a few close girlfriends she had for years, Noah, and me. Our parents moved out of state a few years ago so it's just the two of us here."

This might just have been the first stranger murder for the killer. "Do you know what time you had a fight with your boyfriend?"

"It was probably thirty to forty minutes before Haley and Noah left. Brent, my boyfriend, was angry that I ran into some friends. Sometimes he's like that. He wants all of my attention and when I wasn't focused on him, he went over and grabbed Haley and Noah another drink to be nice and said goodbye. He left right after that."

"How much longer did you stay?" I asked, trying to piece together a timeline.

"It was probably about ten minutes or so, but I couldn't find Brent. He wasn't here at my place, but his car was still in the driveway so I knew he didn't go back home to his apartment. I walked around for probably an hour trying to find him. I went in and out of different bars here in the Heights, but couldn't find him anyplace. Eventually, I came back home and he was in the shower. He said he'd gone to another bar and had a few more drinks, then got into a fight with a guy on the way home. His face and hands are pretty busted up."

I bit my lip to keep from asking what I really wanted to know – could your boyfriend possibly be the killer? Fights on the streets of the Heights were not common at all. Actually, I'd never heard of one before. But I couldn't ask that. I couldn't give it away. I had to play it cool. "When did you try to reach your sister?"

"Brent was still in the shower so I told him I was going to check on Haley. He gave me a hard time, telling me to let her live her life. That she was an adult. Well, of course, she's an adult, but we watch out for each other. I had already felt bad leaving her at the bar so I tried to text her. I still hadn't heard from her and I was worried. Probably twenty minutes later, I still hadn't heard so I went over there…" She choked up. Fat tears rolled down Madison's cheeks.

"Did Brent go with you?" I asked, sitting on the edge of my seat. I was sure my voice cracked as I spoke.

"No, he had already gone home to his place by then. He got so angry with me for going over to Haley's house, he left."

"Have you seen him since?"

"No," Madison said slowly, confusion in her voice. "Is there a reason you're asking about him?"

I pulled my phone from my pocket and texted Luke that he should come to Madison's house immediately. I locked eyes with Madison. "I don't want to alarm you, but is there any chance that Brent might have killed your sister?"

Madison stood, her face growing redder by the second. She let out a string of curses at me.

"Madison, calm down and think about what you just told me," I said slowly. "You said Brent brought your sister and her boyfriend a drink before he left the bar. The killer drops GHB into his victims' drinks. You said Brent was gone, you couldn't find him. Then he shows up at your place beaten and bloody. Noah fought back before he was killed. The killer would have been badly beaten and bloody. Brent didn't want you to go over there. And in your time of need, he's nowhere to be found."

Madison's eyes grew wide both in recognition and in fear. "Actually, he's right behind you."

CHAPTER 53

"What's going on here?" a man asked from the living room doorway. "Who is this?"

I stood and spun around to cover my back. I assumed right away that it was Brent. Madison had been right, he looked like he'd gone several rounds in the ring and lost. I appraised him probably longer than I should have.

Brent took several menacing steps towards me. "I said what's going on here. Who are you?"

I didn't respond. It was Madison's place to let him know who I was if she chose to. I had no reason to disclose who I was or why I was there.

Brent looked to Madison and back to me. He pressed, "I asked a question."

Finally, Madison spoke up, her voice suddenly timid. "This is Riley. She's working with the Little Rock Police Department to help find my sister's killer. She just had a few questions for me."

Brent turned angrily on me. "I don't think we have anything to say to you on the matter."

"That's not really your choice, Brent," I said firmly. "You'll have to excuse us. I wasn't done speaking to Madison. Maybe you can come back later."

"Don't tell me…" Brent started to yell, but Madison reached for his arm.

"This is really important to me. I have to find out who killed my sister," Madison pleaded with him.

The strong confident woman who had stood in front of me mere moments ago dissolved into a pleading little girl, bending over backward to appease a bully. I didn't like it one bit. If my radar about Brent had been up before, it was screaming now.

Brent didn't budge or respond to Madison's plea. He shook free of her hand and folded his arms across his chest, staring down at me.

I didn't move. I wasn't going to cower to him. "I really don't understand what your issue is," I said, propping my hands defiantly on my hips. "What happened to you? You look beat up."

He tried to stare me down. "None of your business. If you don't leave, I'll force you to leave."

I actually laughed out loud. Sometimes being a bit of a bigger girl had an advantage. I considered myself immovable unless I was willing. He took a step towards me. His hands balled into fists at his sides. Madison cowered. I held firm.

The knock at the front door did little to ease the tension. Madison moved quickly between us and went to answer the door.

Luke's voice boomed in the entranceway of Madison's house. All at once, Brent's face lost its tension and anger. It softened and his posture relaxed. His eyes, nearly navy in color, still told the same tale. He was red hot with rage and hiding it in front of Luke.

As Luke entered the kitchen, he drew back, surprise blanketing his face. "Brent, what are you doing here?"

I had no idea that Luke knew the man. I hid my shock and explained, "Brent is Madison's boyfriend. He was with her last night at the bar."

Luke turned to me. He had read my text about my suspicions about Madison's boyfriend. It's why he had come to the house so quickly. He locked eyes with me, and we communicated without words, the way two people could after knowing each other for a long time. Luke's hand instantly went to his hip where he had his gun. He shifted just his eyes towards the living room, indicating he wanted me out of there. As I took a step to do just that, I was met with Det. Tyler and Madison.

Det. Tyler also drew up short when he saw Brent. Taking in Luke's stance and then at me, he said slowly, "Riley, why don't you take Madison in the other room and continue your conversation."

I don't know if it was because Madison knew she had the protection of the three of us or if the last day had finally closed in on her, but she swiftly shoved past Det. Tyler and launched herself on Brent. She punched him in his already battered face and kicked his shins. She clawed at him with her fingernails. As she pummeled him, Madison shrieked words I couldn't make out. Brent didn't even have the chance to defend himself before Luke pulled Madison off of him.

Brent's hand went up to his bleeding nose. "What is wrong with you, Madison?" Brent grunted.

"You killed my sister…you son of a…" Madison cursed, screamed and cried. She tried to pull out of Luke's grasp to go at him again. Luke held her firmly while Det. Tyler gripped Brent by the shoulders and dragged him from the kitchen.

"Madison, calm down. We can take care of this," Luke said, wrapping both arms around her from the back, trying to help her regain control of herself. "I know you're upset and you have every right to be. My own sister was murdered. I get it, but this isn't the way."

Madison's breath came out in heavy rapid sobs. She slid to the floor and sat there in a heap at Luke's feet. She dropped her head into her hands and cried, sobs wracked her whole body.

"Can you stay with her?" Luke asked me. He came over and whispered, "He's connected to another case. He told Tyler that he was with his girlfriend during all the murders, but the girlfriend never called Tyler back to confirm. We had no idea of the connection until just now. See if you can confirm his alibi."

Luke left the room while I sat down with Madison on the floor. I handed her some more tissues. "Can I get you a drink of water or anything?"

Madison blew her nose. "No, I'm okay." She hiccupped once and then twice, trying to hold back tears. "Is what Det. Morgan said true, that his sister was murdered, too?"

"Yes, it's true. Not on this case, but back when they were in college. Actually, Luke just brought his sister's killer to justice. He lived years not having any idea what had happened to her the night she was murdered. Answers don't necessarily make it easier. Like you, his sister was his only sibling."

Madison looked toward the living room where Det. Tyler, Luke, and Brent were talking in hushed voices. Turning back to me, she asked, "Do you know why Det. Morgan and Det. Tyler already know Brent?"

"Luke told me that Brent is connected to another one of these murder cases. I don't know what connected means though. He might have been a witness or knew someone."

Madison bit at her lip. "Brent never said anything to me. Do you really think he could have killed my sister and Noah?"

"I don't know," I told her honestly, "but Brent's story about coming back here all beaten up certainly sounded suspicious to me. And he's unaccounted for during the time of the murder."

Madison nodded along. "That was the first thing I thought of, too, after you said it."

I dropped my voice lower. "Brent told Det. Tyler that he was with you during the other murders. Is that true?"

"What are the dates?" Madison asked me, nervously.

I detailed the date and time of each murder and when I was done Madison started to cry again. Through tears, she said, "He wasn't with me any of those times. He's lying."

CHAPTER 54

C ooper and Adele had spent the day together canvassing all of the spots Cooper frequented. He wasn't going to give up until he figured out how he knew the killer. They had already been in and out of Cooper's favorite bars and restaurants, showing the composite sketch to bartenders, waitstaff, other patrons, and pretty much anyone that would give Cooper a moment of their time. He found nothing and was even more frustrated than when he had started the day.

They were both hungry so they stopped at Dugan's Pub to have a late lunch. Cooper checked his phone. Actually, at near four, it was closer to dinner. As they were seated, Cooper pulled out the sketch again and showed it to their server, Rhoda, who frequently waited on him at Dugan's. She took the photo from him and looked it over.

"It's the guy from the news, right? The one suspected of killing those women?" Rhoda asked.

"It is, but he looks familiar to me. I know I've seen him someplace so I'm just trying to figure out from where. I'm assuming it's from someplace I go to often."

"I can pass this around here and ask, but he doesn't look familiar to me." Rhoda took the sketch and walked away from the table.

Cooper went back to looking at his menu. He scanned two pages and then stopped to look at Adele, who sat reading her own menu, seemingly lost in thought. His heart ached with fear that she'd leave him and sheer anger with himself that this was how they were starting what should be the best time of their lives together.

The stress of it all had also finally set into Cooper's muscles. He kicked his legs in front of him and rubbed at his arm. Living in the hotel had also worn on him. He didn't have the comfort of home. He was tired of living out of a suitcase.

Almost as if reading his mind, Adele dropped her menu to the table and turned to him. Out of nowhere, she said, "I think we should redo your condo and live there. Before you argue, I know that you want to move and think it isn't fair to have me live there, but I like your place. More importantly, you like your place. Jenny, your neighbor, seems great, too."

"I don't know," Cooper said, cautiously. He really didn't think it was a good idea.

Adele tugged at his arm. "We can take the next week or so and redo the place. We can pick out a new paint color for the walls, buy new bedroom furniture, and completely redo the room. When I was there the other day, I felt at home. I know something horrific happened there for you, but I think you need to reclaim your space. There is no reason to let what happened to you also be a financial drain."

"I would probably lose money on it…" Cooper said, his voice trailing off. Could it work? Could he really go back and sleep in the same room where Holly was murdered? He didn't know, but fair or not, the idea that Holly would drive him from his home even in death pushed Cooper to a fast decision.

Reaching for Adele's hand, he asked, "Is it really what you want to do?"

"Yes, I'm sure," Adele assured him. "I really think once we are back in the space and fix it up, we can reclaim it and the bad memories will fade. You'll always have them, but we will be so busy making so many new memories that you won't think of it as often."

Cooper smiled and he felt it, too. "I assume you're going to want to handle decorating?"

Adele laughed. "Yes. You have good taste, it's just very masculine. It needs a softer touch."

"Eight million throw pillows?" Cooper laughed for the first time in two weeks.

"We can compromise at four million." Adele squeezed his hand.

They were brought back to reality when Rhoda arrived at the table with their drinks. She also handed the sketch back to Cooper. "Our cook said this looks like a guy that came in here looking for a job not too long ago. He said he had been a cook, but he'd been in prison and not someone our cook wanted to hire."

"Do you have a name?" Cooper asked.

"Jim, that's all our cook remembered."

Cooper and Adele placed their food order. After Rhoda walked away from the table, Adele said, "Yesterday, you thought Jim Jennings looked like the sketch, and now we have outside confirmation. Riley said last night she sent his photo to Luke. I wonder if he's done anything with it."

Cooper heard what Adele said, but his eyes were focused on the television across from the table. He kept his eyes glued to the screen and stood and walked towards it. The killer had struck again last night in the Heights. Cooper sucked in a sharp breath as he watched the report.

Neither Riley nor Luke had told him, but maybe they hadn't had time. The news report mentioned that there was a suspect with the police right now.

Adele put her hand on Cooper's back, and he flinched in surprise. "Sorry," she said, "I didn't mean to startle you. What's going on?"

"There's been another one. Last night. This time he killed both the man and the woman."

"Cooper, will this never end?" Adele stood by Cooper's side and thread her hand through his.

The murder wasn't that far from Luke and Riley's house. Concern grew in the pit of Cooper's stomach. He hoped the killer wasn't trying to target them somehow. Riley and Luke had always done a good job of keeping their information as private as possible, but with the internet, things slip through.

"I'm surprised you're out to wander the streets. Shouldn't you be in jail?" Don Jennings hissed from Cooper's side.

Cooper glanced over at the assistant prosecutor. Calmly, without any hint of emotion, he said, "You and I both know that I didn't have anything to do with this. Keep saying it, and I'll sue you for slander."

Adele stepped around Cooper and reached her hand out to Jennings and introduced herself. "I'm his lawyer. I've handled cases like this in Atlanta and won."

"Well, that's Atlanta. We do things a little differently here," Jennings said with a smirk.

Cooper laughed. "If you want to handle it that way, I'd be happy to step outside with you. I've got some frustration I need to work out. But I can guarantee you won't win that way either. Why don't you just back off and worry about your own family?"

"What's that supposed to mean?" Jennings barked.

"I don't know," Cooper drawled. "Maybe just that your brother, Jim, who has been out of prison and here in Little Rock for a few months looks strikingly similar to the composite sketch the witnesses made. And he's already served time for a violent sexual assault."

Jennings stepped back. "How do you know about Jim?"

Cooper turned on him. "I know all about your whole family. Back when I put your other brother in jail, I found a wealth of information. How'd you turn out on the right side of the law?"

Jennings didn't say another word. He disappeared from Cooper's side as quickly as he had arrived. Cooper wasn't even sure where he came from or went off to. As Cooper and Adele sat down at their table, Jennings was nowhere to be seen.

Their food arrived, and they ate while talking over the recent murder. When they were done and Cooper paid the check, he received a text from Luke asking him to come to the police station. Luke wanted Cooper's eyes on the suspect they had brought in.

CHAPTER 55

Luke watched Brent through the two-way mirror. Brent sat ramrod straight, hands folded on the table, with the righteous indignation of a man who couldn't possibly have committed a crime, and anyone who thought so was insane.

Luke didn't have enough direct evidence and information to arrest Brent for the murders of Haley and Noah, or any of the others for that matter, right now. But he had enough to bring Brent in for questioning and get a search warrant for his place and office. Brent had refused Luke's request to search his home and office so the warrant was needed. The judge wasn't pleased to be called in off the golf course on a Saturday to sign the warrant, but it was done. Det. Tyler headed up the team executing the search.

Luke checked the time on his phone. The search would be well underway by now. He hadn't spoken to Brent yet because he had hoped Det. Tyler would have found evidence, some leverage Luke could use during questioning, but so far, nothing. Luke knew he was being impatient. A search could take hours, but it was time he didn't have.

Captain Meadows opened the door and hitched his jaw in the direction of Brent. "He asked for a lawyer yet?"

"No, thankfully. I'm going to need to get in there and start questioning him before he does. He's been in there stewing for at least an hour."

"You call Cooper and ask him to come down?" Captain Meadows asked, folding his arms across his chest appraising Brent.

"He's on his way. If you could text me when he gets here that would be great." Luke headed into the interrogation room, which wasn't any bigger than a square room big enough to hold a simple square four-person table. There was just enough space on each side to walk around the table, but not much more. The lighting was bright and harsh on purpose. Nothing about the room was designed for comfort.

As Luke opened the door, Brent shot up from his seat. "I don't understand why you're keeping me in here. I haven't done anything wrong."

Luke didn't react. He pulled out the chair slowly and placed the thick case file folder in the middle of the table in front of him. "If you didn't do anything wrong, then you should have no problem talking to me. You could be a critical witness, Brent. This killer could be someone you know. You're connected now to people in two of the cases. Little Rock is small, Brent, but it's not that small."

Brent's eyes darted toward the door and then back down at Luke. He eventually sat back down. "I didn't kill anyone. I came to you willingly, remember. I'm the one that told you about Tom. A killer wouldn't do that."

"I do remember, a few days after your co-worker confessed to waking up with a dead woman. That seems odd to me. If it were me, I'd be scrambling to tell someone. I wouldn't want to live knowing that."

Brent let out a frustrated sigh. "I told Det. Tyler why. I was worried about my priors. I was worried you wouldn't believe me or worse, accuse me."

"See that's a little different than what you said before, Brent. Before you told us that you didn't know if Tom was being serious. Now if a man isn't serious, what could you be accused of if he did nothing wrong?"

"Well, I…" Brent started, fumbling over his words. "You know I lied to you before. I had to in order to come forward and tell you."

Luke smiled. "Okay, so you admit you lied to a detective. What makes you think I should believe anything you're telling me now?"

Brent had nothing to say. He sat back in his chair and folded his hands on the table.

Luke thought as much. "Speaking of your past priors has that kind of behavior continued in your relationship with Madison? You came across as fairly controlling and ready to pounce on Riley when we arrived at Madison's house today."

"That girl Riley is infuriating. Some man needs to rein her in and get her under control. She has no right to speak to a man like that."

Brent was making this easy for Luke. "Does it make you angry, Brent, when women don't do what you want them to do? When they stand up to you?"

Brent pounded his fist down on the table. "It would make any real man angry. That's not a woman's role. Women have no right to question a man. We rule the relationship. Our word is final."

"So, the women you were involved with in the past, they didn't do what you said so you had to get rough with them, right? Keep them in line?"

"That's right. Our laws have made men weak. They have made our family structure weak. Sometimes a woman needs a firm hand to get her head right again," Brent said proudly.

Luke had never been hit as a child. There had been no need, but he was fairly certain that if he had ever expressed this kind of attitude about women in front of his mother and father, he might not have lived to tell the tale. If Luke went home and even thought about treating Riley like this, she'd have thrown him and his stuff to the curb.

Luke changed tactics. He sympathized, "I get it, Brent. I understand. Women are weaker than men. We have to protect them, but we also have to keep them in line for their own good."

"Not many people get it these days," Brent said, finally relaxing his posture.

Luke spent a few minutes regaling Brent with his own fake views on women and how women were indeed hard to get under control but stressed how necessary it was for a good relationship. Luke finished by asking, "You've some really good thoughts on the subject, Brent. Have you ever written these things down, you know to share them and help educate other people?"

Brent smiled. "No, but that's a good idea. Most people don't really understand."

Luke had him primed. He might as well go for it. "After talking to Madison, it seemed like Haley was the kind of girl who wasn't going to listen to anyone. Noah seemed weak. I mean he couldn't even protect her from the killer. He certainly wasn't going to keep his woman in line."

Brent leaned across the table. "You're right about that. Haley ran that relationship. Noah barely had any say at all over what she did or where she went. Haley didn't like me much. She couldn't have handled a man like me. I know she told Madison more than once to cut it off with me."

"Wow, she went as far as to interfere in your relationship? That takes some balls. That must have really made you angry."

"It did," Brent said. "Haley meddled all the time in our relationship."

"It will be easier now that she's gone, I'm sure," Luke said straight-faced.

"Darn right it will," Brent said loudly, slapping at the table, completely unaware of the corner he backed himself into.

"Well lucky for you then," Luke said evenly. "Tell me what happened to your face last night? Madison said you got into a fight with someone on the street? That must have been rough."

Brent exhaled and his eyes shifted ever so slightly. "It was, man. Some drunk guy on the sidewalk when I was walking home from the bar. I was down Kavanaugh on my way to Madison's house, and he bumped into me walking past me. Then he got in my face for bumping into him. He threw a punch and I threw a punch and it went from there. You know how these things go."

"That happened after you left Mickey's?"

"Not right after. I walked down Kavanaugh and had a few drinks in Prospect Bar & Grill. It was when I left there."

"Did you know the guy? Did anyone see the fight?" Luke needed to establish his story so he could prove it true or false later. The goal was to box Brent into his story now and give him no wiggle room later.

Brent shook his head. "No, I didn't know the guy. No one saw that I was aware of. At least I didn't see anyone."

Luke nodded along. "What time do you think the fight happened?"

"I'm not sure, but I went to Madison's right after."

"You were in the shower when she got home. Is that correct?"

"Yeah, that guy hit me pretty hard in the face a few times. I had a bloody nose and busted lip. I had his blood on me too. That's why I threw out my clothes."

"You what?" Luke said leaning forward, not sure he heard the man correctly.

"Yeah on the way home, I ripped off my shirt and threw it in the trash. My jeans I threw in another trash bin. I had to walk home in my boxers. I was a mess."

CHAPTER 56

"You threw your clothes in the trash on the walk home?" Luke asked, incredulously.

"With that amount of blood, they weren't going to get clean. I knew Madison wouldn't want bloody clothes in her place," Brent explained with an air of arrogance like what he was saying was common sense.

If this was a true story, it was the stupidest one Luke had ever heard. "You took off your bloody clothes at night in the middle of the neighborhood and walked home in your boxers?"

"Nobody was around. It was a warm night. I don't see what the big deal is."

"What about your shoes?" Luke asked.

"I hosed those off in the backyard at Madison's before I went inside," Brent explained.

"You went through an awful lot of trouble to clean up from a fight."

Before Brent could respond, Luke's phone buzzed on his hip. He excused himself and stepped out into the hallway. Captain Meadows and Cooper were headed to the observation room. Luke met them at the door.

"Cooper, I just want you to take a look at this guy. I know you don't remember him, but I want to see if anything sparks a memory or if he's familiar in any way." Luke walked with Cooper right up to the window where Brent was clearly visible, sitting at the table. Luke realized that he had left the case file sitting on the table, but Brent made no move to touch it, probably assuming he was being watched. He'd been in trouble with the law before. He knew how things worked.

Cooper took his time. His face was pensive as he looked over Brent. "I don't know. He seems like he'd be the right height and build, but when I saw him standing outside of Dugan's his face was partially obscured by a hat."

"Anything about him familiar to you?" Captain Meadows pressed.

"No nothing about the way he looks. His voice might be. Luke, can you go in and talk to him a little? This way I can see if his voice is familiar. If we could also get a writing sample, we can see if the way he writes is similar to how the killer texts."

Luke agreed. As he exited the room, he remembered that Det. Tyler had a St. Louis Cardinals baseball cap tucked away in his desk. Luke went to grab it. While he was doing that, Luke also grabbed the recording of the voice message the killer had left Leslie, the only woman they knew so far who had been wary of the killer and never met him.

Luke stood at his desk and played the recording again. Unfortunately, the killer was screaming so loud and violently into the voicemail that it was nearly impossible to tell if Brent's normal speaking voice was a match or not.

Luke left the recording at the desk and went back to the interrogation room. "Sorry, Brent, I had to speak with someone." Luke sat down at the table.

"Are we nearly done here? I have things to do."

"Just a bit more. I appreciate you answering my questions so far. Would you mind putting this hat on for me and turning to look at the mirror?"

Brent smirked. "Is there someone watching on the other side?"

"There is. I just want to rule you out, and this is the fastest way to do it."

Brent took the hat and slid it on his head, but didn't pull the bill down very far. Luke asked him if he could, and he obliged. Brent got up and brazenly stood in front of the mirror, a smirk plastered all over his face.

"You can come back and sit down," Luke directed him. While Brent was showing off in front of the mirror, Luke had pulled out a pad of paper and pen. He slid it in Brent's direction. "Now if you could, write how you'd text someone if you were messing with their head. Threatening them maybe."

Brent looked at Luke quizzically. "I'm not sure I'd even know how to do that."

"Come on, anything. Your style of text is what I'm aiming for really. Are you formal? Informal? Abbreviate? Use slang? Emojis?"

"Emojis are for little girls." Brent laughed. He took the paper and pen and scribbled out a brief message. He slid the paper over to Luke. "This is the best you're getting from me. As I said, I'm not much of a writer."

"I'll be right back," Luke said, standing and heading for the door. On his way to Cooper, he read over the message Brent had scrawled. It read: *You know I can find you. I will kill you when I do.*

Simplistic and straight to the point. Things were spelled correctly. It was basically what Luke had asked for. Luke had no idea what Cooper hoped to gain from it.

Once inside the observation room, Luke handed the note to Cooper. "What did you think when Brent put on the hat?"

Cooper read the note and handed it back to Luke. "I really don't think he's the guy."

Eyes wide, Luke asked, "Are you sure? His story about last night makes absolutely no sense. He doesn't have an alibi for the other murders either. His misogyny and violence towards women are more than apparent."

Cooper shrugged. "I wish I could tell you something different, but even with the hat on, he doesn't look like the guy that shot at me." Cooper pointed to the note. "I realize that's a very small sample, but the only thing familiar is the way he texts. The killer was simple, clear and direct like this. But I still don't think it's him."

Luke nodded in understanding. It didn't change his mind about Brent though. Cooper's memory was not necessarily something he could trust at the moment anyway. For Luke, if Cooper thought Brent might be the killer, it would be just one more confirmation, but if not, Brent still couldn't be ruled out.

Luke explained, "I'm still waiting for Det. Tyler to get back to me about their search. I'm going to continue questioning him."

Cooper left quickly after that. As Luke went to leave the room, Captain

Meadows pulled Luke back. "Do you find any validity to what Cooper said?"

"Cap, he doesn't remember anything. I have to rely on what's right in front of me. I've got a suspect who admitted to throwing out his bloody clothes, has connections to two homicides, and has no alibi. He's the best lead we have, and I'm going to take it as far as I can. I need to place a call to the crime scene unit to send someone out there to start looking for his bloody clothing."

"I can take care of that for you, Luke," Captain Meadows said. "Listen though, call it a feeling or just an old man losing his touch, but my gut tells me that Cooper's got something in his head that once it's knocked loose will solve this whole thing."

"I'd love to believe that, but until then, I have to run with the evidence in front of me. Do you think there's any chance we can get a warrant to take his bitemark impressions?"

Captain Meadows shook his head. "We need something more solid to connect him directly to the Nikki Eagan case before a judge is going to allow us that. Let's see what Det. Tyler turns up first."

Luke checked his phone again. Still nothing from Tyler. Luke took a deep breath and went back into the interrogation room.

Luke pushed open the door, sat down at the table and looked Brent dead in the eyes. "Let's stop playing games here. You and I both know that your alibis for all of the murders didn't check out. Your girlfriend confirms that you were in fact not with her on any of those nights. Where were you really?"

CHAPTER 57

Cooper had been back at the hotel for probably an hour after meeting Luke at the police station, but he couldn't sit still any longer. Even though Luke had told them not to, Adele had left Cooper there alone, fed up with listening to him. She said she was going to take a drive and visit Riley. That was good. Cooper wanted to go back to his condo alone anyway and had been trying to figure out how to make that happen. He worried telling Adele that he wanted to go without her might worry or offend her. They were still learning the moods and rhythms of each other.

Cooper's plan was to retrace his steps again from Kepler's. He had no idea what he would find, probably nothing, but still, something in him pushed to do it again. Weeks had gone by and the killer struck again and again. Something needed to break.

From the walkway in front of Kepler's, Cooper started his path home. It was a route so familiar to him, he could probably do it in his sleep. This time, unlike when he was with Riley and Adele, he was ready to go down the alley to the side entrance of his condo building. Cooper no longer felt the fear that had kept him from doing it the other day.

Cooper walked the few blocks to his place and ducked down the alleyway to take his shortcut. Everything looked exactly the same. The space was just wide enough for a delivery truck and a few feet on each side. Cooper stepped around the mail truck, which was parked a few feet from the door. He punched in the numbers on the keypad next to the condo's side door and entered into the first floor. Cooper walked the long narrow corridor to the main lobby of the building.

The corridor led directly into the area that held residents' mailboxes. Each box, small and rectangular, had a solid metal door that the resident opened with a key. The postman stood in the small room behind the mailboxes shoving stacked mail into each box. Cooper said hello to the man as he passed by, and the man nodded in return. Cooper went to the elevator in the main part of the lobby and rode it to his floor.

At his condo door, Cooper paused for only a minute before unlocking it and stepping through. Immediately, the tension left his neck and shoulders. Cooper wondered if it was real or just muscle memory. It was always how he felt coming home, but he figured over the last few weeks he'd never feel that again walking into his home.

The air still held an antiseptic smell from the cleaners. Being completely closed up probably hadn't helped any. Cooper shut off his central air and opened the row of front windows. He went back to his bedroom and did the same. Fresh air flowed into the space. Cooper started to walk back toward the living room but decided to try something first.

Standing right on the edge of where his bed would have been, Cooper closed his eyes. He counted each breath slowly and let his mind relax. After a few minutes, his mind peeked at the edges of a memory. A blip really. That night after entering his condo, Cooper had left the man and Holly alone in the living room. They had refused to leave, and Cooper hadn't wanted to cause a fight and wake his neighbors. Really Cooper hadn't had the energy to force them to go. A wave of nausea rumbled through his stomach as it had that night. Cooper saw himself standing in the bathroom, feeling as if he might be sick to his stomach. When the feeling passed, Cooper asked them once again to leave, even yelling at them to leave, but they didn't budge from his couch. Cooper had simply given up and gone to bed alone with their voices still echoing in the living room.

Cooper's eyes flew open, and he centered himself back in the present. Did he simply go to bed and pass out? He couldn't be sure, but he felt like that's exactly what had happened. That's exactly what Cooper would have done if he were drunk and sick. He had no tolerance for any craziness. If Cooper had felt as bad as he thought he might have felt that night, it was reasonable that's what he could have done.

Cooper went to the kitchen, grabbed a glass from the shelf, held it under the spigot on the fridge door and waited for it to be filled. He took his glass of cold iced water and sat down on the living room couch, stretching his long legs out in front of him. He rested his head back and stared at the ceiling.

Cooper tried to reconcile the fact that he may never fully remember what took place that night. For weeks now, he had pushed and prodded at himself, feeling like a failure. But maybe the answer was as simple as what Adele had said to him – that maybe his mind was protecting him from horrific memories that wouldn't serve him in the long run. Maybe it was better that he didn't remember.

Adele had told him that he'd have to adjust to a new normal, much like she had to after she found out how her sister was murdered and who had killed her. It was a shift in thinking and perspective. Adele told him that she couldn't change the past so she had to create a new way of thinking about it all. She was still working through it. Maybe the answer was as simple as that.

Cooper closed his eyes to rest. He lost himself in a pleasant daydream about living with Adele, making dinner with her, and spending lazy Sunday afternoons on the couch. Peace and calm washed over him. He was warmed by the thought in every muscle in his body. Cooper rode a wave of happiness for as long as he could.

In the distance, his neighbor Jenny's door opened and then closed. Cooper assumed she had just arrived home from a shift at the hospital and made a mental note to go talk to her before he left. A few minutes later, someone knocked on Jenny's door. For a second, Cooper thought it was his own the raps against the door had been so loud, but Jenny's voice echoed in the hall.

The other voice, a man, drew Cooper's attention. With his eyes closed, Cooper focused only on the man's voice. The tone and how he said his words. All at once, Cooper knew. It was the killer – the man he had spoken to that night. Most importantly, it was the voice that filled his living room when he had gone to bed and left the man and Holly alone. He was sure now that's what happened.

Not paying attention to anything but getting to the door to see the man, as Cooper pushed himself off the couch, the water glass slipped from his hand. It shattered as it hit the floor, and water pooled around the broken pieces. As he stood, Cooper slipped on the water on the hardwood and twisted his left knee. Searing pain coursed through his body. Immediately, Cooper dropped down on the floor unable to put weight on it. He used the couch as leverage and pulled himself up, but as Cooper got himself upright again, his left knee buckled under his full weight.

Cooper was forced to stand still, working out the pain in his knee. When he could tolerate it, Cooper hobbled to the door, yanking it open. He was too late. There was no one there. Cooper turned to the right just as the elevators opened, and the man stepped in. As he turned in the elevator and reached for the button, Cooper got a good look at his face and the familiar uniform he wore. He was sure the man was the one who had killed Holly and had shot at him.

"You!" Cooper shouted. The man's head snapped up. Cooper hobbled down the hall as fast as he could to reach the elevator in time, but the pain made him lightheaded. His vision blurred, and he was forced to stop.

"You're too late, Cooper." The man's mouth turned up in the same menacing grin as it had before. He chuckled as the elevator doors slid closed.

Cooper jerked forward trying again to run after him, but his knee wouldn't cooperate. Cooper went back down the hall to Jenny's door as quickly as he could, favoring his knee. He banged his fist and called her name.

"I'm coming, Cooper, hold on," Jenny yelled from behind the door. Jerking it open, out of breath, she asked, "What's the matter?"

Cooper's words rushed together. "Who was the man at your door?"

"You mean Eddie, our mailman?" Jenny asked, confusion blanketing her face. "He brought me up a package."

"Do you have a full name?" Cooper pressed.

"Eddie Russo, I think, but I can't be sure. Cooper, what's the matter?

You're sweating. Are you okay?" Jenny reached for him.

On the verge of tears from the pain and sheer frustration, Cooper's voice broke. "That's him. That's the killer. I'm sure of it."

"No, Cooper. Remember I saw the man that night. I would have known. He…" Jenny started to say, but she stopped and stepped back suddenly unsure. Her hand flew to her mouth. "You're right! Cooper, you're right. That night I only saw part of his face briefly, but his voice…"

Cooper cursed under his breath and punched at the doorframe. He hobbled back toward his door.

"What happened to you?" Jenny asked, her voice as shaky as Cooper's.

"I slipped trying to go after him. I messed up my knee. I need to call Luke."

Jenny stepped out into the hallway and tried to help Cooper, but he brushed her off. He told Jenny he'd be okay, but to go back inside and lock the door. Cooper told her not to open it for any reason. Cooper navigated back to his place, stumbling back inside. He found his phone on the kitchen counter and called Luke, but it just rang and rang. Cooper left an urgent message, trying to explain. He did the same for Riley and Adele – no one was answering his calls.

CHAPTER 58

As the minutes ticked by Cooper grew more frantic. He tried Luke's office phone and cellphone. He left several messages and texts. The same with Riley and Adele. Neither answered their phones. Adele had a terrible habit of keeping her phone on silent because she had to so frequently when she was in court. Riley though should be answering.

Cooper tried to walk. With each attempt, the more his knee pain grew. While Cooper hadn't pulled off his jeans to see the injury, he could feel that his knee and the area around it had swelled considerably. His shirt stuck to his back from sweat. He wiped a hand across his brow. He couldn't just sit there while the killer roamed the streets. Cooper grabbed his phone and tried Det. Tyler, but that went to voicemail, too.

Finally, he reached Captain Meadows at his desk. When the man answered, Cooper blurted, "I know who the killer is. He's my mail carrier!"

"Cooper?" Captain Meadows asked. "Is that you? What are you saying now?"

Cooper forced himself to take it slowly. He detailed for Captain Meadows the entire course of events leading up to the man leaving in the elevator. Cooper finished by saying, "He's been gone now for about thirty minutes, but he knows I know. I hurt my knee and couldn't go after him. I've been trying to reach Luke and Riley and Adele. I can't reach anyone. He's just out there roaming the streets. We have to do something."

Captain Meadows didn't even argue with him or second guess him. "Let me grab Luke. He's still in the interview."

A few minutes later, Luke was on the line. "Cooper, what's going on? You know who the killer is?"

Cooper went through everything again for Luke. He grew frustrated not being able to move from the couch. "Look, Luke, you have to find this guy. He knows I know it's him."

"Did he say that?" Luke asked hesitantly.

"He said that I was too late a second before the elevator door closed. But from the look on his face, he knew that I recognized him. Jenny believes it might be him, too," Cooper pressed, growing frustrated. "I can't reach Riley or Adele either."

"Riley was with the victim's sister all day. She's probably still there or maybe she went home and took a nap. Either way, I'm sure she's fine."

"Adele was going to your house to meet with Riley," Cooper explained.

"They are probably talking and not paying attention. I'll try Riley when we're done. I'll go down to the main branch of the post office and talk to someone. What's this guy's name?"

"Eddie Russo, but he's probably not going to go back to work. You need to send a police unit to his house right now. Come get me, and I'll go with you to the post office. I'll know him if I see him."

"Cooper, if you're that hurt, you need to get to a hospital," Luke stressed.

"No, I can't. Not until we catch him."

Luke said something to Captain Meadows that Cooper couldn't hear. When Luke got back on the line, he said, "Captain Meadows is tracking down an address, and we will send a unit over there. Let me wrap up this interview, and I'll be over to get you."

It was the longest forty minutes of Cooper's life. He stopped counting how many times he tried to call and text Adele and Riley. When Luke finally arrived, Cooper pulled himself off the couch, putting all his weight on his other foot and hobbled to the door.

Luke got one look at him and expelled a breath. "Cooper, you can barely walk. Are you sure you don't want to go to the hospital? I really think you should."

Cooper shook his head adamantly. "I'm going with you. I can take care of this later."

Luke bent down and felt Cooper's knee through his pant leg. "That's bad, Cooper." Luke pulled a photo up on his phone and showed it to Cooper. "Is this the guy?"

"Yeah, that's him. Does he have priors?"

"No, clean record, but he'd have to, to work at the post office. I got the photo from Facebook. We've sent a unit over to his house in West Little Rock. I don't think there's going to be anyone at the post office this late. I tried calling and didn't get anyone."

"That's why I said we need to go over there," Cooper pressed. "The mail trucks come back after their deliveries. If there's not anyone answering their phones, we can at least talk to some of the other mail carriers and see what they might know. They will know who I'm talking about. I know his route."

Cooper tentatively took steps toward the door, putting only so much pressure as necessary on his bad leg. He wasn't moving fast, but he was moving. That's all that mattered right now. Luke followed behind him.

Once in the elevator, Cooper asked, "Why aren't you in more of a hurry? This is serious, and you're treating it like it's no big deal. We have to find this guy."

Luke cleared his throat. "I don't even know what we are working with here. You're telling me you just figured out today that your mailman is the killer, but you're not offering any proof of that. Even with what he said to you, it doesn't make a whole lot of sense to me. Too late for what?"

"To catch him. To stop him. I don't know," Cooper said, growing more frustrated and impatient with Luke by the second. "Did Brent confess?"

"No," Luke admitted. "Det. Tyler found a gun legally registered to him."

"Did he find GHB?" Cooper pressed.

"No. I didn't have enough to hold Brent. I was nearly done with him when you called. He asked for a lawyer right before I talked to you. I had to let him go."

"Okay so you at least can consider he's not the guy," Cooper said, hobbling out of the elevator at the ground floor. Luke pointed through the main lobby to his car parked at the curb. He helped Cooper through the lobby, out the door, and into the car.

"Tell me again why you think it's your mailman," Luke said, sliding into the driver's seat.

As Luke drove, Cooper explained. "It all makes sense now. I kept telling you the killer was familiar to me. I've seen the mailman on and off in my building for years. I saw the man in passing, but never really met him. I didn't even know his name. Jenny told me. Our mailman has the passcode to the side door. He knows the ins and outs of not just my building, but probably every other on his route. If he's paying attention to any particular person, he knows where they live and even if they live alone. He's got all that information right at his fingertips. I bet that's how he stole Johnny Smith's identity, too."

Cooper took a breath. "They also have odd days off because they work Saturdays. The day I saw him outside of Dugan's was probably his day off. They also wear those same black shoes. Who better to hide in plain sight and not question than someone who provides a vital service to us every day and is legitimately in and out of buildings? Think of how much information you could gain if you were up to no good."

Cooper watched Luke. He knew the man's responses. Cooper knew when Luke was considering and weighing the information carefully, which he was doing. Cooper drove home the final point. "The thing that got me was the voice. I was quiet in my apartment, lost in thought. As soon as I heard his voice in the hall, I knew. I remembered something earlier today about that night."

Luke looked across the car. "What did you remember?"

"When the three of us went into my apartment, I felt really sick that night. I didn't want Holly or the guy there in my place. I left them in the living room and went into the bathroom. I thought I was going to be sick. I tried to get them to leave, but they wouldn't. I finally gave up and went to bed alone with them still in my living room. I was feeling too sick to force them to leave. I truly believe now I was passed out when Holly was killed. But I fell asleep listening to his voice. I'm sure of it."

"Okay, I believe you, Cooper. I'm not doubting what you believe. We are just going to need more proof, but let's go get him and see," Luke reassured.

CHAPTER 59

I arrived home late in the afternoon, nearing four o'clock, exhausted after spending nearly all day with Madison. The sheer emotion of the day and the last few weeks had worn me down physically. My lower back ached and my forehead throbbed. I sat in my car in the driveway processing everything that had transpired while gently rubbing my temples.

A crime scene unit had arrived mid-afternoon to search Madison's house for the clothing that Brent had worn the night before. They grabbed his black sneakers from the backyard where Brent had left them after apparently hosing them off. As the crime scene tech slipped them in the bag, I had wondered if they were similar to the kinds of sneakers Cooper said the killer had worn when he saw him standing outside of Dugan's.

Madison knew the clothing Brent had worn the night before, but could not find them anywhere in the house. When the crime scene tech mentioned that Brent indicated he had thrown them away on his walk home, Madison had been as horrified about the potential implication as I had been. Who gets that bloody from a simple street fight?

After the tech left, I made Madison some tea, and she settled into the couch in the living room. I didn't even try to make her feel better with trite words or a pep talk. There really was nothing to say. From experience, I knew she had to feel the worst of it to get through it. Madison was strong. She'd get through with time.

Before I left, I had assured her I was there for her anytime she wanted to talk. She'd have to make a formal statement to Luke. But he was going to give her until Monday, on the promise that she'd answer his calls if he needed anything sooner.

Dragging myself from the car and walking in my house, I dropped my purse on the couch and kicked off my shoes. I made a beeline right for my chair. I snuggled back into it and propped my feet on the ottoman. I rested my eyes for what I thought was a few minutes, but I must have dozed off, enjoying the comfort of my home and the cool breeze from the air vent above my head as the central air kicked on and off.

The next thing I knew Adele was knocking on my front door and calling out my name. I struggled to rouse myself and shuffled to let her in. As I pulled open the door, Adele handed me an iced coffee and bag from my favorite bakery. I peeked inside and spotted a perfectly frosted chocolate cupcake. Laughing, I said, "I guess Cooper told you how to win me over?"

"I already ate mine in the car and thought about going back for another," Adele admitted, kicking off her sandals and sitting down on the couch. "Cooper's back at the hotel. He told me at least twenty times that he is sure the guy Luke is questioning right now isn't the killer, but Luke is focused on him anyway. I know Luke said not to leave him alone, but I got tired of listening to Cooper gripe and figured you might want some company."

"I was with the victim's sister all day so I really could use some downtime. Glad you're here." I grabbed a napkin from the kitchen and then sat back down in my spot. One bite of the cupcake and my day was already remarkably improved. I held it up. "This is not going to get me into the wedding dress of my dreams."

Adele laughed. "Has Luke proposed yet?"

"No, but I feel like it's soon," I mumbled through bites of the gooey cupcake. I took a sip of coffee and washed it down. "I think if it hadn't been for this case, he would have done it already."

"You were married before, weren't you?" Adele asked, tucking her feet under her and settling back farther into the couch.

"In my twenties for like five minutes. Okay, more like a couple of years, but still it was over in the blink of an eye. He's dating my sister now."

Adele's mouth dropped open. "Are you okay with that?"

I waved her off. "Completely. Jeff and I weren't a good fit. We got married too young."

"Still, I don't think I'd be okay. Have you decided how you want to get married?"

I nodded enthusiastically. I had already planned it but hadn't told anyone. I hadn't really been excited to get married the first time around so the wedding planning had felt like a chore. This time, I suddenly couldn't wait to be Luke's wife. I opened my mouth to tell Adele when I spotted Emma through the front window. She was struggling up my porch steps. I jumped up to give her a hand.

As I reached down to take her hand and help her up the last step, Emma groaned. "I'm ready for this baby now. Sophie is out with Joe and I needed a break."

Emma stepped inside and noticed Adele on my couch. "I'm sorry, I didn't realize you had company. I tried calling you, but you didn't answer."

"My battery died, and I need to plug it in. I just haven't had the energy yet." I introduced the two of them and pulled a chair from the kitchen for Emma to sit. If she sunk into my couch, she was sure it would take all of us to get her back out. She sat, catching her breath and rubbing her enormous belly. "What were you talking about before I interrupted?"

Adele smiled. "I was asking Riley how she wanted to get married when Luke finally proposes."

Emma clapped. "I'm ready to hear this!"

I took a sip of my iced coffee, leaving them on the edge of their seats. They both had their eyes glued on me. Finally, I told them. "Lake Placid in the fall. There are a few resorts up there that are gorgeous at that time of year. I think it's perfect for a small intimate wedding."

"Sounds absolutely perfect," Emma said. "My mother-in-law can have the kids that weekend."

I told them a little bit more about my perfect wedding. During a lull in the conversation, I asked Adele, "How's Cooper doing really? He's been putting on a brave face, but I'm sure he can't be doing as well as he wants us to think."

Adele shrugged. "He's not. He's obsessive about recovering what he can't remember. I told him the more he tries, the less he will remember. I understand. I don't know how I'd react in his situation. I don't really know how to help him, but Cooper's going back to the therapist next week so hopefully, he can talk it out there."

"Did you decide when you're moving?" I asked.

"Within two months. I called yesterday and gave notice on my place in Atlanta. We decided to make some changes to Cooper's condo and live there."

Emma cringed and wrinkled up her nose. "Do you really want to do that?"

"Believe it or not, it was my idea. I think Cooper needs to reclaim his space. I think it would be good for him. Plus, there's some office space near there that I'd like for my new office. I'd love to be able to walk to my office and court."

"That's good then. What kind of law are you going to practice?" Emma asked, shifting in her seat to get comfortable.

"Probably the same. I've specialized in criminal defense. With Cooper's job as a private investigator, I'm sure I'll have work for him too."

I barely registered what Adele said. A postal truck pulled up into the driveway. It was much later than they normally deliver. A postman hopped out, went to the back of the truck and walked up the driveway carrying a sizeable box. I met him at the door before he had a chance to knock.

"This is for Luke Morgan. He needs to sign. Is he home?" the postman asked.

"No, I'm sorry he's not. Is there any way I can sign?" I hadn't realized we were expecting a package.

"You are?" he asked.

"His girlfriend. I'd be happy to sign for it. He won't be home until you're done for the day."

The postman stood quietly, I assumed debating. The box seemed heavy and awkward in his hands. He shifted his weight from one foot to the other. He relented, winking at me. "If you can grab a pen, I've got the slip in my pocket."

"Sure, why don't you step inside and set the box down." I held the door and let him in. As I turned my back to look for a pen in the basket that I keep on the table in the foyer, the box dropped heavily to the floor. Much too heavily. No regular postman would slam a box into the ground like that. My hair stood on end.

As I turned to signal to Adele something was wrong, a heavy object crashed down on the back of my skull. Before I lost consciousness, he uttered, "This is going to be fun. I've got three for the price of one."

CHAPTER 60

At the post office, Cooper gave Luke directions where to pull in around the back of the building. He had been there before on a surveillance case and knew although there was a gate, it was never closed at the very end of everyone's shifts.

Cooper had a case a few years ago where a woman had been having an affair with her mail carrier, and she'd meet him at the post office after work. Cooper had learned more than he had ever wanted about mail delivery and more jokes than he thought possible about a mailman delivering his big package. Cooper shook his head just thinking about it. The woman's husband left her when Cooper confirmed the affair, but she had ended up marrying the mailman or at least that's what he had heard. If it were true, Cooper thought they probably deserved each other. But the case gave Cooper some insider knowledge he might not otherwise have.

Luke pulled the car around back, and Cooper breathed a sigh of relief at the number of mail carriers still at work. Luke maneuvered the car to the side out of the way. He asked, "Do you want to stay here or come with me?"

"I'm going. I'll know him when I see him. You only saw one photo from social media. I've seen him up close." Cooper opened the car door and put his good leg firmly on the ground. He nudged his bad one out and was on his feet.

Slowly they made their way into the back of the post office. The garage-like doors were opened, and they walked right through one of the open bays. Immediately a mail carrier approached. "You can't be back here," the man said seriously, blocking the path.

Luke flashed his badge. "We are looking for one of your carriers." He turned to Cooper to explain more.

"Eddie Russo, I believe. He's got the route downtown that covers Rock Street, Third Street and some of the condo buildings in the vicinity."

"Yeah, that's Eddie Russo. He's not back from his route yet. He should be here any minute. Our supervisor, Carla Berk, is inside if you want to speak with her." The man pointed to a side door up three steps inside the warehouse-like interior.

Cooper and Luke followed, passing by large mail baskets and stacked boxes. The hum of postal work created a din of noise in Cooper's ears.

"Can you do the stairs?" Luke asked.

"Even if I have to drag myself up them." And that's basically what Cooper had to do. He put his good leg up a step and gripped the railings, pulling his other leg up and then the next until he was to the top.

They found Carla Berk sitting behind a desk, clicking away at her computer. She barely picked her head up when they entered her office. She simply cast her eyes upwards.

Luke introduced Cooper and himself and said, "Ma'am, we need to speak with you about Eddie Russo in reference to an ongoing murder investigation." He flashed his badge.

Finally, Carla picked her head up. "Yeah okay when he gets back. We have to do this all the time with you guys. You are always hounding us thinking we see things on our routes. We keep our heads down and do our job. We aren't here to be your informants."

Luke cleared his throat. "He's not a witness. He's a potential suspect in what the newspapers are calling the Missing Time Murders."

The woman rolled back in her chair and lost her balance as she stood. When Carla recovered, she brushed past them and shut her door tightly. "You should have said that when you came in. That would have gotten my attention. Eddie's always been an odd duck so it doesn't surprise me you'd be here asking about him."

"In what way is he odd?" Cooper asked.

Carla looked him up and down. "Aren't you one of the guys involved in one of the cases? I've been following this on the news."

"Yes, but I'm also a private investigator working as a special consultant with the cops. Eddie is my mail carrier. I think that's how he knew my building so well."

"That makes sense." Carla tapped at her head. "We've got a lot of info up here that's why we screen our carriers so well, but you know, once in a while like any profession, there's a bad one in the bunch."

"You're saying that you've known Eddie was the bad one of the bunch?" Luke asked.

Carla waved for them to sit down at her desk. "Yes, in a way. Now don't get me wrong, I'm not saying that any of us knew that Eddie could be a killer. That's not what I'm saying. What I am telling you is that it doesn't surprise me, and probably wouldn't surprise anyone here, because he's always been weird."

"You've said that now twice. What does that mean?" Luke urged her, sitting on a chair across from her desk. Luke held the other chair steady for Cooper to sit as well.

Carla tossed her hand around in the air dismissively. "Most of the guys here are married. They talk sports out there, who should be coaching the Razorbacks, stuff about their families. Most of the guys here are really humble hardworking folks. Eddie's a braggart. He didn't just do something well. He was the best at it the world has ever seen. He bragged about how many women he's gone to bed with. Every weekend he'd have a different story, but some of the guys started catching him in lies. Eddie couldn't keep his stories straight, and people took notice. People stopped talking to him. They gave him the cold shoulder."

"How long ago was that?"

"I don't know, let me think," Carla said, and she sat there counting back on her fingers. Finally, she continued. "I'd have to say a few months, around the start of March there was a big blow-up out there. One of the guys didn't like the way Eddie had been talking about women and he told him. Eddie got really cocky. But all it took was for one of them to break the silence, and they all must have finally felt free because they ganged up on him. I've never seen a man break faster. Eddie's face got all red. I wasn't sure if he was going to shoot us all or run out of here crying."

Cooper shifted in his seat. The pain in his knee was almost unbearable now. He needed Carla to get on with it. He pushed. "What happened next?"

"Nothing really. Next time Eddie came to work, he stopped speaking to everyone. He did his shift, and he left. He even filled in for the others a few times. He wasn't friendly at all, but he put his head down and went to work like he should have been all along."

"Did he work any route other than this one downtown?"

Carla clicked a few keys on her computer. "He's covered a few areas when people have been sick. He bid on another route a few times. These guys move around, you know."

"Has he worked in midtown, specifically behind Cantrell down near Hughes and Mellon Streets?"

Carla checked her computer again. "Sure did. Eddie covered one of those routes this week actually."

Luke demanded, "I need his schedule this week."

Carla clicked a few buttons and printed out a report and his employee badge photo. She handed it to Luke.

He read it over and expelled a frustrated breath. "I think I actually saw him delivering mail the day I went to talk to Johnny Smith. We were that close and didn't even know it."

Luke handed the page to Cooper. Eddie was off the day Cooper saw the man at Dugan's. He had figured as much. Cooper nudged Luke's leg and pointed to a line in Eddie's schedule. "It's him."

Luke's cellphone rang. He looked at the screen and excused himself from the door.

"Where is Eddie now?" Cooper asked.

Carla picked up her desk phone. "Let me give him a call. He should have been back by now." Carla sat with the phone propped between her shoulder and her ear while she clicked away on the computer. She tried one number and then another. After leaving Eddie a message, she slammed the phone back down. "He's not answering, and he's supposed to answer."

Luke came back into the room, holding his phone. His brow furrowed and his eyes pinched. He explained, "Eddie hasn't come back to his house, but it's surrounded by cops so even if he did, I don't think he'd approach. I had asked them to hang back and observe, but they made it a little obvious. If Eddie's the killer, he's probably on the run by now."

"How can we find him?" Cooper asked, antsy and ready to search the streets if he needed.

"Hold your horses. I'm lookin'," Carla said. "We've got GPS trackers on all their phones. I can tell you at any time where my carriers are." She clicked a few more keys and then cursed under her breath. "I don't know what he's doing all the way up there, but he's at a house in the Heights."

"What's the address?" Luke demanded.

Carla stared at him blankly.

Luke slammed his fist down on her desk. "Tell me where he's at right now!"

Carla looked back at her screen and fumbled to get the words out.

Luke shoved a chair out of his way and went around to the back of Carla's desk. He peered down at the computer screen.

Luke's eyes snapped up to meet Cooper's. "He's at my house."

CHAPTER 61

I slowly opened one eye and then the next. I was lying face down, the cool hardwood floor against my cheek. The back of my head throbbed. I struggled to sit up but couldn't do it from the position I was in. I rolled to my side and with my hand flat on the floor pushed myself into a sitting position. I was in the same spot in my foyer as I had been when I was struck from behind.

I blinked my eyes once and then twice. There were two of my couch and chair. Two of everything, in fact, between fuzzy lines. I closed my eyes and rubbed them gently with my hands. I opened them again and tried to focus. The double vision subsided some, but it was still cloudy, like looking through plexiglass.

"I thought for a minute that you were dead," a man said, smirking down at me. He had on a white tee-shirt and the blue pants a mailman wore. His dark hair was sweat-soaked and messy, sticking up in several places. He stood less than six feet and had a medium build. I realized his strength as he reached down and pulled me up by my hair, pain searing through my scalp. "We need to get out of here."

I swung at him, but it was no use. "Where are Adele and Emma?" I demanded.

He shoved me towards the kitchen. Emma sat on the edge of the chair at the table, holding her belly. Tears streamed down her face. Adele stared straight ahead. Blood dripped from her swollen lip. I rushed to both of them at once. The man kept his gun on us the whole time.

"What happened?" I asked Adele, while I reached over and rubbed Emma's arm.

"Eddie, at least that's what he says his name is, knocked you out. When he shoved Emma, I took a swing at him, and he punched me," Adele explained. Her voice was unnervingly calm.

I was pretty sure she was in shock. Turning to the man, I asked, "Who are you? What do you want with us?"

He snickered and waved his gun around. "Are you really that slow? I'm the Missing Time Murderer or whatever they call me. You are my insurance policy to get out of here."

"I'll get my keys, take my car and go."

He shook his head. "It's not that simple. I need money for an escape. Since your boyfriend cut off access to my house, I'm going to get mine one way or the other. Here's how it's going to go. I'm trading you three for cash, and if I don't get it, they can claim your bodies. They might just be doing that anyway. It's going to be a while before I can scratch my itch if you know what I mean." Eddie lewdly grabbed himself.

There was no way that was happening. "Where do you think the money is coming from? I don't have it and neither does Luke."

"Trust me, the cops will give me what I need. Now, let's stop playing games and get out of here. I know just where we can go."

I stood up and faced him. "I'm not going anywhere with you."

He closed the distance between us in seconds and smacked me hard across the face. "You'll do what I tell you to do when I tell you to do it or I'll put a bullet in Preggo's head. Got it?"

Emma looked up at me her eyes pleading. I wouldn't give him the satisfaction of rubbing my stinging cheek. "Where are we going?"

"A house out in West Little Rock. It's foreclosed and secluded. It's perfect for my plan. You're driving. Come on we are wasting time." Eddie pointed the gun at us and shooed us toward the living room, but none of us budged.

"My keys are upstairs," I said defiantly while I desperately tried to formulate a plan.

Eddie sighed. "Well, now that's a problem. I can't let you go get them."

"Come with me."

"Do you think I'm stupid? As soon as I do it, these two will escape."

"Then stand at the bottom of the stairs with Adele and Emma, and I'll run up to get them. Emma is not going to make it up the stairs. That's the best I can tell you if you're planning on taking my car. The keys are up there."

Eddie looked down at Emma who was clutching her belly now and breathing rapidly. "No funny business, got it? I have no problem killing a pregnant woman. Trust me on that."

He tried to yank Emma up by the arm, but she shrieked in pain. "I'm in labor," she cried.

Eddie let out a string of curses. He pointed the gun at me. "Get the keys now. Before you think you're calling anyone, I've got your phone." Eddie pulled my phone from his pocket and waved it at me.

It wasn't charged anyway. It didn't matter. That's not what I was after. I ran through the kitchen and into the living room, taking the stairs two at a time. I knew I only had a few seconds, but luckily my keys were in my pocket the whole time. I slipped quickly into my bedroom and pulled my Glock from my drawer and slipped in the seventeen-round clip. I couldn't remember exactly if it was fully loaded or not. It didn't matter, I probably wouldn't get off more than a shot or two. I couldn't believe it didn't even occur to him that I might be armed. When you routinely underestimated women, it might eventually come back to bite you, and I was hoping it bit Eddie right between the eyes.

I jammed the gun in my pants at my hip, pulling my tee-shirt down over it. I hoped my natural padding might give it some cover. I jingled my keys loudly and yelled, "I found them."

By the time I reached the bottom of the stairs, Emma was in full-blown distress. She sat on the edge of the chair, crying and breathing hard. I ran to her, slipping past Eddie, and rubbed her back. "Breathe slowly. It's okay. It's going to be okay." I just kept saying it over and over again, not even believing it myself.

"Let's go, now," Eddie called out.

"You can't take her. Leave Emma here. She's in labor. The cops will never negotiate with you if you have her. It's only going to slow us down, and if we aren't out of here, Luke will get here soon."

Eddie stared at me but didn't say anything. He looked down at Emma and rubbed the side of his head.

"I don't know what your plan is. But do you really want to do it here in Luke's house? He's got a tactical advantage over you."

"I could just kill her," Eddie said finally.

Adele, who had been quiet, leaped to her feet. I moved in front of Emma as did Adele.

Adele sneered at him. "You'll have to go through both of us, and then you'll have nothing left to barter."

Eddie let out a string of curses at us, but we weren't budging. Finally relenting, he waved the gun at us. "Let's go then. Leave her here, but I'm taking everyone's phones. If she wants to reach someone, she's going to have to walk."

Eddie apparently had no idea Emma only lived next door. I wasn't cluing him in. I leaned down and gave her a hug. "We'll be okay. I'll see you as soon as you have that baby." Then as quietly as I could, I whispered, "Tell Luke my iPad is in my car."

Emma shook her head not understanding. She reached for my hand and didn't let it go. I squeezed it reassuring her. Eddie shoved me out of the house.

Eddie kept his gun out and put Adele in the back seat. I took the driver's seat. As I buckled myself in, Eddie climbed into the passenger seat. He jammed the gun into my side. "I swear if you make one false move, I'll blow your head off as you drive."

I believed him.

CHAPTER 62

"Riley's car is gone," Luke groaned as he pulled up in front of his house. He took in the mail truck parked in the driveway, but Riley's SUV was gone. Tire marks tracked across the grass where Luke assumed Riley must have had to pull around the truck to leave.

Luke raced out of his car, leaving the engine running and door open. He took the porch steps up in one leap and pushed open the slightly ajar front door.

"Riley!" Luke yelled as he entered the living room. "Riley, are you here?" He knew she wasn't but it was instinct to call for her more than anything. Some small sliver of hope that the worst hadn't happened.

The living room was empty, but Riley's purse was tipped on its side on the floor near the foyer table. As he bent down to pick it up, noise from the kitchen drew his attention. Luke drew his gun, checked the hallway off the living room, and made his way into the back of the house to the kitchen. He kept the gun pointed in front of him and took the turn into the kitchen with force. He dropped his weapon when he found Emma sitting on the edge of a chair, holding her belly, and softly crying.

Through tear-stained cheeks, Emma said softly, "He took her, Luke. Riley convinced him to leave me. He wanted to kill me, but Riley and Adele stopped him."

"Is anyone still in the house?" Luke asked, still on edge.

"They left about twenty minutes ago. He said he had a foreclosed house in West Little Rock that would be perfect for his plan."

Luke knelt down in front of Emma and checked her over. She didn't appear to be hurt. "Are you okay?"

Emma held the sides of her belly. "I'm in labor. I've been in labor for probably an hour. I need to get to the hospital, and I need my husband."

Luke's instinct as a detective drove him to push ahead and ask Emma questions until he got what he needed to find Riley. As a man and Emma's friend, he knew she needed a doctor. Before Luke asked anything else, he called for an ambulance and his neighbor Joe. When Luke was done, he assured Emma that Joe would be there shortly and an ambulance was on its way.

Luke held her hand and asked, "Did he say anything that might give me an idea of what his plan is?"

"No, he just said that he needed money to escape. That you had blocked his way out, and this was his only way to be free now. He said he was going to trade Riley and Adele for money, but Luke, he also said he might kill them anyway."

"Trade them for money? Like ransom?" Luke had no idea what she meant.

"I think so. Riley said that she didn't have any money, and he said the police department would pay."

Luke made another call to the SWAT unit at the police department, to a hostage negotiator, and to Captain Meadows while they waited for the ambulance. He didn't have an address yet, but Luke needed everyone on standby.

Cooper yelled from the living room. He had made it into the house from the car. "Where's Riley and Adele?" he asked when he saw Emma.

Emma strained to tell the story again, but Luke stopped her. "Cooper, Emma is in labor. I have the information so let's give her some space. I've called an ambulance, and the medics can take a look at your knee, too. Let me handle this."

When Cooper didn't budge, Luke pressed, "Go now, we are wasting time." Luke was screaming inside, terrified at the thought of losing Riley, but he had to maintain his composure for everyone else right now.

After Cooper went into the living room, finally, Luke knelt back down in front of Emma. "Were either of them hurt when you saw them last?"

Emma swallowed hard. "He hit Riley in the back of the head pretty hard, and he punched Adele in the face when she tried to help me, but they both walked out of here. Riley said she needed to find her keys and he let her go upstairs before they left. I hope she was able to grab her gun."

Luke wasn't sure if the idea of Riley being armed with a madman was comforting or terrified him more. If he ever found the gun on her...Luke couldn't think about that right now.

Before Luke could ask Emma anything else, the siren from the ambulance and a rush of medics filled the house. Joe arrived just as the medics strapped Emma to the stretcher. Captain Meadows and Det. Tyler rushed in after them.

After making sure Emma was okay, Joe gripped Luke's arm. "What's going on? Is everything okay?"

"Just take care of Emma. That's all that matters right now. I'll tell you everything later," Luke reassured him.

Joe went right to Emma and walked by her side as the medics wheeled her out of the house. As she got to the door, Emma called out. "Luke! Luke! I forgot to tell you something."

Luke rushed to Emma's side.

She reached for his hand. "Right before they left, Riley whispered to me to tell you that she left her iPad in her car. I have no idea what that means, but she told me I had to tell you that. She said she'd be okay. She promised me."

Luke knew exactly what that meant. He and Riley had gotten into more arguments than Luke could count about the things Riley left in her car. He worried someone would break in. But this time, what Luke saw as Riley's carelessness might just save her life.

Luke could track the location of Riley's iPad, and therefore, track her. Luke could find them, hopefully before it was too late. He thanked Emma and assured her he knew what Riley meant.

Luke raced up the stairs to Riley's office. Once there, he dug around on her desk to find her password. He quickly logged into her account and searched for the navigation to find her device. Within thirty seconds, Luke zeroed in on the address. A subsequent search indicated the property was, in fact, for sale and foreclosed on from the previous owner. This had to be it.

Downstairs in his living room, Luke found a medic putting Cooper's leg in a brace. Captain Meadows and Det. Tyler stood close by talking. Luke explained everything he knew up to that moment.

"We need to call SWAT in immediately," Captain Meadows said.

"I already called them. I just need to give them the address, but I want to get there first before they swarm. I don't want anything spooking this guy. We get the search warrant for his house yet?"

"It just came through. The cops on the scene are checking the house now. I've got a crime scene unit heading that way, too," Captain Meadows explained.

Luke wanted to tell Cooper to stay at the house, but he knew it would be a losing battle. Luke gave Captain Meadows and Det. Tyler the address, and he'd call SWAT on the way. Luke helped Cooper out to the car.

They drove in silence. Luke was keyed up and he was sure Cooper was the same. As soon as Luke turned onto the road in West Little Rock, he spotted the two-story brick colonial with Riley's SUV pulled up far into the driveway. He had no idea if they'd really be there or if it was a ruse.

Luke stopped the car far back from the house. As he slid the car into park, his cellphone rang. He glanced down and shook his head. "No idea who this is." He answered it on speakerphone.

As soon as the call engaged, Eddie's voice blared through the speaker. "You come any closer, I'll kill them both."

"Eddie, listen. I don't know what's going on, but there's time for you to back out of this."

Eddie let out a maniacal high-pitched laugh. "What's the news calling me – The Missing Time Murders Killer? We both know that's me. If you get your hands on me, you know I'm not coming out of this alive, especially after what you probably already found in my house. That's why I have two insurance policies with me."

"What do you want?"

Silence filled the other end of the phone for far too long. Eddie was breathing but not saying a word. Finally, he barked, "I want a car with no GPS or anything like that and two-hundred-fifty-thousand-dollars cash in unmarked bills. You have an hour to make that happen."

The line went dead.

CHAPTER 63

The SWAT team positioned themselves around the perimeter of the house. They covered the front, sides and the back in the woods. There was no way Eddie was getting out of the house alive, but right now, they didn't have a clean shot. Eddie was smart. He stayed far away from any window.

Luke spent the hour preparing everything that Eddie had requested. At first, Luke didn't understand the request for cash and why Eddie would kidnap Riley and Adele instead of just leaving town. It wasn't the typical act of a serial killer. Then Luke learned what the crime scene techs uncovered in Eddie's house.

The search turned up GHB and other drugs, scales, stacks of cash, and a cache of weapons. There was also a pile of watches, some with straps attached and others just the faces. Eddie had writings on his computer going back years indicating his frustration with life, everything from money to women to friends. He expressed a pathological desire for money, power, and fame that his normal life would never have afforded him. He also was obsessed with the passage of time, and his inability to have the life he wanted as he aged. Eddie noted, "I want the power to stop time and to erase it." That was probably the best indicator Luke would get about the GHB and watches.

Luke suspected that Eddie was the elusive Ghost that Det. Romero had been hunting for a long time. Eddie was his own supplier of GHB and would have to have been a part of a broader criminal empire to have that much money and drugs on hand in his house. It meant that Luke wasn't going

284

to be the only one hot on Eddie's trail. He'd need the cash to disappear for good. Otherwise, whatever drug operation Eddie was a part of would be hunting him. The kidnapping and money were signs of a desperate man.

Eddie refused to speak to anyone but Luke. The hostage negotiator had tried to speak to Eddie, but he flat out refused to speak to the man. In fact, Eddie told Luke that if he tried to make him talk to anyone else, he'd shoot Riley or Adele. Luke assured him it would just be him from that point forward.

Over the hour, Eddie called and spoke to Luke in small bites and then he'd hang up again. Luke didn't have any real sense of what was happening inside the house or if Riley was okay. He'd have to ask for what they called proof of life when it came time for the money exchange. The only saving grace for Luke was he knew how smart and calculating Riley could be. Adele was as much a wildcard for Luke as Eddie was. He had no idea how she was responding and hoped she kept her head about her.

Luke had enough to deal with especially with Cooper. Keeping Cooper back behind the barricade that had been set up was a full-time job, which Luke had assigned to three uniformed officers. Even not being able to walk, Cooper could overpower most men but not three at once. Luke understood his fear and frustration, but there wasn't anything for him to do. With emotions running hot, Luke worried what Cooper would do if let loose.

Luke made his way back to Captain Meadows and the rest of his team. They stood across the street from the house behind patrol cars and the SWAT van. There really wasn't a better position for them. If Eddie had really wanted to take a shot at them, he probably could have. But he'd have to get in the line of sight of one of the SWAT team members who would probably kill him before he got the chance to squeeze off a round.

Luke placed the call. It rang only once and was answered. "All right, Eddie. We have your money and the car. You can let Riley and Adele go now."

Eddie snorted. "I'm not letting them go until I have my money. Once I have my money, you'll get one of them. The other is coming with me to make sure no one follows me. Once I get out of town, I'll let her go."

Luke knew that whoever he chose to take with him would be killed once

Eddie got far enough away. He wasn't going to let that happen. "That's not the plan, Eddie, and you know it. Now we need to work together on this. They aren't going to let me send in the money if that's the deal."

Eddie breathed heavy on the other end. "You'll just come after me. What assurance do I have you'll let me leave freely?"

Luke didn't have any reassurance to give him. Eddie wasn't going anywhere. "You have my word, Eddie. That's all I can give you. Now you wanted the money. I have that for you. You wanted the car. I have that, too. If we weren't going to let you go, we'd have already stormed the house."

"You wouldn't if you want your hostages back. They'd get killed in the crossfire."

"Maybe, Eddie, but not always. SWAT is very precise. Now, do we have a deal?"

Eddie still hesitated. Luke needed to redirect him and keep him on the line.

"Eddie, tell me about the drugs. Are you Ghost?" Luke asked, keeping his tone calm and even.

"You know I am. What did you all expect, some gang members in the wrong part of the city could pull that off? He'd have been caught in a month. I've been at it for years, and no one was the wiser."

"I'm impressed. Det. Romero couldn't get to you, and he can get to anyone. You were that good. How did you pull it off?"

"I'm a mailman. Nobody was looking at me. I'm in neighborhoods all day. I used some message boards to start out and then I used a series of dead drops later on with messages for where they should drop the money and when. Once you establish that you're golden. I deliver mail and make a drop or pick up. Who'd even suspect?"

Luke wanted to know about the murders. Turning from running a drug empire to a serial killer didn't make any sense to Luke. "You were running a good drug empire, getting away with it, Eddie. All that money. Why give it up to kill some women?"

"I have nothing to say."

"You had a lot to say when you wrote that manifesto," Luke reminded him.

"That's all everyone wants to know – what's Eddie thinking? Stupid question if you ask me. Why does anyone do anything?"

Luke pressed, "You talked in the manifesto and in the writing in your house about how men are losing control and women are ruining society. I don't get it, Eddie. You seem like enough of a charismatic guy you could have anything you want in life. I just don't understand the murderous rage."

"Who said anything about rage?" Eddie barked back. "You're looking for something that isn't there. There's no sob story. No parents who beat me and caused this. Men aren't men anymore. It's time we take that back by force if necessary. You of all men should know that. You really want to know why I killed them all?"

"I really want to know," Luke stressed. He cared more about keeping Eddie talking than he did his reasons for killing, but knowing why might make it easier to take him down.

Eddie laughed. "Because I can. Now don't think I'm stoppin' either. When I'm done here, I'll move on to the next town and out of your way. You're not going to catch me. If you keep pressing me on this, you and Cooper might as well look for a grief therapy discount because I'm going to put a bullet in the head of your ball-busting wife. How you live with her I don't know. Now I'm getting out of here. Tell me how we are doing this exchange."

"I need proof of life, Eddie, from both Riley and Adele. I need to speak to both of them and know they are okay."

Luke heard Riley's voice first through the phone. It was far off though like she was across the room from the phone. Riley indicated she was fine. Adele was next. She sounded weaker and nervous. Eddie yelled to Adele to come over to him. Luke couldn't tell what was happening.

Eddie was back on the line. "Now I want my money and the keys in the same bag. Cooper can come up to the front door and throw in the bag and turn around and go."

"Cooper can barely walk. He can't do it," Luke argued. That's all he needed right now. Cooper was unpredictable. Forget not being able to walk, Luke worried about Cooper's mental stability.

"That's the point. He's no threat. Strap the bag around his neck for all I care. Send Cooper or no deal. And Luke, no funny business either. One false move, I'll kill them. I'm standing here right now with the gun to Adele's head. Cooper opens the front door and tosses in the money. Got it? Any false move, it would be a pleasure to kill her, so don't tempt me."

The line went dead. Luke closed his eyes. At this point, he could only hope for the best.

CHAPTER 64

When the time came, I'd really have no problem shooting Eddie. I wanted to shoot him right then and there, but I still hadn't had a good enough shot. Thankfully, Eddie still had no idea I had my gun on me. I remained as annoying and unpredictable as possible so he mostly stayed away from me. The car ride was uneventful, but I didn't do anything stupid. Neither did Adele. Once we had arrived at the house, Eddie was more focused on negotiating with Luke than he was on Adele and me, but he kept us close enough we couldn't escape.

Adele and I had been sitting on the floor against a wall at the far end of the living room. Eddie paced back and forth while on the phone with Luke. I knew SWAT was probably surrounding us by now. I knew how this worked. Eddie refused the hostage negotiator and stayed far away from any window or door. They didn't have a shot.

We waited while Luke prepared Cooper to drop the money into the house. I knew that was the only chance I'd have. It would be enough distraction for me to take my shot – literally. I wasn't going to have much time, and I wasn't the best shot in the world so I tried to plan it out in my head. There were too many variables at play though.

I jumped and exhaled a breath when a knock reverberated off the front door.

"I've got your money and keys, Eddie. Let the girls go." Cooper's voice echoed through the living room.

Eddie had his arm around Adele and held her tightly with the gun pressed against her temple. I couldn't take a shot as long as he held her like that.

Eddie shouted, "Don't come in here or I'll kill her, Cooper. It will be one more death on your hands."

"I'm not going to do anything stupid, but I have to know where you want this bag."

"Step into the foyer and throw the bag into the living room, but don't take another step. Got it?"

"Got it." Cooper stepped into view. His leg was braced. Cooper carried the money in one hand and leaned on a crutch with the other. His eyes widened when he saw Eddie holding the gun to Adele's temple. He locked eyes with me, and I patted my hip, hoping he understood my meaning.

"Where do you want me to set this down?"

"Right there, that's far enough. Now get out!" Eddie shouted.

Cooper hesitated, but Eddie screamed it again. Slowly, Cooper backed out of the foyer and back outside.

As soon as the door clicked in place, Eddie tossed Adele violently to the floor and went for the bag of money. He unzipped it tentatively and pulled out stacks of cash.

Adele landed with such a hard thud right next to him on the floor, I was sure she had been injured. She tried to move her arm first, which was bent under her body at an odd angle. As she fully opened her eyes, Adele looked in my direction. She gasped when she saw the gun in my hand.

"What is wrong with you?" Eddie shouted over his shoulder while he counted the stacks of cash. He had several small piles lined up in neat rows.

Adele recovered quickly enough. "You hurt my arm when you threw me to the ground."

"Doesn't matter," he grunted, "you'll be dead soon enough."

I motioned for Adele to try to move out of the way. I didn't have a clear shot with her so close. I hoped Adele could get up and move in that direction, but she was clearly hurt. Adele pushed herself up off the ground with her good arm and tried to get into a standing position, but she couldn't do it and slumped down again, wincing in pain.

With Eddie distracted, I sprung up from my position and took several fast steps toward Adele. I knew he'd see me eventually, but my whole goal was to put my body between hers and Eddie, but I wasn't fast enough for even that. He whipped up from standing over the money and yanked Adele by her good arm off the ground before I could get to her. He pointed the gun at her head.

"What's going on? Where did you get that gun?" Eddie shouted, confused and scared. He stumbled back with Adele in his grasp.

I had my gun pointed at him but had no shot. "Eddie, you came for me. Let Adele go and take me."

"Not a chance. I'll have you both. You'll be dead by the end of this one way or the other."

"That's not going to happen," I said slowly, punctuating each word.

Eddie stared me down. "Put the gun down and kick it over to me."

I hesitated, and he pressed the gun harder into Adele's head. Her eyes pleaded with me. I didn't drop the gun, but I moved closer to the front window. Eddie turned following my movements.

"What are you doing? I said drop the gun now or I'll kill her!" Eddie screamed.

I got exactly to where I wanted to stand and then placed the gun on the ground and pushed it over to him. I stood with my hands up. The gun landed too far away from him to bend down and pick it up. He'd have to move his position and get closer to the front window where SWAT could take him out.

Eddie inched towards it and then stopped as if debating what to do. There was a method to my madness. It was like juggling now. If he went for my gun, he'd be in the line of sight of the sniper.

Eddie had been in charge, and now, there were too many variables at play for him to juggle. His controlled environment slipped away.

"Do you have another weapon?" Eddie pointed the gun at me. Adele tried to jerk free, but he tightened his grip around her shoulders.

"Do you really think I brought an arsenal?" I said sarcastically.

"Is there something wrong with you? Are you insane?" Eddie asked, squinting at me. He bounced from foot to foot, seemingly not sure what to make of the whole situation.

"Eddie, you're the one that's killed several people, kidnapped me and are holding a gun to Adele's head. Don't you think it's kind of strange to ask me if I'm insane?" I lowered my hands and stood casually like we were having a nice chat in the grocery store. Maybe Eddie's assessment wasn't far off.

"I don't get it," Eddie started. "You're not afraid of me."

He was wrong. I was terrified. My heart thumped loud enough in my ears to deafen me, but I wasn't going to show him. "Eddie, you came to my house. Obviously, you wanted to kill me. You had no idea Adele would be there, and besides, she and Cooper broke up. Who'd want to date a man who couldn't save a woman from a killer? Cooper's already lost. You don't need to kill Adele. The worst thing you could do to Cooper now is let Adele live so he feels her rejection. Killing her just lets Cooper off the hook to continue with his old ways. Make him really feel the loss for the rest of his life. Let him know Adele is out there choosing now to live without him."

For the first time, Eddie twitched. It was like a slight crack in the ice. "Is that true?" he asked Adele.

"That's why I was at Riley's. I was saying goodbye before I left town."

I took a step toward him, but when he pointed the gun at me again, I stopped. "Eddie, why did you do all this? You were getting away with it."

"It wasn't my plan. I knew today when I saw him that Cooper had figured it out. I needed to do something."

"You could have just left town."

"I told you I couldn't. The cops were already at my house. I had nowhere to go and no money to leave. I needed a way out."

"This isn't a way out, Eddie."

Eddie steadied the gun on me. "It's the only way out I have. I'm not going out alone. You're coming with me."

CHAPTER 65

"I'm not going anywhere with you." I moved an inch closer to the window. I knew I was in a position now that SWAT could see me clearly. I just needed to draw Eddie a few inches over and get him to let go of Adele.

"Help me understand something, Eddie. If you don't like strong women who are equal partners in relationships, why aren't they the women you went after? You went after weak women who couldn't get what they wanted."

He eyed me. "They weren't all weak."

"You knew one of them, didn't you? It was Nikki Eagan," I pressed.

Eddie twitched but didn't say anything. It was starting to make sense. I goaded him. "Tell me, Eddie, did she break up with you?"

"She wouldn't even give me a chance, but every other loser guy out there she had in her bed. I got my revenge," Eddie spat.

"Is that why you changed how you killed?"

Eddie shrugged. "It was more fun with the knife."

"The rest were weak though, Eddie. Are women like me and Adele too much for you? Can't manipulate and control us so easily?"

I locked eyes with Adele. I hoped she could take some action to wriggle free of him, but all I read was defeat on her face. I needed her to get some fight back into her.

"Women like you just think you're better than everyone."

"That's because we are," I said defiantly. "Adele is about to start her own law firm. I run my own business. We want it, we achieve it. If you can't handle that, that's not our problem."

"You chose weak men you can control."

I smirked. "That's not a true partnership, Eddie. Luke isn't weak because he doesn't keep me barefoot in the kitchen. It takes a strong man to love a strong woman. Something you'll never be. You'll never get a woman like me or Adele."

"I've had women like you."

"You've drugged and sexually assaulted women, Eddie. It's not the same thing. I mean you had to drug them. You couldn't even sexually assault them with them conscious for fear they'd fight back."

"You don't know anything," Eddie spat at me.

"I know you'll never have a woman like me or Adele willingly. You aren't on our level. Do you think you have us under your control right now? I'm in control, Eddie. Adele is in control. She's allowing you to hold her like that. She could break free anytime she wanted. You aren't man enough to control women like us."

Adele zeroed in on me. She had fear in her eyes but there was also recognition of what I was trying to do. I again stepped closer to the window, and Eddie followed this time. His face grew redder by the second. I pricked up his anger.

"You don't know anything about me!" he shouted.

"Eddie, come on. You're easy to read. Yeah, you killed because you can, but they were weak women too stupid to see you for the psycho that you really are. Those women were too stupid, and I'm here because you're too stupid to know when I went upstairs to get my keys, I got my gun instead. I could have shot you at any time."

Eddie's hand that held the gun shook. He gritted his teeth. I'm pretty sure he was deciding who he was going to kill first – me or Adele. My money was on me.

"You don't know anything about me," Eddie said, his voice low and the anger simmering.

I shrugged. "You keep saying that. If I'm wrong, and I don't know you, then it's because you're not really worth knowing."

As soon as the words left my mouth, Adele bit down hard on Eddie's arm.

He yelped in pain and threw her to the floor. Eddie lunged for me and got me by the shirt. We both fell to the floor in a heap. He slammed a fist into my stomach, knocking the wind out of me. He punched at me as I kicked at him. In the struggle, Eddie's gun bounced out of his hand. As he reached for it, I kicked it hard sending it away from his grasp.

Eddie was stronger than me and pinned me to the floor. As he straddled me, his face contorted in rage. I wiggled free enough to grab for my gun, which was only inches from my fingertips now. As Eddie reached over me for his gun, I gripped mine quick enough to squeeze off a round. The bullet struck Eddie's shoulder at near point-blank range.

He jerked back, gripping his shoulder and fell off of me. Before I could shoot him again, the room exploded in utter chaos. Glass shattered and heavy-booted reinforcements stomped around my head ripping Eddie up off my lower half. I rolled to my right out of the way. Eddie screamed and struggled. SWAT had him on his face inches from my own. They cuffed him and yanked him up off the floor.

I laid my head back and looked up at the ceiling, annoyed with myself that even at close distance all I could manage was a shot to the shoulder. I had every intention of killing him.

To my left, Cooper talked softy to Adele asking her if she was okay and helping her to her feet. Paramedics rushed in as SWAT and the Little Rock police rushed Eddie out. I stayed exactly where I was, unmoving.

"Are you hurt?" Luke asked, suddenly standing right over my head. His hands were on his hips as he peered down at me. He had tears in his eyes but was struggling to keep his composure in a room full of cops.

"Just my pride," I grimaced.

His expression softened. He let out a relieved laugh and reached his hand down to help me up. "Why would your pride be wounded?"

I got myself upright and brushed off my pants and straightened my shirt. "I'm a terrible shot. I was right next to him and only got his shoulder."

Luke wrapped me in his arms and told me how much he loved me. I snuggled my cheek against his chest. "I'm glad you didn't kill him. We can bring him to justice this way."

"Yeah, okay," I muttered.

Luke pulled back and looked down at me. "Do I need to be concerned that you're upset that you didn't kill a man?"

I reached up and touched the back of my head. "He hit me in the head earlier. It's been bleeding for a while. I'm feeling kind of woozy. Can I sit down?"

Luke guided me out of the house. I saw the destruction that SWAT had made on the way out. The entire front window of the house was broken as well as the front door.

Luke guided me over to a waiting ambulance. Cooper and Adele sat together in the back of another ambulance. They were putting her arm in a sling and tending to some of her other injuries. The medic cleaned up the blood in my hair and stitched me up.

"Have we heard from Emma?" I asked Luke.

"Not yet. I figured you'd want to go straight to the hospital. I have to go back to the station and process Eddie and take care of things. I'll need you to make a statement later. There isn't much evidence we can get from your SUV so you can take it if you want if you're really feeling okay. If not, you should go to the hospital in the ambulance. You might have a concussion."

"I'm fine, just a little shaken up still. I'll meet you back at the house later."

Luke handed me my car keys and leaned in, planting a sweet kiss on my lips before he headed back to the crowd of Little Rock police that stood in front of the house. The medic finished up with my head. When I was done, I waved to Cooper and Adele before they left in the ambulance. I assumed both needed some serious treatment to their broken limbs.

I navigated through the crowd of cops, several congratulating me on a job well done. I reached my SUV. Nothing looked any different from the last time I had been sitting in it.

I could feel the emotion welling up inside of me, and I wanted to be far away from the scene before I broke down. This was common for me. I could hold back the fear, worry, and even the tears long enough to get through anything. Once it was over, all my defenses were suddenly down and the emotion that I had been holding back hit me like a tidal wave.

I made it out to Cantrell and then a mile down the road far enough to stop at Kroger. I parked in the far back of the lot away from everyone. As soon as I put the car in park, I couldn't hold it back any longer and the tears flowed down my face. I sobbed and sobbed until I was pretty sure there was nothing left. If Luke had any idea how these cases really affected me, he'd probably never let me near another criminal or crime scene for the rest of my life.

Epilogue

A *few weeks later*

Luke stood in our backyard wearing shorts, a tee-shirt, and flip-flops as he manned the grill. It was the most casual and relaxed I'd seen him in a long time. He had corn on the cob and steaks grilling nicely. I finished mixing the salad and smiled at him through the French doors that went directly from the eat-in kitchen to our back patio. He smiled back.

"You guys are really happy, aren't you?" Adele asked, sitting at the kitchen table watching me work. A cast on her arm had replaced the sling. The doctors had reset her arm but told her the prognosis was good, and she'd be back to herself in no time.

"I really am. Cooper seems just as happy. I'd say that after everything, we are both pretty lucky."

Adele readily agreed. "We just need to get Cooper through surgery and settled into his place and life can resume as normal."

Cooper's knee surgery was scheduled in a few weeks. He had torn his ACL. Cooper and Adele had been alternating taking care of one another. They were still living in the hotel while waiting for painters to finish their work at Cooper's condo and the new bedroom furniture to be delivered.

We had asked them to come and stay at our house, but they had declined. I think they wanted some time on their own. Even for as much as Cooper complained about the hotel, now that the case was over, he seemed fairly happy. He was still going to therapy though to address his missing memories and work out some of the guilt he felt.

Cooper sat at the table near the grill giving Luke grilling tips. He didn't need any, but Cooper had always said he was better at the grill than Luke. Their normal banter was back in full swing now that the case had closed. I was glad that they could get back to normal.

Eddie pled not guilty although there was a mountain of evidence against him. He had confessed to Luke back at the station after his arrest. He told Luke he had drugged the couple, and when they got back to the woman's house, or in Cooper's case, his condo, he'd sexually assault the woman and then move her to the bedroom and kill her. The biggest surprise for Luke was the first case, there was no man. She had been a trial run so to speak. Eddie later claimed he made it all up because Luke had threatened to kill him if he didn't confess. No one believed that.

The public defender was hard at work trying to convince him to accept his fate. Either way, even if we had to testify, Luke didn't see a chance that he'd ever see beyond prison walls again. Some had even speculated that if Eddie made the prosecutor's office take it to a full trial, it would be a capital case with the death penalty on the table. Eddie's fate right now rested in his own hands. Bringing him in solved a major drug operation case and the Missing Time Murders case. He had more charges against him than most criminals saw in a lifetime.

All of the funeral services had been held for the victims, and the city was still in a state of shock and mourning. It would be a long time before things returned to normal, or at least, it felt that way.

The police department officially cleared Cooper, Scott Davis, Brendan Howe, and Tom Sharpe, who finally came back to his parents' house after taking off, of any wrongdoing. Luke searched for a reason to arrest Brent but never could find anything to explain his odd behavior. It seemed he really did have a street fight in the Heights and took off his bloody clothing. A crime scene tech found both his shirt and pants in separate garbage cans.

It turned out that Don Jennings had been pressing the police department so hard to arrest Cooper because he was worried his brother had been the killer or involved somehow. It was a diversion technique. All in all, the case was wrapped up, and now, Luke and I finally had a real chance to relax.

"How's Emma doing?" Adele asked as I finished making the salad.

"She and the baby are healthy and amazing. Emma is incredibly strong. Joe said they made it to the hospital in time and she had the baby about an hour later. They named him Daniel after Joe's father."

Luke popped his head inside the house to let me know the food was done. I grabbed him and Cooper another beer from the fridge. I carried that with the salad outside.

"Was Joe or Emma angry with you about what happened?" Adele asked as she sat.

I handed Luke his beer. "Not really. Joe was more upset than Emma. He got over it pretty quickly though. I don't think Emma gave him much of a choice."

I put the salad bowl on the table and admired the steak on my plate. Luke really was a good cook. It was seared to perfection. Each of us helped ourselves to the rest and dug in, letting Luke know how good it was.

The four of us spent the evening talking and laughing. As night turned and it got dark, we heard fireworks off in the distance but couldn't see any from the back of the house. The weather was unseasonably cool, and a nice breeze blew through. Luke started a fire in the firepit, and we turned on the outdoor lighting, which left everything awash in white twinkly lights.

Luke regaled Adele and me with funny stories about Cooper going all the way back to college, long before I had met either of them. Cooper, in turn, shared his funniest and most embarrassing about Luke. It was all good-natured. Our little foursome felt like family.

Later, after Adele and Cooper left, I sat looking at the stars in the backyard. The fire was dying out, but I was comfortably curled up in the lounge chair. Luke insisted on cleaning the kitchen and wanted me to do nothing but relax. I could handle that.

When Luke was done in the kitchen, he joined me in the backyard. He took the chair next to me and reached over and held my hand. "I forgot how nice our backyard is. The lights give it an almost magical feel."

I smiled over at him. "There was so much I wanted to do when I bought this house, but I knew back here would be special once I was done landscaping it. With your help, I made it happen. It's felt more like home since you moved in. It feels like our forever place."

Luke stared up at the sky. "Do you really mean that? Forever?"

There was something about the soft tone of Luke's voice that made my heart beat a bit faster. I squeezed his hand. "Absolutely. It took us a little while to get here, but you know I want to spend the rest of my life with you. Who else is going to put up with me?"

Luke met my gaze and leaned over and took my face in his hands. He kissed me sweetly. When I opened my eyes, he was on his knee in front of me holding the most gorgeous diamond engagement ring I'd ever seen. Even though I knew Luke would propose at some point, it still hit me by surprise.

"This isn't exactly the romantic night I was planning, but something about tonight, being here feels right. I have loved you from nearly the minute I met you. When you came back to me, I promised myself I'd give you time, and I kept that promise. I promise now to love you and take care of you for the rest of our lives. You make me happier than I ever thought it was possible to be. Will you marry me, Riley?"

The tears came quicker than I wanted them to, but I said yes while choking them back. I practically leaped into Luke's embrace, nearly knocking him over. "Yes, yes, yes," I said again and kissed his face. "This is the only place I want to be – here with you forever."

Luke slipped the platinum French-set halo diamond engagement ring on my finger. It fit like it had been there all along. It was the same feeling I had every time Luke kissed me.

About the Author

Stacy M. Jones was born and raised in Troy, New York, and currently lives in Little Rock, Arkansas. She is a full-time writer and holds masters' degrees in journalism and in forensic psychology. She currently has three series available for readers: paranormal cozy Harper & Hattie Magical Mystery Series, the hard-boiled PI Riley Sullivan Mystery Series and the FBI Agent Kate Walsh Thriller Series. To access Stacy's Mystery Readers Club with three free novellas, one for each series, visit StacyMJones.com.

You can connect with me on:

- http://www.stacymjones.com
- https://twitter.com/SMJonesWriter
- https://www.facebook.com/StacyMJonesWriter
- https://www.goodreads.com/StacyMJonesWriter
- https://www.bookbub.com/profile/stacy-m-jones

Subscribe to my newsletter:

✉ http://www.stacymjones.com

Also by Stacy M. Jones

Read The Next PI Riley Sullivan Mystery
  WE LAST SAW JANE

Access the Free Mystery Readers' Club Starter Library
  PI Riley Sullivan Mystery Series novella "The 1922 Club Murder"
  FBI Agent Kate Walsh Thriller Series novella "The Curators"
  Harper & Hattie Mystery Series novella "Harper's Folly"

Sign up for the starter library along with launch-day pricing, special behind-the-scenes access, and extra content not available anywhere else. Hit subscribe at
  http://www.stacymjones.com/

Please leave a review for Missing Time Murders. Reviews help more readers find my books. Thank you!

Other books by Stacy M. Jones by series and order to date

FBI Agent Kate Walsh Thriller Series
  The Curators
  The Founders
  Miami Ripper
  Mad Jack
  The Fuse
  Dead Senate

PI Riley Sullivan Mystery Series
  The 1922 Club Murder
  Deadly Sins
  The Bone Harvest

Missing Time Murders
We Last Saw Jane
Boston Underground
The Night Game
Harbor Cove Murders
The Drowned Boys

Harper & Hattie Magical Mystery Series
Harper's Folly
Saints & Sinners Ball
Secrets to Tell
Rule of Three
The Forever Curse
The Witches Code
The Sinister Sisters
Scandal Knocks Twice

We Last Saw Jane

A senator's missing daughter. The suspicious death of a teacher. The prestigious all-girls boarding school that holds the secrets to it all.

In the days leading up to her wedding, PI Riley Sullivan is supposed to be taking a break at her mother's home in upstate New York. But when Jane Crandall, a powerful senator's daughter, goes missing blocks away, Riley is pulled into a mystery that draws her in deep. For the idyllic setting the school provides, something sinister lurks behind the perfection.

Forced to work with a local police detective until her team arrives, Riley must convince him something bad has happened to Jane. As Riley starts her investigation, a series of crimes come to light. But the questions remain - where is Jane and what does she know?

Riley isn't the only one on the hunt for Jane, but finding her may be the key to solving it all.

Buy it on Amazon: https://www.amazon.com/gp/product/B08HY7SXVX

Made in United States
North Haven, CT
15 March 2023

34114579R00188